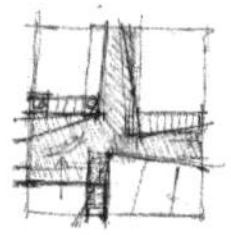

Secret Paths Editions presents

We Girls

The Boy & Girl Saga - Book Three

Alan McCluskey

ISBN 978-2-940553-24-2

Other books by the author

The Boy & Girl Saga
Boy & Girl - Book One
In Search of Lost Girls - Book Two

The Storyteller's Quest
The Reaches - Book One
The Keeper's Daughter - Book Two
The Starless Square - Book Three

Chimera
Stories People Tell

Coming soon
Local Voices

1.

"Peter! The postman's brought you a new dress," Kate called out from the foot of the stairs. That she spoke Swiss German was no longer a problem. Peter had quickly picked up the local dialect in the six months since he arrived in Luzern. That she drew attention so openly to his dressing as a girl was more of a problem. Not because it was a secret. It wasn't. But having it blared for all to hear embarrassed him.

The girls, who had free run of the house with the owners Lydia and Klaus out, peered over bannisters and out of doors as if prompted by Kate's call, laughing and calling out, watching him hurrying down the stairs two at a time. Some smart Alec whistled the tune of Oh, She's a Pretty Girl and the other members of the Lost Girl's choir took it as a cue and broke into song, the stairwell resonating with their voices amid giggles and wolf whistles.

"Thanks," Peter said, pulling a face as he took the parcel from Kate. Brown paper, trussed up with string, stamped with her Majesty's crest and a label listing the contents in English, it was surely from England. "Did you put them up to that?"

Kate's expression was all innocence as she took him by the arm and ushered him into the study, closing the door on the final bars of the song.

Peter was upset. The all-girls choir didn't usually single him out as different or apart. He lived amongst them as a girl amongst girls. At least, that's how he saw it. By singing about him as a girl, were they celebrating him? Or had they been mocking?

"I'm sorry," Kate said, contrite as they unpacked the dress. "It's your birthday. I thought you'd enjoy being serenaded as a pretty girl."

"I do. I'm flattered." He made a show of curtsying. "But I can't rid myself of a nagging suspicion I'm being made fun of."

With the dress was a card and a photo of him in the dress. Fi had her arm slung around his shoulder and was kissing his cheek. She was flushed with excitement while he was just as flushed, but with embarrassment. He remembered the occasion well. It was the first time his new parents had seen him decked out as a girl.

Turning over the card, he read: Found this photo in the pocket. Thought you'd like to have both as keepsakes. Hope we see you soon. Happy birthday. Do write. Miss you. It was signed, Christina and John. His adoptive parents. Fi's mum, Christina, had taken him in when his own mother and sister had threatened to kill him. Both had to be locked away in a mental institution.

Peter chose not to show Kate the photo or the card for fear they'd upset her. He laid them face down on the table. She must have recognised the dress though because she said, "Let's see if it still fits." She held it up in front of him as she returned to their earlier discussion, "The girls do accept you as you are, you know."

He slipped out of his blouse and skirt and she helped him pull the dress over his head. It was pale green and flared out at the hem, reaching to just below his knees. "Maybe you should change your name," she suggested. "Being called Peter does make a statement. As if you were holding back. What was that girl's name you adopted in England?"

"Wendy." Saying the name made him shy. He wasn't sure why, but he felt vulnerable. The name also made him sad. Like the card and the dress, it reminded him of Fi with all her gay colours and her boyish airs. She'd encouraged him to be what she called a 'pretty boy'. Poor Fi. He shuddered. She'd been killed by an angry youth, despite Peter and Kate's desperate efforts to save her.

"Ah yes. Peter Pan and Wendy," Kate continued. "And who am I? Tinker Bell, here to sprinkle fairy dust over you and turn you into a girl?"

Was that irritation? It would be understandable. He too would be irritated if he were taken for somebody else. "For me, you are Kate." He wrapped his arms around her. "You're my soulmate."

She nuzzled his neck. "You remember the first time we met?" she said. "You'd travelled to my world and were in my head. You thought you'd become a girl."

He remembered well enough. How could he forget that initial shock? "What about the time you wore this dress," he replied. It had been one of Fi's. She was always encouraging Peter to wear her clothes. "You were in my head and I let you take over my body for the evening." He'd wanted to console her, miserable as she was at no longer having her own body.

"But now we are two separate people." Stepping back, she held his shoulders and smiled. It made him want to kiss her. "Do you ever yearn to be a part of me or me of you?" she asked.

Her question took him by surprise. He did regret those long conversations when he was in her mind or she in his. He also regretted no longer being able to feel her body as if he were her. They hadn't lost the ability to 'travel to minds' as they called it. They just didn't do so any more now they were together. "I do miss not feeling how you feel. I have to rely on your words, your expressions to guess."

She closed the distance between them and kissed him gently on the lips. "I love you, my girlie boy," she whispered.

He would willingly have kissed her more but she drew back. "So should we baptise you Wendy?"

Why was he reticent? As she moved behind him to button up his dress, he said, "I think I've stumbled on something. But it's not easy to explain. If I were to become a girl I would lose an extremely important part of myself." He giggled, realising what he'd said. "No I don't mean that." He blushed. "Well, that too. Especially that"

"I like you as you are," she said, running a brush through his shoulder-length hair.

He pressed on, needing to pursue the idea. "When I look at a girl, the girl's in the choir for example, what strikes me is that being a girl comes natural to them. They don't give it a second thought. If I were a girl there would be nothing special in dressing or acting as one. But for me there is something special about being a boy who dresses as a girl. I'm attracted to girls, I identify as a girl, I feel like a girl, especially when I'm dressed as one, it makes me feel more alive, but I am not prepared to go the whole road and become a girl. In a strange way, refusing to choose is an important part of who I am."

"Are you sure you're not just trying to get the best of both worlds?"

She was joking and he grinned to acknowledge it, but he considered the possibility all the same.

A loud hammering at the front door interrupted his train of thought. Normally Klaus or Lydia would go, but both were out. The insistence of whoever was knocking didn't bode well. Peter instinctively wanted to hide, but he accompanied Kate to the door.

A man in a dark grey suit stood stiff on the doorstep flanked by two men wearing the uniform of the Luzern municipal police. The man peered over his spectacles at Kate and Peter, his look disdainful. "I am here to fetch a certain Peter McCloud," he said in English.

"I'm sorry," Kate said, her English hesitant. With Peter learning Swiss German she had little chance to practice. "I didn't catch who you are."

"I'm a bailiff sent from a court to accompany Peter McCloud back to England."

"Excuse me if I don't understand," Kate said, sounding very formal and polite. "Why should the young man need to go to England?"

The man sighed, as if explaining was beneath his dignity. "The boy's mother sought an injunction to nullify the adoption of her son. The judge ruled the adoption illegal and ordered the court to restore her son to her."

Peter was seething. His birth mother was raving mad. Had she not threatened to kill him? The police had had to restrain her. She'd been locked away and as far as he knew she still was. If she got free, she would stop at nothing to prevent him parading as a girl. How come Christina and John had not warned him? Surely they would have said. No. These were not the doings of his mother. She would have sent an assassin, not a bailiff. This was the work of someone else, someone more lucid in their madness. He shuddered. He knew exactly who.

"The person you are looking for did live here," Kate said, as quick thinking as ever. "But he no longer does. He left a few months ago."

"That's not what the authorities told me," the man said turning for confirmation from those accompanying him. The men nodded. "They said he was still registered as a resident in this house."

"Wendy, would you go and tell the others I will be with them in a moment," Kate said. "I'll accompany these gentlemen to the door. They're leaving."

Peter wanted nothing better than to flee, but he wouldn't leave Kate alone with the brutes, even if she was a champion at unarmed combat.

"Now look here, Miss," the man said, taking a step forward. "I have a warrant to search this house." He waved an envelope in front of Kate's nose. "So I suggest you cooperate, or we will have to use force."

Kate snatched the envelope from his fingers, much to his surprise and annoyance. "Hey! That's not for your eyes," he exclaimed, trying to grab it back.

She dodged - easy enough for an expert in unarmed combat - and handed the envelope to Peter. Opening it, he scanned the contents. It was a letter from a judge authorising the man to fetch

Peter McCloud. There was no mention of a search warrant. Peter handed it back to Kate, saying mind-to-mind, *It says nothing of a search warrant.*

Kate was visibly startled by his voice in her head, she'd got out of the habit, but quickly recovered and glanced at the letter as if reading it. "This is no search warrant," she said in Swiss German, handing the letter to one of the two policemen for him to see. "Why don't you come back when you have one," she added in English.

Hearing quiet steps behind him, Peter glanced over his shoulder to see the whole choir massed, the Lost Girls looking none to friendly. The girls had been through tough times, so being menacing came easy.

The man glared at the girls, turned on his heals and headed for the door followed by the two policemen. Peter let out a sigh of relief, but he knew full well it was only a reprieve.

2.

"What the hell was that about?" Tania asked, her hands on her hips, her eyes flashing.

"They want to force Peter to return to England," Kate said sounding weary.

"No way!" Suzanne, one of the smallest and youngest, exclaimed, distressed. "Who's gonna teach me healing?"

"Let them damn well try!" Tania added, flinging an arm around Peter's shoulder as if to protect him. Everyone knew he was off limits but she wasn't interested in him. It was just her way of baiting Kate.

Extracting Peter from Tania's grip in return for a kiss, Kate said, "You need to prepare the concert. I suggest you go with Clara and practice." Clara was the best of their singers, apart from Peter, and led the choir.

"What about you?" Tania challenged, apparently still game for a fight.

"How good is your English?" Kate asked.

"Why?"

"'Cause we need to talk to Viktor."

Kate was right. They should inform Viktor. He was Peter's singing teacher and mentor. He'd travelled from England with Peter and had opted to stay in Luzern with his long-lost love Beth.

"Oh," Tania muttered, crestfallen. Peter chuckled inwardly. Viktor spoke fluent German and was pretty good at the dialect too, but Tania seemed to have forgotten.

An hour later Viktor opened the door dressed as usual like a Russian spy with his round Cossack cap, his long leather coat and his beard. That he really was Russian didn't help. "You're eager," he said ushering them in. Responding to Peter's evident incomprehension, he added, "Your singing lesson isn't till tomorrow."

Peter groaned.

"Are my lessons that daunting?" Viktor pursued, unable to suppress a grin.

Next to him was Beth in her wheelchair. She looked much like an older Kate with her hair cropped short, her high cheek bones, her arched eyebrows and that same intelligent smile. "Stop teasing the poor girl," she said, taking hold of Peter's hand and pulling him towards the sitting room.

Peter had to smile at being called a girl.

"Let's have a cup of tea," she continued, "and you girls can tell us why you came." Peter wheeled Beth into the sitting room while Viktor slung an arm round Kate's shoulders and followed.

A plate of biscuits and an array of tea things were set out on a low table in the middle of a circle of armchairs. Peter pushed Beth to her space between two armchairs. Viktor took the chair next to her while Kate joined Peter on the settee.

The maid, who entered carrying the teapot, halted, staring, mouth half-open, at Peter. "Thank you, Tricia," Beth said, raising her voice to get the girl's attention. "Put it on the table."

Visibly startled, the maid tore her eyes from Peter and set the teapot next to the cups and saucers. Once she'd left, Beth said, "How embarrassing. I'm sorry about that. She's new."

"Poor girl," Kate said, with a grin. "She was completely smitten."

Peter grimaced, twisting his fingers through his hair, a habit he copied from a girl in the choir. "The few who realise I am anything other than a girl seem to get sucked in…"

"Like insects to a naked bulb," Viktor. "Except they don't fizzle up when they get too close."

Beth spluttered and placed a restraining hand on Victor's arm. "I imagine you didn't come to talk about fizzling up my maid."

"No," Peter began. "Although, it does have to do with overblown reactions."

Once tea had been served, Kate described the bailiff's visit.

"What I don't understand," Peter added, "is why Christina and John said nothing. I just got a parcel from them."

"Parcels take time," Beth said. "They must have posted it before."

Peter nodded. She was probably right, but it didn't explain why they hadn't warned him. "My birth mother might have wanted my downfall, but I can't see her going to court and winning back guardianship. She'd only have to open her mouth for anyone to realise she was nuts."

"Sounds like the work of Priscilla's aunt, if you ask me" Viktor said.

Peter agreed. If anyone was capable of ruining his life, it was her. Not only did she have the necessary clout, but she had the will. The woman had already attempted to oust Peter's adopted father as headmaster and heap disgrace on him. She hated Peter for what had happened to Priscilla. That the girl had been unhinged and attempted to kill Peter didn't deter her, on the contrary. She'd taken up her niece's crusade to rid the world of people like Peter.

"You could always stay with us," Beth suggested. "No one would dare search here."

It was a generous offer, but he didn't want to get in the way. Beth and Viktor had only recently got back together. At the same time, the thought of not being with Kate and the Lost Girls pained him. "Thanks," he said. "But I wouldn't want to bother you."

"We'd be delighted to have you," Beth insisted.

Kate frowned. "As long as you steer clear of Tricia."

Viktor chuckled. "We'll have to keep Peter locked up."

Peter winced. "Maybe I'd be better off returning to England."

Beth waved a reprimanding finger at Viktor. "I'd rather find a new maid than force you to return to that nightmare," she said.

"Seriously though, what about the concert?" Kate asked. "You'll hardly go unnoticed. You've got several solos."

"Surely that bloke will be too busy getting his search warrant," Viktor chipped in.

Peter was about to express his scepticism when a tiny voice in his head whispered, *Peter?* He didn't recognise it at first. *Peter, can you hear me?*

Suzanne?

Yup. She sounded relieved. *I wasn't sure this would work. What's up?*

That horrible man came back with the police and they're searching the house.

That's awful.

Worse. There are several priests and they're rummaging through our healing stuff.

Peter was afraid they were looking for proof of occult practices. Since the Lost Girls escaped the convent, the church had sought a pretext to get back at them. The ill-treatment of the girls at the hands of the nuns had caused such an uproar the clergy weren't ready to forgive. *That's dreadful. I need to alert people here. Let me know what else happens.*

"Are you alright, Peter?" Beth asked. "You've gone dreadfully pale."

Peter drew in a deep breath. "We have a problem." He shook his head. "Several of them." He related what Suzanne had told him.

"How on earth do you know that?" Beth asked, turning her wheelchair to face him. "Do you have a secret telephone?"

Owning a telephone was not given to everyone. His father had had one installed because of his work, but Fi's mum had readily done without.

"Or have you mastered telepathy?" Beth pursued, grinning.

Telepathy? No. Talking mind-to-mind was not telepathy. But this was no time to explain. Peter and Kate invariably avoided the subject. Experience had shown doing so was far safer.

Kate glanced at Peter, then said, "We have developed a limited form of communication mind-to-mind as a consequence of the way we do healing."

Beth's eyes lit up. "I'd really like to learn."

Peter shot a warning look at Kate, before saying, "Talking about it properly would require peace of mind. At the moment, we're sick with worry."

"Of course," Beth said, contrite.

Having steered her back to the raid, they discussed how to react. Beth had an appointment so it was agreed Viktor would drop her off before accompanying Kate to negotiate with the police and try to get the priests off the property. Peter wanted to go with them, but Viktor was categoric. It was too dangerous. "Catching you would be exactly what they want," he said. "You're going to have to sit this one out."

"I'll keep you posted," Kate said as she pulled on her coat and kissed him on the cheek.

"You can use the bedroom at the end of the corridor," Beth said indicating where she meant. "Or you can stay in the sitting room till we get back."

"No cavorting with the maid," Kate said with a grin. Peter blushed. He'd completely forgotten Tricia. Luckily Kate's attention was elsewhere as she helped Beth pull on her jacket.

Once they were gone, Peter returned to the sitting room, meaning to contact Suzanne and inform her help was on its way. He'd barely settled in an armchair and closed his eyes than a timid knock came at the door. The maid peered in. "I need to clear away the tea things," she said, stepping into the room. "If that's alright."

"Go ahead."

Tricia stacked the cups and saucers on a tray, but was in no hurry to leave. Dressed in a traditional maid's uniform with a lace pinafore, her unblemished face made her look like a porcelain doll. That she wore her hair in plaits only accentuated the impression of youthfulness. Peter guessed she must be sixteen. Taking a step closer, the girl said, "You're a boy, aren't you?"

"What makes you say that?" he asked, getting up and taking a cautious step back. There was none of the antagonism he'd felt with Priscilla, but he was wary.

"I can feel it," she replied, glancing sideways at him from under her lashes. "Why do you dress up?"

The question was blunt and made him feel exposed and vulnerable. He had no wish to reply and resorted to shaking his head. A feeling of foreboding stole over him.

Tricia seemed oblivious to his horror. She extended a hand and ran her fingers through his hair making him cringe. "I could help you get dressed," she said, her voice taking on a strange compelling tone as she took a step closer, so close he could feel her breath on his cheek.

He was reminded of Andrew's stories of his uncle. The man had forced his nephew to dress as a girl for his own perverted pleasure. Could Tricia somehow be similar? He glanced up at her. Her eyes glistened with excitement and her cheeks were flushed as she licked her lips. When she reached out to grab him, Peter ducked and stepped away. He was tempted to use one of Kate's moves, sweeping sideways with his foot, knocking the girl's legs from under her. He had visions of her screaming as she crashed headlong onto the low table, scattering cups and saucers everywhere.

Instead he said with all the authority he could muster, "You don't want to do this." He held up a warning hand. "You will lose your job … and your reputation. You might even get arrested."

She faltered, her hands sinking to her sides, defeated, and tears welled in her eyes. A stifled shriek escaped her lips and she turned and fled, muttering "I'm sorry. I'm so sorry."

3.

" Hey!" Kate cried out in alarm as Viktor swung the car off the main road and, slowing, drove down a narrow, tree-lined street. "Where are you going?"

"Remember Regina and Heinz?" Viktor asked, ignoring her protests. "The journalist and the photographer."

How could she forget? She owed them an immense debt. They'd prepared a special supplement for the local newspaper denouncing the exactions the girls had been subjected to. "Sure," she said. "But this is no time for social calls. The police are searching our house and priests are ransacking our apothecary."

"I know," he said, ignoring her exasperation. "But having the press with us will dampen the ardour of even the most enthusiastic villains."

He was right, of course. A bunch of young girls didn't hold much sway against the combined force of good and evil that were the police and the priesthood. Kate swallowed hard. Colouring from a mixture of embarrassment and irritation, she muttered, "I'm sorry."

They reached Regina's house only to find her out. Sick with worry, Kate pleaded with him to drop the idea, but he insisted they drive to Heinz's place. Luckily the photographer was at home and Regina was with him.

"Come in," Heinz said, delighted to see them. They hadn't met since the publication about the Lost Girls. "I'll make tea while you tell us the latest..."

"No time," Kate insisted, beside herself with worry. Her

tone startled both Regina and Heinz.

"What's up?" Regina asked.

"We need your help. It's urgent," Kate replied, turning to go. "I'll explain on the way."

Kate knew full well adults in this world didn't appreciate being ordered about by children. But this was an emergency and they were sensitive and understanding. It was one of the reasons they were so good at their jobs.

"So the church is out to get you," Heinz said once Kate had finished. "Doesn't surprise me. I would've wagered they'd try to get back at you."

Heinz was right, but she didn't bother saying so. They were nearing the farm on the hillside overlooking Luzern where Kate and the Lost Girls lived. The moment the car stopped, she was about to jump out when Viktor grabbed her arm. "I know you're worried," he said, a firm grip on her, "but you can't just barge in. It could be dangerous."

Kate twisted free and ran a few steps only to halt and look around. How come theirs was the only car? There was nowhere else to park and the police couldn't have come on foot. *Suzanne?* Kate called mind-to-mind, wondering why she hadn't done so before. What a mess. How could she have been so reckless?

Kate?

Yes. Where are they?

Gone. Five minutes ago.

Kate turned to find the others had joined her. "They've gone," she told them.

They were greeted by Tania and Suzanne who burst from the porch with the Lost Girls spilling in their wake. Spotting Kate, Suzanne blurted out, "It was terrible." A dark bruise was blossoming on the side of her face and her clothes were tattered. Heinz promptly took a photo. "For evidence," he said. Suzanne was such a mild girl and unusually small for her age. Kate couldn't imagine her getting into a fight. But then bullies always picked on the smallest and weakest.

"What happened?" Kate asked.

"I tried to stop them."

The memory of the ordeal must have been fresh in her mind because she was still trembling when Kate put an arm round her. As she tried to reassure her, they were surrounded by a bevy of girls, each vying to tell their version.

Eileen raised her voice, saying, "Don't crowd our guests." When the noise subsided, she sent a couple to prepare tea and two others to fetch cake from the kitchen. The owner of the property, Klaus, was a baker, and he often brought cakes home. Turning to the adults, Eileen said, "The kitchen is too small for us all. Let's go to the common room."

The common room was on the ground floor of a two-storied wooden building the girl's had commandeered. They had installed a canteen with an adjacent kitchen next to the common room. Their bedrooms were on the first floor. The building also housed the music room where the choir practiced as well as several smaller study rooms used for talks and lessons.

"While the girls prepare tea," Eileen said, "maybe you should see the apothecary." The neighbouring outhouse which they called the apothecary consisted of a large room that acted as a store for dried herbs and other medicinal supplies, several preparation rooms and an office in which they received the growing number of people that consulted them.

Suzanne tried unsuccessfully to push open the door. "Something's blocking it."

Viktor put his weight against the door and, letting out a grunt, shoved. There was a grating sound as something gave, the door flew open and he fell inwards onto a confused heap of dried plants. Kate stepped into the room to help him up and gasped. The place had been ravaged. Plants that once hung drying from the ceiling had been yanked loose and lay strewn in a muddle on the floor. Jars containing painstakingly prepared powders and creams had been smashed making any hope of salvaging impossible.

"What the ..." Kate began, only to be interrupted by Heinz.

"Don't touch anything," he said, pulling a camera from his

bag. "I want photos."

"That's months of work!" Kate exclaimed. "How could people who preach loving your neighbour be so hateful?"

"Some priests don't always practice what they preach," Regina commented, putting a comforting arm around Kate's shoulder. "Believe me, it's more common than you'd think. Abuse of power by the priesthood just happens to be the subject of our current investigation."

"Let's talk about that later," Heinz said as he finished taking photos. "I believe tea calls." Eileen, who'd just joined them nodded. "Indeed. And home-made birthday cake."

The girls had pushed several tables to make a large rectangle so everyone could sit together. No one wanted to miss out. Kate sat at one end with the three adults. They were flanked by what Kate called the Five, except they'd become Seven with her: Eileen, Tania and Clara on one side and Suzanne, Christine and Claudia on the other.

Once everyone was seated, Kate said grace, one of the rare customs they'd kept from the convent. She ended by adding, "May we be protected from those who wish us ill."

"Amen to that," Tania said, reaching for a piece of cake. "Happy birthday, Peter." She brandished the slice in salute, acknowledging his absence.

"You might like to offer a piece to our guests first," Christine chided.

Tania pushed a plate of cake in their direction then started in on her piece. "Shouldn't we go to the police?" she asked, her mouth half-full.

"Sorry? I didn't quite catch that," Suzanne said. She was fond of baiting Tania and it never failed. Tania spluttered, half choking on the giant morsel she was trying to swallow.

"Enough!" Kate said. "You two can settle your differences later."

"I don't think going to the police would be a good idea," Suzanne pursued, taking advantage of Tania's momentary handicap. She might be small, but she was tenacious. "The priests came with the police and they didn't lift a finger to stop them ransacking the place."

"Did any of you see what happened?" Regina asked. "Having eye-witness reports would help."

Heads shook around the table.

"That's a shame,"Regina said.

"Would photos help?" Suzanne asked. The way she stared naively at Regina had Kate suspecting the girl was hiding something.

"I took photos," Heinz said, sounding disappointed. "But they don't prove who did it."

Suzanne pulled out a camera she'd concealed under the table, a giant grin on her face. "No. But I have photos of the priests going berserk."

"How on earth did you manage that?" Tania asked.

"I tried to prevent them entering," Suzanne replied, her fingers lingering on the bruise to her face. "When they kicked me out, I remembered the camera I used to snap plants. There was a new film in it. So I sneaked outside and took photos through the windows."

"And they didn't try to stop you?" Heinz asked, incredulous.

"They were so set on doing as much damage as possible, I could have danced a gigue in the buff and they wouldn't have noticed."

Heinz chuckled. "Excellent. I didn't know you took photos. Do you develop them yourself?"

Suzanne shook her head. "Never had a chance," she said. "I thought to take them to the chemists."

"I could teach you," Heinz offered, eliciting a satisfied grin from Suzanne. "And it would be better if other people didn't see them just yet."

"I think those priests were a bit dim," Suzanne pursued.

"What makes you say that?" Regina asked.

"They went on and on about Devil's Claw. I tried to explain it was a herbal remedy that got its name from the shape of the flowers. They paid no attention. To listen to them you'd think the stuff had been brewed by Satan himself."

"Doesn't surprise me in the slightest!" Regina said. "To prevent women from healing, the church accused them of witchcraft and burnt them at the stake."

The mention of witchcraft unleashed a flood of questions, leaving Kate concerned about the girls' fascination, but Regina steered the conversation elsewhere with details of their latest investigation.

Kate pushed her chair back and slipped away. She needed to tell Peter what had happened and warn him to be vigilant. It would be easier to converse mind-to-mind if she were alone, so she climbed to the bedroom she shared with him. It too had been visited but there was none of the chaos of the apothecary.

She sat on the bed and called Peter. He listened in silence as she described the state of the apothecary. Even without him saying a word, she could sense his distress. The two had worked so hard to get the apothecary up and running. They'd been counting on income from the sale of herbal remedies to help pay for the Lost Girls.

Did they search our room? Peter asked.

Yeah. But they were light-handed. Just some photos missing and the wrapping from your parcel screwed up on the floor. She picked up the ball of paper and unscrunched it. *That's odd,* she said. *Didn't you get a card with your dress? I don't see it anywhere.*

There should also be a photo of you, or rather me, with Fi. She sensed his guilt at not showing it to her. *I was afraid you'd be upset,* he explained.

There's no sign of it, she replied, opting not to object to him keeping secrets.

That's torn it.

Why?

Because if they've got that photo, they know what I look like.

4.

Kate shuddered. He was so reckless. "You can't!" She insisted. "It's too dangerous."

"But it's my birthday and I've got several solos," Peter retorted, turning to Viktor for support. "The audience will be expecting me."

"Exactly. That's the problem," Kate countered, raising an imperious hand to silence Viktor. "We'll just have to change the programme."

Peter shook his head. "I can't spend the rest of my life hiding."

"True. But that bailiff will give up soon enough," Kate said.

"What if you stayed behind the altar screen," Beth suggested. "You'd be heard but not seen." They had sung from there at their first concert in the church. They hadn't needed to hide. It was for effect. "You could enter by the vestry door. No one would be any the wiser."

"Great," Peter said. "Glad that's settled."

Kate was peeved at him cutting short all discussion, but she knew how much he needed to sing so she kept quiet.

"Does anyone know what's wrong with Tricia?" Beth asked, looking questioningly at Peter. "She's locked in her room and won't come out."

Following Beth's gaze, Kate caught Peter blushing. She'd never experienced jealousy, but his embarrassment stirred feelings she guessed must be just that. "What did you do to her?" she asked, feeling an unwelcome surge of anger. He was reluctant to reply, which only fuelled her suspicion. "Well?" she snapped.

"I… didn't do anything," Peter replied, looking more hurt than embarrassed. "It was her."

"Yeah! You bet," Kate said, unable to rein in her runaway emotions.

"Let him speak," Beth said.

"It was all wrong…" Peter began.

Kate spluttered in indignation. To which Beth shot her a "Shhh…"

Peter drew in a deep breath, looking beseechingly at Kate who folded her arms across her chest. "When she came to take away the tea things," he began, "she asked me embarrassing questions."

"Like?" Kate interjected.

"Like was I a boy or why did I dress up."

"I'm so sorry," Beth said. "That was completely out of line."

"She didn't stop there. She wanted to help me dress. And her eyes! They were wild and greedy. I think she might be a bit crazy."

"That's terrible," Beth exclaimed. "I'll send her away post-haste."

"Don't be too harsh," Peter said. "I don't think she can help it."

"That's the problem," Beth replied.

Kate felt ashamed and miserable. "I'm sorry," she muttered, tears creeping into her eyes.

Viktor joined Beth saying, "Do we have to tell you young folk everything?" He laced his arms around Beth's neck and planted a kiss on her forehead.

Kate took a hesitant step towards Peter. It was all very well for those two. They might have just met, but they'd known each other for years even if they hadn't been together. And they lived as man and wife. Between her and Peter, it was different. They avoided being openly intimate around the other girls, out of respect. They certainly didn't kiss in public. What would people think if two girls kissed, especially ones so young? With the strong religious feelings rooted in the town, it would surely provoke outrage. All the more so if they found out Peter was a boy in disguise.

Peter reached out and took hold of her hand. His touch sent tingles down her spine. Not to be outdone, she took his other hand and pulled him closer till they were nose to nose.

At that moment, Tiana burst into the room laughing, closely followed by the entire choir. "Oops. Sorry," she said, stopping short as she took in the scene. A mischievous smile spread across her lips. "I hope we are not interrupting. It's time to go. Our audience awaits..."

Kate let go of Peter's hand and took a step back. "Did nobody ever teach you to knock?"

As infuriating as ever, Tania shrugged and blew her a kiss.

"Peter will not be coming," Kate announced. They hadn't discussed logistics, but she thought it better to let everyone know.

"What about his solos?" Clara asked, worry creasing her forehead.

"We've figured out a way for him to sing without being seen," Kate replied, hoping some smart-Aleck like Tania wouldn't want to know more. "Just in case those men try to grab him."

Luckily Tania's thoughts were elsewhere. "Surely he'll need a chaperon to keep an eye on him," she suggested, bent on mischief, as ever. "As a stranger in town, we don't want him getting lost." Several girls sniggered.

"Yeah!" Eileen exclaimed, shaking her head. "As if you could be trusted not to lead him astray." Tania feigned innocence. "Come on girls," Eileen continued, linking arms with a reluctant Tania and leading her away. "We should head for St Leodegar. It's time."

"I'll catch up," Kate said as the choir left. Once the girls had gone, Kate turned to Viktor, "Can you smuggle Peter in?"

He nodded, donning his Cossack's hat as if it were a disguise.

If anything, he was the least likely person to go unnoticed.

"Don't mind me," Peter exclaimed, slumped in an armchair. "Does me being under threat give everyone the right to treat me like a mindless pawn?"

"That happens to girls all the time," Kate retorted, planting her hands on her hips, a pose she'd never tried before. She rather liked it. "You remember our discussion about wearing cute dresses and lovely colours…Now you know what it feels like to be a girl."

"Kate," Beth said, a hint of a smile on her lips. "I see your point. But now is maybe not the time. The longer we wait, the more risky it'll be. Pretty or not, we don't want him hustled off to England."

"True," Kate said, grimacing, and set off with Beth, heading for the church. Peter and Viktor trailed some twenty yards behind, talking in hushed tones. One of the few accesses to the cathedral for a wheelchair was round the back via a short bridge that spanned a road sunk in the rock then plunged through the high wall surrounding St Leodegar into a cloister that doubled as graveyard.

Viktor scooped Beth in his arms while Peter and Kate heaved her wheelchair down three short steps and through the archway into the church grounds. Following them, Viktor settled Beth in her chair and made sure she was comfortable. Meanwhile, Kate and Peter exchanged a hasty kiss and, filled with misgiving, Kate whispered, "Be careful." To which he replied, "I love you too."

Viktor pulled a large key from his pocket and, hugging the walls, he and Peter slunk clockwise round the church to the vestry door. Kate pushed Beth in the opposite direction intent on reaching the main entrance at the top of the stairs up from the lake. They were to greet those come to attend the concert.

The moment they arrived at the entrance with its sculptured wooden doors, they were caught in a flurry of polite greetings. As patron of the most important choral festival in Luzern, Beth knew anyone and everyone who had anything to do with music and she made a point of introducing Kate as the leader of the choir. From those who knew the history of the Lost Girls came enquiries about the wellbeing of the choir. Others recalled recent concerts and were full of praise. A few enquired about herbal remedies, having learnt of the girls' efforts to set up a dispensary. There were even those who were already regulars at the apothecary.

It was Clara who came in search of Kate, no doubt intending to rescue her from the swell of well-wishers. Something of a darling with those women who followed the choir, Clara was immediately swept up in a sea of admirers who flooded her with compliments. Unwilling to deprive the little girl of well-earned praise, Kate was hesitant about interrupting, but they were running late. Finally, it was Kate that had to rescue Clara and lead her into the church.

The choir would normally wait unseen in the vestry, but as Peter was hiding there, they huddled in the shadows off to one side of the nave, silently watching the audience fill the remaining pews. When the main door was pulled shut and the lights dimmed till only candles lit the nave, Clara got to her feet and gave the note.

The first words of the song on their lips, the girls rose and strolled down the aisle. Clara led the way with Kate bringing up the rear. Halting before the wrought-iron screen erected to mask the inner sanctum, they took up their places on the steps in front of the altar and turned to face the congregation.

Kate shot a look over her shoulder, but couldn't make out Peter in the flickering gloom. Applause had died down and the audience sat in silent expectation. Time for Peter's first solo. As the silence prolonged, Kate tensed, her breathing shallow. Then Peter's treble voice soared over the gathered listeners and everyone let out a sigh of relief as if they'd shared Kate's fears.

Midway through the solo, Peter broke off and let out a strangled cry. There were sounds of a scuffle, a door slammed and a shocked silence settled in the church. As one, the choir turned to look where Peter should have been. The congregation gasped. Kate was the first to react, abandoning the others, she sprinted round the screen and ran to the vestry.

Pushing open the door, she narrowly missed tripping over Viktor sprawled on the flagstone floor. She placed a hand on his shoulder, at which he groaned. "Stop them," he mumbled. Crossing the vestry, she struggled with the door. It was locked. "The key," Viktor croaked, holding out his hand.

The door unlocked, Kate emerged amongst the gravestones and shot a glance in the direction of the archway they'd used earlier. Nobody. No one the other way either. Hearing noises behind her, she turned to see the girls helping Viktor to his feet. "What happened?" Eileen asked.

"Don't know," Viktor mumbled. "Everything went black."

Susanne sniffed the air. "Chloroform," she pronounced.

Kate was about to return inside when she was shoved aside by two policemen who shouldered the girls out of the way and seized Viktor. "You are under arrest," the taller of the two informed a bemused Viktor.

"Whatever for?" he asked, trying unsuccessfully to shake loose.

"For assaulting a policeman."

"What nonsense," Viktor spluttered. "I never attacked a policeman in my life."

"You tried to prevent the arrest of a young man."

They must be talking about Peter. So the police continued to abet the bailiff and now they sought to blame Viktor. Kate was deep in thought when a hand on her shoulder made her jump. "It's me," a male voice said behind her. She turned to find Heinz stepping into the room, closely followed by Regina. He swung up his camera and snapped the two policemen flanking Viktor, much to their annoyance. "I'd let that man go if I were you," he said.

"Keep out of this!" the taller policemen said, raising a forbidding hand. "It's police business."

"Is it?" Regina said. "We witnessed the supposed altercation. Contrary to what you claim, this man was assaulted by your colleagues and drugged before they made off with an unconscious child."

"What rubbish!" the policeman exclaimed. "You have no proof."

"Wait till you see the photos in tomorrow's paper," Heinz retorted.

The two policemen abruptly relaxed their hold on Viktor. He would have fallen had not Eileen offered him a hand. "Mistaken identity," the tall one muttered as the two made their getaway.

From within the church, Kate could hear a rising buzz of conversation. Something had to be done. She strode round the screen and breasted the noisy speculation. Silence fell the moment the congregation caught sight of her.

Halting at the top of the steps, Kate surveyed the audience then drew in a deep breath. "One of our number has been kidnapped," she said, her tone grave. A gasp went up from the audience. She was about to apologise and cancel the concert when the girls, who must have followed her out, took up the song they'd sung at their dear friend Sister Teresa's funeral. Kate had tears in her eyes as she added her voice to that of the choir. To her astonishment here and there members of the audience stood, heads bowed as if in prayer, only to be joined little by little by all the others.

5.

Peter awoke to the clatter of wheels on rails and a filthy taste in his mouth. He raked his fingers through his hair struggling to untwine his thoughts. His throat was parched and his belly complained. The blinds were drawn but the absence of light hinted at night.

Only when he got to his feet did he realise he'd been stripped of his girl's clothes. With a sinking feeling, he looked down at a loose-fitting, grey tracksuit. His feet were bare, but socks and sandals lay strewn nearby. He shot a look round the compartment. He was alone. His dress was nowhere to be seen. He shuddered. A stranger must have undressed him. Surely not the bailiff!

He tried the door. Locked. Of course. He struggled with the blinds. They too were fastened shut. Then he spotted the emergency cord. He shouldn't. He couldn't. Come off it! Why ever not? He'd been abducted, damn it! He seized the cord and yanked. Unsure what to expect, he braced himself should the train brake abruptly. Nothing of the kind. They continued unabated into the night.

Peter had just sat down and taken his head in his hands when a key turned in the lock. The bailiff burst in, closely followed by a ticket collector. "What the hell...?" the bailiff began, rounding on Peter, only to be interrupted by the ticket collector.

"You can't just pull the emergency cord," the man said in German, not in the Swiss dialect. They must have crossed the border.

"I was frightened," Peter replied in German.

"Stop that!" the bailiff said in English, shifting to shove Peter into a corner.

Peter dodged and took refuge with the ticket collector. "This man kidnapped me," he exclaimed, sticking to German despite the bailiff's remonstrances. "He locked me in. I've had nothing to eat or drink all day."

The collector looked from Peter to the bailiff who'd gone red in the face. Seizing Peter's arm, he said, "Come."

"You can't do that," the bailiff blustered, trying to block the door.

"Do want I call police?" the ticket collector menaced in broken English

The bailiff's mouth snapped shut and he scuttled after the collector.

"Where are we going?" Peter asked as the collector hurried him along the darkened corridor.

"The restaurant car. To get food."

The restaurant car was surprisingly full given the late hour. Solitary men sat slumped over drinks, shooting furtive glances at two young girls, twins most likely, who leaned together whispering, oblivious to the attention, a slice of cake half-eaten between them. All the passengers turned as one to eye Peter, the twins unashamedly sizing him up. He must look odd in his ill-fitting tracksuit and bare feet, in the grips of a ticket collector, trailed by a bespectacled man swearing in English.

The ticket collector sat Peter down at one of the few remaining free tables and ordered a sandwich and a bottle of water. When the waiter returned, he handed Peter a ham sandwich. Peter set about unwrapping it while the man poured him a glass of water.

Biting into the bread, Peter let out a sigh. "Thanks," he managed to say, despite the mouthful. The ticket collector nodded then got to his feet and began checking tickets. The bailiff would have sat opposite Peter, but the waiter beat him to it, pushing a slice of cake in Peter's direction. The bailiff turned even redder, if that were possible. On the verge of exploding, he launched into a diatribe in English about meddling Germans and how they were losers who had been thrashed by the English during two wars.

The waiter asked him to translate, but Peter was so embarrassed and upset, he replied, "He's beyond himself. He knows not what he's saying."

Several passengers got to their feet and rounded on the bailiff. What if they understood what the idiot was saying? Peter was afraid they'd come to blows. The bailiff was so insensitive and exasperating. Luckily the ticket collector intervened. "Leave boy alone," he said, stepping between the bailiff and the men. "He going nowhere."

"You wait till I get my hands on you, brat. I'll make you pay!" the bailiff muttered as he retreated to a seat across the car.

"What did he say?" the waiter enquired under his breath, pouring Peter more water

"Threats," Peter said, shooting the bailiff a look. He didn't want to make things worse.

"So what's all this about?" the waiter asked.

Seeing the bailiff glaring at him through oversized spectacles like an owl furious at prey for getting away, Peter hesitated. Even if he'd won a temporary reprieve, the man could still make his life hell.

"I travelled with my adopted parents to Luzern for a choir festival," Peter began.

"You sing?" one of the twins asked. Her obvious delight surprised him. The two had been so engrossed in each other, he hadn't thought they were listening.

Peter nodded. "After the festival my parents returned to England, but they let me stay in Luzern and join a choir."

"So, are you going to sing for us?" the girl asked, clapping her hands like a tiny tot about to get a treat. Peter was confused. For all her childish outburst, she must surely have been at least fourteen. But he had no time to wonder as several people joined her in encouraging him.

"To pay for your supper," the waiter recited with a grin.

"Like in the nursery rhyme."

Peter didn't want to cause trouble, but he loved singing and he might never get another chance. It was the scowl on the bailiff's face that made up his mind. He got to his feet, drew in a deep breath and launched into a German love song Viktor had taught him.

The moment the last note settled, the car was rocked with applause. "Wonderful," the girl said, when the clapping ceased. "You have such a sweet voice," she said, batting her eyelids at him. Her conduct was such a caricature, it had to be an act. She concluded, "You could be mistaken for a girl."

Several of the travellers chuckled quietly as they rose and headed for the door, understanding the performance was over. Peter blushed, unsure if he'd just been insulted or complimented.

"Enough nonsense," the bailiff said, elbowing the two girls aside.

"Hey!" they objected rubbing bruised arms, but the man paid no attention. He grabbed Peter by the wrist and wrenched him from his seat. "Now you've eaten, it's time to return to the compartment."

Peter searched for allies, but most passengers had left. It was late. His saviour, the ticket collector, was nowhere to be seen and the waiter had disappeared into the kitchen amid a clatter of plates. Only the twins remained and they were little use against the brute who tugged Peter towards the door?

"Can we help?" one of the twins asked in impeccable English.

"Mind your own business!" the bailiff snapped, and, yanking open the door, shoved Peter down the darkened corridor. Preoccupied by the girls and what they were up to, Peter failed to notice the small suitcase planted mid corridor and tripped over it, sprawling head first to the floor.

"Get up!" the bailiff spat, aiming a kick in Peter's direction. If the man had not been so clumsy he might have broken Peter's leg, such was the violence of the blow. Instead he missed and kicked the case. Letting out a shriek of pain, he hopped on the spot, cutting an absurd figure as he tried to grasp his injured foot.

Seeing the bailiff distracted, the twins slipped past. They helped Peter to his feet and stood flanking him like bodyguards or was it jailers? Their grip was so tight, he winced as their nails dug into his flesh. To his horror, he realised he might not be any safer with them than the bailiff.

"Girls!" a deep female voice called out. The accent reminded him of Viktor. The woman must be Slav. What's more, she had Viktor's build and even wore the same ankle-length leather coat.

The girls relinquished their hold, but not before digging their nails one last time into his skin, and stepped away looking contrite. Grasping them by the collar, the woman marched them away without a word.

Peter stood wide-eyed watching the girls meekly follow the woman. He'd passed within inches of disaster, although he had no idea what he'd escaped. A groan behind him reminded him the nightmare was not over. Fingers grasping his throat confirmed it. "I'll teach you," the bailiff growled, his nails digging into Peter's flesh, cutting off the air to his lungs.

Survival instinct kicked in and Peter did something he hadn't done for ages. He lashed out mind-to-mind, sending a mental strike ripping through the bailiff's head that had the man reeling in confusion. For all the desperateness of the situation, Peter immediately regretted acting impulsively. He and Kate had vowed never to resort to such radical means again, having seen the damage it could cause.

Peter managed to catch the bailiff before he fell. Staggering under his weight, he inched the man towards their compartment. Once inside, he let the bloke collapse onto the bench and made sure the door was properly closed. Rummaging through the bailiff's pockets felt like breaking a taboo, but he had to find the key. His imagination was probably running wild, but he didn't want those twins bursting in.

Once he was sure the girls were safely locked out, he let himself slide to the floor and stared at the bailiff who stared unseeing back. Peter was loathed to use mind-to-mind healing on such a person, but he had to undo the damage. He couldn't just leave him a zombie. Entering some else's mind was always tricky, but it was far worse when the person was hostile.

The prospect of righting a wrecked mind was daunting. The brain was so complex. Better to tackle a simpler task first. He closed his eyes, and placing a hand on the man's ankle, went in search of the damage to the bailiff's toes. A bone was broken, another bent. Ligaments had been torn and a clot of blood was forming just beneath the skin. Peter let energy flow into the man's foot and encouraged the many cells to do what they did so naturally, shift to a state of health and harmony.

It was the secret of healing that he and Kate had uncovered. Every cell contained a blueprint, all the necessary information for how it should be. To set things right, it sufficed to provide healing energy and coax the body to follow that blueprint.

Peter sat back, leaning against the bench opposite. He opened his eyes and drew in a long breath. There was a deep satisfaction to setting things right. Next to singing, healing was the most wonderful thing you could do.

He closed his eyes again. Now came the real challenge. Like every other part of the body, the brain had its blueprint, but much of the working of the brain depended on those ideas and patterns that went beyond the original schema. He would have to mentally jump to the man's mind if he were to undo the damage. Steeling himself, he launched across the space between them.

It wasn't the overriding confusion that trouble him but what he could only describe as the stench of putrid thoughts. Protecting himself as best he could, he drew in positive energy and channelled it to the blueprint. The impact was immediate. A good deal of the confusion lifted but the unpleasant odour persisted. It was tempting to tamper with the thought patterns and flush away the filth. Doing so would make his life a lot easier and might do the man some good. But such changes were not up to him. Interfering wouldn't be right.

Sensing that the man was on the point of rousing, Peter withdrew, glad to be free of the stink. Opening his eyes, he was about to get to his feet when he realised the bailiff's eyes were open and fixed on him with a look of pure hatred.

6.

"What the hell?" the bailiff exclaimed, springing to his feet, only to keel over, bounce off the bench and sink with a thud to the floor.

Peter had seen it before. A residue of confusion could cause problems of balance or even a feeling of nausea. It was generally short-lived, but could be alarming. "Easy does it," he said. "You fainted." With anyone else he'd have laid a reassuring hand on the person's shoulder, a discreet way of topping up the person's energy. But the man was far too hostile for such kind attention.

The bailiff stared at Peter, uncomprehending, then rubbed his foot as if the memory of the injury persisted even though the damage had been repaired. Confusion gave way to suspicion only to be replaced by anger. "You need to stay calm," Peter said, hoping he could stave off the coming storm. Instead veins bulged in the man's neck and his face turned a vivid red. "Getting worked up might not be good for your heart." In the man's case his heart was surprisingly healthy, but fear of a heart attack might hold him in check.

"There's nothing wrong with my heart," the man snarled, struggling unsteadily to his feet. "That blasted waiter must have drugged me." He rummaged through his pockets, no doubt looking for the key, the very one nestling in Peter's pocket. Peter slid a hand in his pocket, praying the move would go unnoticed, located the key and pulled it out concealed in a clenched fist.

Giving up on his search, the bailiff tried the door, only to find it locked. He spun round, his eyes boring into Peter. "You've got it!"

"Got what?" he asked, slipping the key between the seat and the back of the bench. The dull clunk as it fell to the floor had Peter terrified, but the man continued his rant unabated.

"The blasted key, boy." The man threw up his arms in exasperation. "Are you daft?"

"I don't have any keys." To drive home his point, Peter made a show of turning out his pockets.

The bailiff took a step closer, no doubt aiming to frisk Peter, but didn't get very far. A resounding knock shook the door. "Everything alright?" It was the ticket inspector.

"We're locked in," Peter managed in German before the bailiff clamped a hand over his mouth. The skin-to-skin contact gave him direct access. He could easily have launched an attack but was loathed to do so again. It proved unnecessary.

The ticket inspector opened the door, presumably with a master key, and stepped inside. A look of horror darkened his face seeing what must have looked like the man trying to suffocate Peter. "What the hell are you doing?" he asked in German.

The bailiff replied with a scowl, then said, "Tell this idiot to mind his own business."

Peter stared at the ticket inspector, at a loss what to say.

"Tickets, please," the inspector demanded in English, holding out a hand.

Pulling an envelope from his inside pocket, the bailiff handed it over. The inspector examined the tickets for so long Peter wondered why he was stalling. Then the inspector put one ticket back in its place and, pocketing the other, handed the envelope to the bailiff. The latter was on the verge of exploding, but the inspector gave him no chance. He took Peter by the arm and led him to the door, saying, "I'll make sure this boy reaches his destination safely."

If Peter had imagined he could convince the inspector not to deliver him to England, he was soon set right. The man was a stickler for rules. At least Peter was treated better and fed regularly, but he was still a prisoner in his first class sleeper. "For his protection," the inspector insisted as he locked Peter in.

Shaking off the ill-fitting sandals, Peter lay fully-clothed on the neatly-made bed, closed his eyes and went in search of Kate. What with the bailiff and the inspector, he hadn't had a moment. She must be anxious.

For a long time he couldn't locate her. At first he wondered if he was out of practice - they hadn't spoken mind-to-mind at such a distance for a long time - then he realised she must be asleep. And, sure enough, she was. So much for worry keeping her awake.

Kate, he said, his mental voice sharper than he'd intended.

Peter? She sounded confused as she emerged from sleep. *Am I dreaming?*

No. It's me.

Where are you? I was so worried. Her words were thick with concern.

He described where he was and related what had happened. *They even replaced my dress with a tracksuit while I was unconscious.*

Poor thing. He sensed no irony in her words, only compassion. *Is there no way you can escape?*

Peter shook his head mentally, relaying images of an over-protective ticket collector and a zealous bailiff hovering like a vulture waiting to strike. *They're waging a bitter war that can only have one outcome, me returning to England.*

Have you tried contacting Christina or John? Surely they can help.

I only ever spoke to them mind-to-mind once and that in their presence. It terrified them. They were worried they'd be manipulated. Reassuring them was not easy.

He nodded mentally, acknowledging her intention to contact them. *Good idea. You might have more success than me.*

Things here were a mess. The police tried to arrest Viktor, accusing him of obstructing their work. She shared a couple of memories of the scene. *But Regina and Heinz saw what happened and Heinz threatened to publish photos of the police attacking Viktor and you.*

Lucky they were there.

I think they suspected something was afoot. They came prepared.

If they had their doubts, why the hell didn't they warn him? He thought he'd kept his ideas to himself, but something must have seeped through. Kate replied, *I don't think they were sure. It was a hunch.*

His reply was little more than a grunt, keeping a tight rein over what he shared. Even if it was only an intuition, they might at least have said.

Changing the subject, Kate asked, *Do you know when you reach the coast?*

Not sure. In a couple of hours, I believe.

You should get some rest.

He felt her readying to sever the communication. *I love you,* he thought and, taking her mentally in his arms, hugged her tight, unwilling to let her go.

Love you too. She planted a kiss on his lips, the memory of which lingered long after the contact had been broken.

The remainder of the journey to the coast was uneventful, apart from a nightmare in which the terrible twins sprang from the shadows and grabbed him, dragging him off to a destination he never reached. When the girls didn't turn up at breakfast, he asked the ticket collector. Apparently they rode the train once a term on their way to school in England. But that was all he knew.

The bailiff, on the contrary, was present wherever Peter went, keeping a wary eye from a distance, but the inspector made sure the man didn't pester him. That protection would necessarily end the moment he stepped off the train to board the ferry. Peter had visions of being tossed into the Channel, but the inspector assured him the bailiff wouldn't dare. "He won't get paid if he doesn't deliver the goods."

Peter grimaced at the expression. The bailiff probably did

see him as 'troublesome merchandise'. When the train sidled to a halt in the terminus, the inspector was busy with paperwork but insisted Peter wait, saying, "I'll get one of my colleagues on the boat to keep an eye on you."

Peter watched the passengers trundle heavy cases from the train and shuffle along the crowded platform towards the docks and the waiting ferry. During the night they must have travelled into France. Calais, the sign read. The announcements were in French. His knowledge of the language was rudimentary, but he knew enough to recognise it.

He had no luggage. He could easily have bolted, disappearing in the seething mass, or, even better, hid in the train, but doing so would have been futile. He had no money, no papers. What's more, the bailiff was watching his every move, waiting for a chance to grab him.

"This way," the inspector said, surprising Peter, whose mind was elsewhere. Instead of following the remaining stragglers towards the exit, the inspector led him down a narrow alley to a door. If Peter did nothing, the boat would carry him off to England. And there, without the hormones, his voice would break and all those transformations that would mark him as a man would proceed unchecked and irreversible. Blocking the way, he turned to face the man and said, "I can't go. I don't belong in England. My place is with the choir in Luzern. If you force me to go, you'll be helping that bailiff abduct me."

"Listen, I've done my best to protect you from that odious man. But I can't go against a court order. You need to be re-united with your rightful mother. If I go against the law, I'll be abducting you, not him."

Peter wanted to point out that his rightful mother was Christina, not the mad crone who'd been used to justify dragging him back against his will. But arguing was pointless. The man was unbending in his correctness. That was why he'd protected Peter, but it was also why he slavishly obeyed official documents.

With a sinking feeling, Peter stepped through the door to

find himself on a wind-swept quai, the ferry towering over him and men in overalls scurrying here and there, loading cargo.

"I don't know if that horrible man has papers for you," the ticket inspector said, following him through, "but I have nothing, apart from your ticket. So I'm going to have to smuggle you on board ."

The cry of a horn rang out startling gulls. They shrieked, lifting into air only to circle then land nearby. "We must hurry," the ticket collector said, jostling Peter up a narrow ramp onto the ferry. "The boat is about to sail."

They'd just reached the top when a customs officer stepped from behind a crate and barred their way. He said something in French but Peter didn't understand. The ensuing argument between the two men went back and forth with growing acrimony. Fearing a fight, Peter was about to step away, when a hand grabbed his shoulder and a familiar voice said, "There you are." It was the Bailiff.

7.

Peter gripped the railing and turned to face the wind. They'd sailed out of Calais smack into a storm. The ferry bucked time and time again as it crested giant waves and plunged into deep troughs. The deck was littered with passengers heaving up their breakfast. He'd left the bailiff bent over double, one hand grasping his belly, the other cupped over his mouth. He could have helped, after all was he not constantly healing any trace of nausea in himself, but he didn't feel charitable. And anyway, the man's indisposition left him free to roam the boat.

As they neared the coast, the sight of the white cliffs filled him with despondency. They could have been a welcome sign, especially as they promised an end to the heaving nightmare. Once upon-a-time Peter would have risen to the pull of home, the deep Englishness of it, like Elgar and Blake at the Last Night of the Proms, but now the chalk cliffs reared up like the walls of a prison whose door was about to slam behind him.

"Oh, look," a girl's voice stage-whispered close to his ear making him jump. He spun round to find himself face to face with the twins. "It's the pretty boy who sings like an angel," the shorter of the two said, her tongue darting out over moistened lips.

Being called 'pretty' reminded him of Fi. He'd been her pretty boy and she'd been his handsome girl. But there was none of Fi's playfulness in these two. Whatever they were up to, it was deadly serious. They planted themselves on either side of him, standing so close the smell of their soap engulfed him. Cornering him against the railing, they exuded confidence, convinced he wouldn't dare push past and escape.

"Sing us that love song," the taller sister said, moving closer till her lips were only inches from his face. For one horrible moment he was terrified she might kiss him. He had visions of being sucked dry. "I haven't been able to get it out of my head," she added, her voice husky, her scented breath caressing his cheek.

"Girls!" The sharpness of the word cut knife-like through the twins gruesome game. They jumped back. "Leave the boy alone..." The speed at which their expressions switched from sinister and scheming to submissive and contrite was alarming. Such cunning and deception filled Peter with foreboding.

The girls trotted meekly after the matron who busied herself fixing her hair that had been ruffled by the wind. In that moment of distraction, the shorter of the two shot him a glance over her shoulder. She licked her lips lasciviously before giving him the finger then, turning away, giggled with her sister.

He breathed a sigh of relief once they disappeared below deck and was about to search for the bailiff, preferring to find rather than be found, when he spotted a crumpled paper at his feet. It must have fallen from the girl's pocket. Rescuing it before the blustery wind could blow it over board, he smoothed it out and began to read.

The missive dated from a year earlier. Addressed to the twins, it cautioned about their behaviour and informed them they were on probation during the coming year. If they didn't amend their ways, they'd be expelled. No mention was made of what they'd done.

Glancing at the letterhead, Peter was horrified. It had been sent from Our Lady of Grace and was signed Christina, his adoptive mother. She'd been administrator there for many a year. Our Lady was a private girls' school from which his nemesis Priscilla Wit had been expelled. She'd turned up at his school and latched on to him threatening to torture and kill him. After a stay in a mental institution, she'd taken her life.

That any girls from Our Lady should be interested in him was completely out of character. If they had eyes for anyone, it was the girls from his former school, but only to glare at them as vermin to be exterminated. The thought of bumping into the twins down a dark alley filled him with dread. As if he didn't have enough problems.

Peter was about to shove the letter into his tracksuit pocket when a violent gust of wind ripped it from his fingers and sent it soaring over the railing and out to sea. The bailiff chose that moment to step unsteadily onto the deck and stagger towards him. Still grasping his stomach, the fellow was even more sour-faced than usual. Peter braced himself for a torrent of abuse, but all he got was, "Come."

They reached London without further ado and, despite Peter dragging his feet in the hope of delaying their arrival, just managed to catch the local train westward. The bailiff refused to say where they were heading, but the more they travelled the more Peter became convinced Tallford, his old home, was their destination. If he was right, he would be close to his adoptive parents, Christina and John. The prospect filled him with hope. Surely they'd be able to help.

They did indeed end up in Tallford where the bailiff hailed a taxi from the rank in the forecourt. Peter even caught a glimpse of his former school out of the rear window. He'd only been away six months, but the place felt intensely foreign. He wondered if he'd spot anyone he knew, but it was early afternoon on a Wednesday and everyone was in class. Even the playing field was deserted.

The bailiff had said his mother had ordered his return. That she was out and about, capable of arguing her case before a judge, was so unlikely he suspected a lie, but the man insisted. If it were true, they'd surely drive to her house on top of the hill outside town. Last time he'd visited the place, it'd been populated only by dust motes and painful memories. Their home had been abandoned shortly after he fled the cruelty of his mother and sister. The police had had to intervene and the two were carted off kicking and screaming to the local clinic.

Having biked those lanes at least twice a day for several years, he knew the route by heart. When the taxi driver turned the wrong way, Peter was about to set him right, but the bailiff shot him a menacing look, silencing him. It was only as the car pulled into a wooded park and came to a halt in an ugly car park in front of a stylish brick mansion that he realised with a sinking feeling where they were. Our Lady of Grace.

How could that be? Boys didn't attend Our Lady beyond the age of ten. He wasn't even sure boys still went there after the tragedy in which one died at the hands of Witless. For a hopeful moment he wondered if he was being taken to see Christina, but as he followed the bailiff into the building, the woman behind Christina's desk was someone he'd never seen before. She couldn't have been less like Christina. Her black hair hung mat around a miserable face and her beak-like nose and pinched lips gave her an air of a carrion bird. Her stoop accentuated the impression as did the claws disguised as nails. He was so shocked, he blurted out, "Where's Christina ?"

"That woman no longer works here."

Christina gone. It was unthinkable. She'd worked there for ages. She'd been such an integral part of the place, girls would come back years later just to see her. "That's not possible," Peter insisted, raising his voice. "Our Lady of Grace wouldn't be what it is without Christina."

"You are sorely mistaken," she replied, staring down her nose at him. "That women was a disgrace. The headmistress did well to fire her."

Her words were like a punch in the gut. Peter stood gaping in disbelief. He was about to object when a door opened and out stepped a woman he knew only too well. Priscilla's aunt. The very woman who'd tried to orchestrate John's downfall and subsequently pursued her niece's witch-hunt against Peter. He stared at her with undisguised hatred and she stared back with equal animosity.

"Madame Headmistress," the new administrator said with a

deferent nod. "As you predicted, we're already having trouble with our new pupil."

Those two sentences rang like a death knell. He clenched his fists, furious. He wouldn't go down without a fight. "How many innocent people did you assassinate to get this job?" he snarled, beside himself with fury. His voice was so unlike him, he shuddered. He hated it. Never had he sounded so like an angry young man.

Easy does it, a soft voice whispered in his head.

Kate, he gasped, a deep feeling a gratitude flooding him. He calmed as Kate's presence had its effect. He'd been so caught up in his emotions he hadn't noticed her join him.

I'm your guardian angel, she purred.

Peter drew in a shuddery breath. His attention was focused on Kate rather than what was happening in the room so he was surprised when he felt her tense. *You're going to have to apologise*, she warned.

Looking up, he saw the headmistress glaring at him with pointed hatred. Both the administrator and the bailiff stood silent, their expressions disapproving. Kate was right, he should apologise, but he found it hard. "I'm sorry," he mumbled. "I don't know what came over me."

"It would seem the whole family is unhinged," the administrator said flicking through what Peter supposed was his dossier. "Maybe we should call the clinic."

Peter shuddered. He'd visited his sister and mother there. It was the worst sort of asylum, the likes of which should exist only in novels. Ever present staff in white coats brandishing syringes and confused patients bound in straight jackets, their temples sporting burns from excessive electroshocks. He'd stand no chance.

"No," the headmistress said, a twisted smile spreading across her lips. "Not yet."

Peter took an involuntary step back, horrified at the implied threat. As if fearful he might make a run for it, the bailiff blocked Peter's retreat, placing a heavy hand on his shoulder. "Going somewhere?" he growled. Peter didn't even bother to reply.

"You can let him go," the headmistress said. "He's going nowhere." Turning to the administrator, she added. "I want a private word with him first, then see he gets a uniform. We must have a used one lying around that would fit, and have a prefect show him to his new room." Addressing Peter, she said, "Follow me."

In his earlier visit to Our Lady he'd not entered the headmistress's study. He expected something akin to his new father's office. After all, he too was head of a school. John's study was lined from floor to ceiling with shelves of books, a fitting reflection of the man who occupied the room. In comparison Priscilla's aunt's office was like a parched desert. The walls were bare, the only decoration being a life-sized portrait of herself hanging behind her desk from where it glared down at him.

The woman took up her place behind the desk, resting her arms on the otherwise empty work surface. Peter was forced to stand, no chairs having been provided for unfortunate visitors.

Impressive, Kate said. *Talk about power-crazed.*

Peter didn't reply. He was busy steeling himself from what was to come. Not that he had any idea what that might be. The woman was silently sizing him up in a way that was meant to intimidate and it worked.

"We have rules," she began, running a hand across the desk as if she could further smooth the surface. "You'll find them behind the door to your room. But as you are a special case, I am laying down additional rules." She paused as if mentally drawing up the list. "We need to wean you off your filthy habit of dressing as a girl. Some would oblige you to dress as a boy, that would make eminent sense, but I prefer to force you to mascarade as a girl. You'll quickly get sick of it."

Never, Peter thought.

There must be a catch, Kate warned.

"Whenever in school, you'll wear the uniform you've been allotted. If you refuse, I'll personally see you join your mother and sister in that clinic."

Peter was tempted to shoot back, 'I suppose you imagine me hanging myself like your niece?'

I have to go, Kate said during a brief pause in the conversation. *I'll be back as soon as possible.*

Contact Christina and John, if you can.

Will do. Love you. And she was gone.

"You'll attend classes like all the girls," the headmistress pursued. "I see no reason to single you out. You'll eat your meals in the refectory with the others. You'll use the same bathroom facilities. In addition, I've asked the administrator to organise weekly visits to a psychiatrist. The doctor has been given explicit instructions to undertake whatever necessary to straighten you out. That is the only time you'll be authorised to leave school and then only accompanied by a prefect."

8.

Kate sat on the edge of the bed and stared out over the lake at the snow-capped mountains beyond. She would willingly have stayed with Peter, worried as she was about him. That headmistress was vicious and clearly had a vendetta against him. He was going to need all the support he could get. But she had an appointment with Viktor. He'd promised to introduce her to a Russian scientist on visit to Luzern, saying she might glean information to help Peter stave off the onset of puberty.

One thing remained to be done before meeting Viktor, contact Peter's adoptive parents. John would probably be at work, but Christina might well be home given she'd lost her job. Lying back on the bed, she closed her eyes and reached out to the woman. When she pictured Peter's adoptive mother she inevitably saw Fi who'd looked so much like her mum. The memory of the girl who'd been Peter's close friend and a good friend of Kate's had tears welling in her eyes. What a waste. Fi had died far too young.

Finally locating Christina, Kate remained in the background, not wishing to startle the woman who sat alone in her kitchen, a pencil in her hand, a draft application for a job in front of her. Gone was the light-heartedness that had characterised both Fi and her mum. Christina's thoughts were heavy with melancholy and there were distant rumbles of anger.

Christina, Kate said quietly. *It's Kate.*

The woman spun round in search of the source of the voice.

Don't be alarmed. I'm talking in your head, Kate explained.

You remember, Peter showed you we could do it.

"Kate?" Christiane exclaimed, her hands flying to her head as if she could grasp Kate that way.

I wouldn't normally encroach on you like this, Kate apologised, *but it's an emergency.*

"What's up?"

Peter has been dragged back to England. She went on to describe the bailiff's visit and the news that Peter's birth mother had gone to court to get him back.

"Yes I know," Christina said. "But his mother had little to do with it. It was the work of that woman..." she almost choked on the word "...who tried to discredit John, the aunt of that crazy girl who attacked Peter, the one who ousted me from Our Lady of Grace."

Peter suspected as much, but he wondered why you hadn't warned him.

"We received a restraining order forbidding us from having any contact with him."

They've taken him to Our Lady of Grace.

Christina gasped. "Was that woman there?" she asked, an angry edge to her voice.

Yes. I don't know why, but she insisted he dress as a girl. It doesn't make sense. She was dead set against him doing so.

"Poor Peter. That woman is pure evil. I bet she's got some twisted scheme to humiliate him."

That would make sense, Kate replied, her heart sinking. *I have to go, but if you agree, I'll contact you again. Maybe we can help Peter.*

"Okay," Christina said, although, being in her head, Kate could sense her reluctance.

Can I tell Peter he can contact you? It was worth a try. She knew the woman didn't like such mind talk, but Peter would be relieved if he could talk to her and John.

There was a long pause while Christina debated whether she should agree. Not wishing to spook her, Kate kept silent about being able to read her thoughts. It was the very reason the woman was wary of mind-to-mind communication. "Yes," she finally replied. "But no one must know."

Of course. I'll tell him. Give my love to John.

Viktor was waiting in the drive. When he saw her coming he waved his hat, as enthusiastic as ever. She waved back. She liked the man. He'd been a true friend to Peter and her. "Any news of Peter?" was his first question the moment they were seated in the car. She related what she knew while Viktor interrupted her with questions, many of which she couldn't answer. She also told him about the restraining order and that Christina had been sacked.

He whistled between his teeth. "That Witless woman is a scheming witch."

Witless had been Peter's nickname for Priscilla because her surname was Wit. "She hardly sounds witless to me," Kate said as they pulled out of the drive. "Tell me something about this scientist we're to meet?"

"Igor was a molecular biologist. He did research into sex hormones, those that are responsible for men growing beards and girls breasts," he began. Apparently the man had been secretly coopted by the Russian elite gymnasts federation.

"Why would they do that?" Kate asked.

"Because the hormones he was investigating could give a considerable advantage to young girl gymnasts."

"That's cheating!" Kate exclaimed.

"Exactly," Viktor replied giving her a wide grin. "Igor's research is far in advance of other countries which means people are unaware of the potential…"

"And he gets away with it?" Kate muttered, disgusted.

"Sure. But don't criticise him too much. He's the source of the hormones Peter takes. Without Igor's help, Peter's voice would have broken a while back."

Kate winced. She knew, of course. But she would have preferred the changes took place without drugs or a scalpel. There were always undesirable consequences. She wished they could use their form of healing, but the method involved restoring a natural balance not changing it. What's more, she knew so little about hormones. "I know it's top secret, but would your Igor talk about these hormones?"

Viktor chuckled. "You won't be able to stop him, but you'll probably learn little about his work."

Igor greeted them warmly in a rundown apartment a mutual friend had loaned him. Kate had imagined a larger-than-life figure like Viktor, but instead the man was nondescript. A stoop made him appear shorter than he was and his shabby suit further diminished him. His brown hair was turning grey and his hairline was receding. He wore horn-rimmed spectacles perched on a vaguely pointed nose and the smile on his round face formed wrinkles around his mouth. Were it not for his heavy Russian accent, he could have been mistaken for a shopkeeper from Luzern.

"Kate," the man exclaimed, holding out his hand for her to shake. "Viktor has told me a lot about you and your choir."

"Pleased to meet you." Kate said, wondering how she could steer the conversation to the man's work. She needn't have worried.

"How's your friend? The one who wants to be a girl," Igor asked with a chuckle.

She explained that Peter had been forced to return to England and would no longer be able to take the hormones.

"That's a shame," he said. "I was hoping to meet him. Or should I say her?"

Kate shook her head. The question was too complicated to answer. "What'll happen now he's stopped taking the hormones?" she asked.

"The onset of puberty should kick in quite quickly. Remind me how old he is and how long he's been taking the hormones."

"Twelve and just over six months," Viktor replied.

Igor began detailing the characteristic signs, but Kate interrupted. "Excuse me. There's something I don't understand. What exactly do these hormones do?"

"They are not hormones but hormone suppressors," he

replied, shifting from foot to foot in an excited little dance.

"How do they do that?" Kate asked, delighted at the prospect of finding a way to simulate their action.

"Puberty is brought on by sex hormones secreted by the pituitary gland…." He snatched up a pen and scribbled a drawing of the brain on a scrap of paper, encircling a small point at its base.

Kate nodded. She knew exactly where it was and could picture it seen from within. She'd explored it as part of her efforts to bridge the gap between her experience of healing from within and the medical vision of the body as a set of organisms to be treated from without. Of course, she couldn't tell him that. He'd probably dismiss it as childish nonsense. But if he took her seriously he'd sink his claws in her and never let her loose.

"…but it's other hormones created in the hypothalamus which sits just above the pituitary gland…" He drew a cross on his sketch. "…that trigger the so-called sex hormones when puberty begins. Rather than stop the flow of hormones that dictate the sex of a person we suppress those that trigger their release. Depending on what you do, puberty can be a real nuisance, so, in some circumstances, putting if off for few years can be a real boon."

That was surely what he'd been doing for those top-notch gymnasts. Unfortunately, it wasn't going to help her. It was all very well knowing what did what and where, but the difficulty was elsewhere.

The method she'd developed with Peter involved helping the body right itself. To do so you didn't need to know a lot about anatomy, although it helped. All you had to do was have confidence in the body and the blueprint each cell contained and nudge it along. But to solve Peter's hormone problem required changing the blueprint. The prospect was daunting. What if she got it wrong?

"Maybe we can smuggle hormones to your friend in England," he suggested. "Although the English are opposed to anything that smacks of gender ambiguity. I had a friend…."

With that he was off on a tale about a Russian ballet dancer who passed himself off as a woman. It was a gruesome story that didn't end well. Kate wondered how the Swiss would have reacted.

As Igor launched into a third tale, Kate got to her feet. "Sorry to interrupt but we have choir practice and I really must get back!" she said. The two men also stood, Viktor looking a little perplexed. "It's been really nice meeting you," she continued, "I've learnt a great deal."

"My pleasure," Igor replied, handing her his card. "If ever you get to Moscow, give me a ring."

"Thank you," Kate said extending a hand to shake his but he hugged her instead. Being enveloped in a stranger's arms was uncomfortable and struck her as invasive, but she managed not to cringe.

Once in Viktor's car, he was quick to ask, "What was all that about? You don't have choir practice."

"I know. But there was so much to think about, I didn't want my emerging ideas carried off by a flood of stories."

Viktor chuckled. "I did warn you he talked a lot."

Kate thought over what she'd learnt. She wished she could talk it through with Peter. He was the only person who could really appreciate her dilemma, but he had problems of his own. "I'd like to discuss some questions? Do you have time for me?" Kate asked, deciding Viktor was her next best bet.

"Sure. Let's go to Beth's place. She's out, but I can rustle up a snack."

Viktor let them into Beth's house and led Kate to the kitchen where he indicated various ingredients. She washed the salad, adding slices of tomato and cucumber to the mix. Meanwhile, Viktor cut bread and, having dowsed the slices with a little white wine, he placed a piece of cheese on top, adding a sliver of gherkin and some paprika powder before laying the result on a dish ready to go in the oven. "How many do you want?" he asked.

Seeing the thickness of the cheese, Kate replied, "Two will

do fine."

Once the cheese had melted and the edge of the bread was a crispy brown, they sat down to eat. Pouring her a glass of fruit juice and himself some wine, he asked, "What did you want to talk about?"

9.

Kate stared at Viktor seated across the kitchen table wondering how much to tell him. Keeping their healing work a secret had always seemed the safest bet. How could children possibly achieve what experts barely managed after years of study? Peter and Kate's way of healing called into question not only accepted approaches to medicine but also how people learnt. Opting to develop healing as an activity of the Lost Girls had forced them to be more open. Alongside Klaus and Lydia who'd taken the girls in, Beth and Viktor were their principal sponsors, so Kate and Peter had shared the basic outline with them.

"You know Peter and I have a new way of healing," Kate began.

Viktor nodded, saying, "From within."

"Exactly. Rather than intervene with drugs or a scalpel, we work directly with the body to right whatever imbalance or damage is making the person ill or injured. To do so, we rely on a blueprint in each cell which dictates how the cell should be and how it should function. All we do is encourage the body to follow the blueprint and supply extra energy if needed."

"That much I knew," Viktor said. "So what's troubling you?"

"With Peter hostage and having no access to his treatment, we need to find a way to continue blocking puberty."

"And you think you can do so with your healing method?"

"No. That's the problem. The way we heal only works if you stick to the existing blueprint. We want to change something, stalling on-coming puberty. Some boys who dress as girls are convinced they are in the wrong body. In their case, our method might work. They probably have a blueprint that corresponds to a girl. But Peter wants the best of both worlds and I doubt the body's blueprint caters for such a creative coexistence." She had to smile at the expression. "Some day maybe the blueprint will change to accommodate ambiguity, but at the present it's not on the 'cards'."

Viktor looked thoughtfully at his empty plate. "Even if the possibility is not written in the blueprint…" he began hesitantly, "that doesn't mean it's impossible. After all, with the aid of Igor's hormones Peter's body can achieve what he wants and it doesn't seem to make him ill or damage him."

Kate nodded in agreement. "I don't see how that helps."

"Well, the blueprint is a plan for a particular form of body." He scratched his head, caught up in a thought. "Not just at a given moment but all along its life. It's been proved to work both for the individual and the species. It's developed over centuries if not millennia. But what if there were an all-embracing 'blueprint', a sort of blueprint for possible blueprints, that dictated all viable bodies. Of course, never going beyond puberty would not work for humans in general because the species would peter out." He chuckled at the pun. "Sorry. My brain is working overtime." His expression became serious again. "The period is probably short because circumstances require children to get out into the world and have their own children. But extending the period a few years would work fine, at least in some places."

Kate jumped to her feet in her excitement and began pacing the kitchen. The prospect had her mind racing. "That would mean that what Peter wants might be an alternative blueprint. If we could access that, our method would work." She turned to Viktor, who had also got to his feet, and hugged him. "You're a genius!"

Viktor chuckled as she released him. "Don't celebrate victory too quickly. You still have to access that meta blueprint - if it exists - find the right alternative and substitute it for the existing one." He began clearing away the dishes. Kate helped, drying what he washed. "Modifying the blueprint for the future of mankind sounds mighty like usurping the prerogatives of God. Or evolution if you don't want anything to do with gods," he said, chuckling again. "If the church got wind of what you're up to, they'd reintroduce the inquisition just for you and burn you at the stake as the devil incarnate."

Kate shuddered. The church's fear made sense. Being able to substitute one blueprint for another could prove far worse than opening Pandora's box. In the wrong hands it'd be catastrophic. Being exploited by Igor's Russian masters to win athletics competitions would be kids' play in comparison. Of course, it was all hypothetical. She had no idea if a radical change from one blueprint to another was viable.

At that moment Kate's thoughts were cut short by Beth who rolled her wheelchair into the kitchen. Lifting her nose to flare the air, she asked, "Kept any for me? I'm starving."

"No," Viktor replied with a grin, "but I can make some. How many do you want?"

"A couple with a bowl of salad would be fine," she said, heading for the larder. When she returned, the remains of the salad cradled in her lap, she addressed Kate, "Good that you are here. I have something to tell you." Judging from the look on her face, the news was not good. Kate was impatient, but there was no hurrying Beth. She chewed her meal with application and said not a word.

It was only when Viktor rose to make coffee that Beth spoke. "I had a call from the Episcopal See."

"See?" Kate asked, perplexed.

"The Bishop's office. His Excellency wishes to talk to you."

"Now?" Kate exclaimed. "But why?"

"I don't know. They wouldn't say."

Kate sprang to her feet, readying to leave. The offices were only a short walk away. "I'll drop by when I've finished."

"You can't go alone," Beth said. "Where you come from being young is not looked down on, but here, being a child makes you a third class citizen."

"Who's second class?" Viktor quipped.

"Women," Beth snapped.

"I have nothing to fear from these people," Kate insisted. "I have arms they couldn't imagine." Her bravado was a bit over the top, but the persistent opposition of the church annoyed her.

"Be careful," Beth said, "they are cunning and ruthless. The church has a long history of brutally suppressing rivals."

When Kate walked into the Bishop's offices, she was greeted by a tall, emaciated man in a black robe that reached to his ankles. Around his neck on a heavy chain he bore a wooden cross. She shuddered, remembering the sinister warrior priests who'd overrun her home and finally executed her. She owed her reprieve to Peter who'd helped her spirit escape just in time.

"Come this way," he said without the slightest introduction or explanation. Clearly they'd been expecting her. He led her into a library, one of those dim affairs in which all the books on display were leather bound and probably never read. A low table sat in the centre of the room on which tea things had been laid out with a small plate bearing a single, delicate pastry. The table was flanked by upholstered armchairs in one of which a round faced man was seated. Seeing her enter he got to his feet smoothing out his purple robe with the flat of his hand. He too bore an immense wooden cross suspended over his heart.

He extended a hand. She thought he was offering to shake hands but he turned his palm down. When she realised he was inviting her to kiss the back of his hand, she shoved her hands in her pockets, pursed her lips and gave him a challenging stare. The sour expression that crossed his face clearly said what he thought of ignorant, disrespectful pagans.

Resuming his seat somewhat stiffly, he indicated she should sit and he poured them both tea. He then pushed the plate with a small sugar-coated pastry in her direction saying, "I am told they are the best in Luzern. Unfortunately I can't eat them. Doctor's orders."

Offering a single pastry did seem stingy. She ignored it and got straight to the point. "You wanted to see me?"

He glanced from the pastry to her, then, clasping his cross, looked like he was about to excommunicate her. Instead, he said, "I heard one of your concerts. The music was truly lovely."

She stared at him in disbelief. Surely he hadn't summoned her urgently just to praise the choir. She took a sip of the tea. It was particularly bitter. Instinctively she reached for the pastry with its inviting sugar. Despite the liberal coating, it tasted as bitter as the tea. What was wrong with these people that they needed so much bitterness? She couldn't spit it out, not in front of the Bishop, so she swallowed the morsel whole, almost choking on it, before returning her attention to the man.

"We have heard disturbing reports about the activities of the girls in your choir…"

Kate stared at him in disbelief.

"Luzern is small city, you realise. People talk. It would seem that your choir has attracted unwanted attention." His face twisted in a look of distaste. "You will admit that having such a large group of unmarried girls alone in an isolated house is not wise."

"What are you insinuating?" she demanded, her voice rising.

"Nothing," he replied, gifting her a smarmy smile that made her stomach lurch. "It's just that a number of our congregation are concerned. That's why we have decided to revoke permission for the choir to use Saint Leodegar."

"But…" Kate was flabbergasted. The church was their main venue, their biggest audience, their largest source of revenue. "You can't. Just because some twisted minds …."

"We take our flock very seriously," he interrupted, affecting a pained smile. "The devil takes on many forms," he said, shifting to a more fatherly posture, his expression the epitome of benevolence. "Even that of pretty young girls like yourself."

Kate cringed at the implied lecherousness masquerading as righteous indignation. He got to his feet. "I will fetch the official letter," he said, pointing to the unfinished pastry. "But do finish the pastry. It would be shame for it to go to waste."

There was no way she was going to swallow another mouthful of their bitterness. Instead she wrapped the remaining morsel in a paper napkin and stuffed it in her pocket.

The letter in hand, Kate hurried back to Beth's place where the two were anxiously waiting.

"They've decided to stop us singing in Saint Leodegar," Kate said in reply to their unspoken questions.

Beth didn't seem surprised. "What excuse did they give?"

"Apparently they have doubts about a group of unmarried girls living alone in the mountains." The implied innuendo sickened her. Young girls in this world often bore the brunt of the twisted imaginations of men who hid like cowards behind their righteous indignation. "It's all rubbish!" she exclaimed. "They can't stop us using the church."

"They do have god on their side," Viktor quipped.

Kate shot him a withering look.

"There's more," Beth said, "I've heard from a friend working at the Episcopal See that a recent visit to your house uncovered troubling evidence of activities that are not Christian."

"That's nonsense. Although, it would explain why they were so interested in the jar of devil's claw when they ransacked our workshop."

"Sounds sinister," Viktor continued, pursuing his jarring humour.

"It's a traditional remedy for pain, in particular from arthritis," Kate shot back. "It got its name because of the spiky nature of its fruit not because of any affinity with Satan."

"But how did they know about your workshop?" Viktor asked, pouring the coffee.

"Someone tipped them off," Beth said. "At least, that's what my friend told me. The bailiff that came to fetch Peter dropped by to see the Bishop's staff. He isn't really a bailiff, he works for a Catholic school in England."

"Our Lady of Grace," Kate muttered.

"How did you know?" Beth asked in surprise.

"That's where they've taken Peter."

"This is beginning to look like a sinister plot worthy of the KGB," Viktor said. "Is there any way you can get round the church's ruling?"

"I don't see how," Beth said. "I fear they won't stop there. They wouldn't have raided your workshop if they didn't plan to corner you about what they call your 'non Christian' activities."

"This has all the marks of a witch hunt," Viktor mused.

"I would like to talk to the Lost Girls before deciding," Kate said, "but my idea would be a two pronged response: promoting both the choir and our work with natural medecine. I imagine stands at the market or events in venues other than churches."

"I'm sure Heinz and Regina would willingly help," Viktor said. "Maybe they could bring out a supplement like they did about the abuse of you girls." It had been hard hitting stuff that had not only protected them from the nuns who sought to get back at them, but also contributed to the early success of the choir.

"I don't think visiting the market would be wise. Too many risks of disruption by troublemakers," Beth said. "I'll use my contacts to find more suitable venues."

"Thanks", Kate replied. Being in close contact with the audience would probably work better. They could shift easier from singing to demonstrating their work with plants. "Aim for smaller places to achieve a more intimate atmosphere."

"How much do you depend on the concerts for financial support?" Viktor asked.

"The concerts are two thirds our income, the other third comes from the sale of medicinal plants." Lydia, who grew such herbs with the help of the girls, had contacts with chemists and they'd become their clients. "Only a very small part of our money comes from actual healing. We try to avoid competing with doctors and other professionals. They get upset if mere children steal their customers." She shrugged as if dismissing their reactions as a poor joke. "Without the money from concerts we would be in a real mess. How else are we supposed to pay for the board and keep of twenty hungry girls?" And one half-girl she thought with a mental nod to Peter, even if he couldn't see or hear her.

"I'm sure we could find rich benefactors who would be delighted to get back at the church," Viktor said.

"That wouldn't work," Kate retorted. "The church would just accuse us of trading services for money." Her turn to use innuendo. "And anyway, I don't want to spark a religious war. I have nothing against people worshiping a god even if I come from a place where no such thing exists." She had to wince, her island having been overrun by priests bent on imposing their god on Kate's godless people. "What I find intolerable is their claim to have a monopoly. You know, the one true god!"

"I'll figure something out!" Beth said, with a smile, "I'm quite good at raising funds for lost causes." Viktor came to stand behind her, placing a hand gently on her shoulder as if to underline what she said. "Like me," he said with a grin.

Back in the converted outbuildings that housed the Lost Girls, the assembled choir was complete with the exception of Peter. It was time for choir practice. Despite a growing headache, Kate chose that moment to inform the girls. "That's terrible," Clara burst out, tears in her eyes. All her ambitions centred on the choir. Claudia slung an arm round the little girl's shoulders to comfort her, although she looked like she needed comforting herself.

"They can't do that," Tania insisted, clenching her fists, ready as always for a fight.

"They can and they have," Kate said dryly. "It's just another step in a war they've waged against us since we were entrusted to their care in the convent. Judging from what I've heard, their next move will be to prevent us from selling herbs."

Suzanne groaned. "I knew their trashing our workshop was a bad sign."

"They won't halt till they get us back in one of their filthy convents," Tania groaned, uncharacteristically deflated. Of all the girls, her body bore the worst marks of her stay in a convent.

"Maybe we should run," Claudia suggested, her eyes

darting around as if an army of nuns might burst in at any moment. As personal slave to the Mother Superior, she'd borne the brunt of the woman's pleasure at hurting girls.

"We can't run," Kate pointed out. "There's nowhere to go. These people have roots all over. That guy who dragged Peter off comes from the same church in England. No. We can't escape. Either we give in or we confront them." Not that she'd ever give in.

"What can girls like us hope to do against the weight of the church?" Clara asked, drying her eyes.

"You are forgetting that we already stood up to them," Kate said, remembering how they'd taken over the convent and driven the remaining nuns out. She also remembered their triumphant first performance in Saint Leodegar before an audience shocked at the state they were in.

"We will politely thumb our noses at them," she continued and as she spoke she saw the girls' enthusiasm return. "Our own version of girls' guerrilla warfare. Popping up in unexpected places. In disguise. Singing. Dancing. Giving samples of our herbs. Talking to people. Helping the sick. Handing out leaflets. Pinning up posters… The sky's the limit."

10.

Birgit, the name tag read. Just below, a prominently displayed badge screamed, PREFECT. The blond-haired girl was a couple of years older than him. She'd have been as delicious as her uniform were it not for her scowl. Dealing with him was clearly a chore she'd gladly have dumped on a hapless underling.

Peter stared at her uniform, transfixed. Chocolate brown trimmed with a narrow yellow band at the cuffs, around the lapels and along the hem at the bottom of the blazer, the same yellow was used for the school crest on the breast pocket. The blouse underneath was crisp white while the tie, neatly knotted around the girl's neck, sported yellow and brown diagonal stripes. The knee-length skirt was a matching brown as were the court shoes. Finally, the socks were yellow, trimmed at the top with brown.

In normal circumstances, the prospect of dressing in such a uniform would have made Peter's mouth water. But these were no normal circumstances. He'd been brought back to England to punish him for dressing as a girl. At least that's what he'd deduced. His birth mother, his sister, Priscilla Wit or Witless as he called her, and her heartless aunt, now become headmistress of Our Lady of Grace, had all been furious about him donning girl's clothes. They'd wanted to stamp out the habit even if that meant stamping him out too. Now the headmistress insisted he dress as a girl. Her about-face was incomprehensible. Where was the trap?

"Come!" Birgit ordered, turning on her heels, and strode

down the corridor with a haughty sway to her hips. She reminded him of Witless. Surely not all girls in private schools were so stuck up and hostile.

Peter trailed after, following her out of the administrative building, along the winding path past the newly-built glass and steel block housing classrooms and on to the much older brick mansion that served as residence. Prominently displayed by the door was a sign warning 'Girls only'. The girl shot him a filthy look before pushing open the door and indicating he should enter. Clearly, it was one thing to obey the headmistress's orders, but quite another to agree with them.

They halted at a door on the ground floor on which a large text had been painted, 'Attention: Pervert. Kept out!' Peter stared at the humiliating words in disbelief. Humiliation? Was that the name of the game? The prefect gave him no time to ponder. She opened the door and shoved him inside.

The room was tiny with a narrow bed, a small wardrobe, a wicker chair, a minuscule table and a window high on the wall that was far too small to climb out. Visions of prisons sprang to mind, although there was no way to lock the door. He shuddered. If he couldn't be kept in, he couldn't keep others out either.

Laid on the bed was his uniform. Well, all of it except the blazer.

"Undress," Brigit snapped, leaning against the door frame. Peter blushed. He couldn't possibly take off his clothes with the door wide open and the girl staring at him. He'd only ever stood naked before two girls, Fi and Kate. Without clothes he couldn't deny he was a boy. It was a truth he hated to share. "Hurry up!" the girl growled.

"Could you turn round?" Peter asked, his voice trembling.

She snarled. "If you think I get kicks out of watching you, think again." If anything, her voice had got even posher, as if her upper crust accent made it clear he was little more than worthless vermin. "Get on with it!"

He hung his duffle-coat over the chair, pulled off his shoes and socks, abandoning them on the lino floor, dragged the tracksuit top over his head folding it on the chair, then, turning his back to the girl, drew off the tracksuit bottom which he held like a shield in front of his groin as he stood otherwise naked. He shivered. It was December and the room was poorly heated.

"Give me that," the girl said, yanking at the trousers he was hiding behind. "Aren't boys peculiar," she said with distain, staring pointedly between his legs. His hands flew to conceal himself. If he could have shrivelled up and disappeared, he would have.

"Get dressed," she ordered, scooping up his clothes.

He did as he was told. When he came to pull on the skirt, it was far too short. It barely reached mid-thigh leaving him feeling dreadfully exposed. In comparison, the knee-length socks were too big, constantly sliding around his ankles. She nodded in approval as he bent down to pull them up for the third time.

"Turn round," she said, opening the wardrobe. He couldn't understand why he should turn away but he obeyed. She pulled the blazer over his shoulders and spun him round to examine him. For the first time she smiled, although the expression was distinctly predatory. He wondered what gave her such satisfaction. If only there were a mirror, but there wasn't.

Brigit glanced at her watch. "English," she said. "You'll just be in time." She fished a plastic bag from the bottom of the wardrobe and shoved his clothes in it before hustling him out. At the entrance she tossed the bag in a large waste bin before stepping outside.

He wished he'd held on to the duffle-coat. Without it and in such a ridiculously short skirt, the biting wind was bitterly cold, especially around his bare legs. Peter was grateful for the regulation cotton knickers he wore under his skirt. Inside the building the temperature was a little warmer.

Stopping in front of a door, the prefect knocked. "Come in!" a deep female voice called from within. The girl opened the door and pushed Peter inside. A sea of grinning faces looked up to scrutinise him. Not the grins of a friendly welcome. More a savage hoard catching sight of an easy prey.

"This is the new girl," Brigit said, emphasising the word 'girl' which had many of the class sniggering. Apparently everyone was in on the joke.

"Stop slouching girl and pull up your socks," the teacher ordered, more like a parade sergeant than a teacher. She was massive. At least six foot six with the build of a weight-lifter. Peter sent up a mental prayer that the school didn't allow corporal punishment. "What's your name?"

Peter was at a loss what to reply. He was forcibly reminded of his conversation with Kate about names. Peter or Wendy? Neither would work. Seeing the whole class waiting for him to make a fool of himself, he took a risk and replied, "Grüße, ich heiße Wendy."

The girls stared at him dumbfounded but the teacher snapped angrily, "English! We speak English here."

"Was ist, wenn ich kein Englisch kann?" he responded. It was downright stupid provoking her by suggesting he couldn't speak English. They presumably all knew he could, but he enjoyed a brief moment of rebellion. The English were renowned for their poor grasp of foreign languages. His satisfaction died the moment the teacher's hand connected with his face sending him flying. Her slap had stars shooting before his eyes as he staggered against a desk.

He nursed his face, trying to ease the sting. In his fury, he said, "What a friendly way to say hallo."

The teacher's hand flew out to slap him a second time, but Peter saw it coming and used one of Kate's favourite moves to dodge. There was a collective gasp as the teacher spun off balance almost falling as she did, but he was granted no respite. Recovering quickly, the woman bore down on him, a murderous glint in her eyes. He knew exactly how to better her. All that practice with Kate had left him well prepared and the bigger the opponent, the harder they fell. But in the long run he couldn't win. She had a whole institution behind her and beyond that the might of the church.

Rather than attack, he dodged, shifting to put some distance between them. The woman was breathing hard now, apparently not as fit as her build would have people believe. "Let's call a truce," he said. "Before someone gets seriously hurt." He shot a quick glance at the class. Despite the overall hostility, several girls were looking at him in surprise, if not admiration.

"Brigit! Take him…" the woman began, only to correct herself, "…her to the headmistress," she ordered. "Tell Miss Wit I will be along shortly." Straightening her blouse and skirt, the teacher turned back to the class to resume her lesson as if nothing had happened.

As he stood outside the headmistress's door waiting - the woman was apparently absent - every girl that went past sniggered. Was the whole school in on the plot? Some of the younger girls pointed fingers, one even made the sign of the cross as if to ward off evil. It was only when a little girl came to stand next to him that he understood. Her slight build and her mousy brown hair reminded him of Clara, but her skin was swarthy, not at all like Clara's pale features. Absently, he wondered if she could also sing so well.

"It's your blazer," the girl whispered without the slightest introduction.

"What about my blazer?" Peter asked, startled that anyone should dare talk to him.

"Take it off and look," she suggested, darting a nervous glance down the corridor.

He did as she said, only to discover a notice embroidered in yellow on the back which read, 'Pervert! Keep clear!'

He chuckled, despite himself. It was the childish sort of prank boys from his old school would have played.

"Why do you laugh," the girl asked, alarmed. "It's serious. They're poking fun at you."

"I know," he said. "But you have to admit it is rather silly."

She stared at him as if uncomprehending for a long moment, then said, "You're not like the others."

He chuckled again. "That's true."

The girl blushed. "No. I didn't mean that." Her hand flew to her mouth to hide her embarrassment. "I meant the way you react."

"I understand." Taking an instant liking to the girl, he held out his hand, saying, "I'm Peter. What's your name?"

"Sarah," she replied, shaking his hand.

"You waiting to see Heartless?" he asked, jerking his thumb over his shoulder at the closed door.

"Heartless? Fits," she said, nodding.

"I think God forgot her heart when he cobbled her together from left-overs. Not up to his usual perfection." He grinned. Sarah did too. "What did you do?" When she looked confused, he added, "To be hauled up before Heartless, I mean."

"Nothing. I swear," her look earnest. "The other girls wrote rude words on the board and told the teacher it was me."

"Do you often get bullied?"

The girl stared at her shoes in silence for a long moment, then muttered, "It's their sport. I'm the ball they like to kick."

Peter winced. He was little for his age and some of the school rugby team had tried to bully him. If it hadn't been for Kate teaching him to defend himself, he'd have been toast. "Yeah," he said. "I know what it's like."

"How come? I heard you fought off Miss Superwoman."

News travelled fast. "Is that really her name?"

"No. It's Tumball. That's just what we call her…" She broke off abruptly as the click of heals on the linoleum announced the arrival of the administrator.

"You're not to talk to her," she reprimanded. "Take an hour's detention."

Sarah groaned.

"Give me detention instead," Peter said. "I forced her."

"Who said you were allowed to speak?" the woman snapped.

Peter shrugged. There was no point in baiting her, even if he sorely wanted to. For the moment he had to live with these people. "Sorry. I thought talking was the polite thing to do. Which reminds me, you know my name, but I'm afraid I don't know yours..." Peter didn't expect an answer and he didn't get one.

"You talk too much." She waved a dismissive hand, her newly polished claws glinting in the light. "Now get back to class. The headmistress will see you some other time."

Once the administrator had gone, Sarah said, "Batch!"

"Sorry?" Peter asked, perplexed. He thought he heard 'bitch', but he couldn't imagine the girl swearing.

"Miss Batch. The new administrator."

"Ah!" he replied. "Good name. Seems appropriate."

Sarah grinned and offered to show him the way to the classrooms. In the course of their quiet conversation about the school, Peter said, "My room is on the ground floor. Come visit me."

"That'll be difficult," Sarah sighed. "We have strict instructions to avoid you and the night guard has her room next to yours. If we're lucky it'll be Eloise, she won't bother so much. But even if it's her, the others'll keep their beady eyes on you. There's no lack of girls willing to spy."

"Well, know you're welcome if you can."

When Peter entered the classroom the lesson halted abruptly, everyone turning to stare at him.

"What do you want?" the teacher snapped, clenching her fists.

"To learn English," Peter replied, straight faced. "I gather this is my new English class or am I mistaken?"

"Sit down," the teacher said, pointing to the only free chair at the back.

By the time Peter had reached his place, the teacher had resumed the lesson. He had no book to follow, so he listened while girls read out extracts. They were reading Lord of the Flies which he'd read with Kate. Being part of a choir themselves, they were fascinated by the behaviour of the boys choir stranded on an island. The two had debated whether it was because they were all boys that things had gone awry or because the author believed adult control was necessary to stop children turning savage.

They'd just reached the famous kill-the-pig scene when the teacher turned to Peter asking, "New girl, what do you say to this behaviour?"

No doubt she wanted to make a fool of him, thinking he hadn't read the book, but he was delighted to disappoint her, "There seem to be two possibilities. Either boys are inferior to girls and more likely to become savages…" several girls laughed out loud, others sniggered behind cupped hands.

"Silence!" the teacher roared. She was about to move on when a girl put up her hand. "Yes?" the teacher asked.

"What was the other option?" the girl asked, clearly addressing Peter.

Peter looked to the teacher for permission. She shrugged. "The other possibility, which does not exclude the first, is that the author was trying to point out that children naturally go wild if they are not restrained by adults. Rather like the idea of original sin, thinking that children are born wild and need to be educated is a dubious claim that gives all the power to priests, parents and educators."

A deadly silence filled the room with several girls nervously crossing themselves. Too late Peter realised he'd let himself get carried away, forgetting he was a prisoner in a catholic girls' school.

11.

The smell of baked beans had Peter's mouth watering. It wasn't nostalgia for English food - he hadn't missed eating such fare for months - yet surprisingly it exerted an undeniable pull on him, but above all he was starving. He hadn't eaten since breakfast a day ago.

As the girls refused to point him to the canteen, he followed his nose. He could just as easily have followed his ears. The chatter from the canteen was considerable. However, the moment he stepped into the room with its rows of benches and trestle tables dancing brown and yellow with excited uniformed girls, the babble of voices ceased and all heads turned to stare at him.

He had no idea where to go or what to do. Seeing the school motto painted in Latin in gold letters below the crest above the dais, he had a crazy idea. He knew he shouldn't, but it was tempting. If he was lucky the surprise might hold long enough for him to slip away should things turn nasty. He'd have to keep it short. He strode between the tables, feeling all eyes on his back as he struggled to appear confident. When he reached the raised area at the front of the refectory he turned to face the assembled girls. Sucking in a deep breath, he launched into a short transcription of a longer, more elaborate grace, singing as if his life depended on it. Maybe it did.

When he finished, his performance was greeted by a stunned silence and stony faces. He bowed stiffly then said, raising his voice to be heard by all, "That grace in Latin was based on a longer piece composed by the great English composer Orlando Gibbons. Enjoy your meal."

His words must have freed the girls from the spell because chatter broke out and rippled round the room. Spotting an empty table at the back, he took refuge far from the others. Servers began carrying in baskets of toast and tureens filled with beans to waiting tables, but none approached his. Were they going to starve him too?

It was Sarah that saved him. Joining him, she bore a plate piled high with toast and beans. Sharing her meal must have taken guts, because everyone else pretended he wasn't there. A good many even shot Sarah murderous looks.

"That was lovely," Sarah said between mouthfuls. Peter wondered if she meant the beans, but she added, "You have such a delightful voice."

He was about to thank her when he spotted a prefect heading their way. This one was less imposing, despite being a few inches taller than Birgit. Maybe it was the limp. "Now we're in for trouble," he said in a low voice.

The girl halted opposite them, her face stern. Her name tag read 'Eloise'. "Don't pull a stunt like that again. You were lucky the headmistress is not here. And if you want to eat, next time sit at a table with other girls, not on your own." With which she turned and limped off.

"Was she being kind?" Peter whispered.

"Eloise? She's okay, once you get to know her."

Peter watched Eloise join the others at the top table. He couldn't hear what was said, but, judging from Birgit's pointed finger and the general throaty laughter, the others were making fun of her. The girl stoically got on with her meal, not responding to their taunts.

Sarah followed Peter's gaze. "She's often forced to keep an eye on us in the evening and during the night," she said, keeping her voice low. "The other prefects hate doing it, but Eloise doesn't mind. She spends much of her time reading."

"What happens in the evenings?" he asked, not relishing the

idea of being shut in his tiny room all alone.

"Most people study. I prefer to go to the library and read. When the weather is good, the slackers wander the grounds. The older girls escape into town. Being from rich families, I suspect their parents buy them permission. Not having the means, I've never been let out. I've heard they generally pick a fight with girls from the local school who willingly oblige."

Peter chuckled. "That doesn't surprise me. Shame really. There are some interesting girls at the local school." When Sarah looked put out, he hurried to add, "There are some dreadful ones too."

"How do you know?"

All around girls were getting to their feet and carrying their dishes to a serving hatch. Sarah did so too and Peter followed. "Is there anywhere we can talk?" he asked once they left the refectory.

They were alone in the corridor and she was on the verge of answering when she halted, staring at him. "Whatever have they done to your skirt? That's ridiculous."

"I imagine it was shortened to make me feel uncomfortable."

She got down on her knees and examined the hem. Her fingers against his bare thighs were more than embarrassing. He held his breath, keeping stock still. Sarah, in comparison, behaved as if it was the most natural thing in the world.

"As I thought," she said, accepting a hand up. "It's been turned up. Really shoddy work. All I need is a pair of nail scissors and we'll get your skirt back to regulation length." She took his hand and pulled him in the direction of the residence, saying, "I've got some in my room."

As Peter walked beside her, he was overwhelmed with gratitude. It was a rare gift to be so readily accepted, especially in Our Lady. So much so, he was afraid someone would dart out and snatch her from him. The moment he thought it, he wished he hadn't. A soggy, rotten tomato smashed into Sarah's back splattering her blazer. A second hit Peter on the back of his head and juice dribbled down his neck. More tomatoes followed.

Weaving left and right, the two made a dash for the Residence, avoiding the worst of the attack.

The moment Sarah was safely inside, Peter spun round to face the attackers, a group of girls all older and bigger than him. To his horror, the twins from the ferry were amongst them. They grinned at him in a way that had his skin crawling. He was tempted to launch a mental strike, but he didn't want to play that card unless he really had to. *Kate*, he called. When he felt her presence, he said, *I need your fighting skills*.

I see, she said, a grin colouring her words.

Nothing too spectacular, he replied. *Just frighten them. They've been pelting us with rotten tomatoes.*

Okay. Let me take over.

He relinquished the hold on his body. He hadn't done so for quite a while - there'd been no need with the Lost Girls - so the feeling of taking a back seat while someone took control was very strange.

Kate eyed the group of girls who were staring at her in surprise. They clearly hadn't expected to be countered. Bullies rarely did. Kate singled out the largest and strode up to her. When the girl tried to shove a tomato in her face, Kate deftly swung round, twisting the girl's arm so that the rotten tomato landed on the bully's nose. "Ugh!" the girl squealed.

The twins moved forward to challenge Kate, balancing a tomato in each hand. The others hung back. Suddenly slipping between the two, Kate banged their heads together. Collapsed on the ground, she freed them of their tomatoes and pressed the juicy fruit into their pristine uniforms. Ducking and spinning, Kate narrowly missed several tomatoes that had been thrown at her. Catching one out of the air, she sent it on its way straight into the face of one of the remaining attackers.

The other girls were backing away, not daring to confront her.

That's enough, Peter said.

Just let me mark them so we know who they are, Kate insisted.

Let them go, Peter said, seizing control. *They'll hesitate about doing that again.*

I hope you're right, Kate retorted, still worked up from the fight. She sounded sceptical.

Thank you.

Always a pleasure. Oh, by the way, I spoke to Christina. She said you could contact her mind-to-mind providing nobody knows. Peter wanted to know more but Kate said, *I have to go. We've got problems here too.*

Before Peter could ask what, she was gone. Turning back to the Residence, he saw Sarah staring wide-eyed at him through a window. Abruptly her expression changed to one of horror and she began waving wildly. Her meaning quickly became clear when a final tomato smashed into the back of his head knocking him forward against the door. Some people always had to have the last word.

Sarah stepped out and helped him inside. Producing a large handkerchief from her pocket, she began wiping squished tomato from his face and hair. "That was…" she began, when a muscular hand clutched his shoulder and wrenched him away.

"Enough of your wasteful games," the administrator said. "Tomatoes are meant to be eaten not played with. The plentiful God gave us food to eat, not to squander."

"Your god was right, Miss Batch," Peter muttered, furious. "Go tell that to those who pelted us with tomatoes. We are just the victims of their generosity."

She raised a hand to slap him, but Peter saw it coming and dodged. "What's wrong with you? Did nobody tell you the eye-for-an-eye approach was revoked in the New Testament?" A noise behind him had him glancing over his shoulder to see a crowd of girls pouring out of their rooms. If he hadn't looked away he might have avoided the second slap. As it was, it caught him square on the jaw and sent him flying into Sarah. The two tumbled to the ground in a sticky mess. An answering cheer went up from the gathered girls.

Shaking his head to clear it, Peter helped Sarah to her feet.

They were caught between a vengeful woman flexing her boney fingers and a blood-thirsty crowd of girls baring their teeth. So much for his theory about Lord of the Flies. Girls were no better.

"Let's get cleaned up," Peter said to Sarah, in an effort to remain calm in the face of multiple threats.

"You aren't using our bathroom," one of the elder girls snarled. Those around her nodded in agreement as they closed ranks to stop Peter and Sarah getting through. "Look," Peter said, in a last-ditch appeal to reasonableness, "I didn't chose to come here. It was Miss Heartless, your charming headmistress, who forced me to." A couple of girls sniggered at the name, but most looked shocked or disapproving.

This time he did see the slap coming and side-stepped, giving the woman a gentle push as he did, sending her sprawling into a squealing mass of girls, crushing more than one. Spluttering and furious, the woman scrambled to her feet, clearly game for more.

"Is this all you have to say?" Peter challenged. "Hitting people solves no problems. What would your Jesus have said about such behaviour?"

The woman glowered at him. "How dare you quote the Bible at me, heathen."

Not that he had. "I could. It's an interesting book," he said. He knew it well enough. Having had a lot of it quoted at him over the years in church. But instead he shook his head. "I doubt it'd make much difference."

"The devil was always the one to twist the Almighty's words to suit his own ends," the woman flung at him.

"Your Headmistress has had Satan's name embroidered on my back but that doesn't make me a devil," Peter shot back, getting ever more furious as the battle of words escalated.

Easy does it, Kate's voice said in his head.

You're back, he said just as he was about to accuse Heartless of being the devil incarnate.

Just thought you might need more help. He could feel the knowing grin in her words and, despite himself, that further fuelled his anger. *Seems I was right,* Kate continued. *I can't believe I'm saying this, but you are being reckless.*

These are desperate times, he thought between gritted teeth as he stepped in front of Sarah to protect her from the woman who advanced on them.

My father always insisted on level-headedness in difficult times, especially when up against religious bigots.

It seemed so long ago, Peter had to remind himself that Kate's father had been a mage who had led a community of mage families on an island in another world till they'd been overrun and enslaved by an army of warrior priests.

Miss Batch raised her hand to slap him but when Peter held his ground and didn't flinch, she hesitated, presumably fearing another manoeuvre on his part. Spotting Eloise enter, Batch called out, "Deal with this Eloise," and stomped off.

12.

"Give me that," Eloise ordered, taking Peter's stained blazer. "Yours too," she said to Sarah. "Now go wash your faces and hands. And don't forget your hair. She handed them two towels and a bar of soap.

Luckily the crowd had dispersed and they were able to access the bathroom unhindered. It was little more than a long, narrow room with multiple sinks aligned along one wall and a wooden bench stretching the length of the wall opposite. There were no mirrors.

Sarah unbuttoned her blouse and tossed it onto the bench, standing in front of him in only her skirt. "Can you wash my hair?" she asked, not the least abashed at being half-naked.

Peter looked away, making a show of unbuttoning his own blouse to conceal his discomfort. "Sure," he said, his voice trembling. "Lean over the sink." When she did as told, he gingerly stood behind her and began scooping handfuls of water over her head. The water was barely warm and he couldn't help noticing the goose bumps that formed on her upper arms. They were otherwise so smooth.

As there was no shampoo, he rubbed the bar of soap between wet fingers and applied the lather to her shoulder-length hair. Washing a girl's hair was a first. He hadn't even washed Kate's or Fi's.

"Rub it in well," Sarah said, "or I'll stink of rotten tomatoes tomorrow."

He'd been cautiously adding soap as if she were a porcelain

doll, but when she insisted, several times, he rubbed with more vigour, massaging her scalp as he did. She laughed with pleasure. "You should be a hairdresser," she suggested. "You do that so well." Fortunately, with her back turned, she couldn't see his burning face. Despite his momentary discomfort, he was surprised to find washing someone's hair was a real pleasure. Who would have thought?

"Enough," she said, startling him from the circular movements which had completely absorbed him. When he'd finished rinsing, she rubbed the water from her eyes and said, "Hand me a towel."

With the towel wrapped like a turban around her head, she faced Peter. "Your turn," she said inviting him to bend over the sink. Like him, she scooped water over his head, making him shiver as some ran down his back and over his chest.

"You have quite muscular arms," she said, her wet hands straying over his shoulders. "Shame you don't have breasts. You'd make a pretty girl."

Peter stiffened, fearing a repeat of the scene with Beth's maid, but Sarah just chuckled and returned to soaping his hair. She too massaged his scalp, but far more adventurously and less mechanically than him. "That's a real pleasure," he admitted. "No one has ever washed my hair."

"Not even your mother?"

"If she did, I don't remember. She was always so busy…"

"That's sad," she said, her fingers lingering on the hairline at the nape of his neck.

Inexplicably Peter felt like crying and he had to fight back tears. "Do you think that prefect will check on us? What's her name again?" he said, in an effort to distract from his emotions.

Sarah immediately halted and set about rinsing his hair. "Eloise? I doubt it," she said, handing him a towel. "It would be far too devious to trust us only to burst in in the hope of catching us doing something we shouldn't. She's probably got her nose in a book."

It was true, the prefect had been much more easy going than

the administrator. Apparently, the night-watch fell to a different prefect each day, although Eloise often did the job as the others hated the chore.

He thought over what Kate had said. That he might be parading his violence or pig-headedness like other boys was a horrifying thought. What if all that he hated about boys was already bursting through. Surely not. He'd been off the hormones for only a day. And anyway, did he depend on medecine to be a good person? Did being born a boy necessarily condemn him to being an insensitive ass?

His confused emotions had him struggling to button his blouse. Sarah offered to help but he held up a hand in refusal. "I may look like girl dressed like this, but for people here I'm a boy in disguise. If they caught us in a compromising situation they'd only see the boy and jump to unsavoury conclusions."

Sarah scoffed. Clearly that was not how she saw him.

"You're one of the rare people who accept me as I am, like the girls I live with in Switzerland." Sarah's face lit up at the mention of his home, clearly eager to know more, but Peter pressed on. "Most people see an aberration or a 'pervert' as they so tellingly scrawled on my back. What I am makes them so angry they'd willingly shove me under a bus."

"Is that why the headmistress hates you so much?"

"It's a long story." He hesitated. Leaking the tale might rebound in ways he couldn't anticipate. Seeing the longing on Sarah's face, he gave in. "Heartless, that's what I call her, has a niece who used to go to this school till she got kicked out. She bullied a young boy so much he ended up taking his life."

"Oh! That's so sad!" Sarah exclaimed, instinctively clutching his hand.

Gently freeing himself, he went on to describe how Witless had come to his school and latched on to him, doing everything she could to destroy him. When Witless had been locked away as mad and finally took her life, he told how her aunt, Heartless, had unsuccessfully tried to discredit both him and his adoptive father. "Now," he finished, "she's manipulated my mother, who's in the mental clinic Witless was. Using her, the headmistress forced me to return, no doubt aiming to break me with her humiliation." He chose to make no mention of hormones or visits to a psychiatrist.

"Something doesn't make sense," Sarah said, removing the towel from her head for a final rub. "Why ever would the two react so violently?"

Peter sighed. The girl was far too perspicacious. "Heartless's brother, Witless's uncle, was suspected of abusing little boys, but before the police could confront him, he hung himself in the stairwell at their home. Witless discovered his lifeless body strung up. It drove her over the edge. As for the aunt, I believe she always blamed boys rather than her brother. That's why she hates me. For her, I epitomise all that led her husband astray" He hastened to add, "Not that I like boys. I prefer girls. I just like dressing as a girl." There. It was out.

The door burst open and Eloise strode in, a carrier bag grasped in her hand. "You take your time, I was able to read a whole chapter," she grinned. "There's no way I can remove the stains. You blazers will have to go to the dry cleaners." She huffed. "Which means muggins here," she jerked her thumb at herself, "will have to undo all that stupid embroidery," she said to Peter. "Can't have anyone in town getting wind of the madness thriving here." Apparently not everyone was dupe to the headmistress's schemes.

"There are no spares in your sizes," Eloise said. "So you'll just have to wear Our Lady's tracksuit jackets." She rummaged in her bag and pulled out two jackets, handing one to Peter and the other to Sarah. Peter's had clearly been someone else's, judging from the perfume that clung to it. That it had been worn by a girl remind him of the times he secretly donned his sister's clothes. Hers too had smelt of perfume. It was a smell he'd come to look forward to. As if to confirm his suspicions, Eloise added, "They belong to the netball team. Try not to get stains all over them."

He and Sarah promised not to, although, if they were

attacked again, there was little they could do.

"Let me see your hair," Eloise said, running her fingers through Peter's then Sarah's. "Good. Hand me that soap and the towels." They did as they were told. "Now get to your rooms. It's almost time for bed."

"Can we share?" Sarah asked, a pleading look on her face. "There's a spare bed in my room."

"That's not very wise," Eloise said, turning to go but then halted. "As the headmistress is away I suppose it might work. But make sure no one sees. No one!"

Sarah grinned so wide, Peter wondered if it hurt. Both nodded their assent. As they emerged from the bathroom, girls were still out and about. "I'll come and fetch you," Sarah whispered and headed off down the hall.

There was nothing to do in Peter's room. There wasn't even a book. He wasn't allowed out and even if he did risk a tour of the grounds, he was fearful some enterprising girl would attack him. Worse, he could be set on by the dreadful twins. Rather than lie on his bed, where he might fall asleep and get savaged by someone pushing open the lockless door, he sat on the chair and closed his eyes.

Early evening. Christina should be home. She didn't reply immediately. When she did, her tentative question underscored how unsure she felt about using mind-to-mind communication. *Peter?*

Yup. Great to talk to you, he said. *How are you? I heard you lost your job.*

A tidal wave of angry thoughts accompanied a growl. *That woman is pure evil*, she spat.

Tell me about it! You know she's forced me to attend Our Lady. He told her about the uniform with the label sown on the back.

How you holding up? she asked.

What worries me most are the hormones. He mentioned the puberty blockers. Christina had never heard of them so he explained. *Being here, I can't get my daily dose. I'm worried what I'll become without them.*

Can they be found here? Christina asked, concern in her voice.

I doubt it, he said. *We'd have to get them through Viktor's contact.*

I'll see if I can organise something with Kate, she said.

So should we try to meet? he asked tentatively.

We'd need to be very careful. None of us wants to get arrested, she replied. *Ah, there's John. I have to go. Speak to you soon. Love you.*

Love you too.

Alone again, Peter wondered about the pesky male hormones. Retreating inside his body, he went in search of signs that puberty was kicking in. He had no idea where to look. He might be capable of healing someone - he'd even healed a man with cancer - but he relied entirely on the body's blueprint which he couldn't actually read. He wasn't even sure it could be read.

Apart from growing facial hair and his voice breaking, the most obvious sign of nascent manhood was the development of his testicles. He'd always shied away from exploring down there. When he'd tried to conceal his sex from that prefect it was obvious enough why he didn't want anyone to see what he was. He now realised he even hid his sex from himself.

As he directed his attention down between his legs, he felt squeamish. Ridiculous really. He was not looking at the appendage that hung there somewhat forlorn, the one that seemed so out of place on his girlish body. No. He was looking from within. Looking was maybe the wrong word. Sensing. Everything seemed in order, but that didn't mean they were not growing.

He withdrew, not wanting to remain staring, albeit mentally, at his own sex. He meandered around his body till he reached his brain. There was an immediate shift in perception. Instead of sensing tissue with all those firing neurones, he became aware of feelings and thoughts and memories. He'd taken it for granted that he could read thoughts, but now it seemed odd. It was as if he saw mind instead of brain. What exactly happened when that shift occurred? Could he do the same elsewhere? Don't be silly, he berated himself. Thoughts are only in the brain. But there are other messages elsewhere came the excited reply. Maybe he could read the blueprint if he looked at it like he did mind.

He was about to try when he heard the quiet click of his door opening and, rising to the surface, he steeled himself against an attack. He needn't have bothered. It was Sarah.

"Peter?" she whispered. "Do you always sleep in a chair?"

He blushed, glad night had fallen and she couldn't make out his face. He couldn't possibly explain he was studying his testicles. "I was meditating," he lied. Well, not exactly. What he did was akin to meditation.

"Let's go," she said, clearly more interested in what was to come. "Everyone's in bed." Hearing the excitement in her voice, he once again worried about her motives. He had no wish to be an object of someone's twisted desires. But intuition told him Sarah was okay.

Grabbing the nightdress that lay folded on his table, he hurried after her down the corridor. They were just turning a corner when someone stepped from the shadows and confronted them. Sarah squealed only to be silenced by a hand clamped over her mouth. Peter's heart was hammering so hard he had to reach mentally inside to calm it.

"I told you not to get caught," the person hissed.

"Eloise," Peter whispered. "You terrified us."

"I don't think you realise how dangerous this all is. If Miss Wit were to hear, you'd be roasted alive in hell. And so would I. Rest assured, there are plenty of smug little girls who'd rush to tell on you and me."

Eloise sounded so bitter, Peter wonder what she had against the others. Or against Heartless. But in that darkened corridor, in the dead of night, it was hardly the time or place to ask. "Get to bed," Eloise ordered. "And, for god sake, be careful."

13.

Kate got precious little combat practice in her role as head of the Lost Girls so fighting, even using Peter's body, was welcome exercise. Not that she didn't have her fair share of battles, but they rarely involved physical conflict. It was all manoeuvring and word play, politics and sleight of hand, the kind of games her father had been caught up in on the Mage Council. She preferred direct, physical combat, matching body against body. Of course, being the daughter of a mage, learning combat skills had also involved using magic. She'd never tried to wield magic in Peter's world. Maybe she should.

Despite her lack of practice, her legs and arms shouldn't have ached so much. She massaged them as she lay on her bed. That she no longer did magic was not strictly true. Talking mind-to-mind had been her and Peter's discovery, as was their way of healing. Both would certainly be classed as magic in this world, if not satanism, she thought with a shudder. The herbal medicine she taught the girls had all been learnt from her father who'd been a master in plant magic. But he'd always refused to teach her battle magic. He disliked hand-to-hand combat and the use of magic to fight as much as she despised the conniving of politics. Most of what she'd learnt came from Zhuru, her father's arms master and her marshal arts teacher.

Talking of battles with words, the meeting with the Lost Girls had not gone well. She'd felt uncharacteristically tense. She put it down to the loss of Peter and the decision of the church. In a bad mood, she found it hard not to snap at the whining girls.

The younger ones were terrified they'd be forced back into a convent. Some had even cried. The older ones, like Tania, were spoiling for a fight, indignant that the church, which had already done them so much harm, was allowed to go on hurting them. It'd taken all Kate's power of persuasion to reassure the young ones and calm the firebrands. She'd been obliged to promise reconsidering in a week. Not a good idea. It left little time for a strategy.

A timid knock at the door brought Kate back to the present. It was Suzanne, her second when it came to healing. "How're you coping?" Kate asked, patting the bed as an invitation to sit down.

"Not so well," the girl admitted, her face creased with worry. "Life in the convent was really hard." Tears sprang to eyes. "I don't think I could stand going back."

Kate put an arm around the girl and pulled her into a hug. The world was beastly unfair dealing such a rotten hand to such a wonderful girl. Suzanne was so kind and considerate. She hadn't spared in her efforts to learn healing, driven by an innate desire to be of service. Yet adults, the church in particular, hadn't ceased to hurt her and put her down. The injustice of it made Kate clench her fists and grind her teeth. Suzanne's story ought to be shouted from the roof tops instilling shame in all those who'd mistreated her.

"Any news of Peter?" Suzanne asked, wiping her eyes.

"They've taken him to a girls' school run by the very woman who tried to get rid of him…"

"Oh no! Is he alright?"

"The last I heard, he was holding his own. But we urgently need to find a replacement for those hormones he was taking."

"A herbal remedy, you mean?"

"No. I don't think that would be enough. We need something more radical. Ideally, we should realign how his body works to make the hormones unnecessary."

"Can we do that?" She looked both excited and incredulous.

"It should be possible. But, for the moment, I don't know

how."

"Have you spoken to Peter about it? He always has good ideas."

Kate was miffed at the suggestion Peter would have the answer. She was about to make a caustic remark when she remembered Suzanne worshipped him. How could it be otherwise? He'd taken her seriously when no one else had, apart from Kate, and he helped her learn to heal.

"No!" she said, biting back her anger. "He's got a lot to think about. I talked to an acquaintance of Viktor's who synthesised the hormones Peter has been using. But it wasn't very helpful. Like all doctor's, he comes at the body from the outside. His knowledge and approach is 'outside in', if you see what I mean. What we need is 'inside out' knowledge."

Suzanne chuckled. "Indeed."

"I'm glad you came, it's important to talk about these things, but it's getting late," Kate said, feeling a wave of tiredness sweep over her. "You should get a good night's sleep. We have a lot to do tomorrow to protect our world and you have an important contribution to make."

Smiling, Suzanne said "Thanks", gave her a quick hug and left.

Their discussion had given Kate an idea. She wanted to talk to Heinz and Regina about it. She knew they had a phone, but it was surely too late to bother them. Tiptoeing down the stairs to avoid further heart-to-heart conversations with other desperate girls, she left the Lost Girls' house and headed to the main house where Klaus and Lydia lived. In the kitchen he was finishing off a cake and she was bottling dried herbs. They both looked up as she entered.

"Heard from Peter?" Lydia's asked, setting her herbs aside.

Kate gave a quick update before asking, "Do you think I dare phone Heinz and Regina at such a late hour?" She glanced at the clock over the range. Half past ten.

"Sure," Klaus said. "They're both night owls."

When she looked questioningly in the direction of the phone,

Klaus said, "Go ahead."

The phone rang only once before Regina picked up. "Were you expecting a call?" Kate asked.

"No. But Heinz is asleep. He has a photo shoot early tomorrow morning."

"I'm sorry. Should I phone back tomorrow ?"

"No. Fire away."

Kate told her about the church's decision and the threat hanging over their herbal business. "I was talking to Suzanne and I had an idea. It struck me as terribly unjust that she should be hounded by the church when her intentions and her actions are all for the good. What if we published a short illustrated interview with her in the form of a pamphlet calling out those who put her down? If it worked, we could do others with other girls."

"You'd have to be careful to get the tone right," Regina said, "but I think it's an excellent idea. What else do you plan?"

Kate outlined their idea for girls urban guerrilla tactics, mentioning the spontaneous performances and the health and healing actions.

Regina chuckled. "You lot could probably overthrow the government, if you put you minds to it."

"We have no such ambition. All we want is for people like the church to leave us in peace to do what we do best." She realised as she said it that the church was probably incapable of encouraging people to fulfil their potential. After all, their starting point was that people were inherently bad. Was that not what they meant by their 'original sin'? She preferred the option that people were born good and that their task in life consisted of uncovering and developing their potential.

"That may be a tall order," Regina replied. "It would require turning the church on its head and that isn't for tomorrow, but you could probably shame them into leaving you alone. Especially if you got enough people on your side."

They agreed that Regina would drop by in the morning to interview Suzanne. With that Kate hung up. She informed Klaus and Lydia that Regina would be coming and, wishing them good night, she returned to the Lost Girls' house. Her legs, her arms, her shoulders ached. Surely that brief fight in Peter's body couldn't have done that.

Back in her room, she was exhausted, but far too strung up to sleep so she went in search of Peter. No luck. He was asleep. She lingered a moment in his mind, tempted to thumb through his memories. At least that way she'd know what had happened. Of course, doing so was something they'd agreed never to do unless absolutely necessary. An insidious voice in her head whispered, 'What harm could it do?' She knew the answer, 'A lot.' Despite that, she lingered, basking in the feel of her sleeping friend, refusing to be goaded into prying.

Kate? a sleepy voice asked in her head.

She blew him a mental kiss in reply, only to be acutely aware of his embarrassment. *Peter?* she asked. *What's up?* In was then she became aware that he was lying in the arms of a sleeping girl. With a raging surge of jealousy, she took a mental step back. *Who's that?* she blurted out, readying for a fight.

Peter sighed. *It's a long story.*

Furious, she almost broke the contact for fear she'd smashed something irrevocably. The feeling of betrayal was terrible. He'd hardly been away a day and he was already sleeping with someone else. *Explain,* she hissed.

She felt him sending out a calming influence, but shook it off. In the circumstance, his 'healing' efforts were akin to manipulation. *Just explain,* she snapped.

So Peter told his tale. When he reached the bathroom scene, Kate stiffened. *Washing each other's hair!* she spluttered. *How could you?*

Because our hair was plastered with tomatoes, he said, his tone exasperated. *You saw that much yourself.*

She couldn't shake her indignation. *But we've never done that!*

Maybe we should.

She huffed. The idea was far from appealing. Would she not

always think he'd done it first with someone else?

Listen, he said. *Being who and what I am can be very lonely. When I stumble on someone who accepts me as I am, that's like a breath of fresh air. People here hate me. With Sarah, in comparison, everything was so simple. It was like being with one of the Lost Girls. I felt at home. Are you jealous of the Lost Girls?*

Begrudgingly she had to admit she wasn't, with the exception of Tania. But that was different. The rivalry between the two had more to do with Tania's possessive love for her than Peter.

I'm not normal, he continued. When she objected he added, *No moral judgement implied. I'm just different. I'm in-between. Maybe one day I'll be considered 'normal'', but for the moment I'm the odd one out.*

She had to agree. *I've been thinking about that.* She spoke of changing the blueprint. His excitement was palpable.

How's that for a coincidence, he replied. *I was thinking of ways to read the blueprint.* He talked of seeing mind differently from brain. It was her turn to get excited.

Their conversation was interrupted by a sleepy girl's voice saying, *Who're you talking to?* The voice startled them. Whoever spoke was doing so mind-to-mind.

Sarah? Peter exclaimed. *How come you can talk to minds?*

"What's that?" she asked, reverting to speaking out loud.

You were speaking directly into our minds, Peter said. *Try doing it again.*

"But I don't know how."

Sure you do. You just did.

Instead of speaking out loud, think your thoughts to us, Kate said.

"Who's that?" Sarah asked, alarmed.

I'm Kate, she said, *Peter's friend from Switzerland.* She had been sorely tempted to say 'girlfriend' and lay claim to him.

"Wow!" was Sarah's immediate response. "So far away."

You have to talk mind-to-mind, Peter insisted. *Someone might hear you if you speak out loud.*

Like this, Sarah said.

Exactly, Peter said, delighted. *I told you you could.*

Kate could feel the girl's excitement and it worried her. Sarah had no idea what she'd stumbled on. *It is very, very important that you tell no one you can talk mind-to-mind. Nor that Peter can. If people find out they'll turn on you and tear you apart. Literally.*

Sarah terror was evident, she even began trembling.

Kate is right, Peter insisted, place a reassuring hand on the girl's shoulder. *You must never breathe a word to anyone.*

I understand, Sarah said, her words shaky.

Kate remained wary, even if the girl did have a simple and direct way of being that was appealing. *It is understandably more difficult when you are on your own,* Kate said, her mind scrambling to find a way to bring the girl into the fold, as it were. *So if ever Peter gets out of there and you are free to travel, you should join us in Luzern.*

14.

The moment Kate's eyes cracked open, the early morning light was so stark she snapped them shut. She must have fallen asleep during her visit to Peter because she was lying fully dressed on her bed. She had a splitting headache, not to mention every muscle ached. What's more, she was uncharacteristically short of breath.

She'd been talking to a girl named Sarah in Peter's head when she'd felt giddy. The memory of that dizziness was alarming. She'd tumbled as if falling in slow-motion.

It wasn't the first time she or Peter had fallen asleep in each other's mind, but normally they slept then returned to their own mind when they awoke. This was different. Something had gone wrong. Had Sarah done it to her? It didn't make sense. But she had no other explanation. Not that she imagined it was deliberate. It was just that there was something unusual about a girl who spontaneously spoke mind-to-mind.

She wanted to check on Peter. Maybe he too had had a malaise. But she couldn't risk contacting him if Sarah was around. What if she was struck down again? Should Sarah realise she had such an effect, she might be tempted to use it against her, possibly even blocking her access to Peter. Visions of being cut off from him had her gasping in a panic. She sprang to her feet, meaning to open the window and breath some fresh air, but the world spun violently and she collapsed on her bed.

She didn't black out, but she felt weak and nauseous. Her instinct was to call Peter. But if Sarah were the cause, doing so would be a disaster. Instead she called Suzanne.

What's up? Suzanne asked.

I'm not feeling well.

Within minutes Suzanne was at her side along with a worried looking Tania and Eileen. "Symptoms?" Suzanne asked, donning her healer's cap.

"Giddy," Kate said, her words coming out as if she were short of breath. "I almost fainted."

"When did you last eat?"

"With you, yesterday evening."

Suzanne placed a hand on Kate's brow, wincing as she did. "You're burning up! I'm going to go inside and look around," Suzanne said. Turning to Tania and Eileen, she added, "Can you wait outside? I have less experience with healing than Kate and I don't want to be distracted."

Tania, who was holding Kate's hand, was reluctant, but Eileen took her firmly by the arm and led her out. "Call us if you need us," Eileen said over her shoulder. "We'll be just outside."

I'm going to contact Peter, Suzanne said, *he has far more experience than me.*

"Don't do that," Kate pleaded, unable to get up enough energy to reply mind-to-mind.

Why ever not?

It sounded silly to voice her fears, but how else was she to explain? "He's with someone I suspect of sapping my energy. If you link to him I'm afraid I'll only get worse."

Suzanne looked sceptical but nodded, saying, *Ok. I will only reach out to him if I have to.*

Kate was aware of Suzanne's ghost-like presence shifting inside her but she no longer had the strength or lucidity to guide her. In her feverish state she drifted in and out of consciousness. At moments she could have sworn she heard Peter's voice. She wanted to send him away, but was too weak. The whispered words that did reach her rarely made sense, as if speech was garbled. Were they deliberately scrambling their words to hide their plotting? After ages prowling on the verge of delirium, a cool breeze rose and blew through her, chasing away her fears and doubts. Her whole body heaved a sigh of relief and she fell into peaceful sleep.

When she awoke, from what she could hear the whole choir was gathered around her bed singing quietly. Keeping her eyes closed, she listened. The lyrics struck her as particularly appropriate, "…May there always be angels to watch over you, to guide you and keep you safe from all harm…" Tears filled her eyes and flowed freely down her cheeks. "Thank you, my angels," she said, opening her eyes as the song came to an end.

"Welcome back," Suzanne said from where she was perched on the side of Kate's bed.

Looking round the room, Kate saw that the girls, who'd taken up every space in chairs and on the floor, were eagerly eyeing her. Several of the younger girls had tears in their eyes.

"You gave us a real fright," Tania said, sounding genuinely alarmed as she voiced what was probably a feeling shared by all.

"So," she asked, turning to Suzanne, "what was wrong with me?"

Suzanne shifted uncomfortably on the bed, staring at her hands.

"Well?" Kate pursued, worried she might have been more ill than she'd thought.

"You were poisoned," Suzanne said, her words falling with all the finality of a death sentence.

"What?" Tania gasped. "Surely not?"

Suzanne just shook her head. "I found traces of strychnine which I was able to eliminate with Peter's help. You are lucky there was so little. More and you would have suffocated to death."

"How on earth did I absorb strychnine?" Kate mused. She'd neither eaten nor drunk anything special. "We certainly don't have any in the workshop, as far as I know."

Suzanne nodded. "It can be used as rat poisoning and it is even employed as a remedy in very small doses, but it is far too dangerous to leave lying around. We have none here."

Kate thought back over the past day. She'd visited Beth's place at midday and she'd gone with Viktor to see Igor but they'd neither eaten nor drunk. When they returned to Beth's, she'd gone on to … she let out a gasp which had the girls looking at her in alarm. Her hand flew to her pocket, rummaging in the depths till she felt a soft lump. She pulled it out, revealing a folded paper napkin clearly stamped with the Bishop's insignia. Cautiously unfurling the little bundle, taking care not to touch its contents, revealed a squashed, half-eaten pastry. No wonder it had tasted like it did. With hindsight, the thick coating of sugar made complete sense. It'd been there to conceal the bitterness.

Susanne stared at the insignia as realisation dawned. "The Bishop!" she exclaimed. "I know the church is capable of terrible things." She glanced round the choir. "We are all proof of that. But cold-blooded murder!" She shook her head. "How could they dare? Not only is it against the law, it's against everything the church stands for."

"They do it," Tania said with a scowl, "because they're confident they can get away with murder." She pointed to the poisoned pastry. "What proof is that? We probably made it ourselves. After all, don't we dabble in potions and poisons? Who will believe us. We're just insignificant little girls and girls are known to be born liars. And of course, important as those men are, everyone will believe them."

"Who can get away with murder?" Regina asked, standing in the doorway. With the attempt on Kate's life, everyone was on edge so an unexpected adult voice made more than one jump.

"The Bishop," Kate said wearily, "and his clerical cronies."

"Explain," Regina said, weaving her way between the girls to join Kate on the bed.

Kate described her visit to the Bishop and her subsequent malaise. When she mentioned the pastry, Regina reached out to touch it. "Don't," Kate said, "it's probably laced with strychnine."

Regina snatched back her hand as if she'd been burnt.

"This is far more serious than the question of concert venues you mentioned over the phone. What makes you sure it's strychnine?"

"Partly the symptoms," Suzanne said. Kate was afraid the girl would reveal their way of healing, a fact that rarely went down well with adults, even those who supported them, but instead Suzanne added, "but mostly the urine."

Kate realised they must have forced her to eliminate the poison, but she hadn't bothered to think it through. "You kept the stuff?" she asked, her embarrassment quickly giving way to admiration. "Smart!"

"Indeed," Regina said, her face grim. "We need to have it analysed. The cake too. But not here. Too many people are dependent on the church. Heinz will know where. And he should take pictures of the evidence."

"I wondered where you'd all got to," Lydia exclaimed from the open doorway. "You trying to break a record for how many people you can pack into a tiny room." She laughed, but when no one laughed with her, she must have become aware of the tension in the room because she asked, "What's up?"

When Kate briefly explained, Lydia made a face. "Strychnine? I've seen that." She'd been a nurse at the hospital. That's where she first met Kate. "Not a pleasant way to go." Looking Kate over, she asked, "How do you feel?"

"Starving," Kate said. Several girls giggled.

"That's a good sign," Lydia said.

"Off you all go," Kate said. "I need to get washed and dressed." Above all she wanted to reassure Peter. If he'd seen her flake out, he must be worried. "Can you stay a while?" she asked Regina. "We can talk over breakfast."

"Sure. But judging from the time," Regina chuckled, "that's more likely to be brunch. I had breakfast ages ago." Getting to her feet she followed the others out and closed the door.

Having been surrounded by so many, having room to think and breathe was a pleasant relief. Lying back on the bed, she reached out to that familiar mind. *Peter*, she called.

Kate, he answered, *sounds like you're recovering well.*

Of course. He knew. He'd been there to help. How could she have forgotten? Suzanne had mentioned it. *Yes. We have a lot to do, but I wanted to check on you.*

I'm fine. But maybe not for long. I've been summoned to the headmistress's office. She's back. Kate heard a sharp voice call Peter's name. *Got to go,* he whispered.

Downstairs in the refectory, a noisy brunch was in full swing. Tania was holding court at one table with most of the girls, while Suzanne talked earnestly to Lydia and Regina at another. Kate helped herself to a bowl of muesli and yoghurt then joined the table with the adults.

"Is Peter okay?" Suzanne asked.

Kate blushed. Suzanne knew her too well. She nodded, then dug into her breakfast.

"They won't stop at that," Lydia said, presumably pursuing an earlier conversation. "When they realise their attempt on Kate's life was unsuccessful, they'll try something else."

Regina nodded. "And if we publicly force their hand by guerrilla action like you suggested," she nodded in Kate's direction, "there's a strong risk they'll step up their attacks."

Lydia passed Kate the tea pot. "Regina told us about your plans," she said. Her smile was pinched. "Maybe you should tone it down a bit. At least until the church eases off."

Capitulating before they'd even started seemed over hasty, especially as they'd yet to evaluate the extent of the threat. "Hold on a moment," Kate said, putting down her cup to have her hands free. She pulled a pencil and a piece of paper from her pocket. She'd already participated in this sort of discussion when she attended Zhuru's war councils. "What form do you think their attacks will take?"

15.

"I hope it won't be necessary," Kate said, getting to her feet to address the girls, "but as a precaution, I propose to teach you to detect poisons."

When she'd discussed warding off attacks, she'd hesitated about sharing her father's magic. It wasn't without risks. Everyone had something akin to magic, although it was often limited and remained locked away, safe from temptation some might say. In her world, most young people destined to be mages were rarely granted access to magic before they were older. Given that her father was on the Council, she probably could have started earlier. But she hadn't needed to ask. Her abilities had developed spontaneously when she was little.

As a result her teachers spent hours instilling a respect if not an awe of magic. So much so, she'd always been circumspect about using it. Unfortunately, in the current situation there was no time for lengthy preambles. And anyway, the circumstances were different. In this world magic was not taken seriously. If it was considered at all, it was seen as something to fear, if not as evil.

"A few of you may not manage," she went on. "Don't worry. There's nothing wrong with that. Not everyone can. Your contribution may lie elsewhere. Those who do succeed will check your food and drink for you, should that be necessary."

Teaching a novice to detect poison was a long process, but Kate and Suzanne had an enormous advantage. They could enter a person's mind and guide her, sharing their own feelings and experience first hand and directing the girl's attention to the right sensations.

Eileen, with her shock of black hair and her infectious smile, was the first off the starting blocks. As she took her seat between Kate and Suzanne she looked uncommonly nervous. Tension was hardly conducive to learning, so Kate placed a hand on her shoulder and shared calming energy.

"Don't be alarmed," Kate said, "I'm going to talk directly into your mind."

Eileen nodded.

Good. Kate indicated that Suzanne should close her eyes. Kate did so too. *While I teach you, I will also teach Suzanne how to teach, so please bear with me. If talking to her distracts you, let me know.*

When you do this, Suzanne, communicate mind-to-mind and get the girl to respond in kind. If that doesn't work, let it go. She opened her eyes and shifted an apple onto the table in front of Eileen. *Now, Eileen, I want you to hold out your hand palm down.* She guided the girl's hand over the apple. *Once you've got the knack of this you'll be able to do so with your eyes open. I want you to sense the fruit on the table as if you can see it through the palm of your hand. To make things easier, I'll show you what I feel.* She placed her hand over the apple and sent her impressions to Eileen.

Oh, an apple! Eileen said.

See what I did, Suzanne? The girl nodded mentally. *Now you show her what you feel.* Suzanne did as Kate had done.

Oh! They are different, Eileen exclaimed.

Good that you can spot the difference, Kate said. It was indeed a positive step. *Now try to see what you feel.* At first Eileen's vision was hazy. *Watch carefully what I am about to do, Suzanne. I'm going to focus Eileen's attention on different aspects of the apple.* She took hold of Eileen's attention and zoomed in on the core of the apple. Both girls gasped.

That was weird, Eileen said, *like having a magnifying glass shoved in front of your mind.*

Good lord! I didn't know that was possible, Suzanne added.

Now you try, Suzanne, Kate said. Kate had to show her exactly what she had done before the girl managed to replicate it.

I feel like my mind is being pinched and squeezed, Eileen joked.

Is that uncomfortable? Kate asked.

No. Just weird.

Now look again, Kate said. *This time I want you to look at it differently. Healthy food, like a healthy person, has a healthy 'ring' to it. Let me show you.*

I get what you mean, Eileen said. *It's a bit like instruments being in tune. They sound right.*

Kate had Eileen sense several different foods and drinks, insisting on her looking for the harmony, before sliding a fruit with poison in it under the girl's outstretched hand. *What do you feel?* she asked.

Ugh! Eileen exclaimed. *It's completely out of tune.*

Good. You've seen how I zoomed your mind in on a part of something. Now you focus in on the part that is at odds.

Not only does it jar my musical senses, but I swear it stinks.

Well done. That's the poison. With practice, you'll be able to recognise them. But don't linger too long. Even at a distance and through mind communication, those vibrations are not good for you.

They cut the communication and opened their eyes. "That was extraordinary," Eileen exclaimed, a broad grin lighting up her face. "I'm a very practical, down-to-earth person. I never imagined I could do such a thing. It's like magic."

If only she knew. "You'd be surprised the things you could learn," Kate said. "You are a remarkably talented young woman."

It didn't matter that Kate was a few years younger, Eileen glowed with pride.

"Once we get a couple more girls taught, could you set up a place for them to practice? Just samples of food and fruit, no poison. You could try rotten fruit, though. The more practice they get, the better. Have them work in pairs, talking mind-to-mind, watching from within, coaxing and coaching each other."

Kate was about to tell her to send in the next girls when she remember something important. "All this must remain a secret. If ever it got out, being poisoned would be the least of our worries." At her words, both Eileen and Suzanne shuddered. "Make sure the girls know."

By the time the last girl had left, both Kate and Suzanne were exhausted and starving. They'd managed to teach all the girls, despite the difficulties a few had encountered. With their efforts, the whole choir had taken a big leap forward. Nothing could have been clearer than when the two walked into the refectory to find the girls eating high tea in animated silence. Kate halted in horror, wondering if she'd stepped into a nightmare.

"Cut that out," Kate exclaimed, her strangled voice shattering the silence. "Its way too creepy."

"You did ask us to practice," Tania retorted, gifting her a wide grin that pointedly bragged, 'I win!'

"I did. But not like that. Imagine what Lydia or Klaus would think. You look like a clutch of children begat from alien spawn."

Several girls giggled nervously. A couple looked confused. Not everyone was as widely read as Kate.

"Talking mind-to-mind is a natural human ability," Kate said. "The proof? You all learnt in one short lesson. But arguing that it is normal will protect no one. People have forgotten how to talk to minds. Worse. Doing so or doing any of the many other incredible things you are probably capable of have been labelled evil."

She sucked in a deep breath. "People are so afraid of those abilities, or what they imagine them to be, they would willing slaughter anyone suspected of wielding them. Forget the accusations that, as a group of young girls, we are on a rampage leading the men of Luzern astray." Shocked gasps erupted around the room. Only Tania seemed to find it amusing. "If the church discovered what we can do, they'd burn us at the stake."

"So there are other things we can learn," Tania said.

Kate sighed. Teaching them to detect poison had been a risk, but she'd judged the threat merited it. Had she not almost died? But girls like Tania seemed to court risks. She thought only of herself and her kicks. "You're not listening," Kate said sternly, getting to her feet. "Eating poison might get you killed. But openly using mind-to-mind communication will inevitably bring on a death that will be far worse."

Tania just grinned, much to Kate's exasperation. The girl's defiance and recklessness was plain stupidity. It was gentle Suzanne that set things right. "Wipe that stupid grin off your face," she snarled, standing up. Tania looked at the little girl, stupefied. No doubt she'd expected Kate to fight it out with her. That was what normally happened. She'd never dreamed Suzanne would put her in her place. "You are a laugh," Suzanne said, glancing at the others who nodded in agreement. "We all appreciate that. Even if your constant feuding with Kate is a pain in the neck."

Tania plastered an innocent expression across her face as if to say, 'Who? Me?'

"Clearly you don't know when to stop," Suzanne pursued, shaking her head. "This is deadly serious. Your foolishness could get us all killed. The church tried to assassinate Kate. Just think about that. Do you imagine they'll hesitate before wiping the rest of us under the carpet? Flaunting our ability to do things the church has branded black magic is suicidal. Do you want to destroy our choir, our community, our future?"

As Suzanne sat down, the silence in the room was palpable. Tania tried to shrug it off to the disgust of several of the older girls, but Christine, true to form, moved to smooth things over.

"This is not a time to fall out," she exclaimed. "That you have unresolved issues with Kate," she said to Tania, "everyone in this room knows." Tania looked ready to dismiss it, but Christine stopped her. "But we also know we're under serious threat. If this goes wrong, at best we could end up in a convent. At worst some of us might die." Her words had everyone holding their breath as they eyed Tania.

"If we're divided," Christine continued glancing around the room at the serious faces turned to watch her, "we don't stand a chance. I implore you," she said turning to Tania, "tone it down and try to listen to Kate without rearing up as if her every word were a challenge. We all know you love her, but that doesn't mean you can possess her. There's no way you ever could. And trying to claw Kate into your arms certainly doesn't give you the right to jeopardise all our futures."

To have both Suzanne and Christine confront her so eloquently in front of the whole choir left Tania speechless. Never before had the situation been laid bare so explicitly. Kate got to her feet and walked between the tables, laying a gentle hand on each girl as she did, till she reached Tania who stood with her arms crossed over her chest. She took the pouting girl in her arms. At first Tania resisted, her body rigid, only finally to let go and begin to sob.

16.

Sarah shuffled out of the headmistress's office, tears streaming down her cheeks as she nursed her right hand.

"What happened?" Peter asked full of concern.

Sarah wiped her running nose with the back of her left hand, a sob bursting from her lips. "Cane." It was more a gasp than a word. She uncurled her fingers, revealing bright red wheals across her palm.

"That's barbarian!" Peter muttered. The teachers in his old school hadn't resorted to caning. John would never have allowed it.

"Worse," Sarah added. "She threatened to kick me out."

"What?" he exclaimed, furious that Heartless was destroying yet another life.

"There's nothing I can do. I have nowhere to go. No parents. No home. Just the orphanage. If I talk to you, she swore I'd be expelled. But you're the only person I have. I can't give you up."

"We'll see about that," Peter said, as a voice called, "Come in!" He wasn't sure what he could do, but he wasn't going to stand for this. He shoved the door with such force it flew open banging against the wall.

The woman looked up from behind her desk in alarm, her startled expression quickly morphing into a sneer. "Get out. And enter properly."

"What's all this about expelling Sarah?" Peter shot back, beside himself with rage. Even to his own ears, his outburst sounded over the top.

The headmistress's laughter was frankly maniacal, making Peter flinch. He'd had his fair share of nutters putting him down and was sick of it.

"If you weren't such a disgusting pervert," the woman said, a twisted grin on her lips, "your pathetic outburst might even be funny."

He was sorely tempted to return the compliment, but he wanted more than insults. She'd deliberately hurt him and the people he loved. He'd had enough. "Do you get it from your brother?" he asked, unable to quell his anger.

Heartless's head shot up at the mention her brother, a growl on her lips.

"He liked to torture little children, didn't he? It must run in the family. Your niece was expelled from this school for hurting young ones too."

Heartless lurched to her feet, her fists clenched white, her eyes boring into him. He'd do well to cut his losses and run, but he was so angry he battled on. "Are you going to expel me too?"

Her tight-lipped anger gave way to a sly smile. "You'd be so lucky!" she said, easing herself back onto her chair. "No. Your education clearly has a way to go." She began sorting through the papers on her desk, ignoring him. When she picked up the phone and dialled, he turned and stalked out, not bothering to shut the door.

He found Sarah huddled on a bench, her injured right hand clutched in her left, whimpering. "Let me have a look," Peter said, but she clung to it, not answering. He knew he shouldn't. Doing so would only bring more trouble, but he placed a hand on her shoulder. When she didn't flinch, he quickly shifted his attention to the raw wheals across her palm and set about healing them.

"What are you doing?" she whispered in alarm, staring at the wheals as they faded.

"That's odd," he replied, removing his hand from her shoulder. The healing was incomplete, but most of damage had been set right. "Wow! Looks like it was only superficial. Maybe she didn't hit so hard."

Sarah ran a finger over the faint red lines that remained. Looking up, her eyes met his, brimming with questions. He didn't doubt she'd get her answers, one way or another. "Make no mistake, she hit hard," she said, shaking her head.

Peter glanced over his shoulder at the open door to Heartless's office, worried she might step out and catch them. "Let's go somewhere safe," he whispered, although he had no idea where. Luckily, Sarah knew of a place.

Taking his hand, she led him. They had to dodge the administrator who was prowling the corridors like a starved wild cat. When they finally reached their destination, she whispered, "It's the one place that's never locked and at this time of day will be deserted."

Peering in, he discovered a chapel just big enough to seat the whole school on regimented rows of pews. The scent of incense hung in the air, a penetrating reminder they were in a sacred place. He shivered. The sanctuary lamp burnt red over the altar. Like the royal flag fluttering over the castle roofs, it symbolised the presence of god, or so he'd been told. If god there was, would he or she watch benevolently over two fugitives? Would they be offered sanctuary?

God might be portrayed as stern but benevolent, but the church apparently found benevolence difficult. He'd attended church regularly, singing in the choir, but his relationship to the church was ambivalent. Had not the church been responsible for the suffering of the Lost Girls? Although he was unsure if it was the institution or the people that made it so.

Sarah wove a path between the pews till she halted at the lone confessional. He pulled open the door and peered inside. He had no experience of confession. Such organised forgiving was not part of the church he'd attended.

Sarah wanted them to squash into one side, but there was hardly room. "I could sit on your lap," she said, looking coyly at her shoes as she did. Her attitude had warning bells ringing in his head. He imagined the priest's reaction should he find them cuddling in a place dedicated to driving out sin. He doubted the man would grant them absolution.

"No," he replied. "What would the priest say if he stumbled on us? Better we separate. We can talk mind-to-mind. No one will know."

"That won't work," she said, pointing to the cubicle for the penitent. She was right. There was neither door nor curtain. Anyone walking into the chapel would spot them, especially with the bright yellow of their uniforms. So much for godly discretion.

Peter felt cornered. What they were about to do was surely a sacrilege. He didn't relish sitting in the dark with a girl he hardly knew cuddled on his lap, for all her cuteness and her easy going manner. He'd have preferred to search for an alternative, but they'd probably get caught looking.

Reluctantly he slid into the priest's place having just the time to straighten his skirt before Sarah clambered onto his lap, giggling as she wriggled to get comfortable. With her perched on his knees, no amount of wriggling could rid him of his discomfort. As she lent forward to pull the door closed she almost tumbled out. He was obliged to shoot an arm round her waist to prevent her from crashing to the floor. Perfect. All he needed now was for Kate to contact him. He'd die of embarrassment if she didn't kill him first.

So you have no family? he asked, preferring talk to embarrassment. The moment the question was voiced, however, he realised it made both of them even more embarrassed. She squirmed on his lap as if a change of position might help dodge the question. *Sorry. I didn't mean to embarrass you. Don't feel obliged to answer...*

Her body shifted as she shook her head. *That's ok. I never knew my parents. My mother died giving birth to me, or so I've been told. As for my father, I can only suppose he bolted.*

Weren't there any relatives? Peter asked, tucking a strand of her hair behind her ear when it kept falling over his face.

In the dim light he caught her smiling. *No. My parents were only children. At least my mother was. No brothers. No sisters. No aunts or uncles. Not even grandparents. No one to come forward and own me,...* The word 'own' shocked him. Were children the property of their parents?*...so I was trusted to a home. Till I came here, I'd lived in orphanages all my life.*

How did you get into Our Lady?

My orphanage was run by the church which offered a few scholarships to children in need. There was stiff competition...

But you fought and won. He understood why being expelled would be a terrible punishment. Heartless was really cruel. Yet for all that, Sarah opted to be with him.

It's one thing to get in, she said, *but quite another to be accepted. As a scholarship kid when all the others pay for the privilege, well their parents do, belonging is nigh on impossible.*

Is that why the others treat you so badly?

Not having mastered how to nod mentally, she did so physically, dislodging the strand of hair behind her ear which promptly flopped in Peter's face. *Sorry,* she said, tucking it back behind her ear, her fingers lingering a moment against his cheek as she did.

He was not averse to signs of affection, they seemed to be the hallmark of Sarah, but cooped up in the dark with a girl he didn't know who couldn't sit still, planted on his lap, 'affection' was a trifle too much. He tensed, expecting to be kissed at any moment.

I don't know if you can imagine what it's like to go through life without a friend...

He could. The loneliness, the desperate need for someone, anyone to talk to, to confide in, someone to be with without having to constantly protect yourself. For quite different reasons, he'd also been friendless till he met Fi. She'd been a friend, a first real one, someone he could trust with his secrets, that he could be himself with. By way of answer he hugged her. At which she began to cry softly.

I'm sorry, she said.

That's alright.

You're the first person who's taken the time to talk to me, to listen. You can't imagine how much that means. For the other girls, I don't exist. Except as a nuisance or the butt of their jokes. She laid her head on his shoulder and continued to cry.

Her words reassured him. She sought a sister, a friend, a confident. That he could be. *You realise she's mad*, he said.

Who? The headmistress?

Peter nodded. *Yes. Miss Wit. Heartless.*

Heartless? She's that alright. As for mad, you may be right.

He was about to reply that mad people could be violent and unpredictable when the chapel door crashed opened and Heartless stormed in. He knew it was her because no one else had such a voice.

"No. They need to be taught a lesson. What he's done, with his foul mockery, disdains God's sacred vision of life. Men are men and women are women. If we let pests like him spread they'll contaminate humanity, just like he's infected that girl. It wouldn't surprise me if he hasn't convince her to dress as a boy."

Sarah drew in a sharp breath, shuddering in Peter's arms. Luckily someone shifted a chair, the noise covering Sarah's gasp.

"We should lock the door," she said. "We don't want them taking refuge here."

"I can't." Whoever it was sounded stricken.

"The priest," Sarah whispered in his ear.

"Why ever not?" Heartless asked.

"Because I don't have the key. It's been lost for years. And anyway, the chapel is a holy sanctuary. People are meant to be able to take refuge here."

"These aren't people. They're vermin. I'll have a locksmith change the lock."

The priest sounded as if he were choking, but he didn't object. The chapel door closed behind them and silence rushed in, leaving Peter and Sarah trembling in the dark.

17.

If they're going to lock the door, Sarah said, *we need a new place to hide.*

Peter was not so sure. Hiding wasn't going to solve their problems. As for running, he didn't value their chances. Heartless would set the police on them, feeding the authorities some story about him being crazy. *No*, he said, *I think we have to return to class.* Sarah groaned. *We can't hide indefinitely,* he continued. *We have no food, no drink...*

We could run.

I've thought of that. It won't work. He explained why.

Sarah gave in, although not without complaining, *I was looking forward to hearing about where you live and the people you live with.*

I'll tell you, I promise.

Sure, she said, sounding sceptical. *I'm not allowed to talk to you. Remember?*

I know. But we can talk mind-to-mind.

By the time Peter returned to class, the last lesson was drawing to a close. He was tempted to wait outside for the bell, but a stern reprimand from the administrator who was prowling the corridors had him scuttling inside. It quickly became clear the lesson was French. He apologised to the teacher, his politeness earning him a filthy look and a torrent of French he didn't understand. "Excusez-moi," he muttered - that much he knew - and hurried to his place at the back.

Well he would have if one of the two twins, who ill luck

had placed next to the only free desk, hadn't stuck out her foot, sending him sprawling. His knee took the brunt of the fall, sending a searing pain up his leg. When he tried to get up, the knee gave out and he collapsed, provoking laughter from the girls. The teacher was still spouting French, apparently reprimanding him, not the girl who'd tripped him.

He hopped his way to his desk to the sniggers of his neighbours and managed to sit down without bending his leg. Placing a hand over his knee, it was hot and beginning to swell. He closed his eyes and went inside. The damage wasn't serious. He encouraged his body to heal and reabsorbed the blood that was accumulating so he wouldn't have an unsightly bruise.

"Should we get a wheelchair?" the twin asked with an all-too-familiar malicious grin as the bell rang.

"No thanks," he said, shaking his head, and got cautiously to his feet. To his relief his knee held. Not that he doubted his healing ability but the memory of the pain lingered. The girl rose too, blocking the passage. Peter darted a glance over his shoulder, making sure the other twin wasn't waiting in ambush. He went to step round the girl but she moved to shove him. Using the momentum of her thrust, he sidestepped, gently guiding her on her way. She would've fallen flat on her face had he not held onto her blazer, stopping her mid-flight. When he was sure she wouldn't fall, he let go.

"I wouldn't try that again," he said. "Next time, I might let you fall."

By way of answer she kicked out. He dodged, and, catching hold of her foot, upended her, sending her sprawling to the floor, her legs flailing in the air, her skirt caught up around her waist. Aware that boys were always trying to spy under girls' skirts, he looked away, but not before he pulled off her shoe. He was about to leave with his trophy when a voice said, "Give me that." It was the other twin.

She lunged at him and, like her sister, ended up on the floor, the two writhing like snakes as they struggled to get up. He was about to flee when the classroom door slammed and a woman with a heavy French accent said, "What the…?" He felt a firm hand grasp his shoulder and the woman added, "Give me that."

He handed over the shoe and turned to leave. He didn't get far before the teacher called him back. "Two hours detention!" she said. There was a time when he would have objected, but he knew how it would go. He'd accuse. The teacher wouldn't believe him. There'd be an argument and he'd get even more detention. "Where? When?" he asked.

A brief look of surprise flitted across the teacher's face, no doubt surprised at his capitulation, before saying, "Next door. Now."

He was the first in the room, so he chose a seat at the back and settled in. Sometimes detention was used to do homework, but he had none, or if he did he was unaware of it. He wasn't surprised to see Sarah walk in. She'd already told him she was the target of nasty pranks and often got blamed. Rather than sit next to him, she took the seat farthest away, not even looking in his direction.

You alright? he asked. A question that was met with a brooding silence. He tried again, without success. Disappointed, he gave up. Reining in his attention, he reviewed his short time at the school. With hindsight, his hot-headedness had been frankly foolish. The verbal attack on the English teacher. The grace flung in the face of the whole school. The confrontation with the headmistress. The fight with the twins. Why was he being so provocative? If he wanted to survive, he needed allies not enemies. And Sarah was his first.

Sarah, he said wondering what had happened that she refused to talk. *I know this isn't easy, but we've got to stick together. You said so yourself.*

Do you know what I had to put up with because of you? Sarah's angry voice asked.

Me?

Apparently you told everyone I was your girlfriend. So now I'm a pervert too.

What? That's nonsense. I was in French, a language I

hardly speak. Rest assured, I said nothing about you.

Oh! She sounded confused . *They were so sure.*

Proficient liars generally are.

Brigit strode into the classroom and shot him a hostile glare before slumping into the teacher's seat. She pulled a fashion magazine from her satchel and began flicking through the pages, paying neither Peter nor Sarah any further attention. Apparently no one else had detention.

So, Sarah said, pretending to read the book in front of her, *you promised to tell me about your home.*

Peter told her about the choir and how the girls had been held captive and mistreated in a convent school. He'd just reached the moment he was reunited with Kate when the door opened and Eloise stepped in. She pointed to Peter and beckoned. "I'm to accompany you to your appointment," she said.

"Rather you than me," Birgit said looking down her nose at her fellow prefect before returning to her magazine. So it was true, Eloise got the tasks nobody wanted.

Speak to you later, he said to Sarah and followed Eloise out. "What appointment?" he asked.

"You're to see a shrink." She handed him a duffle-coat, saying, "Button it up." When he raised his eyebrows, she said, "You might be forced to dress as a girl in school, but the headmistress doesn't want that to be known."

Made sense. It was tempting to thwart her plans by revealing how he was dressed, but, knowing Heartless, she'd find a way of turning his defiance against him.

Eloise pulled a brown beret from her pocket, where it nestled against a paperback, and set it at an angle on his head. "Suits you," she said, no trace of mockery in her voice. His lips were curling in a smile of satisfaction when, to his surprise, she took his hand and led him across the street away from the school.

Walking through his old town dressed as a girl, hand in hand with another girl, filled him with conflicting feelings. Doing so had always been an ardent desire but also a terrifying prospect. Fi had threatened to walk him down the high street dressed in her school uniform but she'd never followed through, leaving him torn between disappointment and relief. The fact that he was being forced to do what he'd always dreamed of was so weird he both trembled with excitement and felt oddly detached.

Of course. It had to happen, didn't it? They bumped into a bunch of girls from his old school. That there was a war raging between the girls of the two schools didn't help. Eloise groaned, quickly letting go of Peter's hand, as the girls moved to block the pavement and surround them.

"Don't mind us," a girl Peter recognise as having been in Fi's class said, "Feel free to cling to your girlfriend." She sneered at Eloise. "Do you sleep with her? Or is that privilege reserved for nuns?"

Eloise ignored them and tried to continue but the girls linked arms and blocked the way. Peter was terrified they'd recognise him. After all, he'd been openly hanging out with Fi less than a year ago and he'd become quite well known in school, but none of the girls paid him any attention. Their target was Eloise, taunting her into hitting back, but the prefect was not the fighting type. Frustrated by the girl's lack of response, the tension was mounting. He was afraid there'd be a fight and sure enough two girls grabbed Eloise and tried to drag her into an alley.

When someone swung at him, he dodged and shifted to push the passing girl in the back, sending her sprawling to the pavement. For all his momentary success, he couldn't let this degenerate into a brawl. When a hand grabbed his wrist, he made the most of the skin-to-skin contact, leaning against the girl for support as he jumped inside her body. Releasing the content of her bladder was as easy as switching on a light. Jumping free, he left the girl to squeal in horror as she copiously wet herself.

Eloise was still in the grips of the two girls, despite her struggles. Peter moved to free her only to be pushed roughly away by one of girls. Grasping her clenched fist, he used the same ploy. When she halted, her hands flying to stem the flow of pee, Peter made the most of the distraction, grabbing Eloise's hand he pulled her out of fray.

Eloise was still in shock, her mouth open, her chest heaving, as Peter led her into a public garden off the high street. He headed for a bench, partly concealed by bushes, a convenient hiding place he'd discovered with Fi. Seating Eloise, he sat next to her and took her hand.

"I don't understand," she said. "What have they got against us?"

Peter shook his head. He didn't know either. "Maybe there's nothing to understand. They were born savage..." He thought of the horde of rugby players who'd attacked him and Fi. "And I thought it was only boys that were born stupid."

Eloise shot him a shocked look. "I don't know how to say this…" she began, her voice trailing off in embarrassment. "How can you be so harsh on boys? Some of them are cute." She gave him a twisted smile.

"Boys can be so clumsy and ugly both physically and in the way they behave." An intense wave of disgust rolled over him causing him to grimace. "I've never wanted to be one of them."

"Well," Eloise said, glancing over her shoulder to check they were still alone, "Some girls are no better." There was anger and disgust in her voice as she absently straightened Peter's beret which had suffered from the fight. "Although that never made me want to be a boy."

Peter sighed. Why did he always have to explain? Did girls have to explain why they were girls? The truth was, though, he did want to explain, at least to himself. He needed to. "I have an aversion to boys. I certainly don't want to be one," he began. That much was sure. "And although I feel whole dressing and acting like a girl, I stop short of wanting to change into one." He glanced to see if she understood, expecting to be confronted with incomprehension or even disapproval, only to find a thoughtful expression on her face.

"You want the best of both worlds," she replied with a grin.

When he glanced to see if she was mocking him, she squeezed his hand. "I don't like the way the girls pick on you. I too have been bullied, but nothing like you. If I were headmistress, that sort of bullying would have no place, but the headmistress not only accepts it, she encourages it."

"I appreciate your support," he said, glancing around. There was no sign of the girls who'd attacked them. If there was going to be revenge it'd probably come later. "There's a long story behind her aversion, but shouldn't we be going?"

Eloise glanced at her watch, "Oh my God! Yes. You're going to be late." For all her hurry, she made no move to get up. "Are you sure you want to do this?" Her voice was full of concern. "What's about to happen won't be pleasant."

He shook his head. "I don't want to go." In fact the prospect of an hour with a shrink was alarming. He'd seen the impact of such doctors on his mother. "But for the moment I'm stuck with the situation and have to go along with it."

"I'll wait for you," was all she said as they got up and headed for the shrink's office.

18.

Number 12. At last! They'd been searching for ages. The shabby office block squatted between a supermarket and a bank. A recently polished plaque read, Dr Dieter Rogwert, psychiatrist, 1st floor. Finding the street door ajar, Eloise pushed and stepped inside, closely followed by Peter. They climbed the steep stairs and Eloise knocked. There was no answer.

Peter tried the knob and the door cracked open. A bell had been rigged to ring when it opened. Peering inside, Peter discovered a tiny waiting room with a couple of plastic chairs and a low table piled high with old magazines like Woman's Own, Honey and Girl. Judging from the selection, the man catered for older women and young girls. A door led on to another room but it was closed and no sound issued from within. The two glanced at each other and sat down, preparing to wait.

They'd barely taken their seats when the door burst open and a middle-aged man in a worn grey suit bustled in and began removing his cycling clips. Paying them no attention, he opened the inner door and, disappearing inside, closed it after him. And that was supposed to be someone you could confide in! Peter looked questioningly at Eloise, her puzzled look echoing his. Both shrugged.

"Come in!" a voice boomed from within.

The first things that struck Peter were the carpets. Several overlapping layers provided an uneven but comforting surface to walk on. Carpets, or it might have been tapestries, hung from the walls. Under the sole window, a giant porcelain vase harboured an overflowing bouquet of wild flowers some of which had dried up letting their petals fall negligently to the floor. Odd objects were strategically placed to catch the newcomer's eye. A skull. A string of beads, a rosary possibly. Several large shells, worn smooth by the sea. A bunch of rusty keys and, to cap it all, a shrivelled apple.

The man, who was seated in one of the two armchairs studied Peter as he took in the room. When Peter turned his attention to the man, he indicated the boy should be seated. No words were exchanged. As the man seemed in no hurry to speak, Peter pursued his examination of the room. He was quite happy to spend the hour in silence.

"Well?" the man finally prompted, visibly annoyed at Peter's refusal to talk.

"You tell me," Peter glared. "I didn't ask to come here."

"Miss Wit informed me you have a problem."

"If I have a problem, it's her," Peter retorted. "Maybe you should see her. If you ask me, she's in serious need of help."

"It's normal to be angry. Tell me about it."

"Wouldn't you be angry if you'd been ripped from your life and your friends and dragged to another country by a mad woman bent on torturing you?"

"Come now." The man gave him a condescending smile. "Surely even you can hear how unreasonable your claims are?"

Peter was acutely reminded of a story about the confrontation between two psychiatrists who didn't know each other. Each had been told the other was delusional, believing he was a psychiatrist. The ensuing conversation had been an epic battle in which neither could win. The doctor had been told Peter was unhinged and whatever he did would be seen as proof.

"Where did you get the carpets?" Peter asked, trying to shift the conversation. "They're beautiful."

The man's eyes brightened, apparently delighted to be asked. Clearly, he was tempted to reply, but he resisted. "That's not why we're here."

"Then you tell me," Peter said, "because I don't know why

I was summonsed."

The man let out a weary sigh, as if Peter were the last of a long line of difficult cases he'd been lumbered with. "If you unbuttoned that," he pointed at Peter's duffle-coat, "your problem would be visible for all to see."

"Is what I'm wearing a problem for you or for me?" Peter asked.

The man shook his head as if Peter were beyond hope.

"Answer my question," Peter insisted. "Where does the problem lie? With me? With you? With the headmistress? With the church? With society at large?"

"Clearly the problem lies with you," he said, peering over his spectacles at Peter. "You're the one pretending to be a girl."

At last the reason for their encounter was out in the open. Relieved, Peter burst out laughing, causing the man to jerk back in alarm. "I've no problem being dressed as I am," Peter said unbuttoning his coat to reveal his girl's uniform. "In fact, I feel much better like that. The only problem I have is with people like you," he pointed a finger at the man whose face was a picture of disgust, "or the headmistress, people who try to force me to dress the way they think proper. What is wrong with you that you are prepared to resort to violence to impose your will? Why do you feel threatened by my clothes? Maybe you should analyse your own feelings of insecurity about gender before questioning mine."

The man dismissed Peter's words with a wave of his hand. "There's no doubt in my mind, you are a textbook case of gender identity disorder. You're isolated, anxious, lonely, depressed,… and may well have sought to harm yourself. You're obsessed with wanting to be what you clearly aren't and persist in acting out by dressing with inappropriate clothes."

How like a doctor to look at him through a textbook. "How can you be so sure?" Peter asked. "You think you know all about me, yet when I tell you who I am and what I feel, you don't listen. You've only your medical books to guide you."

"It's enough to see you dressed as a girl when you're clearly a boy. Our task is to get you back on track."

"What gives you the right to impose your will on me?"

The man scoffed. "You're a mere child. You know nothing of life. I, in comparison, am a fully trained doctor and psychiatrist, an expert with years of experience."

"What use is all your training if you can't see or hear the person standing in front of you? How can you pretend to treat someone you don't understand? You abuse the confidence vested in you as an expert…"

"Enough!" The man cut him off. "We're not here for you to insult me. We're here to straighten you out. Ingrid!" he called over his shoulder. A stoutly-built nurse hurried into the room from what Peter had taken to be a large cupboard. She carried a tray which she handed to the psychiatrist. Her hands free, she promptly grabbed Peter by the shoulders. He struggled, but the woman's grip held firm. When the doctor lifted a syringe, Peter realised with a shock why he was being restrained. "See what I mean about violence," he spluttered.

"Come now," the man said baring Peter's arm and plunging the needle into his vein, "This'll set things right."

Held upright as he was by the nurse, Peter was free to dive inside his body where he set about pushing the injected fluid back out the way it'd come. He could feel the rejected liquid dribbling down his arm, but he continued driving it out long after the doctor had finished and the nurse had scotched a plaster over the hole. Better to be sure.

Once the nurse released him, Peter staggered, knocking the tray from the chair arm where it lay. The syringe slithered across the floor heading for the nurse who jump out of its way with a squeal. In the confusion, Peter pocketed the tiny flacon which had tumbled into an armchair.

"I'll see you at the same time next week," the doctor said in calculated amiability.

"You'll see me in court," Peter shot back. It was an empty threat. The last thing he wanted was to defend his cause before judges who'd already decided against him.

He found Eloise engrossed in a book in the waiting room. Looking up at his arrival, her expression turned anxious. "Let's get out of here," he said.

The moment they were outside he asked, "Is there clean running water nearby?"

Eloise looked perplexed but didn't question him. "I saw a fountain in that garden." She was right, he remembered. When they reached the fountain, which was actually an oversized drinking fountain, he checked they were alone and pulled off his coat. Rolling up his sleeve, he ripped the plaster from his arm, and tossed it into a rubbish bin. Having examined the damage, he plunged his forearm under the water.

"I don't understand," Eloise said. "Did he bite you or something?"

"Worse," Peter said, "he injected me with a liquid I guess was male hormones."

"If he injected it, no amount of washing will get rid of it."

"It's complicated, but suffice it to say I made my body reject the liquid."

She shook her head in disbelief. "You ask me to believe that?"

He didn't want to reveal he could heal, but he needed her to have faith in him and felt he could trust her.

"Listen," he began, "I'm going to tell you a secret. Can I trust you to keep it to yourself?"

"Depends."

"Fair enough. My friend in Switzerland and I have developed a way of healing that enables me to do such things."

"If you say so." Her tone was sceptical.

He took her hand in his, closed his eyes and peered inside her body. Apart from her limp, which would take considerable effort to right, the only problem he could sense was the kind of delicate topic a girl would shy away from discussing with a boy. He hesitated. "You have a stomach ache," he said. She nodded. "It's because you have your periods." She blushed. "Does it happen every time?"

"Yes." She made a pained face. "The doctor said there was nothing I could do but wait for the menopause."

Typical! Peter groaned. "That's not true." It was a subject he'd discussed with Kate. It didn't need to be that way. "Let me just…" She must have felt something because she squirmed and would have pulled her hand away if he'd not kept a firm grip on it. "Hold on a sec," he said. "There."

"Remarkable!" she exclaimed. "The pain's gone. However did you do that?"

"It would take a while to explain properly, but let's just say each cell has a blueprint of how it should be. Over time your body got out of alignment…"

"How?"

"The knocks and scrapes of life, food maybe, movement or lack of it, or simply your expectations underscored by the words of key people like that doctor. All I did was encourage your body to return to its natural order. It's easy when you know how."

"That's amazing!" Her eyes were bright with excitement. "You could heal all sorts of things with that."

"I could. I can. But I don't…"

"Why ever not?" she blurted out. "Think of all the good you could do."

"You're forgetting people's reactions, especially those of so-called health experts. They'd lock me up. After all, I've done none of the tedious years of training they've had to undergo. All those books. All those lectures. Unlike them, I have no diplomas from prestigious institutions to vouch for my worthiness. The only thing I can do that they can't, but it's what makes all the difference, is listen to the body and encourage it to do what it wants."

"I see now how you managed to expel that liquid. But why would they inject you in the first place?"

He gave her an extremely condensed version of the Witless/Heartless saga.

"Wow! The new headmistress is not much liked, and, it's true, I suspected she did things she shouldn't. But I had no proof." Suddenly her eyes went wide and she stared at Peter in wonder. "It was you!" she exclaimed. "You made those girls wet themselves." She giggled in delight. "It was so weird. I couldn't understand. Now I see. You did it."

"I'm not proud of it," Peter muttered.

"Why ever not?"

"I don't like violence and I hate hurting people. That's why I love healing. In the moment, making them wet themselves seemed like the least bad way of ending the fight." Peter pictured the girls scurrying across town, trying to conceal their sodden clothes, haunted by the smell, hoping no one would notice. "It probably put a big dent in their self-esteem."

"That wouldn't be so bad," Eloise replied. "Did you see how they behaved? A bit of deflation would do them good."

Peter had to chuckle. "As long as I've known them they've been that pig-headed and brash."

"You know them!" Eloise exclaimed.

"Yeah my girlfriend was in their class." He winced at the memory.

Eloise took a step back. "You went out with one of them?" She sounded alarmed.

"My friend would have nothing to do with them."

"But…"

"None of that matters anymore, my friend Fi is dead."

Eloise look at him in horror. "They didn't…?"

"No," Peter said bowing his head. "It was the brother of a friend. He shot her."

"I'm so sorry."

"So am I," Peter replied, tears springing to his eyes. "For all her shortcomings, she was a real gem. She was the first one to encourage me to dress as a girl."

"Oh! You mean girl friend," she said emphasising the separation between the two words. "Not girlfriend."

"I'm not sure what she was. Temptress. Coach. Confidante. Best friend. Lover. Sister. Pretty boy. She played all the roles."

"Sounds like a real handful." She paused a moment,

thoughtful. "There's one thing I don't understand. How come they didn't recognise you?"

"Too focussed on your uniform, probably. That and the fact I was the last person they'd have expected to see. As far as anyone knows I disappeared on the Continent. We should go. Can't have the headmistress any more angry at me than she is already."

"Couldn't you…? You know. Do something like you did to those girls, but to the headmistress?"

Peter smiled. "Tempting. But no. That wouldn't be wise. The miserable sow has a way of twisting every attack in her favour." He chuckled. "But it's a pleasing thought."

19.

"The town is abuzz…" Heinz said, unpacking his camera.

He'd just arrived and was seated at Lydia's kitchen table across from Kate. Lydia was brewing tea while Regina was in the Lost Girls' House interviewing Suzanne.

"What?" Kate and Lydia asked in chorus.

"Rumour has it, at least, that's what I've heard,…" he replied, a hint of a grin on his lips.

"Come on!" Lydia pleaded, throwing a tea towel at him.

"The Bishop has been recalled to Rome."

Kate whistled between her teeth.

"That's incredible!" Lydia exclaimed. "Could Rome have got wind of the poisoning?"

Heinz shot her a disbelieving look. "A poisoning is no big deal." He winked. "No. A large group of orphans from a convent - the very one the Lost Girls attended - ran away and were discovered shortly afterwards cowering in a derelict house. When the police went to check on the convent, the living conditions were atrocious."

"However did news get out?" Lydia said, placing the teapot between them. "The church is normally good at covering things up."

"A leak. After what happened with the Lost Girls, journalists homed in on the convent like hornets, flaring a second scandal. Apparently the girls told the police they were trying to rejoin the Lost Girls, but were too exhausted."

Kate wonder if it was the same group she'd visited. She

remembered them well. She'd managed to get them to sing, despite the intimidation of the nuns. Had she not promised to rescue them? She'd been so caught up with the Lost Girls, she'd completely forgotten.

"One of the nuns broke down under the media's questions," Heinz pursued, "and confessed the children had been badly treated."

"Another reason for the church to silence us," Kate commented, blowing on her tea which was scalding. When everyone looked at her questioningly, she added, "We're a bad influence."

"What's this about bad influences?" Regina asked as she entered, closely followed by Suzanne. Once Heinz had retold his news, Regina said, "You can bet the journalists will flock here too." As if to prove her point, a knock sounded at the door. "I'll slip into the next room … with Heinz," she said, pulling him after her. "You don't want another journalist and a press photographer openly listening in on the work of a competitor." She grinned. "Instead, we'll listen from behind the door."

Once the two were out of sight, Lydia opened the door.

Kate knew the young woman. The journalist had interviewed her after their first concert. She looked very different. Wrapped as she was for winter in fur-lined boots, a thick overcoat, scarf and hat, she was clearly soon to have a baby. "Jo, isn't it?" Kate asked. The young woman nodded. The two greeted each other with a hug.

"When's it due?" Kate asked.

"February."

Kate eased Jo out of her coat while Lydia poured a herbal tea. "To help your body fix the iron," Lydia said, sliding a packet of herbal tea across the table. "A present for the mother to be."

"Thanks," Jo said, bestowing a broad smile on Lydia, "you're an angel." She pulled a notebook from her bag and turned to Kate. "Presumably you've heard the latest scandal in a convent orphanage. I'd be interested to know what you think."

"We whole-heartedly condemn those who mistreat children.

The damage leaves scars for life. We should know. We've all been the victims of such violence and abuse."

"There are rumours you orchestrated this mass exodus. Is that true?"

"No," Kate said, as emphatically as she could. "We didn't know about the escape till just now and we certainly didn't organise it."

Jo paused to glance around the kitchen. "If the authorities were to allow it, would you welcome them here?"

"We'd need to discuss it amongst us," Kate replied.

"But as leader, surely you have an opinion."

The word 'leader' brought Kate up short. She was indeed the leader and it was only right she be recognised as such. Yet she'd already seen how the press singled out an individual as a figurehead and glorified that person, repeatedly talking of her and only her, shaping her public image till she became a currency they could cash in on. That said, there was probably little she could do against it, less it be to push other members of the choir into the spotlight as she planned to do with their pamphlets. Thinking of which, she turned to Suzanne who was busy sorting dried herbs. "What do you think?"

"We would willingly grant refuge," Suzanne said without hesitation. "But it would have to be temporary. We don't have the means to cater for so many for more than a short time."

Suzanne's heartfelt but practical response offered an ideal opening to reveal the negative attitude of the church towards the Lost Girls. Doing so might not be wise, but the occasion was too good to pass up. The deplorable conditions of the girls in the church-run orphanage were just another facet of the church's disregard for orphans and girls in particular.

"I've often wondered where you got your money," Jo asked.

Jo's question bore no hint of innuendo, but it still rekindled Kate's anger at the church suggesting, without the slightest proof, that the girls survived by selling sexual favours. "From concerts and the herbal remedies," Kate explained, nodding to Suzanne who was carefully spooning the sorted herbs into tiny paper bags. "Unfortunately, the church, has decided to forbid the use of its churches for our concerts. As if that loss of revenue wasn't enough, we've learnt they're actively opposing our work with herbal medicine. Only the other day a group of priests broke into our workshop and ransacked the place, pretexting a search for proof of devil worship. You'd think they bore a grudge against orphan girls the way they behave."

Jo was startled at this new revelation and eager to know more. Kate let Suzanne tell the tale. Finally satisfied, Jo turned back to Kate, saying, "Can we take a photo of you in that workshop?"

"That would be Suzanne's domain," Kate replied. "The workshop is her responsibility. If you need a photo of anyone, it should be her."

Suzanne was reticent as was Jo who clearly wanted Kate.

"We have photographic proof of the break-in and the damage done," Kate said. "Suzanne took a whole series of pictures. Maybe you'd find a better illustration for your article amongst them."

"I don't think a photo of a wrecked workshop would work very well," Jo said.

"Wait till you see," Suzanne said, getting to her feet. "I'll go and fetch them."

Kate would have preferred she ask Heinz first, but when Suzanne headed not for the exit and the Lost Girls House, but into the next room, she had to smile.

While they waited, Jo and Lydia talked of child birth and the best herbal teas to help with mother's milk. It was the young woman's first. She let Kate put a hand on her swollen belly saying with a chuckle, "He kicks like a mule."

Kate made the most of the brief physical contact to check on the baby. It was healthy and indeed kicking. To her surprise it wasn't a boy at all. Jo had sounded so sure. "It's a girl," she blurted out before she could stop herself. The future mother stared at her in disbelief. Luckily Suzanne returned at that moment bearing a bunch of photos, sparing Kate an awkward explanation.

"Good Lord! This is extraordinary!" Jo exclaimed as Suzanne fanned out the photos on the table. The girl had chosen a selection in which the priests were clearly visible wrecking the workshop. "However did you get these?"

Kate studied the photos over Jo's shoulder. They really were a prize catch.

"From outside, through the window," Suzanne explained, clearly proud of her exploits. "They were so bent on destruction, they paid no attention to me."

"Have you shown them to anyone?" Suzanne glanced questioningly at Kate, who replied, "As you must be aware, we work closely with Regina and Heinz. I'm sure you know them. They've seen the photos."

"Do they plan to use them?"

"You'd have to ask them," Kate said. She knew full well Heinz had made the selection so she doubted he'd give away anything he wanted to use. "I imagine if you publish quickly, you'll be first off the mark."

"Thanks," Jo said, giving Kate a smile. She bent over the table as best she could with her belly and examined a photo in which a priest held a raised stick poised menacingly over a row of jars. "Did you go to the police?"

Kate was considering how best to reply when Suzanne beat her to it, "The priests came accompanied by two policemen as if it were a concerted effort. Alerting the police seemed pointless."

"Have you got any photos showing the police at work?" Jo asked.

"No," Suzanne replied. "The two stayed in the main house. To be honest, I can't be sure they knew what the priests were up to."

"Can I take these?" Jo asked, indicating the photos.

"Pick a few," Kate replied. "Those you choose you can have."

Jo spread the photos on the table and picked three. "I'll take these."

Kate helped her on with her coat and they hugged, saying their goodbyes. Jo was about to leave when she turned, adding, "The editor will probably want to focus on the fugue from the convent, but I'll do my best to get your story in print. I'm banking on the connection between the two to convince him."

"Thanks," Kate said. "It's important. No one should be allowed to get away with what they're doing. Keep in touch."

Once she'd gone, Heinz and Regina came out of hiding.

"What do you think?" Kate asked.

"I wouldn't hold out too much hope," Regina said taking a seat at the table. "The editor's a good friend of the Bishop..."

Both Kate and Suzanne groaned. "Is there no way round these people and their influence?" Kate exclaimed.

"Your guerrilla idea is the best I've heard so far," Regina said. "Priests preach from the pulpit, newspapers roll off printing presses and television is transmitted from a studio somewhere else. Centralised power broadcasts its message to the masses. It's one-way communication. That's all they know. Your idea turns that on it's head. The central, one-size-fits-all is replaced by many small messages, all different, all unexpected. In dialogue with the people. Popping up. Unstoppable. Uncontrollable... They'll be completely flummoxed."

Kate grinned. "I hadn't seen it like that," she said. "It's the exact opposite of what happened in my world. The local mage councils and the autonomous towns and villages, for all their creativity and diversity, were overrun by centrally organised, highly disciplined, single-minded warrior priests."

"That sounds like the Romans," Regina said. "It was their central organisation, their famously straight roads and the discipline of their army that got the better of Celtic tribes who squabbled so much they couldn't field a united front."

"The church piggybacked on the thrust of the Roman conquest to extend and consolidate its religion!" Heinz added. "The holy church was, and in some ways still is, a military organisation out to reap souls in the name of saving them."

"So if we are to hold them accountable," Kate said, excited

at the image unfolding in her mind, "we must react differently. Catch them off guard, making short, sharp forays then withdrawing to strike elsewhere."

"I much prefer the idea of dialogue and healing," Suzanne said, her face aglow. "Listening to people and helping them suits us much better than metaphors of war and killing. Let's not forget our main mission is to heal. Even our singing might be considered a form of healing. And not just any healing. One that doesn't respond with knives and dangerous drugs to the woes our lifestyle has inflicted on our bodies and souls."

"Are you questioning my leadership?" Kate said, a stern look on her face as she puffed out her chest. "You heard the journalist. Where's your respect?"

Suzanne burst out laughing and, picking up the tea towel Lydia had tossed earlier, threw it at Kate. It didn't reach its target, but was deftly snatched out of the air by Kate who shifted to the sink-side where she began drying dishes. Turning to address those assembled, she said, "Our champion of healing is right, of course. Dialogue not monologue. Healing not harming. Respect not disregard."

"Life not death," Regina added, her face somber.

The reminder was timely. For all Suzanne's good intentions, the church had responded to dialogue with poison. War and destruction were indeed pawing the ground in the wings, ready to erupt onto the stage. Rather than relishing being right, Kate was proud of Suzanne. The girl's positive vision was one she could adhere to.

"What they tried to do to you is unpardonable," Suzanne said. "The way we were treated in the convent is despicable. Their attitude towards the Lost Girls is petty and vindictive. But not all the church is bad. Think of Sister Teresa." Her voice caught on the woman's name. She'd been close to the nun. "She fought and died for us. I'm sure there are scores of churchgoers who have the welfare of others at heart."

20.

"It's Jo," the woman said over the phone. She was clearly distressed. "You remember me. We met earlier."

"Of course I remember you, Jo," Kate said. "What's up?"

"My editor flatly refused your story. He said it was defamatory and he confiscated the photos saying they were fakes." She sounded on the verge of tears. "I tried, but he dismissed all my arguments and finally patted me on the head, saying I was getting over emotional because of my pregnancy. He suggested I take time off, a long time off." The anger alongside the hurt in her voice was palpable. "I felt so humiliated. I'm a serious journalist. I work as well as any man. How dare he pat me on the head, dismissing me as if I were a child?"

"In your place," Kate said, "I'd have been furious too. But I'm not surprised. I heard he was a good friend of the Bishop."

"What am I to do?" A sob burst from her lips. "How am I going to get by with the child coming and me out of work?"

"Out of work? Is that what he meant?"

"I'm paid when I write. If he sends me home with no work, I get no pay."

"I'm really sorry," Kate said, her mind racing. "Listen. Regina and Heinz are coming in a short while. Why don't you join us? Maybe we can dream up a solution. And even if we can't, at least you'll be in good company. The evening meal promises to be particularly good. Klaus has baked a batch of his famous pasties. It's Suzanne's birthday. What do you say?"

There was a long pause as Jo blew her nose, then she said,

"I hadn't realised it was her birthday. If I'd known, I'd have wished her many happy returns. Please tell her from me."

"We didn't mention it, because the meal is to be a surprise. As for wishing her happy birthday, you can do so yourself, if you come."

"Okay. Why not. I'll be there in half an hour." After a short pause, she added, "What should I bring?"

"Just yourself," Kate said with a grin. "But if you're not comfortable coming empty handed, I'm sure a little card would be appreciated."

It was Kate's task to distract Suzanne while the others prepared. Kate suggested they go for a walk. "I haven't visited the herb gardens in ages," she said as they left the Lost Girls' House and wandered up the path. "What was it like being questioned by Regina?"

"Strange. Her questions were far from easy. I was obliged to think about subjects I'd shoved aside for later."

Kate chuckled. "She gets right to the heart of things, doesn't she?"

"She sure does." Suzanne paused, pulling a knife from her apron. She cut a couple of yellow flowers that had long withered on the plant. "St John's Wort," she informed Kate. "They flower late spring and summer. It's a wonder there's anything left."

"What sort of subjects?" Kate asked, leading her back to Regina's questions.

"She wanted to know how I felt when the priests ransacked the workshop. I was at a loss what to say. My feelings were so confused. First of all, I felt disappointed. Despite the nasty things in the convent, I still looked up to the church as a force for good. Those men took that hope, that belief from me. Then there was the fear. They were so big and angry. What could a little girl possibly do if they turned on me? Yet I couldn't run. I had to stay and take photos. To have proof. And I was furious. That was my work they were smashing. Remedies that had taken ages and a lot of love and care to prepare. Remedies that could lessen people's suffering, even heal them. Didn't the bible say you should help the poor and the sickly? I just couldn't understand what drove men of the church to undermine my work, my mission."

As they continued up the path, Kate glanced surreptitiously over her shoulder, checking no one was signalling the meal was ready. "What else did she want to know?"

"One subject touched me more than all others. Why healing was so important to me?"

"Tricky," Kate agreed. It was a subject she'd often discussed with her father both as her teacher and a healing mage. Maybe she should have broached the subject with Suzanne. After all, she was teaching her healing.

"I had to think quite a while before replying. I told her I'd seen so much suffering, it pained me. I have no idea why people harm themselves or others. Stopping them doing so is beyond my power. But I can right some of the damage. That's why I put my efforts into healing."

An owl hooted back down the path. It was the signal. "Oh dear," Kate exclaimed. "I'd completely forgotten. I have several visitors coming to dinner." She glanced at her watch. "We should be getting back."

"What about the gardens?" Suzanne asked, disappointed.

"We'll find time tomorrow," Kate said. "I promise."

When the two reached the Lost Girls' House the refectory curtains were drawn. All was quiet and the dinning room was uncharacteristically dark.

"Where is everybody?" Suzanne asked as they stepped into the unlit room.

The whoosh of a match was quickly followed by the splutter of a candle being kindled. Then another. Then another. In the flickering light, they could make out the girls of the choir huddled in the shadows across the room. It was Clara's hand giving the beat that had them bursting into song. "Happy birthday to you, happy birthday to you, happy birthday dear Suzanne,…"

Suzanne squealed in delight and flung her arms around

Kate's neck, hugging her. "You knew!" she accused. "You knew, didn't you?"

"How could we forget your birthday," Kate replied, freeing herself from the hug as the girls jostled to congratulate Suzanne and give her a kiss. Spotting Jo in the doorway, Kate went to greet her. "How are you holding up?"

Jo grimaced. Kate led her to a table slightly apart from the others, saying, "Regina, Heinz, Lydia and Klaus will be with us shortly." Indicating a chair, Kate said, "Take a seat."

Suzanne had finally got free of her well-wishers and came to join them. The girl was clearly moved by the reception she'd received. "Content?" Kate asked.

"You bet!" She looked sheepish. "I thought you'd forgotten."

"Daft ninny!" Kate chided, slinging an arm around the girl's shoulders. "We wanted to surprise you."

"Happy birthday," Jo said, handing Suzanne as a small package wrapped in brown paper. "I thought you might find this interesting."

"Thank you," Suzanne said, taking the seat next to Jo. She painstakingly removed the sticky tape as if keeping the paper intact was her main goal in life. Once the wrapping removed, the contents turned out to be a beautiful leather-bound book.

"It's a history of medicine," Jo said, "in particular the shift from alchemy to pharmacy, from magic to science."

A broad grin lit up Suzanne's face as she leafed through the pages. "This is wonderful!" Placing the book carefully on the table, she flung her arms around a surprised Jo in an enthusiastic hug. "Thank you. Thank you."

"Somebody's happy," Regina said joining them at the table, a grin on her face.

Extricating herself from Suzanne's hug, Jo greeted the new arrival with a distant, "Regina" and held out a stiff hand for the woman to shake. Regina just stared at the offered hand in disbelief. There was clearly bad blood between the two. Kate was surprised. Regina had made no mention of it.

"I see you haven't forgotten," Regina said, coldly.

"How could I?" Jo shot back. "I lost my job because of you."

It was time to intervene. "I have no idea what past conflict has you two in its grips," Kate said getting to her feet, "but this is Suzanne's birthday and I won't have a personal feud marring it. What's more such tension is not good for the future baby. And there was me thinking you two could work together to help us." Kate wondered if she'd have to revise her plans. To be honest, she couldn't see how she would succeed without their help.

"My apologies," Jo said, looking sheepishly at Suzanne. "I didn't mean to spoil your party."

"You haven't spoilt anything," Suzanne said. "In fact, you gave me the most wonderful present."

"That reminds me," Regina said, "we've also got a present, but Heinz has it."

"Where is he?" Kate asked, looking round.

"Here," Heinz said, arriving at that moment, a brightly coloured packet grasped in his hands. "I heard it was someone's birthday." He grinned at Suzanne. "Happy birthday, Miss." He kissed her on both cheeks and handed her the present before going to stand next to Regina. "It's from both of us."

"Wow. It's heavy," Suzanne said. "Is it a brick? Several bricks?"

"I never thought you'd guess," he quipped.

With as much caution as she had unwrapped Jo's present, Suzanne unpacked Heinz's parcel to find a large book. Suzanne held it up for Kate to see. It was an encyclopaedia of medicinal herbs. "It's just what I needed," Suzanne said, giving Regina and Heinz a kiss.

"I hope you'll loan me that," Lydia said, helping Klaus and several of the girls carry in trays of food and drinks.

"Of course," Suzanne promised. "We're in this together."

No more was said of the conflict between Jo and Regina. In fact the whole meal was devoted to memories of parties past and no mention was made of poisonings or the church or job losses or fights for survival. It was only when the festivities were winding down that Kate suggested they talk. She showed her guests through into the meeting room next door then went in search of the members of what she called 'the council'.

She found Clara and Claudia talking to Eileen about where they could hold their next concert if they couldn't use Saint Leodegar. Having sent them to join her guests, she went in search of Tania. She heard her before she saw her. The girl was in a heated discussion with Christine in a darkened corridor.

"You tell her!" Christine exclaimed, seizing Kate's arm. "She won't listen to me."

It was unusual to find Christine so frustrated. "What's up?" Kate asked.

"Tania insists on getting together a delegation to convince you to teach us new skills," Christine said.

Tania had on her brazen face, her look challenging Kate to contradict her. Kate sighed. The girl could be so self-centred, and when she was, it bordered on destructive. Apparently being confronted by Suzanne and Christine before the whole choir had not deterred her. Kate felt a surge of annoyance. "We have no time for this," she said. "Go get your rebels together. If we have a moment later, we'll hear your complaints. Now we have a meeting of the council to attend."

Kate took Christine by the arm and was about to walk away when Tania blurted out, "What about me? I'm on the council too."

"If you are so pigheaded not to accept when I say this is not the moment to learn such skills, then I suggest you take time to think over your situation."

"You're kicking me out?" Tania said, her voice strangled as she stared at Kate in disbelief.

"No," Kate replied. "I'd never do that. But I can't let you disrupt our work. We have serious problems to deal with. If you persist in your demands that'll only be a distraction. That's why I suggest you pause to think."

"Me? Think?" the girl said, her expression determined. "It's you that needs to think."

The seriousness of her tone caused Kate to pause as she

wondered how to respond. It was Christine that spoke instead. "You should let her explain."

Unsure how to react, Kate nodded, knowing that Christine had good sense.

"To defend ourselves," Tania began, "you wouldn't hesitate to teach us self-defence. You are good at it and you willingly share your knowledge. You also taught us to detect poison and you hinted you had other tricks up your sleeve. Surely it would make sense to teach us more. As young girls, we're particularly vulnerable. Sharing your knowledge could save our lives or at least keep us from harm. So why won't you?"

Kate stood there in the near darkness frozen in indecision. Tania had a point. Why wouldn't she teach them magic? In her world, magic had been common place. Some could do it, others couldn't, but those who were gifted weren't ostracised or persecuted. In this world, magic was either a joke or a cardinal sin. She was worried that teaching it would put the girls in more danger. Then again, harm hovered over them, with or without magic. "Okay," Kate said. "I'm still not convinced, but let's discuss your idea in the council."

She took hold of Tania's hand and linking arms with Christine, headed off down the corridor.

"Where are we going?" Tania asked, digging in her heals.

"To talk to our guests," Kate shot back, tugging on Tania's arm.

21.

"Sorry I'm late," Kate said, taking the seat left free at the head of the table. "You may not all know Jo." She indicated the young woman. "I invited her to join us. She's a journalist who wrote an article about the attack on our workshop. As a result she just got fired."

Several people gasped. "That's awful!" Christine exclaimed.

"What excuse did they give?" Regina asked, seemingly unsurprised by the news.

"My accusations were defamatory."

"What do you expect from a good friend of the Bishop?" Regina asked, sounding bitter. Kate wondered if she too had had a confrontation with the editor.

Jo groaned, nodding. "I misjudged the influence of the church and now I'm paying the price." She placed a protective hand on her swollen belly. "I shouldn't have taken the risk."

"As a journalist, you did exactly what you were supposed to," Regina said, gifting the woman a smile, some of the coldness between the two dissipating. "What I find despicable is the way these men play on the vulnerability of an expectant mother."

Lydia patted Jo on the shoulder, saying, "We'll find a solution."

"If only we had the means to pay Jo as well as Regina and Heinz," Eileen mused. "They could all help us in our combat."

"If we had money, we could also help those poor girls who fled the orphanage," Suzanne added. "They could prepare herbs and in return we could take them in."

"Some of them might even be good enough to join the choir," Clara said, beaming.

"Not having money is one of the reasons we are here," Kate pointed out, feeling a need to calm the enthusiasm. "If the church's boycott works, we'll all be short pretty soon."

"You should make a budget," Klaus said placing a tray of sugar-coated pastries in the middle of the table.

"Make sure there's enough money for food," Tania exclaimed, licking her fingers, having slid a whole pastry into her mouth. Typical Tania. Everyone laughed, of course.

"We might solve most of our financial problems if we could convince Tania to go on a diet," Lydia quipped. At which Tania grabbed a second pastry and shot the baker's wife a filthy look. "Seriously though," Lydia continued, "I like the idea of aiming big. The new girls. Our media allies. The herbal business. And the choir. We should try to estimate how much a global project would cost and aim to raise the money."

"I agree," Christine said, true to form. "Better to be optimistic."

Kate turned to Jo, "Will you work with us if we can raise the funds to ensure your salary?"

The woman looked hesitant. "With the baby coming, I'm wary of taking a job that isn't guaranteed. And remember, from February I'll be on maternity leave. Do you really want that?"

"Only if we get to babysit," Claudia said with an impish grin.

"You can help with the baby even if I don't work for you," Jo replied, blowing Claudia a kiss. Kate marvelled at how some people naturally got on well together. It was at that moment that Jo let out a gasp, clutching her belly.

"Contractions?" Lydia asked.

Jo nodded.

"It's nothing to worry about," Lydia said. "Many women get them well before the birth. Just breath deeply and relax."

Kate wondered how you could possibly relax with a baby kicking around inside you. She was quite used to having others in her head, Peter, for one. But the thought of having another being physically growing in her belly made her shiver with a mix of apprehension and anticipation.

Claudia shifted to Jo's side and took hold of the woman's hand.

You can calm her with your thoughts, Kate said mind-to-mind and mentally showed Claudia how. So much for not teaching them 'magic'. As the pains abated, they pursued their discussion.

"If our stock hadn't been destroyed by those priests, we could step up the herbal business," Lydia said. "We have enough potential customers."

"How long would it take to stock up?" Regina asked.

"It's a long process," Suzanne said. "Plants can only be collected at certain times and drying or macerating them can take a while."

"What about all the stuff in the basement?" Eileen asked. "Could you not sell some?"

"I'd forgotten that," Lydia said. "Yes. It might tide us over."

"What about the choir?" Kate asked Clara. "Have you spoken to Beth?"

Their discussion went on well into the night with Regina, Heinz and even Jo making exciting suggestions of venues and spontaneous events. Kate was pleased to see Jo get involved. She liked the young woman, as did many of those around the table, and very much wanted to work with her. If Jo felt involved, there was more chance she'd agree to work with them. As for funds, it was decided Kate would talk to Beth about sponsors. They'd also talk about drafting a budget. Finally, Klaus and Eileen promised to look into what would be needed to accommodate a group of new girls.

As it was late, and Kate still had to let Tania present her idea, she wound up the meeting. Their guests were on the point of leaving when Jo had another bout of contractions, worry added to the pain etched on her face. "I'll come with you," Claudia offered. "Just in case."

Call me if there's the slightest problem, Kate said to the girl before Lydia accompanied them to the car.

Several of the Lost Girls were about to head to their beds when Kate called them back. "Tania wants to have a word."

"Can't it wait?" Suzanne asked, stifling an enormous yawn. "We're exhausted."

"I'd like to get it settled tonight," Kate said. "Let's see if we can keep it short."

"I'll make hot chocolate," Christine said, eliciting smiles on tired faces. "I already know what it's about."

They shifted to the armchairs ranged around the fireplace. Eileen lit the kindling and quickly had a blaze going.

"Fire away, Tania," Kate said, smiling at her inadvertent play on words. "And try to keep it brief." She groaned inwardly, knowing the long diatribes Tania was capable of.

"I want Kate to teach us more magic," Tania said. "We are battling against forces that are much more powerful than us. If we are to have the slightest chance of winning, we need to make the most of every advantage we've got."

When the girl stopped, Kate stared at her in astonishment. When had Tania ever been so succinct? She was tempted to make a joke about it, but refrained. Instead, she looked at the others inviting reactions.

"I'm nervous about 'magic'," Christine said. "I'm afraid I might make a mess of it or that something will go horribly wrong. I've always been told it was bad. That fear is hard to shake off."

"Me too," Clara said. "But I'm less afraid. I have confidence in Kate not to put us in danger."

"You're clearly reticent too, Kate," Eileen said. "Why?"

"Where I was brought up, magic was natural," Kate replied. "Here, magic is feared and those who practice it are persecuted. I don't want you to be hounded because you can do things others can't or won't."

"Maybe there are ways to practice magic without making a show of it," Suzanne said. "Like healing."

Kate sucked in a deep breath, unable to dispel her worry. "Okay. I'll teach you. We'll begin with the council, on condition that it remain a secret. We'll have to devise ways to conceal what we're doing."

Tania beamed at her, but for once didn't crow at her success.

They were all sipping hot chocolate, staring dreamily at the flickering fire with no one having the courage to climb to bed when a distant voice called out in Kate's head. *Kate! Help!* She recognised Claudia immediately.

What's up?

An accident. A car hit us. We're in a ditch.

Are you hurt?

My head is bleeding. But it's Jo and the baby I'm worried about.

Hold on a sec, I need to tell the others. I'll get back to you straight away. Springing to her feet, her sudden movement startled everyone. "Claudia and Jo have had an accident," she announced. Everyone clamoured to know more, but Kate ignored their questions. "Eileen can you get Klaus and Lydia. We'll need Klaus's van."

"Shouldn't we call an ambulance?" Eileen asked.

"No. We can manage. You wanted magic. Let's use it." Turning to Suzanne, she added, "I'm going to heal Claudia, but to do so I need you to support me."

Glancing at Tania's face, Kate feared a storm. Of course the girl wanted to be the one to hold Kate. "Suzanne's been learning healing," Kate explained, addressing the whole group. "She'll be able to assist me."

Suzanne sat next to her on the couch and put her arms around her. Feeling safe, Kate lent back and closed her eyes. "What ever you do, don't try to wake me till I open my eyes. Suzanne can answer questions if you absolutely need to know what's going on." *I'm going to jump mentally to you, Claudia, so I can stem the flow of blood and make sure nothing else is wrong. I'll stay in contact with Suzanne so she can learn from what I do.* With that she jumped.

That feels really weird, Claudia said, groggily.

Kate wasted no time talking. She staunched the flow of blood from a gash on Claudia's head. *There's a great deal of blood,* she told Suzanne. *There always is with head wounds. But the opening is relatively small.* Kate encouraged the tissues to knit together before checking the rest of Claudia's body. One of her ribs was broken as was a small bone in her wrist. She set them right. *There*, she said. *That should do it. Now I need to jump to Jo. Place a hand on her hand and hold it there till I tell you.*

The moment Claudia laid a hand on Jo's, Kate jumped. The young woman was unconscious but the baby was in a panic, struggling to get out. If she didn't do something quick Jo would go into labour then and there. Kate strove to reassure the little thing. She hadn't realised how hard that would be when you couldn't use language. At first she was at a loss. After several fruitless efforts, she opted to communicate calming feelings. In the circumstances, calm was a hard card to play. Finally, she did so by remembering pleasant moments with Peter. To her relief, it worked and the baby slowly ceased struggling. *You can thank uncle Peter when you meet him*, she told the uncomprehending foetus.

Turning her attention to Jo, she found the woman had concussion. *She's received a massive blow to her head. Several bones in her neck are displaced, muscles have been torn and her ribs had taken a severe beating,* she said, drawing Suzanne's attention to each trouble spot. Working systematically, she began with Jo's head until she'd helped the body set everything right. Once she'd finished, Jo was no longer unconscious, but asleep. Kate encouraged Jo's body to slumber on. *Sleeping will help with the shock*, she told Suzanne. Then she jumped back to Claudia.

You can let go now. Everything's going to be alright. Both Jo and the baby are fine. She's asleep. Should she awake, reassure her that her baby is perfectly ok and that we'll be here shortly. Don't tell her what I did. Just let her believe she had a miraculous escape. Where are we, by the way?

Once Claudia told her, Kate jumped back to her own body, to find Lydia, Klaus and the others standing anxiously around. Suzanne had been too engrossed to tell them anything. Lydia, in particular, was staring at her in awe. She was clearly bursting to ask questions, but Kate left her no opportunity. "Future mother, baby and Claudia are all okay but we need to get to them quickly," Kate said, telling them where the accident had taken place. All the girls wanted to go, but Kate insisted that only Lydia, Klaus and Suzanne come.

"Will we need my medical kit?" Lydia asked.

"I don't think so. But bring it all the same," Kate replied. "They should all be okay, including the baby." To think it had almost been born prematurely. It would never have survived. "The only shock that remains will be in their minds." Judging from her own shock, and she hadn't even been in the accident, getting over it wasn't going to be easy.

Turning to the bunch of disappointed girls, Kate said, "Could you prepare a room for Jo with a comfortable bed? If you can, put a second bed next to it. I think it would be good if Claudia were to sleep by her side. For both of them."

They reached the scene of the accident within minutes, Klaus driving fast on the deserted roads. Kate knew the accident had been bad, but the sight of the car upside down, smoking in a ditch, was terrifying. She'd been so intent on patching them up, it hadn't crossed her mind the car might catch fire or explode. They'd been extremely lucky.

Opening the car doors proved impossible. Klaus had to smash the windscreen with a crowbar. When Jo, who was still asleep, and Claudia were safely in the van, wrapped in blankets, they went back to examine the wreckage. Suzanne had brought her camera and used her flash to take photos.

"Where's the other vehicle?" Klaus asked, looking at the remains of black paint where the other car had hit Jo's.

"Scarpered," Suzanne called out from the van. "The bastards!"

Looking at the skid marks on the road, Kate fought to keep her growing apprehension at bay. After all, the Bishop's gang hadn't hesitated to poison her. "Could it have been deliberate?" she asked.

"She was a threat," Klaus said, recuperating Jo's bag and the car's papers from the wreck. "They seem capable of anything."

Feeling vulnerable standing there in the dead of night with the ever-present screech of owls and only the headlights to reassure them, Kate hurried everyone into the van. "Let's get home."

22.

Peter sat on his bed turning the tiny bottle over in his fingers. Testosterone. He held it up to the light. It seemed innocuous, yet it would've ruined his life. Relief and anger coursed through his veins. How dare these people mess with his body?

A knock at the door had him hastily stuffing the vial in his pocket. Eloise stuck her head round the door, her expression grim as she said, "You shouldn't be doing that."

His face reddened. Reasons for feeling guilty were easy to come by.

"Just joking," she said with a grin.

"Don't do that!" he exclaimed, a hand pressed against his chest. "There are enough threats at Our Lady. I don't need more."

"Sorry. Are you hungry?"

"Starving!"

On their return from the shrink's, he'd told her about his session. She'd seemed sympathetic, almost complicit, although he had no idea how she reconciled her friendliness with being one of the headmistress's minions. When they arrived back, the evening meal was over and the headmistress sent him to his room with nothing to eat or drink.

Eloise pushed open the door revealing a tray bearing a plate of Shepard's pie, an apple and a glass of milk. "You're an angel," Peter exclaimed, accepting the tray. "I just hope you don't get your wings clipped for siding with the devil."

"Knowing my luck, I'll get kicked out of heaven." She made

a face at the word 'heaven', but otherwise didn't sound unhappy at the idea.

"Where would you go?" Peter asked between two mouthfuls.

"No idea."

"You have no family?"

"Sure I do. But I couldn't imagine living with them. What would they do with a daughter who reads books about philosophy and politics when they can't even read a Weetabix packet. No. It's horrible to admit, but they embarrass me. As I do them."

The idea that you could outgrow your family left him feeling sad. He thought of his own. Not that of his adoptive parents, but his birth mother. "My mother didn't embarrass me," he said with a grimace, "she just tried to kill me." He shuddered at the memory.

Eloise gasped. "Really? Why?"

"My sister turned her against me. She was jealous. Her girlfriend, Fi, preferred dressing me as a girl to fooling around with her. You remember, I mentioned Fi when we talked in the garden."

"The one that died."

Peter nodded, sad yet again. "Above all my mother couldn't stomach me dressing as a girl. Not that I ever let her see. The idea alone was enough to drive her nuts. She'd have killed me had the police not intervened."

Eloise shook her head. "I don't see what the fuss is about. If you wanna dress as a girl, why not? Some of those who rage about boys like you, do things in private that really ought to be condemned, but no one says a word."

"Thanks. You can't imagine how comforting your words are." He resisted an urge to hug her. "People like me constantly need to be reassured and accepted for what we are. It's like a craving." He'd seen it with Fi. She encouraged him to be her 'pretty boy'. As a result he'd been beholden to her. He'd had a monumental crush on the older girl. "Most of the population would have us be otherwise. Many would readily resort to violence 'to straighten us out'."

"Like that shrink."

"The name says everything."

There was a thoughtful silence.

"You said you could heal…" she said, her expression turning coy. He wondered what was coming. "Could you teach me?" She let the words out in a rush.

It was tempting. He missed teaching. But was she capable. "Let's test the water, as it were." If she couldn't master mind-to-mind talk there was no point. "I'm going to speak into your mind and you'll speak back the same way. Okay?"

She looked alarmed, but nodded.

This is mind-to-mind communication, he said.

Her eyes went wide and she would have squealed had she not clapped a hand over her mouth. "That's awesome," she exclaimed once she'd recovered.

Try thinking your words to me rather than speaking out loud.

She tried several times without success.

It's a trick, Peter's said, *like falling asleep. You can't force yourself. It's almost as if you have to look the other way and slip past unnoticed.*

I'll never manage, she said.

Sorry? he replied, enjoying teasing her. *Could you say that again?* She obviously hadn't realised.

I said ... She broke off and burst out laughing. *I did it!*

"You did indeed. Okay. I'll teach you healing," Peter said, "but on three conditions. First it must remain an absolute secret. Second you accept that I also teach you self defence. And finally, you let me teach Sarah too."

She raised her eyebrows at the mention of Sarah, but didn't question it. Instead she asked, "Why self defence?"

"Because folks can get really furious if they find out you do healing. I want you to be able to protect yourself."

"Ah," was all she said, her forehead creasing. "All right. I agree."

"Do you want to begin now?" Peter asked. Better to get

started. Who knew what the headmistress had in store for him.

"Can't. I have prefect's duties. How about once everyone's in bed?"

When Eloise left, taking the telltale tray with her, Peter called Sarah. He wanted to reassure himself she was okay, but also to tell her about the healing lesson. *Sarah?* She didn't reply, but he knew she'd heard. *Sarah?* Stubborn silence was her only answer. Was she just obeying orders to avoid him or was she really in a huff?

Giving up, he peeked out into the corridor. It was empty. Where did the girls go in the evening? They couldn't all be shut up like nuns in their rooms. He stepped out and made his way to Sarah's room, a towel over his arm as if he were en route for the bathroom.

Reaching her room without incident, he knocked gently. "Go away," a muffled voice said from within. He couldn't be sure, but he suspected she was crying. He tried the knob. It wasn't locked. Did none of the girls' doors have locks? He'd thought it was a precaution reserved for him.

Inside, Sarah was curled up on her bed, moaning softly as she nursed her arm.

"What happened?" he asked, unsurprised Sarah had once again been on the receiving end of someone's anger. He really did need to teach her self defence. Maybe Kate could give him some tips.

He sat down next to her, placing a hand on her shoulder. She half-heartedly tried to shrug him off, but he wouldn't be deterred. Making the most of the contact he jumped to her body and was horrified to discover a series of burns down her forearm. He set about coaxing her body to reconstitute the charred skin. It was a struggle. Never before had he experience anything like it. The body resisted. Not actively, but rather with a stubborn lethargy. It was as if she'd given up. Even a warrior priest, a sworn enemy, a cancer victim, had still fought for his life when Peter healed him.

Only when her arm was healed did he speak, saying gently,

"We need to put the fight back in you."

"There's no point," she replied, wearily. "They'll only bash it out of me."

She was so dejected, he doubted he could lift her out of her mood. She needed a success to build on. Revenge was the first thing that sprang to mind. But it didn't offer a solid foundation on which to build renewed confidence. No. It had to be positive.

"Listen," he said. "I spoke to Eloise and she convinced me to teach her to heal, rather like I just did to your arm. I agreed, but only if I could teach you too."

Sarah released her arm and rolled up her sleeve only to stare in astonishment at the unmarked skin. She ran a tentative finger over the place where the burns should have been as if touch could dispel her disbelief. "You did this?" she whispered, shaking her head.

"I did. And I'm convinced you can too… if you let me teach you."

She stared wide-eyed at him, clearly unable or unwilling to believe.

"But it'll only work if you want to."

Tears welled up in her eyes and she started to sob. Had he completely misjudged the situation? Maybe depression had too strong a hold on her. He was about to hug her as a consolation when she burst out, "Yes!" And flung her arms around his neck, crushing him against her, the wet of her tears transferring to his cheeks. "Yes. With all my heart."

Several hours later, after a passionate discussion, Eloise joined them.

"Is it time?" Peter asked in surprise, he'd been so engrossed in Sarah's story.

"It is. Everyone is tucked in," Eloise said with a grimace. "If I had my way, some of them would be chained to the bed frame."

"Difficult?" Peter asked, with a grin.

She nodded. Glancing at Sarah, she said, "Let's not dwell on that. We have some healing to learn."

"It might seem self-evident, but the best way to learn healing is to actually do it. Are any of the girls ill?"

"Alexandra, one of the younger girls, is in the infirmary," Eloise said. "The nurse suspects she broke her arm when she fell."

"She didn't fall," Sarah said. "She was tripped."

Eloise shrugged. Apparently such barberry was normal. "She's surviving on painkillers. They're taking her for an x-ray tomorrow.

Eloise led them to the infirmary, keeping close to the bushes as they crossed the lawns. Peter was pleased they'd donned duffle coats. The icy wind was cutting and it looked like it might snow.

Once inside, they crept along the main corridor, past the room where the nurse snored, and on to the dimly-lit ward which housed four beds. Only the farthest was in use. It's occupant was asleep but agitated, tossing and turning, moaning even.

It's probably the pain, Peter told his would-be apprentices. *First we need to ease that. She'll sleep better and won't awake to discover us looming over her. I'll show you how to remove pain another time. For now I'll do it. You can learn how to mend the broken bone.*

He placed a hand gently on the girl's shoulder. Despite his caution, she stirred and he was afraid she might wake. Jumping straight into her body, he hurried to ease the pain and was relieved to feel her breathing steady and become shallower. He rapidly surveyed her whole body to check for damage. Apart from a bout of acne, only the arm was a problem.

We'll work in turns, Peter said. *Who goes first?*

Me, both said simultaneously.

He chuckled mentally. *Okay. Let's work together.* That was surely better. They didn't have much time. *Place your hand on her shoulder. I want you to direct your attention to her arm. It looks like this.* He let them feel and see what he did. He loved this part. Being able to share his feelings and vision with someone was a wonderful way of speeding up learning. All the more so that in healing most things were impossible to explain in words. So many crucial details fell by the wayside.

He watched the mental images of each girl as they explored the arm. *It's not broken, but bent. What we call a green-stick fracture.*

But how do we straighten it out? Eloise asked.

You don't, Peter replied. *The body will do that. All you need to do is encourage it to do it's work. Let me show you.* He showed them how to feed energy into the damaged part to hasten the healing. He let both Eloise and Sarah do some of the healing. He then had them check for nearby damage. *Imagine the body as an orchestra. When it is following its 'score', there's a sweetness and a naturalness to the harmony. The moment you sense discord you know there's damage that needs healing.*

There, Sarah exclaimed, mentally pointing to a bunch of muscles that had been overstretched by the twisted bone.

Well done, Peter said.

So what I do?

Exactly what you did before. Encourage the harmony.

While Sarah did as he said, Eloise found several other pulled muscles which she promptly repaired. Peter was pleased at the speed with which the two girls mastered the task. He could imagine sharing much of what he knew, if circumstances let him.

"What the hell are you doing?" a voice boomed behind them. It was the nurse.

Instinctively they sprang back, breaking the contact. Luckily the healing was complete.

Let me speak, Eloise said. "The girls were worried about Alexandra. They couldn't sleep. So I offered to accompany them to check the girl was okay. I'm to blame if they're out of bed."

"You know full well no girls are allowed out of their rooms after curfew. I'm giving you two," she pointed to Peter and Sarah, "three hours of detention tomorrow, here in the infirmary. There's plenty of cleaning to do. As for you," she turned to Eloise, her lips curved in disgust, "I'll talk to the headmistress about appropriate disciplinary measures. Now get back to bed."

23.

Peter lay on his bed staring at the ceiling, unable to sleep. The hush of the grounds outside was a solid presence. Snow was falling in giant flakes, cloaking the world, as if readying it for a fairy tale. He pulled the covers tight around himself and curled up in a ball. The texture of his nightdress, soft and promising against his bare skin, gave him a deep feeling of satisfaction, but also reminded him where he was which was less pleasant.

He'd promised to teach the girls self-defence. Clearly that made sense. But how did you help someone protect herself against the violence of the headmistress? He had no idea what form Eloise's punishment would take, but it surely couldn't be warded off by traditional self-defence.

Kate? he called out.

Peter? You still up?

Can't sleep. He described his visit to the shrink.

Good you could force the testosterone out, Kate said. *But we still have to find a substitute for those puberty blockers.*

They discussed the mechanisms of puberty with Peter suggesting they block testosterone.

I'm not sure that's a good idea, Kate said. *We can't know what else the hormone does. What if it's essential to your health? No. Ideally we need to rewrite the blueprint to give you a different body. One that remains in between, as it were. That's a completely different game. We know nothing about changing the blueprint...*

The idea appealed to Peter but Kate was right, they had no

idea how to achieve it, so he moved on. *A couple of girls asked me to teach them healing.*

That's a coincidence. The girls on the council want me to teach them magic.

You agreed? He was surprised. He knew her reticence. She hadn't wanted to teach him either.

Yes. We need better defence. She mentioned the poisoning and the car accident. *I thought I might combine magic with self defence.*

If I can, I'd like to sit in on that. I might use some of it here. He described how Sarah had been burnt by fellow pupils and another girl had her arm broken by classmates.

Sounds more like the Middle Ages than a posh girls' school.

There's nothing posh about this school, bar the accents. Peter said bitterly. Shrugging, he returned to his own preoccupations, *such self-defence is useless against attacks that are not physical.* He mentioned the threat hanging over Eloise.

Magic's not the answer, Kate said. *I believe we need to change hearts and minds. We could never have broken free of the convent without the support of all those who read our story and attended our concerts. That's why we're addressing the threat of the church through 'guerrilla public relations'.* She explained the concept. *Maybe you should see if something similar is possible in that school?*

When they finished, it was well into the night and Peter was exhausted. Alone again he expected to find sleep elusive. So many ideas whirled round his head. Despite the agitation or maybe to escape it, he drifted off immediately.

A rough hand shook him awake. "Get up lazy lump!" He didn't recognise the voice. Cracking open his eyes he saw a prefect looming over him. "Where's Eloise?" he asked, still half asleep.

"No business of yours," the prefect snapped. "Get up and get dressed. You'll be late for Mass."

He was tempted to object he was Anglican, not Catholic, but the bad humour rolling off the prefect made him reconsider.

"What time is it?"

"Six. You should've been up half an hour ago. That Eloise was hopeless at her job…"

He didn't like the sound of 'was'. Had Eloise been kicked out? Not that it would've bothered her. She'd have welcomed it. But it bothered him. Just when he'd begun gaining allies.

He struggled out of bed, pulled the nightdress over his head and hung it over the back of the chair. Thank heavens he'd kept his pants on. At least he wouldn't have the added humiliation of standing naked before the sullen girl. The moment he'd donned his uniform, she marched him out with him struggling into his duffle coat.

The corridor was full of bleary-eyed girls yawning, leaning against walls and doorways. No one spoke. Peter couldn't tell if the silence was due to the early hour or the menace of the prefect.

Eloise? he called out. *Are you alright?*

The sob he got in reply had him alarmed.

Speak to me, he urged. *What did she do?*

The cane… Her words were riddled with pain, making him wince as if it were his own.

We're on our way to Mass. The moment I get there I'll heal you. Can you hold out? What a stupid question. As if she had a choice. *Where are you?*

Locked in the basement.

I'll get back to you in a short while.

Kate's conviction that only social pressure would work against such violence was not exact. In the longer term, she was probably right. But faced with unfettered violence something had to be done and it couldn't wait. What they needed was a pause, a respite, during which they could begin their guerrilla campaign without being slaughtered. That meant he'd have to take the headmistress and her prefects off the board. At least temporarily. Put like that, the answer was obvious. He couldn't help grinning.

Sarah? he sent.

Yes, the answer came back immediately as if she'd been awaiting his call. *Where's Eloise.* She sounded anxious.

Peter shared the news. *I need your help. I'm going to heal Eloise. Then I have some other things to do. Can you manage to sit next to me?*

I'll try. But these prefects are beastly. It wouldn't surprise me if they had orders to keep us apart.

If that was the case, healing Eloise would have to wait. He strained to pick out the prefects amongst the girls. There seemed to be three, but he wasn't sure.

How many prefects are there? he asked. *Apart from Eloise.*

Four, Sarah replied.

Where's the fourth? I see only three.

Waiting in the chapel probably. What are you planning?

Of course Sarah would guess he was up to something. *Temporarily ridding us of the prefects.*

Reverse healing, you mean?

Clever girl, Peter said gifting her a mental smile. *Not that I should teach you such bad things.*

She giggled. The sound or rather the feeling was somehow flirtatious and sent a tingle down his spine, but for once it didn't bother him. *I'll take these three first.* He bent down to re-lace his shoes. As expected, one of the prefects grabbed him by the arm and jerked him upright. In that moment, he ploughed a powerful jolt of disharmony into the prefect's stomach causing her face to go green. Lashing out at the girl filled him with a malicious elation that quickly faded, giving way to breathless emptiness. The prefect lurched away and ran down the corridor towards the toilets, one of her colleagues hurrying after.

Working at a distance was more difficult, especially when crouched in a corridor surrounded by potentially hostile girls. But Peter managed to send a spark of similar disarray into the second prefect's stomach.

Two down. One to go, Sarah commented. She was trying to hide a grin several yards down the corridor.

The third prefect was at the head of the procession, trying to bully the girls into hurrying forward. Glancing over her shoulder in search of her colleagues, a worried expression greeted Peter as he looked her in the eyes. "You!" she blurted out. She didn't get any further. Peter's improvised strike had her keeling over in a groaning mass.

Peter pushed through the crowd of anxious girls and kneeled at the prefect's side. "Someone get the nurse," he said, taking control of the situation. "What's the matter?" he asked the prefect, adopting a worried tone as he placed his hand on her shoulder. To anyone else the gesture would be seen as a sign of concern, but in reality it allowed him to heighten the nausea and make her delirious. Doing so filled him with remorse. He hadn't learnt healing to do this. He eased up.

She stared up at him, terror in her eyes. "The devil's in you. We're condemned. Run. The fires are coming. The bells are tolling. It's too late…" she bent forward and threw up across the immaculate floor, causing the girls to scatter. Choking and spluttering, she continued to spout her fears.

That was when the nurse arrived. Pushing Peter aside, she knelt in his place and felt the girl's pulse.

"The other prefects are ill too," one of the older girls said, pointing in the direction of the toilets.

"What did you lot eat last night?" the nurse asked the prefect.

The girl cupped her hands over her mouth to prevent herself from vomiting and muttered, "Nothing special." She scratched her head, then added, "We had some chocolates with the headmistress."

The look on the gathered girls' faces said it all. As one they thought of poison. Perfect. Exactly what Peter needed. Thanks to the chocolates, no one would be surprised when the headmistress also fell ill.

Helped to her feet, the girl teetered on unsteady legs. Meanwhile, the nurse instructed the girls to make their way to the chapel. The moment she left, a buzz of conversation shot through the group. Poison, chocolates and more poison. Nobody was in any hurry to get to Mass, except Peter, who was impatient to be done with his dark deeds. They sickened him. So much so, he began to have doubts. Could what he'd done rebound like curses were said to do? It wouldn't surprise him. The harmony inherent in healing certainly rubbed off on the healer. Could the opposite be true?

He snapped back from his musing only to realise the girls had moved on. They'd stepped out into the snow covered landscape. Hurrying after, he spotted Sarah staring at him with a worried look.

You alright? she asked.

Shaken. I still have to deal with the headmistress. Otherwise removing the prefects will've been pointless. After that, I'll never do this again. Hurting people takes more of a toll than I imagined. He thought of the damage wreaked on the headmistress every time she lashed out. It made him shudder. Her soul, if ever she had one, must be shrivelled up. He vowed to tell Kate what he'd discovered. If she wanted to use magic in self-defence, she needed to know it might have nasty repercussions.

The usually glacial air of the chapel appeared warm after the bitter wind outside. Peter took a seat next to Sarah and looked around for the headmistress. She was nowhere to be seen. Panic surged in his veins. What would he do if she didn't show?

I'm going to heal Eloise, he told Sarah, and closed his eyes. *Let me know if the headmistress turns up.*

Casting his mind out, he went in search of Eloise. *Eloise?* he called.

I thought you'd forgotten me.

Never. We just had a problem on the way to the chapel. He jumped to Eloise's body and set about healing the weals on the girl's palms. *She must have been beyond herself with anger,* Peter said as he worked. *These cuts are deep.*

Can you heal them?

Sure. Watch. He relayed his perception to Eloise who seemed confused at seeing herself being healed. *Sorry,* Peter said. *I thought you'd find it interesting.*

I do. But at the same time I've my own perception and I'm unsure where to look.

He was finishing up when Sarah burst into his mind. *She's here.*

Gotta go, he told Eloise. *We'll come and fetch you as soon as we can.*

Opening his eyes, he saw Heartless staring at him. There was pure venom in that look. She must have heard about the prefects and suspected him.

I'll do the same to her as I did to the prefects, he said to Sarah. If they were suffering from the chocolates, that would make sense.

Make her wet herself first, Sarah said, her tone vengeful.

I can't. I mean, I won't. Doing bad things to people is also bad for the person who does them. We don't need to humiliate her. Just get her out of the way. He muddied the harmony in the woman's stomach. The effect was immediate. Her face turned a sickly green and she shot him a look of hatred before getting to her feet and walking in deliberate steps towards the door.

The priest, who entered at that moment, stopped short, greeted as he was by a barrage of excited chatter. The remaining prefect tried to impose silence, but was promptly struck by the same strange illness and had to run for the door. A ripple of triumph shot through the congregation. Peter was sure the girls would have cheered, had the priest not been there. The man turned on his heals, his robes billowing behind him as he hurried away.

Did you…? Sarah began, a twisted grin on her lips.

Peter shook his head. *I did nothing of the kind.*

The man was replaced in the doorway by the administrator who ordered the girls to return to their bedrooms and stay there until further notice. The nurse would examine each one, she informed them, as soon as she'd tended to the prefects.

As the girls filed out, Peter and Sarah hung back. The last to leave, they didn't follow the others, but were about to go in search of Eloise when a voice close by roared, "Where are you two going?" Peter felt a hand grip his shoulder and spin him round till he was face to face with the administrator. She peered down her nose at him, her lips curled in disgust. "You! Of course. It had to be you."

There was no time for justifications. Eloise needed urgent help. Peter reluctantly sent the administrator scuttling away in search of a toilet, her fists clenched to her belly, her complexion a sickly green colour. "Oh no!" he said to her disappearing back. "You too ate those chocolates." She promptly threw up, her vomit dribbling down the otherwise immaculate wall. Peter grasped hold of Sarah's arm trying to steady himself as his head spun. He hoped the administrator would be the last of his victims. Undermining people's health was draining.

The dingy corridors beneath ground were unfamiliar, but Sarah knew them well. She took the lead. They reached Eloise's makeshift prison, only to find a figure shroud in shadow leaning against the door, a hand clutching its stomach. As the person pushed off the door and stood unsteadily to confront them, Peter was overcome with dread. It was the headmistress. However had she managed to hold out so long? She should be glued to the toilet by now.

"I guessed as much," the woman said, her voice strained. She must be struggling to keep a grip on her bucking innards. Peter was loathed to inflict more, knowing she wouldn't be able to hold out much longer.

"It was good of you to come and let the prefect out," Peter said. "We were worried and wanted to make sure she didn't suffer the same sort as the others. Imagine being locked in a room alone with a bad bout of the runs…" Peter couldn't resist going into details, knowing full well it would make things worse.

The woman was fuming, but couldn't vent her fury for fear that would free the floodgates.

"If you give us the keys," Peter continued, "you won't have to worry about her. You can take care of yourself. You don't look so good." He gave her what he hoped was his most winning smile and held out his hand.

If stares could kill, her look would have roasted him. "Never," she muttered.

"We can wait if you have something to do in the mean time," he said cheerfully, glancing at Sarah as if seeking her approval. "We're in no hurry."

With a growl, she flung a bunch of keys against the wall and sprinted for the stairs. Sarah went in search of them, rummaging in the gloom, only to call out, "Found..." Her words was drowned out by a strangled scream from the headmistress above.

"You realise we're in for serious trouble when she recovers from whatever has got her in its grips," Eloise said.

24.

Kate knocked softly and peered inside. The girls had prepared a cosy nest for Jo and Claudia with brightly coloured eiderdowns and matching curtains. Plump cushions were scattered across the floor. There were even several teddybears and a huge porcelain doll which had belong to Beth. A large vase of flowers stood on the windowsill, gay in the early morning light.

Jo and Claudia were sound asleep, with the young girl's arm slung lightly across the older woman's shoulder. Suzanne, who was seated on a chair by the bed, had an arm outstretched, her palm hovering over Claudia. She turned her head when Kate entered, saying, *They're fine.*

A tap on her shoulder, had Kate glancing back to find Eileen behind her. "The police are here," Eileen whispered. "They want to question Jo. Apparently they found the wreck of the car."

Talk to you later, Kate said to Suzanne and turned to follow Eileen down the stairs and outside on their way to the main house. "What did they say about the accident?" she asked Eileen, concerned the police would cause trouble.

"Nothing much. They found the car and were worried about the occupants."

Two policemen were huddled over the kitchen table sipping coffee from Lydia's best coffee cups. The moment they saw Kate they sprang to their feet and stood stiffly, staring at her, as if being seated diminished their authority.

"Morning Miss," the shorter said. "We've been led to believe the driver of a car involved in an accident is hiding in this house.”

“Nobody is hiding here,” Kate replied, looking the man straight in the eye. “What makes you think that?”

“Because the lady here,” he pointed to Lydia, “said so.”

“That a woman recuperating from a serious car accident is sleeping here is one thing. That anybody is hiding, is a completely different matter. I repeat, nobody is hiding.”

The first policeman sighed as if she were a silly kid wasting his precious time. “We need to talk to her,” he said pronouncing each word with exaggerated care.

“I’m sure you do,” Kate replied, imitating his tone. “And you will. But not today. She’s resting. We can’t let you disturb her.”

“Take us to the doctor then,” the second policeman said. He was overweight and clearly had liver problems, probably the result of drink. And something else was amiss as he kept pressing his abdomen.

“There is no doctor here. I am responsible for the good health of the Lost Girls. I am also looking after the woman who had the accident. What would you like to know?”

The fat policeman scoffed. “I don’t know what game you’re playing little girl,” he said and, stepping forward, grabbed her arm in a move that was none too friendly. She was tempted to make the most of the brief contact to size up his health, but resisted. However obnoxious the man was, prying on his health wouldn’t be right. With a sharp twist of her wrist she sent him flying. He landed with a dull thud on his backside where he sat unmoving, a look of incomprehension on his face. She held out her hand to help him up, but he was having nothing of it. He rolled over and struggled up, clasping his abdomen as he did.

“Are you alright?” his colleague asked.

Having recovered from the shock, the overweight man spluttered with indignation. She held up a hand to silence him.

“You’re probably not interested in my advice, but I’d see someone about that pain in your stomach.” She could see from his worried look that he knew what she meant. “Perforated ulcers can be tricky and all those aspirins I imagine you've been taking aren't helping."

"I've got some very good herbal tea against ulcers," Lydia chimed in.

He literally turned his back on Lydia, just like he'd no doubt refuse Kate's advice. "How do you know that?" he said, his tone accusatory.

"I pay attention," she replied.

"If you think I'm going to listen to the advice of an over-confident little girl, you're sorely mistaken," he blustered, his colleague nodding in agreement.

"Your choice," she said. It was silly really. It would take her less than a minute to spare him a lot of suffering if not death.

"So you won't let us see the victim of the accident?" the first policeman asked.

"Not today. She needs all the rest she can get. Shock takes some getting over," Kate said.

"Tell me, how did you find out about the accident?" Klaus asked, coming forward from the back of the kitchen where he'd been kneading dough.

"An anonymous caller reported seeing a car in a ditch."

"Did you examine the marks on the road and the verge?" Klaus asked, wiping his hands on his apron.

"Of course," the first policeman replied.

"So what happened according to you?"

"The driver lost control and careened off the road. Probably driving too fast. Or drunk."

"And what about the second car?" Klaus pressed.

"What second car?" The policeman's disbelief was evident.

"The one that rammed the first one and forced it into the ditch."

"You're making that up," the policeman accused.

"Not at all. I was at the scene of the accident shortly after it happened. We went to fetch the poor woman. It was clear from the marks on the road that another vehicle rammed the car."

"That's not possible. Our caller told us the car skidded off the road on its own.”

“Did it ever occur to you that your anonymous informant might’ve been the driver of the second car?”

“What nonsense!” the taller policeman scoffed.

“You might like to check the cars in the garage at the Bishop’s palace.” Everyone turned to see Heinz in the doorway, his camera bag slung over his shoulder. “One of them has the front bonnet driven in as if it had collided with another vehicle. And the paint transferred to the bodywork is the same colour as the car in the ditch. I’m sure it’ll be plain to see in the photos I just took.”

“Let me see those,” the first policeman insisted, holding out his hand.

“All in good time,” Heinz said with a chuckle. “I haven’t developed them yet.”

The two policemen left shortly after, making no effort to hide their ill humour. They insisted they’d be back and any further refusal would cause trouble.

Everyone sat around relieved to be free of the grumpy men. “Is being in a bad mood a prerequisite for being a policeman?” Kate asked. Judging from their laughter, they took her question as a joke, but she was genuinely interested. There were no policemen in her world. It wouldn’t have been necessary. Mages made sure people kept in line.

“I don’t think so,” Heinz said with a grin. “But I reckon it may be a product of their job. Not a lot of people like the police and many set out to obstruct their work, for all manner of reasons. I’m sure they were convinced we were doing our best to annoy them.”

Suzanne called Kate at that moment. *Jo is awake. She wants to talk to you.* Her voice conveyed concern although she made no mention of it.

Aware that mind-to-mind communication made people uncomfortable, if it didn’t terrify them, Kate said, “I have to go check on our two casualties.” Getting to her feet she added, “We should discuss what to do with all this evidence. I’ll ask Eileen to organise a meeting. In the mean time, it might be wise to stash the proof in a safe place." At her words, she felt a ripple of fear shoot through the room.

She found Jo sitting up in her bed spooning muesli into her mouth. The young woman greeted Kate with a pale smile. Next to her, Claudia slept on, one arm slung negligently over her face.

"You want some?" Suzanne asked, pointing to the muesli.

She hadn't had time for breakfast, so she accepted. "How you feeling?" she asked Jo as Suzanne went to fetch food. "You had a very lucky escape."

Jo's look was hard to read. Relief. Doubt. Confusion. Suspicion even. "In those final minutes before I lost consciousness I remember vividly what happened. My fear for the baby as the steering wheel shoved into my belly. The searing pain as my ribs cracked. The massive blow on my head before I blacked out. But now, less than twelve hours later, I don't even have a bruise, let alone a broken rib, and the baby is well and kicking." Tears sprang to her eyes. "Both you and I know something miraculous happened and I suspect you know what. I sincerely hope you're willing to tell me."

Kate met the woman's eyes, sensing both the perplexity and concern. "I healed you," she admitted. "You, your baby and Claudia."

Jo's eyes widened. "You." The single word was spoken not in disbelief but in acceptance. The young woman sucked in a shuddery breath and whispered, "Thank you."

Kate nodded in acknowledgement. "For various reasons we keep quiet about such things. The medical profession, not to mention society in general, would be far from happy that a girl of my age without the traditional training should succeed in healing people when doctors make such a messy job of it. Your Jesus healed and look what happened to him. Not that I compare myself to him. But it is pertinent when you consider that the church, built as it is on Christ's teachings, is bent on blocking any efforts we make to heal."

Jo's hand flew to her belly, a smile forming on her lips.

"I believe the baby agrees." There was a brief pause as her attention turned inwards, then she said, "Are you teaching others to heal?"

"Me for one," Suzanne said, sporting an oversized bowl of muesli with two spoons. She handed Kate a spoon and, taking the other, placed the bowl between them.

"Once I've given birth, would you teach me?" Jo asked. A strong desire drove her request but there was also fear and doubt, making it feel both heartfelt and timid.

"I'd love to," Kate replied, pleased at the idea of working more closely with the young woman. "But you have to realise that knowing how to heal might be extremely frustrating."

"Why so?"

"Because, in many cases you won't be able to use your knowledge given society's attitude to healing. Even in cases where action would be urgent. One of the policemen who called earlier was suffering from an ulcer. I could have healed him in no time, sparing him much pain and possible death, but I daren't do so. Such is the prejudice against those who heal differently."

"Policemen?" She sounded anxious.

"Yes. They wanted to question you. I sent them away saying you needed rest. And you do. Shock isn't just physical. There's the mind too. Physical healing is relatively straightforward, but the mind is more difficult. For now, sleep is one of the best remedies."

"I am tired," Jo admitted.

"I do have one final question," Kate said, unsure how to express it. "You never mentioned the father. When you arrived unconscious, we didn't know who to contact. What if someone was waiting for you …"

Jo shook her head, her expression embarrassed. "I'm not sure who the father is."

"So you're going solo."

"I have no choice. I want to have my child."

"I'd have to ask the others, but I could imagine the Lost Girls adopting you, as it were."

"Oh yes!" Suzanne mumbled, stirring at that moment.

"We could be your family," Kate continued, "and you could have your child here. There'll be no shortage of girls to help with your baby."

A smile spread across Jo's face full of warmth and gratitude and relief. "I'd love that," she said. "I was dreading affronting the birth on my own."

"You'll never be alone with us."

<h1 style="text-align:center">25.</h1>

Being generous was all very well, Kate reprimanded herself as Klaus drove her into town. But the Lost Girls revenue had been slashed. They might not even be able to cater for themselves, let alone an additional mother and child. Yet Jo would never have been in such difficulty had it not been for them and, anyway, she liked the young woman and was looking forward to teaching her.

When Beth came to greet her in her wheelchair Kate wondered what had happened to the maid. Had she been sacked? Despite their quasi mother-daughter relationship, it wasn't the sort of question Kate could ask.

"You must be wondering where Tricia is," Beth said, a wry smile on her lips.

"I didn't dare ask," Kate said, taken aback by the woman's perspicacity.

"She insisted she was too embarrassed." Beth shrugged. "I offered to pay for therapy, but she refused." Beth led them into the study and positioned her chair next to the table saying, "Take a seat."

"We had a drama last night," Kate said. She described the accident which, judging from the pained look on Beth's face, recalled unwelcome memories. Kate mentioned the visit from the police, finishing with their suspicions about the Bishop.

Beth ran her fingers through her hair, remaining thoughtful for a while. "We're going to have to do something. It's not going to be easy. The church is woven deep into the fabric of society, playing a central role in local life."

Kate wonder if there wasn't some way to learn from their approach to healing. "If local society were a person, I'd appeal to its underlying nature and apply positive energy to coax it to return to harmony. I'm not sure how that metaphor would play out in practice."

"Well, apart from believing that man comes into the world fundamentally flawed," Beth said, pouring them each a glass of apple juice, "there are still positive tenets at the heart of the church and wider society. If you girls use your music and healing as a constructive force you might achieve the harmony you seek."

If they don't kill us first, Kate thought grimly. "That won't necessarily solve the money problem," she said. "Our survival depends on raking in the funds we need."

"I rather think they are connected. Finding sponsors and raising funds will be much easier if the Lost Girls are seen as a healing force."

Beth reached under the table and pulled out a map. Handing it to Kate, she said, "Could you unfold this and lay it out on the table?"

It was a detailed map of the area around the Lost Girls House and the former farm where Lydia and Klaus lived. Kate studied it. Dotted close to the Lost Girls House were a number of out-buildings, the largest of which they'd imagined using for the other orphaned girls, should they manage to finance the transformations and feed the girls. Behind these buildings was an open area they used to cultivate herbs and medicinal plants.

Beth traced the contours of the plot. "It belonged to my parents, although they rarely went there. It was a sanctuary where I took refuge from the watchful eye of my parents, especially after I met Viktor. The accident happened close by, so my parents were eager to get rid of the place, as if bad memories could be evacuated so easily. As you know, they sold the land and buildings to Klaus's parents for a nominal sum."

Most of the adjacent area was an extensive plateau bordered

by pine forests and a small lake. The only buildings nearby formed a sizeable hamlet that straddled a narrow lane. "In fact," Beth continued, sketching out a much larger area, "this whole region, including the lake, the fields and the forests belong to me. The hamlet, which is currently uninhabited, is also part of the property."

Kate whistled softly between her teeth. She knew Beth was rich but her approachableness and simplicity misled people into thinking she was less than she really was. Kate had had no idea of the extent of her wealth.

For once Beth seemed embarrassed. Surely it couldn't be because of her riches. She'd been one of the richest women in town since the death of her parents over a decade earlier. Beth toyed with the tassels at the end of the silk shawl slung over her shoulders. It was as if she wanted to say something but didn't know how. Her hesitation had Kate alarmed. Bashfulness was really not Beth's style. Something serious or awkward must be coming.

"I'd like to adopt you," Beth finally said, the words tumbling out, "if you agree."

Kate stared at her in disbelief. Adoption? The idea left her speechless. She could never have dreamed of such a thing. Her mother had died in childbirth leaving her the only child. Her father was dead too, killed by invaders, the same religious bigots that had tried to kill her. As for the world she'd grown up in, it was gone for ever.

Peter's adoptive parents, Christina and John, had taken her in when she'd first been severed from her past. They'd willingly have adopted her but she couldn't possibly share Peter's parents. He'd become her brother and their relationship was hardly appropriate for siblings. In many ways Beth was the mother she'd never had. All the more so that the author who'd given Kate form had modelled her on a younger Beth.

Adopting Kate clearly meant a lot to Beth who couldn't have children of her own. "I'd love to be your daughter," Kate replied and, kneeling in front of her, took the woman's hands in hers.

Beth tossed aside all caution and pulled Kate into a passionate embrace. The two hugged in silence for a long moment.

Freeing herself from the embrace, Beth kissed Kate on the forehead. "I'm so glad you accept. I've been mulling over the idea for a while but, to be honest, I was afraid to ask. Viktor and I have decided to get married. Now I have your agreement, we'll officialise the adoption at the same time."

"I must admit, I'm delighted," Kate said, brushing tears from her cheeks. "To have a mother, at last. You can't imagine how much that means to me. My father was a wonderful man, who had my good at heart. A number of women in our household cared for me as if I were their child, but none of them could replace the mother I never had."

"I too am very moved," Beth replied, producing a handkerchief from up her sleeve and blowing her nose. "Believing the love of my life had perished in that accident and me unable to have children, the idea of having a daughter was one of those impossible dreams." She paused, looking off into the distance. "When I look into your eyes, I see so much potential. I want you to have every chance of making the most of that. That's why I plan to transfer ownership of all this land," she gestured to the map, "to you. I want you to have it now when you and your friends need a helping hand."

"Thank you. I really appreciate it, although, for the moment, I am a bit at a loss what to do with it."

"See it as potential you can capitalise on. I don't advise selling it, especially as it surrounds and protects your home, but there are other ways you can use it to make the money you need. Growing herbs, for example. Or setting up a centre for alternative medicine. You're resourceful. I'm sure you and your friends will have ideas. Viktor knows the land, he could show you round."

Kate wondered if she'd ever be able to call Beth 'Mum'. She let out a long shuddery breath. The news of adoption had chased all other thoughts from her mind, sending her soaring into unknown territory. Remembering why she'd come brought her down to earth. "Talking about potential, or lack of it, we were going to discuss sponsors."

Beth grinned. "As focussed as ever! Yes. I suspect being my daughter will help."

Kate was worried, that, on the contrary, being Beth's daughter would make life much more difficult for her new-found mother. The insinuations about the Lost Girls might well rub off on all those associated with them, including Beth and Viktor. "We need to make sure the positive message we deliver is strong enough to ward off the filth the church and others are trying to smear us with."

"You talk about sending out a message. What have you in mind?"

"One idea is to individually highlight the Lost Girls, describing their past in the orphanage and explaining what they are doing and what they plan to do in the future." She explained they had wanted to counter the slurs of the church, but she realised their original idea might have been more vindictive than positive. She discussed the plan with Beth suggesting they emphasise the choir and the work of healing.

"What about those other orphans who wanted to join you?" Beth asked.

"We'd willingly welcome them," Kate said, "but we don't have the means to support ourselves let alone a whole new influx of girls."

"If you had the means," Beth asked, "where would you house them?"

Kate turned to the map. "Next to the Lost Girls House there is a large barn that we could convert into living quarters. We'd have to enlarge our canteen." She pointed to a piece of ground between the two buildings. "We could build a refectory here and convert the existing canteen into kitchens and larders…"

"And what would the new girls do?"

"It'd depend on their aptitude's. A few could join the choir. Others could help in preparing herbal remedies. There might even be some who could learn healing. All the courses and classes we organise, like writing or self defence or healing, could be extended to include them..."

"And how would you protect everybody?"

"Protect?" After the recent attacks, the question shouldn't have surprised her, but it did.

"With so many young girls isolated in the countryside and few adults to accompany them, you could well attract unhealthy attention."

It was exactly what the church hinted at, although they blamed the girls rather than the would-be molesters. "We could hardly build a fence around the whole property..." Kate said, staring at the map. The grounds with the new property were enormous.

"You might have to. If only to be seen to protect yourself, or at least your reputation. Not that a fence would discourage determined ill-doers."

In her old world, the mages would have used wards. Her father had taught her the spells. They were part of any mage's basic training. She wasn't sure the magic would work in this world and some of the effects might be far too spectacular. No. What they needed was gentle, but firm dissuasion. She smiled. She could do that. "If we can put up a fence, I might have a way of discouraging visitors. It's a bit..." she hesitated about the words "...unconventional. But it would deter unwelcome visitors."

Beth looked intrigued but didn't ply her with questions. "Good. Now let's get that money."

Kate looked at her, startled. "Now?"

"I am president of a group of rich and influential women. We meet once a month to discuss good works we want to invest in. It just so happens the meeting is today." She grinned at Kate. "Let's go and present my future daughter's project to them."

Kate! an anguished voice rang out in Kate's head. It was Suzanne.

Kate raised a hand to indicate to Beth she needed a moment, then turned away, replying, *What's up?*

Those two policemen came back and managed to get to Jo. They bullied her so much, the contractions have begun again and I don't know what to do.

The young woman still had over two months till term. It was too early. *You should enter Jo's mind and calm her and above all, you should calm the baby. Try mentally singing it a lullaby. I'll join you in a moment, but I need to settle something here first.* She cut the communication and turned to Beth. "You may know Peter and I developed a way of communicating mind-to-mind at a distance."

Beth nodded. "Viktor mentioned it, although I found it hard to believe."

"That was Suzanne." Beth looked startled, but didn't voice her doubts or fears. Kate explained about the police. "I need to take a moment to help Suzanne calm mother and baby… otherwise Jo will lose her child. Then I can come to your meeting. If you can't wait, tell me where it is and I'll join you."

"How long will it take?"

"Not more than fifteen minutes if all goes well." She didn't like to think what she'd do if the woman went into labour.

"Okay. I'll wait. Is there any way I can listen in?"

"Hold my hand," Kate instructed. "It'll be easier if there's physical contact." Beth did as she was told. *This is how we communicate mind-to-mind,* she said. Beth gasped in surprise. *Now think your words to me.* She could sense Beth's apprehension. *If the daughter can do it, I'm sure the mother can too,* Kate sent with a grin.

You can't imagine how good it is to hear you say that, Beth replied.

Normally Kate would have taken more time, but this was an emergency. *I'm going to jump to Suzanne's mind. I'll take you along. It might seem strange, but there's nothing to be alarmed about. Just relax and watch and listen. If you have questions, don't hesitate to ask. You'll know if I need quiet to concentrate.*

Kate made the most of her contact with Beth to calm the woman's nerves then she jumped, pulling her new mother along with her. She could feel Beth's trepidation. She knew she should never take a complete novice on such a mission but she couldn't see how she could do otherwise.

Suzanne, she said, landing in the girl's mind, *I've brought Beth with me.* She could feel Beth's fear. The woman was afraid she'd get lost or might be abandoned. Having to deal with Beth's emotions made the work more demanding. To avoid further complications Kate made sure she masked her own thoughts and feelings. Realising that you could hear each other's thoughts could be alarming.

Let's jump to Jo, Kate said. No sooner had she done so than Jo's fear and panic swirled around them. Speaking to Beth, Kate said, *The panic you feel is coming from Jo. I'm going to calm her, then the baby.* As the two were inextricably linked, each feeding the other's fear, Kate decided to concentrate on the baby. *Did you try singing to it?* Kate asked Suzanne.

Haven't had time.

Directing her attention to the baby, Kate began humming a lullaby from the choir's repertoire. Suzanne joined in. Even Beth hummed along. At first the baby remained agitated and struggled to get out, but little by little its distress ebbed and calm returned. Once Kate was convinced the crisis was over, she bid Suzanne farewell and ferried Beth and herself back to their respective bodies.

Opening her eyes, she saw Beth staring at her in wonder. She looked like she wanted to say something, but instead she flung her arms around Kate and hugged her tight, a sob bursting from her lips. When she had recovered, she sat back in her wheelchair holding on to Kate's hands and said, "Let's get you girls the money you need and deserve."

26.

The women seated around the dining table were younger than Kate had expected, although, not surprisingly they were all elegantly dressed. She was glad Beth had insisted she borrow a dress from her wardrobe. Luckily Beth didn't like to throw dresses away and in her stock were a number from more youthful days that suited Kate. In trying them on, Kate couldn't help thinking of Peter, a pang of anxiety for him bursting her happy bubble. He would have delighted in wearing such beautiful clothes.

As the women stood to greet Beth, all eyes were riveted on Kate, their expressions astonished. Mother and daughter must have made a striking pair as they looked so much alike, a fact accentuated by their choice of dresses. Kate was intrigued to see how they would react when they learnt she was to be Beth's daughter.

"Let me present Kate," Beth said. "You will all have seen her leading the Lost Girls' choir."

"She looks so much like you," one of the youngest blurted out. "Anyone could be forgiven for mistaking her for your daughter."

Beth grinned. "Not only would you be forgiven, Isla, you'd be right. I intend to adopt her."

A burst of excited conversation rippled round the room, several woman offering their congratulations. One elderly woman stepped forward and shook hands stiffly with Kate. If she hadn't known Beth was head of the group, Kate would have taken this woman, who looked down her nose disapprovingly at Kate, as its leader. "Welcome," the woman said.

"You're right, Mrs Styles," Isla chimed in. "She's very welcome to our club."

The shift from being a wretched, abandoned orphan, beaten and decried, to becoming an exquisitely dressed member of an exclusive club was enough to give anybody vertigo. Just like she'd transported Beth to her world by travelling mind-to-mind to Jo and her baby, so Beth had just plummeted her into her own world of treasures by inviting her to this gathering. In their respective ways, both worlds were beyond belief.

An extra chair was pulled up for Kate next to Beth and a waiter called to set an additional place at the table. A flurry of questions came her way, but, after Isla's earlier outburst, no one dared raise the one question everyone was itching to ask, why Kate looked so much like Beth.

The starters had come and gone and the fish course was on the table before the interrogation abated and Kate could turn her attention to the food. She cautiously took a bite of the salmon, not wanting to be caught with her mouth full if the onslaught were to pursue. When the inevitable next question did come, Beth interrupted saying, "Maybe we should let Kate eat. I'm sure you'll have plenty of opportunity to talk to her later."

Once the meal was over and the coffee and chocolates had been served, the discussion of projects began. One of the women presented a project and the others plied her with questions. If the idea met with their approval, women would bid to finance part or all of the project.

Kate wondered when or if Beth would put her project forward. Each project was advocated by one of the women who took the floor and described what was to be done, but none of the women were directly involved in what they put forward. If Beth were to propose the project for the Lost Girls, her future mother's involvement would set it aside as different. She feared the fact might disqualify it.

When Beth handed Kate the map asking her to spread it

on the table, Kate's anticipation had reached a fever pitch. She was tempted to dissuade the woman from presenting the project. Instead she cleared a space on the table and, unfolding the map, lay it out for all to see.

"I too have a project to propose," Beth began, giving a sideways glance at Kate. "Or rather I wish to commend a project by the Lost Girls. As Kate is the initiator of the project, if you agree, I'll let her explain."

Kate was expecting objections, but, even if Mrs Styles clearly disapproved, judging from the sour look on her face, the rest of the women nodded vigorously and turned their attention to her.

"The twenty-five girls living in the Lost Girls House, here," Kate pointed to the building on the map, "all came from an orphanage where our lives were frankly barely worth living. The generosity of Klaus and Lydia, who bought the land from Beth's parents, made it possible for us to form the choir you have all heard and to begin small-scale production of medicinal herbs. Those two activities would have been sustainable, had it not been for the destruction of our stock by unknown assailants."

Kate paused at the buzz of conversation that erupted. She parried their many questions, insisting they were unsure why the attacks had occurred, being deliberately vague in case the truth came out later. "We'd like to increase security around the site," Kate continued, "but that is only a small part of the project. You may have heard in the news that another group of orphan girls wanted to join us. We'd like to convert this property here," she tapped the building with her finger, "to be able to receive them. Our idea would be to integrate them into our efforts with medicinal herbs and to extend that work by opening a health centre here." She indicated the little hamlet.

"I will bequeath this land to Kate," Beth said tracing her finger around the whole area, "including the little village which is currently uninhabited. What the girls need now are the funds to convert the current building to house the new girls and to refurbish the houses in the village to form the health centre.

They'd also need money to ensure heightened security and to tide them over till the health centre is up and running."

"Have you costed the project?" a stern-looking Mrs Styles asked.

"We were planning to begin this morning," Beth explained. "But we got sidetracked by the question of adoption. As you can imagine, talk of becoming mother and daughter was quite an emotional rollercoaster."

All of the women nodded, knowing smiles on their faces, except Mrs Styles who remained sour-faced and insisted, "You have to cost the project if you want any of us to back it."

"I understand your caution," Isla said, granting Kate a wide smile. "But I'm prepared to finance the lodgings for these new girls and the extension of existing facilities to cater for them." The good news had Kate's heart hammering in her chest. "As for the health centre, I'd very much like to be associated with discussions of the project right from the outset. I have a vested interest."

When Kate looked perplexed, the woman explained. "My mother is seriously ill and none of the doctors here..." Kate wondered why she glanced disapprovingly at Mrs Styles. "...or elsewhere can do anything for her. Even if you won't be able to help her, at least supporting your cause may help others."

Kate would have willingly hugged Isla, but the discussion was not over. Mrs Styles pursued, "I still want to see the complete financial details. I have serious doubts about children meddling in healthcare."

"Justifiable concern," Kate said, resolving never to give the slightest information to the woman. "I'm sure your reservations will find suitable answers in our project."

"You have to forgive Gertie," Isla said, her tone at the limit of condescension. "Her husband is the famous Dr Styles, head of the largest private clinic in Luzern. She has to protect the good doctor from potential competitors who might have solutions he couldn't imagine."

There was clearly venom in Isla's words. Kate wonder what

past history had set the two at loggerheads. Beth stepped in before the conversation flared into a full-blown row. They fixed the date of the next meeting and everyone, except Mrs Styles, enthusiastically invited Kate to join them.

When all the women had left except Beth and Isla, the latter said with a chuckle, "Don't worry about Gertie Styles. She's a bit of a grumpy sow."

"On the contrary," Kate replied. "She raised a legitimate point. One that we'll have to address if we don't want to have the whole medical profession down on us."

Isla stared at Kate in admiration. Beth was grinning. "She's my daughter," Beth said. "Hands off."

"How did you know I wanted to steal her?" Isla asked, pouting.

Beth groaned theatrically.

That they could joke about who owned her left Kate feeling uncomfortable. "I'd like to meet your mother," she asked, cutting through their banter. "If that's okay with you, Beth."

Beth nodded.

"Now?" Isla asked, startled. "Sure. Not that I hold out any hope for her..."

"I just want to say hallo to the person who inspired you to support us," Kate replied, with a smile. What she didn't say was she wanted to know what condition condemned the woman to be beyond medical help.

"Okay," Isla said. "Let's go."

"What do you have against Mrs Styles?" Kate asked as they made their way to Isla's house.

"You're perspicacious," Isla said. "Dr Styles tried to treat my mum. He insisted he could help her. In reality, the treatment just made her worse. He blamed the failure on my mother."

"I'm sorry to hear that," Kate said. "The medical profession has some serious limits, although, the way you describe it, this sounds more like damage caused by an overdeveloped ego."

Beth chuckled, but Isla groaned. "Here we are," Isla said, holding the gate open to let them in.

Isla's mum was in the living room, installed in an armchair with a blanket draped over her lap. A maid stood by, holding a towel and a glass of water at the ready. The curtains were drawn and the air was stale and stuffy. The woman's face was emaciated, her hands wrinkled and bony. It looked as if the illness were sucking life from her and she didn't have much more to give.

Hearing them enter, the old woman cracked open watery eyes and stared at Kate. Clearly Isla's mum stood at the very extremity of life, everything beckoning her to pass over. Was it right to want to pull her back from the brink? Kate took a pace closer. The smell of death and decay warred with soap and perfume. Reaching out, Kate gently placed her hand on the old woman's. It was cold. If she'd had the strength, the woman would have flinched at the touch of so much warmth and life.

Shifting to look inside the woman, Kate was saddened to discover the cancer ran wild. If it'd been caught earlier, Kate might have been able to do something. But this old woman was truly beyond hope. Kate eased the pain as best she could then withdrew and stepped back.

Kate wished she had better news, but there was no point in denying the inevitable. Acceptance was what was needed. "There's nothing I can do," she said. "The cancer has her in its grip. It is everywhere, sapping her life. I managed to ease the pain, but she doesn't have much longer."

Tears streamed down Isla's cheeks as she looked from Kate to Beth clearly wishing Kate's words were untrue. Beth nodded gravely as if to urge her to trust Kate's diagnosis. Isla's attention returned to her mum, her fist pressed against her mouth to stifle a sob. Kate put an arm around her and held her tight, whispering, "You need to let her go. She's ready. It's her time. Would you like us to leave you alone? Or do you want us to accompany you?"

"Stay," Isla said as she knelt at her mother's feet and laid her forehead on her mum's hands. Addressing her mother, the young woman spoke at length, her words barely audible at times. The

long litany of memories embraced hours spent together in joy
and sadness, love shared and lost, disagreements and regrets,…
Ending with a shuddery "I love you," she kissed her mother's
hands and sat up to see that the old woman had slipped away.

27.

Peter paced the room, his pleated skirt swirling at every turn making it hard to concentrate. "Now the prefects, the administrator and the headmistress are closeted in the infirmary, I'm unsure what to do."

On his bed, Eloise was staring at her healed hands in distracted disbelief. Sarah, who sat next to her, looked frustrated. "As if the three of us could do much," she retorted.

Peter was about to answer when the door burst open and the twins marched in. He'd completely forgotten them. Stupid oversight.

"So this is where you hang out with your girlfriends!" one exclaimed, a sadistic smile straining at her lips.

"More like a place for scheming and plotting if you ask me," the other corrected.

"Nobody asked you," Eloise replied, getting to her feet in an attempt to appear imposing. "Get out."

The twins grinned, unimpressed. "Put a sock in it!" one said.

"You're no longer a prefect," the other added.

"Your word doesn't count," the first continued.

Sarah scuttled across the bed, shifting as far from the two as possible. To her alarm, a twin sprinted across the room and grabbed her by the hair, yanking her to her feet. She screamed.

Peter jumped to free Sarah, but he was hampered by not wanting to hurt her. The twin sent him sprawling onto the bed. He'd planned to make the most of the contact to attack her mentally, but to his dismay she was warded. He'd only ever experienced warding with the priests who'd invaded Kate's island. Who were these two?

Kate, he called. She would know. Such was his rotten luck, she wasn't answering. How could she abandon him? Without the use of his abilities and deprived of Kate's support he was in a mess.

"Tie them up," one twin barked. The other promptly let go of Sarah who sank sobbing to the floor. "My pleasure, Sis." She pulled a ball of twine from her pocket and lashed Sarah's hands behind her back. Eloise put up more resistance earning her a punch on the nose. The girl screamed, blood spurting from her nose, and collapsed to the ground. The twin not only attached her hands behind her back but also tied them to the bed frame. With her hands bound, poor Eloise had no way to stem the blood bubbling from her nose and dribbling over her mouth.

Peter figured opposition was pointless so he held out his hands. His goodwill earned him no clemency. The girl knotted the twine as tight as she could. His hands were already tingling from lack of blood as she fixed him to the opposite end of the bed frame from Eloise, making sure the knots rendered sitting or kneeling impossible.

Surveying their work with obvious satisfaction, the twins turned on their heels and left. The moment the door was closed, Sarah shuddered. "They're completely insane." Peter had to agree. Eloise just groaned. He jumped mentally to her and mended her nose, staunching the flow of blood. There was nothing he could do with the sticky mess that marred the lower part of her face. As for Sarah, she was in shock. He did his best to reassure her, not with words, but with waves of positive feelings.

They needed to act. Quickly. God only knew what horrors the twins would dream up. Better not dwell on that. *Would any of the girls help us?* The moment he raised the question, he realised he was asking the wrong people. Both Eloise and Sarah were loners.

Eloise managed to come up with a few names, but wasn't

sure the girls would side with them. Think, Peter urged himself. Surely there was someone in school who'd have the decency to help. Or someone outside the school who knew its workings well. Of course. The answer was staring him in the face.

Christina, he called out. His foster mother had worked there for ages. If anyone knew the place it was her.

Peter, she replied without hesitation, as if she'd been awaiting his call. *Kate said you'd contact me.*

This is an absolute emergency, he said, letting the full weight of his desperation drive home his words. *I'm being held hostage with a couple of friends in Our Lady by a pair of twins who would make Witless look like an angel.* To underline his point he sent her the view he had of Eloise with her bloodied face. He heard Christina gasp and swear. *We're tied up in my room on the ground floor of the residence.*

He sensed her on the move as she said she was on her way. He cut the connection and informed the girls. They'd better be quick, the thread around his wrist was so tight he'd already lost much of the feeling in his fingers. With his healing method there was little he could about such a constraint. In one of those uncanny intuitions, he had a vision of Aslan in the Narnia stories being freed by mice who gnawed through the cords.

A mouse? Yes that might work. If he could inhabit a lion cub, surely he could take over a mouse. He sent out his senses. He didn't have to reach far. A mouse was cowering under the bed. The moment his mind touched it he was overwhelmed by its fear. Everything was so big. The humans had ceased their crashing. But they wouldn't go away. He could smell them. They stank.

As with the lion cub in Kate's world, language was no use. Peter had to resort to feelings and images. How the hell did you tell a mouse to gnaw through a thread around his wrist without bitting him? To make things worse, being in the mouse's head singularly limited his thoughts. Trying to think was like bashing his head against the inside of a tiny box. It made him want to scream.

Getting the mouse to venture from under the bed was hard enough. He wished he'd warned the girls. They might panic if they saw a mouse and frighten the animal away.

His hands were wedged behind his back close to the floor, so he coaxed the mouse to move closer, promising it all sorts of tasty morsels if it bit through his restraints. He hadn't anticipated how odd it would feel to be both inside a mouse and feel that same mouse claw its way up his hands. He also realised he was terrified of mice. So much for poking fun of girls for fearing mice.

The mouse complained bitterly about the nasty taste of the thread but dutifully bit away. It was almost through when a giant crash had it scuttling away. No coaxing could quell its fear, as it squeezed through a hole in the skirting and disappeared into the dark. Peter was just able to jump back to his own body, narrowly avoiding being swamped by the mice's terror.

Through the haze of his initial confusion he realised the twins had returned. He struggled to widen his thoughts which obstinately remained mouse-sized. In that in-between state, the two girls seemed enormous, their movements loud and ungainly. He was seized by a desire to run, but his hands were still tied behind his back. Little by little, his feeling of self came back. The return was painful. He didn't dare speak for fear he'd squeak, but he had enough control to pull on his arms hoping the thread would give. It shifted, freeing the circulation in his wrists, but did not break.

One of the twins was carrying a tray with several little bottles on it and, to his horror, a syringe. It didn't require much imagination to guess what the girls had in mind. He could always push out the fluid as he'd done with the psychiatrist, but what if they tried to inject Sarah or Eloise. He had no idea what a dose of male hormones would do to them. Little maybe. But it was the vindictive nature of the act that angered him. Whatever had Sarah or Eloise done to merit such treatment?

"What've they ever done to you?" Peter asked, his voice indeed a touch squeaky. Appealing to logic was clearly futile.

The twins were beyond reason. But asking made sense, if only to stall for time. Christina was on her way. The twins paid him no attention. One of them began preparing the syringe.

"Which one should I stick first?" one asked. "That one," the other said pointing at Sarah who was terrified. "I've always wonder what male hormones would do to a girl of her age." She cackled. "Maybe she'll grow a prick. That would be fun." Sarah was whimpering on the floor. She was the only one not attached to a fixed object.

Sarah, Peter said mind-to-mind. *Edge closer to me. I'll protect you.* He had no idea how, but his apparent confidence calmed her and she shuffled closer.

The twin brandishing the syringe loomed over Sarah as Peter strained to break the thread holding his wrists. Out of the corner of his attention he sensed the mouse peering from its hole. He slammed into its mind, hoping he'd be forgiven, and drove the little animal wild making it tear across the floor and skitter up the twin's leg, digging its claws into her flesh till it took refuge under her skirt.

The twin screamed letting the syringe fly. It careened through the air and smashed against the wall, showering its manly liquid over the nearby door. The girl threw herself to the floor desperately tearing at her clothes, trying to prisc the mouse free. Ripping off her skirt, she revealed a trail of claw marks dotted with blood. The more she struggled, the tighter the animal clung on. She was sure to kill the poor thing if she continued windmilling. Peter freed the mouse, letting it jump to the floor and shoot under the bed, panting in abject terror.

The other twin screamed too and the tray she carried tumbled to the floor, glass bottles and syringes rebounding miraculously unbroken. Backing towards the door, she seemed set on abandoning her sister, only to discover a policewoman blocked her escape.

"Not so fast," she said, keeping a firm grip on the twin's shoulder as she surveyed the scene. A second policewoman stepped into the room, closely followed by Christina and John.

The school nurse brought up the rear.

"What on earth's going on?" the nurse asked, spotting Eloise's blood-smeared face.

"She punched me on the nose," Eloise replied, pointing at one of the twins.

"And she tried to inject something bad in me," Sarah added, indicating the other twin who was scrambling to pull her skirt back on.

The nurse bent to pick up one of the surviving glass vials, "Testosterone!" she exclaimed, reading the label. Turning on the twin, she blurted out, "What possessed you to do such a thing? You could have killed her. And where ever did you get this from?" She brandished the little bottle of hormones.

"The headmistress gave it to us," the twin replied, suitably hanging her head. "She insisted we inject it in these three. She said it was a scientific experiment. I thought you knew."

It was such an absurd and desperate lie even the girl looked sheepish. However, the nurse felt obliged to shake her head in denial. All of a sudden she'd become a suspect and, judging from the poisoned look she gave the girl, she hated being implicated. "This is the first I've heard of it. Surely even you must know that subjects in scientific experiments are never tied to bed posts. That's called torture."

Peter knew the girl was lying. The two were stark raving mad and quite capable of devising such a nasty scheme on their own. However, it suited him to have Heartless blamed, so he said nothing. Instead, he asked, "Could you possibly free us? These cords are cutting into my skin."

The second policewoman pulled a penknife from her belt and cut them free. Christina hurried to Peter and flung her arms around his neck, asking, "Are you all right?" He nodded, pleased to see that John was enquiring about Sarah and Eloise.

Can you get the three of us out of here before the police start asking questions? Peter asked Christina. The last thing he needed was for them to realise he was a boy in disguise.

"These three have had such a shock," Christina began,

addressing the policewomen. "It might be better if they recovered before making a statement."

"That's no girl," the first twin spat. "It's a perverted boy."

Both policewomen stared at Peter as if they could X-ray him. Luckily, John was quick to intervene. "I'm afraid these two are a little unhinged. I recognise the symptoms. Sometimes the most mundane thing can spark an attack. We've had at least one case like that in my school recently. The poor kid was completely detached from reality, imagining the most absurd situations of which he was supposed to be the victim. Finally we had to hand him over to a clinic. He had become a danger to himself and everyone else."

As headmaster of the largest secondary school in town, John's words carried weight. Grave and a little alarmed, the two policewomen looked at the twins in a new light. "Okay," the first of the policewomen said. "We'll drop by tomorrow to question them." Dragging the reluctant twins with them, they left.

"Oh dear," the nurse said, staring wide-eyed at the chaos. "We'll have to find you another room." She wrung her hands in such a dramatic way Peter began to doubt her sincerity. The feeling was further strengthened by the calculating look she shot him as she said, "That the police should come just when the headmistress, the administrator and most of the prefects are sick."

"Listen Jimena," Christina said to the nurse. Of course she'd know the woman. She'd worked at Our Lady for ages. "It'd probably be better if they weren't surrounded by the scene of their nightmare. At least temporarily. I suggest John and I take them to our place. We have plenty of room. Once they're settled in, I'll come back and give you a hand, if that'd help."

"Yes," the nurse said, seemingly distracted. "As long as SHE doesn't know."

<h1 style="text-align:center">28.</h1>

Memories of wild times with Fi came rushing back as Peter sat in his old bedroom. She'd sneak across the corridor to join him, much to her mother's amused disapproval. Christina had always been easy-going, although she had lines she refused to cross.

As he rummaged through drawers looking for clean pants, he was surprised to discover how many boy's clothes remained. He'd completely forgotten there was a time when he'd been obliged to disguise as a boy. Not that he'd seen it like that. If ever he were to continue living with John and Christina he'd probably have to disguise again. It made him realise how much being with the Lost Girls was paradise.

Admiring himself in the full-length mirror, he decided to continue wearing his uniform even if it was a little grubby. He did so partly out of solidarity with Eloise and Sarah who had no pretty dresses to change into. But mostly because he enjoyed being dressed as a schoolgirl.

The two girls were sharing Fi's old room. He could hear their muted giggles across the hall. Both were visibly intimidated by their surroundings and above all by John. Headmasters and headmistress were never good news in the world they came from.

"Lunch is ready girls," Christina called up.

To his surprise, Eloise had donned one of Fi's dresses, a pretty blue number with frills and tassels that had Peter wishing he too had changed. "My uniform was all bloody," she said by way of explanation.

"I soaked it," Christina said, carrying in a steaming bowl of soup. "You're lucky. I should be able to get the stains out."

John had returned to school, which made for a more relaxed atmosphere, at least for the two newcomers. In his absence, Sarah dared ask a question that must have been bothering her. "I was surprised the headmaster took your defence against the police. Why did he do that?"

"Call him John," Christina said. "He's not a headmaster when he's at home."

"As a headmaster," Peter began, winking to Christina, "long before he became my father, John always took my defence. And if you're wondering how a headmaster could side with a boy who dressed as a girl, it's because he respects my choices. He knows I don't dress on a whim or out of provocation."

"I wish our headmistress were like that," Sarah said wistfully. "She has no respect for anyone."

Peter expected Christina to comment. After all, she'd borne the brunt of Heartless's lack of respect. But she continued spooning soup into her mouth in silence.

"Tell me," Eloïse asked Christina, "why did you quit? It was so unexpected. None of us understood. The headmistress said you'd done very bad things, although she didn't say what. I never believed her."

Christina stared at her empty bowl presumably weighing up her answer.

"We always thought it was because you were so popular with the girls and the headmistress was jealous," Sarah said.

Christina smiled. "Thanks for the compliment. At least, I think that's what it was. I did have your interests at heart." She glanced at Peter, her expression apologetic. "In reality, I suspect she fired me because of Peter. It's a long story that I won't trouble you with."

"You mean that business with her niece. What was her name? Witless."

"Exactly," Christina said shooting an accusatory glance at

Peter. "Few people know the story, so I'd prefer if you kept it to yourself."

"Why?" Eloise asked. "It's a key part of the puzzle. Without it, how can anyone understand her crazy behaviour?"

"Because she has a nasty way of turning everything to her advantage," Christina said, "even the dreadful tales about herself."

"But why Peter?" Sarah asked.

"She blames gay boys for leading her brother astray," he replied. "She's got it all wrong, of course. It was her brother that did the leading astray. That's why the police came to arrest him, but he took his life before they could. What's more, blinded by her anger or misled by what people said, she didn't realise boys who identify as girls are not all gay, nor are they necessarily attracted to older men. I'm certainly not."

The noise of someone at the front door had the girls scuttling to their feet.

"You don't have to hide," Christina said, giving them a broad smile.

"We're tired," Eloise shot over her shoulder as they hurried for the stairs. "Thanks for the soup."

John was not alone. A broad-shoulder man with shocking ginger hair and an equally ginger beard followed him in. His face was a blaze of freckles offset by the deep green of his tartan jacket.

Christina got to her feet to greet the man. Judging from their warm embrace, they knew each other. "My apologies for rushing off like this, but I have to give a hand at Our Lady of Grace."

John looked troubled but said only, "Be careful," and gave her a kiss. "This is Dr Swenson," John told Peter, "he's a mathematician at a university in the north." Turning back to Dr Swenson, he indicated the man should take a seat and went in search of tea.

"What sort of maths do you do?" Peter asked. It was a risky question. He might end up inundated with formulae and abstruse proofs. That's what happened with their maths teacher.

"I work with mathematical models," the man explained.

"Like predicting the movements of planets and stars?" Peter asked, relieved he could understand.

"Sort of. I work on complex systems, like those governing the human body."

Peter's interest spiked. The man might shed some light on the possible evolution of the cell's blueprint. "Can I ask you a question?" he ventured. "It's been troubling me for some time."

"Fire away."

"Well. Every cell in the body has a blueprint…"

"We call it DNA," the mathematician corrected.

"I prefer to call it a blueprint, because that is exactly what it is. It dictates how the cell should be and in so doing ensures good health. On a larger scale it determines our race, our colour, our gender…"

"You speak as one of authority." Peter was unsure if the man's smile was condescending or genuinely encouraging. "How do you know such things?"

"It would be a long story, but for now let's just say I know."

The man nodded although he was clearly curious. John, who returned with a pot of tea at that moment, covered his mouth to conceal a grin.

"That blueprint," Peter pursued, "is extremely complex because it has to tie together so many different processes on which our good health depends. Now here's my question. What if we could change the blueprint, how could we be sure everything would continue to work properly?"

"Your question is challenging, but you've come to the right address, at least for part of the answer. My work consists of understanding change in complex systems. Not the gradual change we call evolution, rather abrupt and unpredictable change. If I'm not mistaken, it is this paradigm shift you have in mind."

Peter pondered the expression 'paradigm shift'. Was the gender system an underlying worldview? Yes. After a fashion.

And could it shift? He hoped so. He nodded.

"I'm going to disappoint you," Dr Swenson went on. Peter wanted to groan. It was like having a sweet dangled before you only to have it snatched away as you reached for it. "I can only predict possible forms of change, not actual content. In other words, I can suggest the type of trajectory your blueprint might follow in changing, but I cannot predict either its state before or after it changes, or when the change might take place."

Peter was discouraged. If he were to change the form of gender, he needed clear guidelines. It was the how and the what that interested him, not the form. "So there's no recipe?"

The mathematician shook his head. "From a theoretical perspective, the actual path of change and the final result are necessarily unknowable till they've happened."

How frustrating. There might well be a solution, but, if Dr Swenson was right, he couldn't deliberately make it come about. His disappointment must have shown on his face because the man muttered, "Sorry."

"However does anyone make decisions in such unpredictable circumstances?" Peter exclaimed.

Swenson chuckled. "That's the key question, although, as mathematicians, we leave that conundrum to others."

"I don't understand," Peter said, perplexed. There was a gaping hole in the man's explanation. "Why can't you know what's coming? Surely all our work in planning and government depends on tracing a line from what is to what probably will be."

"That evolutionary approach doesn't work with complex systems. Let me use a metaphor. A state that appears stable to us, like your cellular blueprint, is in fact perched atop a pinnacle in a delicate balance. That might seem absurd, but complex systems require precariousness to function. As a corollary, change could come at any moment. Abruptly it falls from grace, as it were, and shifts to a new state of balance where it comes to rest. As I said, complex systems are inherently unstable, but they do everything they can to maintain equilibrium because it is only in that state they can work. And they must work or be condemned to break down or die."

"If that were so," Peter objected, "wouldn't we be swinging wildly from one state to another? Clearly that isn't the case."

"One of the odd features of such a system is how it maintains relative stability. Those pinnacles I mentioned, the moments when the system is in balance and functions correctly, they act like magnets, clinging on to stability until something dislodges them and they flip to a new pinnacle. But where that next pinnacle will be cannot be foretold."

The image was odd, but that magnetism would explain why their way of healing worked so easily. "Your explanation might not answer my question, but it does clarify one thing."

Dr. Swenson looked intrigued. "I'm all ears."

"The attractiveness of the cell's blueprint would explain why the body is so willing to fall in line and adhere to those guidelines when it gets out of sync. A little nudge is all you need to bring back health."

It was the man's turn to get excited and he was about to ask a question when Kate's voice rang out in Peter's head, *Can we talk?*

He got to his feet, cocking his ear as if he heard something. "I think the girls are calling. I'd better have a look. We don't want them getting up to mischief." He gave the man a knowing grin. It was a bit mean to suggest the girls were unruly as an excuse to escape, but it worked well enough.

"It's been really interesting talking to you." Peter said, holding out his hand. Shaking hands to say goodbye was a habit he'd acquired in Switzerland. As he hurried up the stairs, he heard the man exclaim, "What an extraordinary girl."

"Indeed," was all John replied.

Once in his bedroom, Peter quietly shut the door. *Kate. What's up?* Her presence in his head was bubbling over with excitement so the news couldn't be that bad.

Beth has offered to adopt me, she blurted out.

The news provoked mixed feelings not least because he'd

been adopted himself, but there was also jealousy and a fear he might lose her. He quickly strove to mask his feelings. *That's wonderful. How did that come about?*

She was too excited to notice his misgivings. *We were discussing finding sponsors.* She related the conversation and her elation at being adopted. She also described the meeting with the rich women.

You're also rich now, he taunted. *Do you still want poor me around?*

A wave of love and affection bowled into him, pushing him back onto the bed. Despite being knocked breathless, he responded in kind, the two revelling in each other for a long moment. *Okay,* he said, sitting up. *I gather you still like me. A bit.* She planted a mental kiss on his lips, silencing any further silliness.

So what's happening to you? she finally asked.

I'm at John and Christina's. He told her how the two had rescued him and the girls from the clutches of the twins. When he explained that the twins had been warding, she grew worried asking him to describe how it felt.

That sounds very much like the way the warrior priests warded. She didn't have to say it, her thoughts were plain enough. She was afraid the priests had located them and sent the twins in pursuit. That they had sent girls did seem strange. Females rarely played a key role in such a male-dominated world. Setting aside her concerns, she reminded him how they'd sneaked round the priests wards.

What are you going to do now? she asked.

Not sure. The police want to question us. I'm afraid they'll discover I'm not the girl they think I am. And there's the restraining order. John and Christina aren't supposed be in contact with me.

Why don't you come home?

I wish I could. But I feel there's something else I must do, as if the situation were unresolved.

Well, hurry back. I miss you.

Me too.

With Kate gone to inform the Lost Girls of her news, Peter lay back on his bed imagining the impact of enlarging the group of girls in Luzern and how he could develop their healing if he had extra money.

"Peter," John called out, his tone urgent. "Can you come down a moment."

He found John alone at the kitchen table, creases of worry furrowing his brow. "I just had a call from the police," he said. "Apparently the twins have escaped."

Peter shuddered, glancing at the back door to make sure they weren't already there. Those two were capable of anything.

"The inspector was afraid they might come after you. He wanted to send someone to watch over us but I told him I didn't think that would be enough."

29.

Being back at Our Lady of Grace was weird, probably more so for Eloise and Sarah than Peter. They'd grown up there. It'd been their home. Peter was only in transit, at least he hoped he was. The three were squashed together on the back seat of John's car in a remote corner of the car park. John had gone to fetch Christina, having instructed them to keep out of sight. They were en route for John's cottage by the sea to escape the twins.

Several times girls chatting animatedly ambled by, much to the horror of the three fugitives. Fortunately, the pupils paid no attention to the cars or their occupants. After ten minutes, Peter was getting anxious. What if the headmistress was up and about and had caught Christina? That'd be a disaster.

"He's taking his time," Sarah whispered, echoing Peter's concerns. "I hope nothing's gone wrong."

"I'm going to call them," he said. He didn't like doing so. Neither adult was comfortable communicating that way and it could be distracting in a difficult situation. But this was an emergency.

Christina? No answer.

John? No answer either. It wasn't that they didn't reply. That he could understand. There was no replying presence, as if they'd disappeared. Surely they couldn't be dead. He shuddered. No. It was as if a ward had been thrown around them.

"Something's wrong," he told the girls. He quickly explained how the twins warded, saying he suspected they were using that to block communication with John and Christina. He wasn't sure they fully understood, but he had no time to elaborate. "I'm going to sneak round the ward. To do so, I'll have to leave my body, mentally at least. Look after it for me."

Sarah giggled nervously. In the circumstances, her reaction seemed inappropriate, but how could he blame her? So much was going on. "If ever there's a problem, try calling me mind-to-mind." He preferred not to tell them they wouldn't reach him if he were on the far side of a ward.

Closing his eyes, he took a deep breath and went in search of Christina. He couldn't sense her. But he encountered a telltale membrane that indicated a ward. Making himself as small and insignificant as possible, he slipped through. Doing so was surprisingly easy. The barrier was rudimentary. Nothing like the reinforced shields the warrior priests maintained around themselves.

Once on the other side, he immediately sensed Christina and flew to her, entering her mind as unobtrusively as possible. He couldn't afford to have her reaction give him away. From there he could see what she saw and hear what she heard. They were in Peter's room. Christina was tied up on the bed while John lay unconscious on the floor, a bloody gash on the side of his head. One of the twins towered over him. The other was lounging against the doorframe, toying with a syringe.

Peter braced himself against Christina's concern which was overpowering and thumbed through her memories. Apparently the headmistress had nothing to do with this. She was still closeted in the infirmary. The twins had waylaid Christina, using her as bait, thinking they'd catch him. Instead they'd stumbled on John. Now they were waiting for Peter to turn up.

His first move was to jump to John. That turned out to be more difficult. A second ward blocked access. Once alerted, Peter was able to wheedle his way through and set about healing the man. He did so cautiously, afraid the twins might realise. He healed the deeper damage to John's head, but left a superficial wound to mislead any watcher.

The twins must have injected him with a sedative. Peter managed to maintain a state of slumber while encouraging John's body to eliminate the toxins. Satisfied the man was going to be okay, Peter jumped back to Christina, unsure what to do next. The only option he could imagine was jumping to one of twins and using her to neutralise the other. It was risky. For starters, they might have stronger wards than those around John and Christina.

In the end, he opted for a tactical retreat, jumping back to his own body. All was quiet. He informed the girls of what he'd found and they discussed whether Eloise and Sarah should go to the police. After much discussion, they decided to stay put. Was that not what John had told them to do?

But he couldn't do nothing. He called Kate, explaining what was happening. She jumped to his body and the two wriggled their way through the ward and jumped to Christina. Unbeknown to the woman, the two observed the situation, gently nudging her to look this way or that. Peter had qualms about such manipulation. If ever she found out, she'd be furious and would forbid him ever to do so again.

When one of twins aimed a vicious kick at John, he could look on no longer. Furious, he flung himself at the twin, smashing into her defences and rebounding. He only just managed to return to Christina. The twin burst out laughing, clearly aware something had happened. "So you did come," she said, scanning the room in search of him. Not finding Peter, she let loose a second kick, planting the toe of her boot in John's stomach. The headmaster groaned but did not wake.

As she raised her foot to kick yet again, it was Kate that jumped. Unlike him, she tread softly, almost caressing the wards as she slipped past. The twin did kick, but her foot went wide, causing her to spin in the air and fall flat on her face with a thud and a scream. Scrambling to her feet, her nose bloody, she struggled with herself. Her arms flayed the air like a crazed windmill. Her legs twisted round each other in what would have been comical had it not been for the infuriated look on her face.

The second twin moved to restrain her, brandishing the syringe as she did. She wouldn't hesitate to employ it, of that Peter was sure. If it contained the same sedative used on John, he worried about the damage it might do to Kate. He jumped, this time following Kate's example.

Once inside the second twin he was almost overpowered by a wave of fanaticism that rose to greet him. He'd only ever felt such a powerful stench in the minds of warrior priests in Kate's world. Gathering thoughts of his affection for Kate as a shield against the fanatical onslaught, he struggled to take control of the twin's body. She fought ferociously, lashing out. He was alarmed at how much her attacks hurt. It was as if she were digging her nails into his flesh.

He dodged, swerving this way and that in her mind, causing her to lose her balance both mentally and physically. She tripped over her twin who was writhing on the floor and fell forward. With a supreme effort she wrenched back control and rolled back onto her feet, standing defiant her arms akimbo, her legs spread in a fighting stance.

You can't win! she shouted. *I'm far stronger and far better trained than you. Why don't you give up while you can.*

She was right. If the warrior priests had taught her, he didn't stand a chance. There was only one domain in which he had the upper hand. Healing. The priests knew nothing of that. Not surprising for a people bent on inflicting harm. As much as he loathed using healing to do damage, this was an emergency.

A quick scan of her body revealed she suffered from migraines. He knew from past experience that the exercises warrior priests were subjected to often brought on splitting headaches. He stoked her blood pressure and ratcheted up the tensions in the nape of her neck. The resulting pain had her clasping her head and crying out. He felt it too, but shielded himself as best he could.

In her distraction, he seized control, forcing her to rummage on the floor for the syringe. Having found it, he made her drive it into her own arm and push down the plunger. He felt her horror as she realised what she'd done and lashed out at him with all her force. He was just able to spring free as drowsiness swept over her.

Once back in Christina, he took stock. Poor Christina watched the scene alarmed. With them in stealth mode, how could she possibly know he and Kate were battling to rescue her? The poor woman was terrified the thrashing twin would inflict further injuries on John. Indeed, Kate was still struggling with the girl who rolled on the floor bashing herself in her effort to drive Kate out. Taking a deep breath, Peter jumped to join Kate.

His first surprise was to discover the twin was a boy. The irony of it. But he had no time to gloat. Kate was receiving a battering and wouldn't hold out much longer. As with the other twin, he scanned her body. Unlike her, nothing was amiss. As the twin was sparring with Kate, and the twins knew little of healing, Peter had free rein. He called on an old favourite, easing the twin's bladder. Urine dribbled into the child's pants despite desperate efforts to stem the flow.

The sensation of telltale warm wetness sparked archaic feelings of shame and disgust causing the twin to cease fighting and freeze in horror. *Take over*, Peter urged. Kate immediately seized control and forced the twin to untie Christina. The twin fumbled with knots trying to resist Kate's hold but Peter increased the pressure on her bladder. With Christina finally freed, neither Kate nor Peter knew how to restrain the second twin who was now curled up in a ball of shame, rocking backwards and forwards. Christina solved their dilemma by knocking the twin over the head with a chair.

In extremis, Peter saw the blow coming and urged Kate to *Jump!* It was a close thing, but they both landed in Christina as the twin crumpled to the floor unconscious. Neither Kate nor Peter hung around. They jumped back to Peter then Kate returned to herself.

The struggles had left Peter exhausted and disoriented. He opened his eyes to find both Sarah and Eloise staring at him.

"Well?" Sarah asked, impatient as ever to know what was happening.

"We freed Christina and John, but not without a fight," he said.

"What about the twins?" Eloise asked.

"Tied up or unconscious or both," Peter said wearily, wishing there was a bed he could flop down on.

"Shouldn't we go and help?" Eloise wanted to know.

Peter shook his head. "They'll be here in a moment." He closed his eyes and drifted off, only to be awoken by Sarah elbowing him in the ribs seconds later.

"Where are they?" she asked.

"Give them a chance," Peter replied groggily.

"We've been waiting more than a quarter of an hour," Sarah pointed out, much to his surprise. "How much longer must we wait before we're allowed to worry?"

30.

Kate paced her room, exhilarated by the fight with the twins. She vowed to programme more combat training, even if fighting with the girls could never measure up to mental battles with foes trained by Warrior Priests. She hadn't realised how much she needed the challenge. That a session of combat training was scheduled early that afternoon was a lucky coincidence. Not that she'd get much done if she broke the news about the forthcoming investments.

She called Eileen mind-to-mind and asked if she could organise a council meeting. Discussing with them first seemed prudent. She didn't anticipate opposition, but a future with a larger group of girls and a new health centre was a giant step. There was an easy-going cosiness to their current life that some might want to hold on to. Well, it would've been cosy had the church not set its sights on bringing their world crashing down.

"Come in!" Kate called when a knock came at the door. Eileen entered, followed by Suzanne and Clara.

"Tania's in town with Claudia. Lydia drove them in," Eileen said. "They went to visit that group of orphans."

The news annoyed Kate. Tania's competitive streak was constantly pushing her to take initiatives that weren't always wise. "We should have discussed that before she went running off."

"She wanted to, but you were..." Eileen hesitated, "...out of it."

Kate was about to apologise when it crossed her mind Tania

could've waited. "What was the hurry?"

"We heard the church planned to move the girls to another orphanage miles away," Suzanne said.

"So what does Tania plan to do?"

"Check if the rumour is true," Eileen replied. "And see what we can do?"

If the church was worried about the Lost Girls interfering, sending a delegation to investigate was the best way to confirm their suspicions and harden their position. "I'll check with Tania," Kate said. *Tania*, she called.

Oh Kate, Tania replied sounding desperate, *it's terrible.*

What's up?

They won't let us in. We've no idea if the girls are still here or have already been spirited away.

Of course the orphanage wouldn't let them in. What else did she expect? A welcome committee with tea and biscuits? Kate made sure to keep her annoyance to herself. *Come home. We'll discuss what to do when you get back.*

"They couldn't get in," Kate told the others. "I asked Tania to come back."

"Why did you call us together?" Clara asked, sitting on Kate's bed. "Did Beth have good news?"

Kate grinned in response. She couldn't help it. The thought of adoption had her all aglow. It would probably be wiser to wait for the others, but she was dying to share the news. "Beth wants to adopt me," she blurted out. She knew full well other parts of her news concerned the girls more, but she couldn't resist telling them. The looks on their faces were not at all what she'd expected. There was a trace of envy and even bitterness, but mostly they looked sad.

"So you'll be leaving us," Suzanne said, tears welling in her eyes.

Kate couldn't help gaping. "Leaving? No. Why should I?"

"Because you have a family now..." Suzanne replied, unable to stem the flood of tears.

"Ah!" Kate said, suddenly understanding. If there was one

thing these girls longed for more than anything else it was to be part of a family. "No. I have no intention of leaving." She took a sobbing Suzanne in her arms, the girl clinging to her in desperation. "I'm not going anywhere. You will always be part of my family. The Lost Girls are my family," she crooned. Glancing over Suzanne's shoulder she saw both Eileen and Clara were similarly afflicted. She beckoned for them to join the huddle.

When the girls had recovered, she told them about the land she would inherit and Isla's promise to invest in building a home for the other orphans. "She'll even help with their upkeep till we can pay our way ourselves."

"That's wonderful," Clara exclaimed. "We should fetch them before they're moved away."

Kate wasn't sure they could handle so many girls before the new building was ready, but it was urgent. "There's more," she said. "Isla also offered to invest in our very own health centre in a hamlet not far from here. It is part of the new property."

"That's wonderful," Susanne cried out, her earlier misery completely forgotten as she launched into a list of what they could do.

"You should write that down," Kate said, gently interrupting her. "We'll need to discuss it with Isla. She'll want to be involved."

"So what do we do now?" Eileen asked. "With the orphans, I mean."

They discussed how best to go about the construction and agreed it would be good to involve the orphans in making plans. They also discussed how to house the girls till the new building was ready. Camping was out of the question. The ground was hard as stone and drifts of snow lay here and there. It was at that point that Tania and Claudia burst in followed by Lydia.

"...it was definitely a mistake," Lydia was saying. "Now they're even more wary of us."

"At least we know what's going on," Tania insisted, dismissing Lydia's accusation with a wave of her hand.

Kate didn't want to waste time on a fruitless battle with Tania. She was about to interrupt when Eileen beat her to it. "Is there no way we can get them out? Like Kate and Tania did with us."

Lydia shook her head. "If I were the church, I'd bus the girls to another orphanage today. They must be eager to avoid any further scandal."

"It's all very well bringing them here," Claudia said. "But we don't have any room and what about the money?"

Eileen glanced at Kate, tacitly seeking permission to break the good news. Kate nodded. "Money is no longer a problem," Eileen said with a grin.

"Have you won the lottery?" Tania asked, her eyes sparkling as if she'd been promised a date with a pretty girl.

"I haven't," Eileen replied, "but after a fashion Kate has."

Tania huffed, clearly struggling with mixed feelings about that.

"Beth has offered to adopt me," Kate said, raising a hand to silence Tania's immediate objections. "And before you ask, no, I'm not leaving. Beth has given me a large area of land around here and one of her friends has accepted to finance the building of accommodation for the new girls."

"That's wonderful," Lydia exclaimed. After a brief pause she asked, "Does that mean we are now your tenants?"

"No. Klaus's parents bought this plot of land and these buildings. It belongs to you. That doesn't change," Kate said. "But I'll be your new neighbour."

Tania aimed a punch at Kate's shoulder that went way beyond a friendly tap. Kate dodged the worst of it. "Look at the rich girl giving herself airs!" Tania exclaimed.

Rubbing her shoulder, Kate pretended to look down her nose at Tania and replied in a haughty tone, "Subjects who can't behave properly towards their new Lord should expect serious trouble."

"Lord?" Tania spluttered, eyeing her in disbelief. "You can't! You wouldn't."

"She's pulling your leg, silly," Eileen said with a chuckle.

Tania sprang at Kate, aiming to get her in what was supposed to be a playful headlock, but Kate was far too quick and ended up sitting atop Tania who lay sprawled on the floor. "What am I supposed to do with these unruly subjects?" Kate complained to a grinning audience. Judging from their evident glee, it was possible Tania's behaviour irritated many of them and part of their good humour came from seeing Tania trounced. "They have absolutely no respect," Kate pursued, and, bending forward, brushed the hair from Tania's eyes and planted a kiss on the girl's forehead. "You could do with some combat practice, my friend. Which reminds me," releasing her hold on Tania and offering her a helping hand, "you've all got a training session I believe."

In the end, Kate did not announce her news to the girls. It could wait an hour or two. Instead she put them through their paces in some basic defence moves. She toyed with adding a hint of magic when repelling an opponent, but opted to keep that for a future lesson. Maybe it was her father's reticence that held her back, but, deep down, she felt uneasy using magic to do harm.

They'd just finished when Lydia hurried into the room. Cornering Kate, she said, "Heinz just phoned. He's heard the church plan to bus the girls out this evening under cover of darkness. He's on his way with Regina."

Kate turned to the girls and called for quiet. "Make yourselves comfortable," she said. "This is going to take a moment." The girls sat in small groups on the tatami and turned expectant eyes in her direction. Behind her, the council assembled, like a reassuring force at her back. "As some of you may have heard, our fellow orphan friends in town are about to be spirited away by the church."

Several girls hissed. One called out, "Can't we spirit them away ourselves?" The suggestion brought a chorus of yeses and nodding heads.

"But where would we put them?" a voice of reason piped up.

"And how could we pay for food?" a second asked. "I thought money was scarce."

Kate nodded, proud to hear the girls thinking things through rather than rushing off and being rash. She couldn't help glancing at Tania before turning to Eileen and indicating she should explain. Eileen was cautious. The news of Kate's good fortune was greeted with enthusiastic 'wows' rather than groans of despair.

"Let's go fetch the girls," one of the smallest called out, echoing the opinion of the majority.

"I think we should," Kate agree. Her words sparked a cheer that almost raised the roof. They were a choir, after all. Raising things with their voices was what they did. Lifting a hand for quiet, she added, "The only question now is how and when."

"I say we hire a bus immediately and snatch them from under the noses of the church before they have time to react," Tania exclaimed, all fired up and rearing for a fight. A couple of girls nodded.

"Not so fast," Kate said, placing a hand on Tania's shoulder. The girl glanced at Kate pleadingly as she tried to shrug off the hand, but Kate shook her head and held on. "Heinz and Regina are on their way. The council has to talk to them first. We will fetch the girls..." She stressed the word 'will'. "...but we don't want to start a war. Things are already tense between the church and us. It won't help us or those girls to escalate to open hostilities. In the meantime, it would be good if you girls could form groups and scour the outbuildings in search of places to lodge some twenty girls, till the new accommodation is ready."

Leaving the girls to hurry off in search of cosy corners, Kate and the council headed for Lydia's kitchen. "Do you ever regret our invasion?" Kate asked Lydia who was busy cutting slices of tart for them. "I mean, life must have been more peaceful without so many young girls kicking up trouble."

"Congratulations," Lydia said, ignoring Kate's question. "I hear Beth is to adopt you. To be honest, she beat us to it. Klaus and I would willingly have adopted you. Ever since that day when we rescued you from hospital, you've had a special place in our hearts."

Kate hugged the woman by way of reply.

"You can adopt me instead," Tania said, sounding both defiant and hopeful.

"In a way, we've adopted you all," Lydia replied, handing Tania a piece of tart. The girl bit into the tart with a sour look on her face.

"Did I not add enough sugar?" Lydia asked, her expression a picture of innocence.

"Poor Tania is suffering from a bad case of neglect," Kate said, keeping her tone as matter-of-fact as possible. "I'm sure a little more sugar would help immensely."

Rather than go in search of a sweetener, Lydia took Tania in her arms and hugged her. "Ooo!" Clara exclaimed, cuing up behind Tania. "Me next."

"Looks like I'm going to have to do the rounds to tuck you lot in and give you a goodnight kiss," Lydia said, letting go of Tania, much to the girl's disgust, and hugging Clara.

"That would be really kind," Claudia said with a sad smile. "Unfortunately, it would be like pouring a bucket of water into an empty well. Being an orphan digs a hole that takes a heck of a lot of filling."

"Wise words, indeed," Regina said, arriving at that moment.

31.

Kate looked around Lydia's kitchen table. A sea of bemused faces stared at the crumbs, all that remained of Lydia's tart. What could they possibly do to save the girls?

"If you're going to act," Regina said, breaking the silence, "it'll have to be before dusk,"

"I spoke to a man from the transport company. The coach is programmed for just after dark," Heinz added. "At this time of year that'll be around five."

"That doesn't leave us much time," Eileen said, absently marshalling crumbs into a pile.

"What if we block the coach," Suzanne suggested, a rare bubble of enthusiasm in the room. "We could give an impromptu concert in the street. A musical vigil. With candles and torches."

"I like the idea, but surely that'll only delay the departure," Claudia said. "What if they call the police?"

"Delaying is good," Kate said, warming to the idea, "and singing will draw a crowd, making it public when they want to hush things up." She glanced at Regina. "With a crowd, we'll have less to fear from the police. But we still need to get the girls to come with us."

"We should make sure we do have a crowd," Regina said.

"How do we do that without the orphanage knowing?" Eileen asked, practical as ever. Regina had plenty of ideas and the more she spoke the more the others were inspired, chipping in with suggestions. That not all of them were viable didn't matter. It was fun and there was hope again.

Heinz produced a plan of the city and laid it on the table, saying, "We're lucky. There are only two exits." He pointed to a wide thoroughfare that ran in front of the orphanage. "The main entrance and..." he shifted his finger to a narrow street at the back, "... the service entrance."

"I know that alley," Eileen said. Most of the Lost Girls had been housed in that orphanage. "They'll never get a coach in there. And the backdoor is so stiff it takes two to open it."

"I wouldn't put it past them to try," Claudia said. She knew something of the spiteful underhandedness of nuns. "We need to make sure they can't smuggle them out the back. And I know exactly how... a simple wedge would do the trick."

"That's all very well," Tania said, having been silent the whole time. "But Kate's question still stands. How do we bring the girls here?"

Kate stared at Tania in surprise as did several other members of the council. The girl was siding with her. Not only that, she was asking constructive questions. Where was the catch? Tania responded by blowing Kate a kiss, then she continued, "We could hijack the bus."

Several girls groaned. Good old Tania was back.

"That's not such a bad idea," Heinz said, startling everyone. Tania grinned in triumph. "But before we do, we need to make it clear the girls want to join you."

"We'd need to warn them," Kate said. "And I have an idea how."

Once details had been discussed and Heinz had made a call to the transport company, everyone went their separate ways to prepare. Heinz drove Kate to Isla's place. She was hesitant about calling on the young woman so soon after the death of her mother, but the gamble was worth a try.

Isla answered the door, a hint of a smile forming on her haggard face. "Come in. Come in." She ushered Kate through a hallway brimming with bouquets of flowers and wreaths. The scent was overpowering. "Let's take refuge in the kitchen," Isla said. "I can't stand the smell of those flowers."

Isla cracked open a window letting in a wintery draught then pulled up two stools, inviting Kate to sit. "I've been meaning to contact you," Isla said. "Do you think the Lost Girl could sing at the funeral?"

"Of course we could," Kate replied. "We'd be delighted." She eyed the woman. They hardly knew each other, but Kate felt a bond between them that seemed much older. "How are you holding up?" she asked.

"It was expected, you know. She'd been ill for quite a while. These last couple of years I found myself wishing she'd let go, but she clung on. She was always in pain and her pain pained those around her. Is it wrong to say her passing came as a relief?" Kate shook her head. "Now all that is left are the unending condolences, the tedious funeral preparations and sorting out the estate. It's exhausting."

"Would you welcome a distraction?" It was a risky question. What if the woman didn't want to be distracted as she contemplated her last goodbyes?

"What do you have in mind?" Isla asked. Kate was unsure if it was alarm or hope she read on the woman's face.

Kate told her about the orphans being bundled off to a far-away place.

"Are those the same girls I offered to help?"

Kate nodded. She explained what they planned. The improvised concert pleased Isla a great deal. "Yes," she finally said. "I'll do it."

"Thank you," Kate said. "I really appreciate it."

"It's me that should thank you," Isla insisted, gifting Kate a pale smile. "For turning me towards the future when everything conspires to drag me back to the past."

Kate got to her feet, meaning for them to leave, time was short, but Isla stopped her. "If you're supposed to be accompanying me, you can't go dressed like that." She laughed. "They'll be taking you for an orphan rather than my assistant."

Kate looked down at her clothes and groaned. She'd forgotten to change out of her tracksuit. Not surprising really.

She felt much more at home in loose-fitting, comfortable apparel. Peter was the one for dressing in fancy clothes. He even liked wearing a bra despite not having breasts, while she preferred to go without. It was so uncomfortable. The thought of him fussing over a new dress and pretty underwear set off a wave of affection and brought home how much she missed him. She sighed.

"Well?" Isla asked when Kate didn't answer.

"I was giving the girls a lesson in self-defence and I forgot to change."

"Don't worry. I'm sure I have something that'll fit."

What was it with these rich women that they always had a stash of clothes for all ages?

Suitably disguised in a smart dress and jacket with a good deal of makeup, Kate followed Isla to the waiting car. "Where would Mistress like to go?" the chauffeur asked.

Isla indicated the direction and they drove across town, skirting the station and the end of the lake as they did. There was no sign of the bus or any of the choir outside the orphanage. That would come later. The building looked even more forlorn than Kate remembered. Rescuing the Lost Girls had been a daring move that, fortunately, had gone successfully. Hopefully luck would be on their side this time too.

Isla marched up to the front door with Kate at her side and knocked as if she had every right to be there. No one came. Isla knocked again, louder. The sound resonated down empty corridors, but no answering footsteps echoed back. It was as if the building were deserted. Could they have already left? Heinz had been sure of the time and, anyway, they'd waylaid the coach. Had the orphanage got word of their plan?

Isla glanced questioningly at Kate who could only shrug. She had no answers, only questions. It was then they heard the rhythmic fall of many feet on the gravel thrown down to stop people slipping on the ice. Turning they saw a long column of girls, two by two, marching towards them led by an imposing nun. Kate shuddered, fearing the nun might recognise her, but the woman was a complete stranger.

"What can I do for you, Madame?" the nun asked Isla, holding up a hand to halt the girls.

"Can we talk in private?" Isla asked, glancing at the girls. "It's a delicate matter." While she negotiated an audience with the nun, Kate discretely scanned the girls looking for familiar faces. To her despair, she recognised no one. Was it possible the group was not there? Then, half-hidden at the back, she spotted the girl who'd been the first to sing with her when she'd come to rescue the others. What was her name? Sandra! That was it!

"Excuse me," Kate said to the nun, then turning Isla added, "I'll just fetch the papers from the car. I forgot them."

"You're such a scatter-brain," Isla said with a chuckle. "If your head wasn't screwed on, I swear you'd forget it at home."

Duly chided, Kate set off along the line of girls that stretched to the gate and beyond. She checked no second nun was bringing up the rear and darted in amongst the girls to stand next to Sandra who jumped back, startled to see her.

Kate took her trembling hand and spoke into her mind. *Do not be afraid I am talking directly into your head so no one can hear but you.* The girl let out a stifled squeal but clung to Kate's hand. *The Lost Girls are coming to fetch you and the other girls in your class. They'll be here in about a hour. You must get the girls ready .*

Sandra gestured to her mouth and flapped her fingers up and down. Kate guessed she wanted to speak. *You can talk mind-to-mind like me. Just think your thoughts to me.*

What about the others? Sandra asked.

What others?

The other orphans.

We can't take everybody. Not this time.

I'm not sure my class will come if you don't take everyone.

Kate felt deflated. They wanted to save the girls. They'd never anticipated they might refuse. She admired the girl's determination and the feeling of solidarity behind it. *How many girls are there?*

About forty.

Kate sighed. There was no way they could accommodate so many. *I'll talk to the others, but I don't hold out much hope.* Kate continued to the car and fetched the wad of papers they'd deliberately left for that purpose. Exchanging a few words of explanation with the chauffeur, she sat on the back seat and called out to the council.

We've got a problem, she announced once she'd assembled everybody. *I spoke to one of the girls we planned to rescue. She insists they won't come if we don't take everyone.*

That's a daring move, Tania replied. *I like it.*

Daring, maybe, but damned awkward, Suzanne said.

How many are there? Eileen asked.

Forty.

That's double what we expected, Eileen replied. *Have you spoken to Isla about it?*

Kate mentally shook her head. *If we can house and feed them, do we take them?*

What do you think? Eileen returned her question.

Kate hesitated. She liked Sandra's uncompromising stance, but accepting was going to create a mountain of problems. *Yes,* she finally said. *If I can raise the money. But first I want Isla to meet the girls. I think that'll help. I'll let you know.* She broke the communication and hurried back to Isla who was still haggling with the nun.

"I have some urgent news," Kate said, her interruption clearly annoying the nun.

"Well?" Isla said, treating Kate like a menial assistant.

Kate put on a show of being embarrassed. "It's private."

"Excuse me," Isla said to the nun and, taking Kate by the arm, marched her some distance away. "Well?" she asked, lowering her voice to almost a whisper.

"I'd like you to talk to some of the girls," Kate said. "They're hesitant about coming." It wasn't a lie, but it wasn't the whole truth either. Whatever they did, they needed to keep up the pretence that Isla had come to pick a girl to adopt. "Maybe you could suggest meeting a girl or two. To help you make a choice."

Returning to the nun, "My apologies. The death of my mother requires so many questions be answered."

The nun effused with condolences, her obsequiousness sickening.

"Humour me," Isla said. "I'd like to talk to some of the girls before I make up my mind. My assistant has spotted a likely candidate. Maybe I could talk to her and her class."

The nun looked fed up with the endless discussions and the girls were getting ever more restless. She probably had the arrival of the coach in mind and wanted to get rid of them before it turned up. "Bring me this girl."

Kate fetched Sandra, explaining mind-to-mind what was going on. *We need to win this woman over if we want you all to join us.*

When the nun saw Kate returning with Sandra her expression darkened. "Out of the question! This girl and all her class are under serious disciplinary action. Go back to your place," the nun said, almost spitting the words at Sandra.

Sandra didn't budge, but glanced from Kate to Isla.

"I'll talk to this girl," Isla said in one of those decisive voices that expects no refusal. She took Sandra by the arm and led her towards the door. "I'm sure you have a quiet place where can talk."

Seething with barely controlled anger, the Nun unlocked the door and let them in. Pointing to a door, she muttered, "In there," before returning her attention to the girls who were streaming in the entrance. Isla ordered Kate to stand guard while she went inside with Sandra and closed the door. That Isla left her outside made sense, but Kate couldn't help feeling nettled. Now everything depended on Sandra.

The longer the discussion went on, the more nervous Kate got, but she couldn't leave her post. The nun had come by several times and would no doubt have eavesdropped had Kate not been there. When Isla finally opened the door and stepped out her face was grave. Sandra, in comparison, was having a hard time concealing a smile.

32.

The moment Isla was in the hallway the nun re-appeared, hurrying to catch her. Isla freed herself from the nun's clutching fingers. "Thank you for the occasion to talk to this girl," Isla said, nodding to Sandra. "I'll be back shortly with my answer, but I have a lot to settle first!" So saying, she strode to the door with Kate trotting after.

"There's a telephone at your place, isn't there?" Isla asked as they climbed into the car. Kate nodded. "Good. Let's go there. I need to see where this new building has to go and I can organise things better from there."

As they drove to the Lost Girls House Isla plied her with questions about the other girls and the way they organised their life. She was particularly interested in the council and who was on it. She also wanted to know about the buildings and the relationship with Lydia and Kurt. Despite all the questions, Kate had time to warn Eileen and the others that Isla was coming.

Isla was surprised to find the council members gathered to greet her. "What a royal welcome," she said with a chuckle. Once the introductions over, she insisted on seeing the site of the future lodgings. "I'm not sure this will be enough," she said as they completed their visit. "You should probably expect more than the forty today. Others will want to come..."

"Forty?" Suzanne exclaimed, wide-eyed. "How is that possible?"

"On Kate's advice I spoke to one of the orphans. A girl named Sandra. The stories she told me were sickening. When

I asked her about coming here, she said the girls would only come if they all could. I agree. That's why I plan to finance a much larger centre than originally planned if you're willing to give them a home. Of course, I can't pay for ever, so you must find ways to become sustainable. Kate tells me you're already thinking along those lines and I can help. I have some experience with entrepreneurship."

She rounded off her speech with a winning smile only to find the girls staring at her in astonishment. All but Kate, that is. She'd warned them Isla was coming but hadn't had time to go into details.

"Let them get over their shock," Kate suggested. "What do you think of the place?" She was expecting Isla to be enthusiastic. Instead she looked sceptical and asked, "You mentioned a hamlet. Can we visit it?"

"Sure," Kate said, although she was not sure at all. The whole project was shooting off in directions she hadn't anticipated. In her mind the hamlet, which she'd yet to visit, was reserved for the Health Centre. "It's about a kilometre away. As we have so little time, we'll need to go by car."

The chauffeur brought the car to a halt in a narrow lane with two-storey houses on both sides. There were many more than Kate had imagined and they looked to be in good shape. It was more of a village than a hamlet. There were even two shops although they were boarded up. Eileen, Tania and Kate stepped out and joined Isla who was admiring the buildings. Lydia's car pulled to a stop behind theirs and the other members of the council tumbled out, wide-eyed.

"I don't think we'll have to build anything for the moment," Isla said as she strode towards the closest of the houses. "Do you have the key?"

"Beth gave me the key to one of the houses," Kate said. It was the former caretaker's. There she could access the keys to all the other houses. Unlocking the front door, they found a cute little house with a living room, a dining room and a kitchen on the ground floor and two bedrooms and a bathroom above.

Isla was particularly interested in the attic which would've been spacious were it not for the bric-a-broc that had accumulated there.

Turning to Kate she asked, "Could you send someone to check the other houses while we looked around the rest of the village? I want to know if they are the same."

Kate was put out by being given orders. Isla was clearly pursuing an idea but not sharing it. This wasn't how she imagined working together. She took Isla by the arm and led her some distance away, causing the woman to look at her in alarm. "Listen," Kate began. "You clearly have something in mind, but if we are to collaborate, you need to share those ideas with us. You can't just give us orders. We may look like children but we're used to running our own lives.

Isla stared at Kate as if she were an alien, her brow furrowed. Several times she opened her mouth to speak but then promptly shut it. "I..." she began. "I don't know what to say." During the long pause Kate kept quiet, wondering what was coming. "I'm sorry," she finally said, looking embarrassed. "I'm so used to treating young people as children..." She must have realised how odd her words were because she laughed nervously. "I mean people not yet responsible for themselves..."

"So what's your idea?" Kate asked, seeking to spare the woman further embarrassment, especially as the other girls were returning from their mission.

"If we use the attics as additional bedrooms," Isla said, "we should be able to accommodate everyone."

"True," Eileen said. "But there's more. These houses were built for families, but we don't live as a family. If we had a central canteen, we could do away with the kitchens and the dining rooms. And if we had meeting places and recreational rooms, we could use the ground floor for bedrooms. We might even install collective bathrooms."

"That's excellent," Isla exclaimed.

"Knowing the weather here," Suzanne added, "if we don't want the girls getting ill, we'd do well to have covered walkways between the houses and the communal centre."

"Indeed," Isla said, looking a little sheepish, an odd look on such a confident woman. "I hadn't thought things out that far."

"Have you found anywhere we could build this centre?" Kate asked the girls.

"There's a big barn with what looks like stables next to it," Tania said. "You could comfortably fit a hundred people in there."

For some odd reason, the barn and stables were in the middle of the village rather than on the outskirts. As they roamed the buildings, an animated discussion began about how best to convert the place to suit their needs. After five minutes and no sign of talk abating, Kate had to remind them they were out of time and needed to fetch the orphans. "If we don't, this discussion will have been pointless. And anyway, we ought to involve the girls in discussing their future home."

"I'll organise food, bed linen and blankets for the weekend," Isla said. "And I'll get a contractor to look at the water and electricity to make sure they are safe and functioning correctly."

Suzanne offered to help with the food and bed things. "We'll need firewood too," she said. "There's more snow on the way and it's going to freeze tonight." She returned to Lydia's house with Isla who needed to make some calls. Lydia drove Kate and the others to join the Lost Girls and travel to the orphanage.

When the coach bringing the choir halted, they could make out a policeman waiting on the pavement. It looked like the nuns had got wind of trouble. Two more coaches drove past and pulled up outside the building, only to be greeted by a questioning look. "I heard there was only to be one," the policeman called out.

"Dunno gov. We were told two," the driver said, leaning out the window to answer. He cut the engine, opened the door and stepped out.

A group of women sauntered up and one asked, "Is this where the concert is?"

The policeman stared at her baffled. "Concert? What concert?"

"The choir..." she began. It was at the moment the Lost Girls moved from their hiding place behind the third bus. Carrying lanterns, they marched in procession along the pavement intoning the opening notes of one of their most successful songs. Kate had borrowed the idea from Peter. He'd once described the solemn moment when the choir marched singing into the church at the beginning of a service.

"Them!" the woman exclaimed in raptures.

More and more people were milling around the two buses, vying for a good place to see the choir. There were soon so many gathered they blocked the entrance to the orphanage. The policeman tried to shoo them away but the audience paid no heed. When he raised his voice calling out, "You can't stay here," he was promptly silenced by the nearby spectators.

As the choir advanced, the growing crowd parted to let them through. There was a slight rise near the entrance to the orphanage and it was there the girls halted. They hung some of their lanterns on the orphanage fence. Others stood at their feet, casting a flickering light over their faces. Turning to the audience, with Clara conducting, they launched into the full version of the song.

The crowd, which by then overflowed down the street in both directions, applauded at the end just as a shout went up from the orphanage. Heads turned, expressions alarmed, to see girls bursting from the building and surging towards the gate, despite efforts of a nun to restrain them. The girls were a sorry sight, their clothes stained and torn, their faces pale, many bearing bruises and cuts, but their eyes were bright with hope.

Some members of the choir went to greet them, offering hugs and a helping hand, while the rest launched into a new song. A bitter wind had got up as the sun set. Blankets were brought from the bus and handed to shivering orphans. Suzanne and a couple of helpers dished out hot soup.

When it was time for a new song, Kate spoke up, addressing the girls. "You must be wondering what's going on..."

The policeman interrupted her. "Stop that! This is illegal. If you persist, I'll have to arrest you."

"Let her speak!" someone from the crowd shouted. "Let her!" chanted others.

"If you insist on disturbing the peace," the policemen blustered. "I'll call for reinforcements."

Kate nodded to Clara who launched the choir into a lullaby sung pianissimo. Moving closer to the policeman, against the soft musical backdrop, she asked, "Do you have children officer?"

He stared at her, his lips pressed in contained anger, refusing to answer.

"He does," someone called out. "I know him. He has four young kids."

"So you know what it's like to be worried about your children, about their welfare, their future," Kate continued. "Look at these children. Do they look like anyone cares for them? They are locked away and probably mistreated. They aren't even allowed to care for themselves."

The policeman sniggered. "They're just kids."

"We might be children," Kate replied, addressing the crowd, "but we're perfectly capable of caring for ourselves. Are we not proof of that?" Several people cheered. "We have confidence in these girls. They too will be able to take their future in their hands. With the help of a generous benefactor we can provide food and shelter as well as a chance for them to grow and develop to their full potential."

She turned to the orphans. "We..." she gestured to embrace the choir, "...know something about living in an orphanage. We managed to find a solution thanks to some kind and generous people. Now we've found a solution for you. We offer you a place that could be your home. Come with us and see for yourselves. Let us talk about how you'd like to live and see how many of your wishes can be accommodated. If some of you change your mind and want to return to the orphanage, we'll bring you back tomorrow."

Many of the children stood shocked, staring, clearly unsure

whether to trust her. Others, mainly the older children, cheered. It was Sandra that stepped forward to speak. "Hope is not something we are familiar with," she said. "We are wary of promises. Constant disappointment is a fact of our lives. But one thing I do know. When you came six months ago, you promised to return and fetch us. Today, you are keeping that promise. When I told you recently we would only come if all of us could come. That too you have honoured. I say we go with you now to see this place we might call 'home'."

"You can't do that," the nun said, struggling through the crowd. "We are the legal guardians of these children. You'd be abducting them."

"Not 'abducting'" Kate retorted, "but rather, 'conducting them to safety'. It is clear they're neither safe nor cared for here."

"What nonsense," the nun exclaimed. "We took them in when no one wanted them."

"You did indeed," Kate replied. "And you should be thanked for that. But clearly it was not enough. Just look at you. Chubby cheeks and not a bruise or a cut in sight. Now look at them. They look starving, each one walking proof of neglect if not mistreatment. By your failure to care for these girls, you forfeit any right to lord over them." Some chuckled at her choice of words.

"It's late and getting cold. We should take these children to their new home. But before we do, and by way of thanks to those who turned up this evening, we'll sing one last song. It's one I taught some girls from this orphanage when I visited them six months ago." Turning to the orphans, she added, "Join in if you can, if only to hum. Let us sing together. You too," she said to the crowd.

33.

Peter didn't need to peer round the door to know it was the headmistress speaking. "What on earth have you done to these poor girls?" she asked.

When Peter did get a peek, to his horror he saw the headmistress helping one of the twins up, the boy in disguise. Rubbing his head where Christina had hit him, the twin railed against Christina. "She set about us like a maniac," the twin exclaimed. "She hit me with a chair. I think she injected my sister with some drug." He began shaking his twin none too kindly, but the girl didn't respond.

That the twin's lies turned everything on its head made Peter furious. He was tempted to step out and challenge him, but he couldn't win against him and the headmistress, even with Sarah and Eloise at his side. They'd have to wait and free John and Christina when the headmistress had gone. To his horror, the twin picked up the syringe and began toying with it. Peter was afraid he might stab Christina.

"Put that down!" the headmistress barked.

What took place next happened so quickly Peter wasn't sure he'd seen it right. The twin sprang across the room and, grabbing the startled headmistress despite her piercing squeal, jabbed the needle in her wrist. There surely couldn't have been much fluid left. Yet the headmistress collapsed to the floor unconscious, probably more from fright than the sedative.

As the twin rounded on a terrified Christina, brandishing the syringe like a dagger, Peter stepped into view. "A curse on your two heads!" he shouted, saying the first thing that sprang to mind, his unconscious taking liberties with Shakespeare. The twin spun round to face him. "So you are a boy," Peter pursued, more out of curiosity than as an accusation. "Do the priests know?"

The twin snarled.

"Apparently not," Peter said conversationally. Out of the corner of his eye he saw Christina raising the remains of the chair to strike. It wouldn't work. The twin was far too quick. "How did you hoodwink them? I'm intrigued. As a boy who's dressed as a girl for a long time, I admire your skill. I'd never have guessed."

Peter wonder absently if the twin had found some way to stave off the onslaught of male hormones. If only he had the secret, he wouldn't be beset by gnawing fears that his voice would break or he'd wake up with a beard. Enough. This was hardly the moment. He took a step closer. It was an invitation. The twin responded by stepping closer and in so doing, moved away from Christina. "Maybe you can slip me some tips."

When the attack came, Peter dodged and shifted further from Christina. As the twin stalked after him, Peter turned and fled causing the twin to pursue only to trip and fall flat on his face, knocking himself senseless. Eloise and Sarah sprang to their feet, using the tripwire to tie the twin's hands behind his back.

Now what? Peter took a deep breath and glanced round the room. Christina had a hand under John's head and was stroking his hair. Eloise and Sarah were trussing up the second twin, delighting in pulling the knots as tight as possible. The headmistress lay abandoned, her arms outstretched, her legs folded under her. No one was in any hurry to care for her. Outside the hall was deserted, but classes would be out in no time and girls would flood the corridors.

They had to get away but they couldn't abandon the twins and the headmistress like that. The police would invariably blame John and Christina, if not Peter. But first he had to bring

John back. He knelt at the man's side and completed the healing, coaxing the headmaster back to consciousness.

Cracking open his eyes, John stared at him uncomprehending. "What the hell...?"

"We'll explain later," Peter said. "You need to get to the car. Christina will help. No one must see you. We'll be with you in a few minutes."

Once Christina and John had staggered off, Peter got the girls to drag the twins to the bed. He was unsure what story to suggest. Something that would speak for itself, condemning the three and making any lies they spun work against them. For all his efforts, no brilliant ideas sprang to mind.

One thing was sure, they couldn't leave the twins tied up. Using healing, he sent them into a deep sleep. Then he had the girls untie the two.

"We just tied 'em up," Sarah protested.

"If we leave them like this," Peter explained, "everyone will wonder who did it. We want people to believe something is cooking between them without interference from anybody else."

"You mean, like a lovers' tryst?" Eloise asked.

"For example," Peter replied, noncommittally. Of course the idea was the first he'd had. But he'd immediately dismissed it, not wanting to venture down such a distasteful avenue. Even if he were to lay all three on the bed and set them up as lovers, why on earth would they be in his room?

"What if they tried to commit suicide?" Sarah asked.

Peter shuddered. Seeing his reaction, the girl quickly added, "They don't have to succeed."

"Imagine the two girls lying on the bed having drunk a potion," Eloise took up the story. "The headmistress finds them. There's a note. She's to blame. There's a glass still half-full of poison. In utter distress, the headmistress downs the rest and collapses next to the bed."

"But we don't have any poison," Peter pointed out. "We don't even have a glass. Not to mention a note written by the twins."

"The note is easy enough," Eloise said. "We write it, then pour water over it so it is illegible."

"Not a glass," Sarah said, following her own train of thought as she gestured to the floor, "a syringe. We have plenty of them."

"But why here?" he asked, acutely aware that time was running out. "Why in my room?"

"Maybe they thought no one would look for them here," Eloise suggested.

Peter glanced at his watch, the one he'd recovered from Christina's place. Time was up. The schoolgirls would be there in minutes. If anyone saw them, the whole plan would be upended and they'd be the villains. Hurrying to the bedside, he turned the twins to face each other. Touching their unresponsive bodies was creepy and gave him an urge to wash his hands. Steeling himself, he wrapped their arms around each other as if in a last embrace. Using his sleeve as a glove, he picked up a vial from the floor and sprinkled the remaining liquid over the girls' hands and arms then laid the little bottle between the two. He added a syringe to the tableau.

"Give us a hand," he said, grabbing the headmistress's arm. Her skin was cold and moist and stained with the smudges of age. He struggled to swallow the bile that scorched his throat. "Let's drag her to the doorway. As if she were trying to escape."

Forcing open the woman's fingers, he placed a vial in her hand. In the other hand he lodged a syringe. The result looked contrived, but time was up. The bell for the end of classes was ringing.

He shot a last glance at the room, picking up the lengths of twine that had served to tie people up and, pocketing them, ushered the girls out. They dashed down the back corridor with Eloise limping as fast as she could behind. Once out the door they sprinted for the shelter of the trees, slipping and sliding on patches of snow and ice.

Peter halted when they reached the wood, waiting for Eloise to catch up. He let out a sigh, but his relief was short-lived. A shout went up behind them. "There! In the trees!" A glance over his shoulder revealed girls spilling from the residence by every door and even some windows, the running mass converging on the copse. At their head ran the twins. How was that possible? They shouldn't have been able to break free of sleep.

"Run!" he urged. They crashed through the wood and burst onto the lane. Judging from the shouts, the twins and their mob were close behind. The lane was bordered by high hedgerows in both directions. They were trapped.

He turned right, hoping they'd find a breach in the hedge. Luckily the lane twisted and turned offering some cover. Judging from the shouts, the mob was already in the lane and rushing after them. As he helped Eloise keep up, he connected to Christina. *We're in a mess again*, he sent.

In broken sentences, his breath coming hard, he explained where they were. *You'll come to a road soon.* Christina said. Peter knew from her thoughts she was already on her way. *We'll meet you there.*

Rounding a corner they stumbled on a wider lane where John's car was parked. The three scrambled in just as the mob caught up with them. Christina, who was driving, shoved the car into gear, but several stones hit the windscreen, one of them shattering it. She pulled on the brake and stormed out of the car to confront the girls.

"What's got into you?" she shouted, her hands on her hips. "People don't go about smashing car windows. It's madness. I know each one of you. None of you would ever do such a thing."

The girls took a step back contrite, dropping the pebbles they clutched in their hands. All, that is, except the twins who stepped forward making a show of weighing up the stones in their fists. Seeing them advance side by side so determined, Peter was afraid. They were capable of anything. John was no use. He lay sprawled on the passenger seat half unconscious. Only Peter could help. But how? He shifted to Christina's side.

Sneering, the twins advanced till they were less than ten feet away. "Get out of our way," the male twin snarled at Christina.

"We're not interested in you."

Sarah and Eloise scrambled from the car and hastened to flank Peter. "Don't let Tweedledum and Tweedledee intimidate you," Eloise challenged, pointing a defiant finger at the twins as she addressed the gathered girls. Peter had never heard her so determined. "They believe they can get away with murder, but you can bet you'll be in for trouble if you follow their lead."

"Shut your mouth," the male twin spat. "Nobody wants to listen to a nonentity like you."

"At least Eloise stood up for us girls," Sarah replied, her voice trembling with anger. "What did you ever do? Nothing. You were too busy fawning up to the headmistress."

Letting out a guttural war-cry, the boy flung himself at Sarah, only to be intercepted by Peter who caught him off balance and sent him sprawling across the road and into the hedge. A cry of triumph went up from the girls. In downing one of the twins, it was as if Peter had broken the hold the two had over their fellow pupils. The girls surged forward and would have set about the remaining twin had Christina not intervened.

"Restrain her only," she called out, an authority in her voice he'd rarely heard. "If you beat the living daylights out of her, you'll be no better than them."

Peter pulled the twine from his pocket and began attaching the hands of the boy behind his back with help from Sarah while Eloise and an enthusiastic gang of girls tied up the other twin. They had just begun to frog march the two back to Our Lady amid laughter and excited chatter when the school nurse burst onto the lane closely followed by the two policewomen who had carted the twins off earlier.

"What's going on here?" the nurse asked. "I found the headmistress out cold..."

"The girls have been wonderful," Christina said, glancing at the many faces turned in her direction. "They helped protect us from these two." She motioned to the twins. "I don't know what got into them, but they set about us with murderous intent."

"Murderous?" one of the policewomen queried, sounding

sceptical.

"They had stones," one of the girls called out.

"As if you didn't have stones too!" the girl twin muttered.

"Silence!" a policewoman barked. "Nobody asked your opinion."

"Look at that smashed windscreen," another girl added, ignoring the twin's accusation as she pointed to the car. "They did that."

The two policewomen stared bemused at the car halted in the middle of the lane its windscreen shattered, with John just visible, slumped in the passenger's seat. The last thing they needed were questions about why the car was there or how John came to be unconscious.

"What did they do to the headmistress?" Peter enquired, making a show of being worried. "Is she alright?" Better to divert attention and make sure blame was heaped on the twins.

"She's been taken to hospital," a policewoman explained. "Apparently these two..." she shot a disdainful look at the twins, "...injected her with something. We don't yet know what. There were several needle marks on her wrist." At the fearful gasps from some of the girls, the woman sought to reassure them. "Her life is not in danger."

"Okay," the other policewomen said. "Let's lock these two away." Turning to Christina, she added, "Do you want us to call a tow truck?"

"No. Thanks. It's not far. I'll drive slowly."

34.

"John's sleeping," Christina said in reply to Peter's worried look. Peter was seated at the kitchen table buttering bread for sandwiches. Sarah added pickles and Eloise ham or cheese. It was four-thirty and time for tea.

He would've liked to speak to Kate, but she was busy. That she had no time for him was upsetting. Apparently she was off saving more orphan girls. With his feelings of disappointment and hurt were stirrings of fear. So much was happening to the Lost Girls he couldn't keep up. Their brief conversation had left him feeling out of touch, afraid he might never catch up and end up excluded from the only real home he had.

"Let's hope they never get out again," Sarah said, placing the sandwiches on a plate and garnishing the pile with a flourish of parsley.

"So what are you girls going to do now?" Christina asked, pouring tea.

"I have no choice but to go back to Our Lady," Sarah said, sounding miserable.

"I don't know how you put up with it," Eloise exclaimed. "Anyone else would be out of there at the first opportunity. Those girls never stop bullying you."

"The other prefects hardly treat you any better," Sarah responded. "At least you have a family to return to. I have nowhere to go."

"If you knew my family, you wouldn't say that," Eloise said, sounding bitter. "There's not a single book in their flat. I'm not even sure they know how to read. That said, I don't want to return to Our Lady any more than you."

"Both of us love learning," Sarah said, "and there's so much to be learnt. Surely the best place for that is in school."

"You don't have to attend school to learn," Peter pointed out, picking up a second sandwich. "In fact, if you know what you want and you're with the right people, you can often learn more elsewhere. Very little of what I know about healing, for example, was learnt at school."

"So can we come with you?" Sarah asked, sounding like she'd been waiting for a chance to ask.

Her request was run through with desire and desperation. Peter was tempted to give in. "Sure you can." Sarah shot him a brilliant smile. "But I'm not going just yet."

"Why ever not?" Sarah exploded, slapping the flat of her palm against her forehead. "Are you mad? You have no reason to hang around."

Peter wanted nothing better than to return to Kate. He yearned to bounce ideas back and forth with her, to be cradled in her arms, to feel her warmth next to him as they lay in bed. He missed singing in the choir and his voice lessons with Viktor. He longed to be free of the constant worry about hormones, of the fear of reprisal from Heartless and the threat of the deadly twins.

Yet he couldn't leave. Not yet. He glanced at Christina, who smiled weakly in return. "On the contrary. I have every reason to delay. My parents have been forbidden to see me. My mother has been kicked out of her job. You girls have lost the very person who watched over you. And all because of me. I have to set that right before I can return home."

Christina smiled, no doubt pleased at being called his mother, but she objected all the same. Of course she would. It was so like her to think of his well-being first. "We can handle this," she insisted. "Not that I want you to go, on the contrary." She gave him one of those equivocal smiles that remind him how much she'd wanted to have a son. "But, for your safety and that of your friends," she glanced at Sarah and Eloise, "it would be better.”

When Peter continued to refuse she gave up, much to his relief, and said, “Eat. I’ll make some more tea.”

“That I have to stay doesn’t stop you two travelling to Luzern,” Peter said to Eloise and Sarah. “I’ll let Kate know you’re coming.”

“I’m not going to abandon you to face Heartless and the terrible two alone,” Sarah said, her expression fierce.

“Neither am I,” Eloise said with as much determination.

Their support was heart-warming and Peter thanked them. “Talking about support, we need to get more girls on our side.”

“Good luck with that,” Sarah shot back. “Nobody ever sided with me, apart from you two that is.”

“I’m not so sure,” Peter replied. “Your courage confronting the terrible two in the lane showed that many girls are willing to side with us if we give then a good reason.”

“A lot are unhappy,” Christina said, returning with more tea. “They’re dissatisfied with the teaching or how the school is run. Most dislike the prefects. They dislike the headmistress even more and find the discipline harsh and unjust. Some are homesick. Many lonely. If you could find a way to tender a helping hand, I’m sure many would side with you.”

“They might talk to you,” Eloise began, pointing her half-eaten sandwich at Christina. “You’re an adult and represent no threat. But few of them would be so forthright with us. They hide behind angry masks, alone or in packs, snarling at anyone who gets too close.”

Sarah nodded. “Exactly!”

“Oh dear!” Christina exclaimed feigning despair, although there was a hint of a smile at the corner of her mouth. She was well aware of the situation. Of course she was. “No wonder so many are unhappy. Surely there must be some way to get beyond those masks.”

Nobody had a ready answer.

“As it’s Friday, would you like to stay till Sunday?” Christina asked. “A rest would do you good. And there are plenty of books to read," she said to Eloise, who grinned back. "And I could teach you a recipe or two," she told Sarah who licked her lips. "As for you," she said to Peter, giving him a wistful smile, "it would be good to have you around."

A short stay at John and Christina's house was appealing. But the longer they stayed away the more difficult it would be to gain support from the girls. Taking such a liberty would surely be held against them. After all, the others had no prospect of a carefree weekend. Instead they were beset by the terrible twins and a half-crazed headmistress, not to mention a band of vengeful prefects back from an unpleasant stay in the infirmary.

"I really appreciate the offer," Peter said. "But we need to be at Our Lady if we are to win the girls over and help them face the trouble that's breaking."

Both Eloise and Sarah looked disappointed but Christina nodded. "You're right. It was selfish of me to try to keep you."

"Not at all," Peter responded. "You were just being your usual generous self. I appreciate that." He glanced at Sarah and Eloise who nodded, albeit without much enthusiasm. "I don't want to oblige you. After all, it is my battle not yours. If you want to stay, I'm sure Christina would be delighted. But I have to go."

"We're not going to abandon you," Sarah exclaimed, jutting her jaw forward in determination.

"And we're not going to let you have all the fun either," Eloise added with a twisted grin.

Christina chuckled. "You make a good team. I'll drive you back and while I'm there I'll have a word with the nurse. Having her on your side might prove useful."

Peter was sceptical. But Christina had a way with people. Maybe she could win her over.

"Talking of speaking to adults, don't bother with that Miss Batch," Sarah said.

"Who's that?" Christina asked.

"The new administrator," Eloise explained.

"Why shouldn't I talk to her?" Christina asked, perplexed.

"She'll never be on our side," Sarah replied. "She prowls the corridors in search of girls to punish."

"Why ever would she do that?" Christina sounded shocked. "An administrator is employed to do paperwork, not police the girls."

"You did more than paperwork," Eloise pointed out.

"You helped us girls," Sarah added.

"Well. Yes. I saw my job as a sort of matron who watches out for the well-being of the girls."

"Batch watches out alright," Eloise said, "but not for our well-being. To be honest, I have no idea what drives her."

"Talking about driving," Christina said, getting up from the table, "it's time. You've probably missed evening meal." She glanced at the remaining sandwiches. "Take these instead. But don't let anyone see you eating in your rooms."

Girls were milling in the corridors when they returned. The evening meal was just over and small groups were chatting before heading for their rooms. Some stared at Peter. Others were frankly hostile. Most just paid no attention.

"You're back," one girl said. "I didn't expect you to return."

Peter recognised her as Alexandra, the girl whose arm had been broken. "How's your arm?" he asked.

His enquiry startled her. "Fine," she said, moving a little closer and lowering her voice. "The nurse was surprised. She was convinced it was broken, but apparently not."

"I'm glad it's better," Peter said. "When you're left-handed, breaking your left arm is not much fun."

"How did you know I was left-handed?"

He knew because he'd seen it when healing her arm, but he couldn't tell her that. "Calculated guess."

"You came to see me," the girl announced. When Peter stared at her as if to say , 'How do you know?', she added, "the nurse told me."

"I heard you'd been bullied and I don't like to see people pushed around. So I came to see how you were."

"Thanks," the girl muttered, embarrassed. "Nobody else came."

"We did," Sarah said pointing to herself and Eloise.

Alexandra nodded her gratitude. "How's you arm?" she asked Sarah. "I saw that prefect brand you with cigarettes."

Peter had forgotten he'd also healed Sarah. With a shudder he remembered the burn marks on her skin. How could he have ever imagined winning over such a pack of vicious barbarians?

Grinning, Sarah rolled up her sleeve and showed off her unmarked arm. "Voilà!" she said with a flourish.

Peter glanced around. They were attracting too much attention. Several girls strained to see what was going on. He ushered his new friends, Alexandra included, into his room. "We'll be in for trouble," he whispered, "if you go on like that. People are watching."

"I'll fetch a broom," Eloise offered, seeing the mess on the floor. She left, pulling the door closed behind her.

Alexandra took hold of Sarah's arm and ran her finger over the faint marks, all that remained of the burns. "Did you do this?" she asked Peter, her words not an accusation but an expression of wonder and hopefulness mixed with disbelief.

"Yes. With help from Sarah and Eloise."

"He's teaching us," Sarah blurted out.

"It's not ..." Alexandra hesitated, sounding worried, "... it's not black magic, is it?"

Sarah laughed. "Good Lord, no! If it were, I'd have nothing to do with it. I'm petrified of such things. No. It's healing."

Peter was about to explain when Eloise burst into the room. "We've got company," she said, glancing over her shoulder. Sure enough, she was followed by Birgit and another prefect.

The two looked pale and out of sorts. "Holding secret meetings is against school rules." Birgit snapped.

Peter rose to confront them, unsure what to say. Sarah and Alexandra joined him on one side while Eloise flanked him on the other. Birgit looked from one to another a hint of doubt in her expression. "I'll give you all detention," she threatened.

"How are you feeling?" Peter asked. "You look a little better."

"My health is none of your business," Birgit shot back, visibly struggling not to appear disconcerted.

"Oh, but it is," Peter replied amiably. "If you are contagious, we'll all be in trouble. I'm surprised the nurse let you out."

The girl did look unsteady on her feet but when Peter reached out to stop her falling, she staggered back with a squeal. "Don't touch me!" There was genuine fear in her voice. "Last time you touched me I fell ill. It's you that should be locked in quarantine."

Sarah giggled. "Seriously? You're hilarious. Quarantine the healthy to protect the sick?"

That someone like Sarah should stand up to a prefect didn't sit well with Birgit, but she was in no state to defend her prerogatives. "You should lie down," Peter advised, his tone that of a worried sister. "We can talk more when you feel better." He was well aware his words only further underscored the girl's weakness. He was clearly in control.

Birgit abruptly clapped her hand over her mouth and bolted for the door, closely followed by the other prefect. Alexandra closed the door after them and, turning to Peter, she tapped her no-longer broken arm, saying, "You were about to explain how you did this."

35.

The air in the barn was surprisingly warm, given that it was snowing heavily outside. Kate removed the scarf from around her neck and wrapped it loosely about her waist. Hastily installed oil-fired heaters were scattered around the large hall, but most of the warmth came from the number of girls seated at row upon row of trestle tables set up in the middle. With all the girls they'd rescued from the orphanage and the Lost Girls who were cooking or waiting on the tables, there were over seventy present.

The constant chatter was like that of starlings about to migrate except these little birds had just arrived. And just like migrating birds, small groups rose and moved about before settling again. She wondered if migrating birds made as much noise at their destination. She'd never noticed their arrival, so maybe not.

"I was surprised they didn't send the police," Eileen said, leaning close to be heard.

Kate thought of all the spectators who'd listened to the choir. There'd been far more than expected and the donations had been generous. "With all those people, they could hardly kick up a fuss. No. They'll wait, hoping we'll get complacent."

"Well I doubt they'll move tonight with all the snow," Eileen replied, glancing out one of the few windows not obscured by makeshift curtains. "We made it just in time. We must be completely cut off."

"All the same, we should take precautions. Just in case,"

Kate said. "Could you organise that?"

Eileen's expression was sceptical but she nodded and got to her feet, taking Tania with her.

Kate looked around for Suzanne. The girl was engrossed in animated conversation with a group of new girls across the hall. Kate managed to catch her eye and beckoned. Once Suzanne was seated next to her, Kate lent close and said in her ear, "We should check if any new girls need medical attention."

"I've already started," Suzanne replied with a grin, "although I've tried to be discreet."

"Good." Kate was pleased the girl saw what had to be done and got on with it. "So, how are they?"

"Cuts and bruises mainly, a blight of infected sores but above all malnutrition. Most haven't eaten properly in months."

"Any contagious diseases?"

"None so far. The worst I found was a girl who'd been raped." She faltered at the word, her expression pained. "I healed the physical damage, but the mind...."

"We'll need to keep an eye on her. How many still need to be screened?"

Suzanne glanced around the room. "About half."

"Would you like help?"

"Nah. I can manage. I'm getting good at it."

Kate chuckled. "Who were those girls?"

"Friends of Sandra. They were in that class you got to sing all those months ago. They want to join the choir, so I introduced them to Clara."

Serious discussion was hard in the noise so they fell silent and watched the girls eating and chatting. By the time desert was over, it was getting late and a number of the youngsters were bleary eyed. Kate got to her feet and, clambering onto a small platform, raised a hand for silence. "It's snowing hard so we're stuck here whether we like it or not. Luckily we planned to sleep in this building till the houses in the village are ready and we have enough supplies for a couple of weeks. Mattresses, sheets and duvets are available for all of you." She pointed to the piles along a wall.

"I suggest you sleep in small groups with an older girl, just in case there's any trouble. We'll be handing out whistles to those girls." The whistles had been Eileen's idea. They had a stock they'd been planing to use in a performance.

"Remember, only use them in an emergency. There are toilets in this building so nobody need go out, which is good because we plan to lock the doors to discourage any visitors crazy enough to brave the snow."

A ripple of fear shot through the hall and several girls looked furtively at doors and windows. Living as they had under constant threat, potential danger, however unlikely, sparked old reflexes.

"Weather permitting," Kate continued, "we'll visit the village tomorrow and talk about how to organise life here. In the mean time, I wish you all sweet dreams and a very good night."

"You too," several girls called out.

It took some time to drag out mattresses and settle girls in bed, but finally the bustle subsided and they were able to lower the lights. Taking Eileen, Suzanne and Tania with her, Kate checked the doors and windows and set powerful wards on each. *Anyone attempting to break in will be overcome by intense nausea and feel weak and helpless*, she explained mind-to-mind to those accompanying her.

What about someone going out? Suzanne asked.

They'll experience nothing. But when they come back the ward will kick in.

That's awkward, Suzanne said.

It's why I told people not to go out. She went on to explain how to set a ward and had them try. Working such magic turned out to be more difficult for the girls than Kate had anticipated. While all had managed to talk mind-to-mind and sense poison, only Suzanne was able to set wards, much to the irritation of Tania and the disappointment of Eileen. Maybe magic was not given to everybody. Certainly in her world only a few were trained.

When Kate finally found a free mattress and lay down it was well into the night. All the girls were asleep. Silence had fallen, a thick blanket of snow masking all sound. Snow had been extremely rare in her world, so the texture of silence that accompanied heavy snow was new. Rather like wading through snow, the silence resisted movement. Her meditation master had taught her the value of silence, but never had she had such tangible proof that there was so much more to silence than the absence of sound.

Replete in that awareness, she closed her eyes and was about to drift off when a faint rattling at one of the windows startled her. Had she imagined it? Keeping as still as possible, she strained to hear. All was quiet. Then the sound came again, more insistent this time. Someone was out there and whoever it was was trying to get in. Had one of the girls inadvertently wandered out? Surely not. They'd need a key and she and Eileen had them all.

The squeak of a rusty door handle being turned on the other side of the hall had Kate standing, readying to fight. There were several of them. A third noise from another door had her perplexed. Whoever was trying doors and windows was making no secret of it. It was almost as if they wanted to be heard. As if they wanted to scare the girls. And it worked. She was terrified. Thank heavens none of the girls had woken. But they would. And there'd be a panic.

It was as if their assailants knew there were wards and deliberately didn't force their way in. That thought had Kate more scared than the presence of people at the doors. *Eileen,* she called out.

Yes. I know. I heard, was Eileen's answer. She sounded scared, but there was also grim determination. *What do we do?*

For the moment they're only trying to frighten us.

They're succeeding. If they wake the girls, we'll never be able to put a lid on the panic.

Eileen was right. If the intent was to have the girls running wild with terror, it would work. The orphans might've been worn down by beatings and poor food, but they were strongly fearful and men, she was sure it was men, trying to get at them would unleash a force that no doors could hold in. She had visions of half-dressed girls spilling out by every entrance, stumbling into deep snow drifts only to be picked off by waiting thugs.

I'm going to stem the panic before it starts, Kate sent. It was a risk but she could see no other way.

How? Eileen sounded alarmed.

I'll send all the girls except the council into a deep sleep.

Kate heard Eileen's in-taken breath from across the hall. *Are you sure?*

Yes. Whoever is outside can't get in. Even if they do they'll fall ill. And I could always wake the girls if necessary. She drew in a deep breath. *Give me a moment.*

Kate closed her eyes and concentrated. Focusing on all the girls except council members and Sandra was a strain. She'd never done anything so ambitious. It made her head pound. Several times her attention wandered as noises at the windows distracted her. She needed to be particularly careful. She didn't want the sleep so deep she couldn't wake them in an emergency. Finally she opted for a special word, a bit like a post-hypnotic command. Once uttered, all would awake immediately. *Done,* she finally announced.

It's a shame we can't capture one... to interrogate him, Eileen said.

I'm sure that can be arranged. But first let's wake Tania and the others. Wake Sandra too.

They crept from mattress to mattress, silencing any cries of alarm as the girls were awoken. Tania was the worst. Kate had to clamp a hand over the girl's mouth to cut off cries of indignation. The girl tried to bite Kate's hand and struggled to get free till Kate shouted in her head, *Keep still you ass. You'll get us all killed!* Even then the girl continued to struggle till Kate threatened to send her to sleep to silence her.

Kate led them to the darkest corner where they squatted behind a pile of mattresses, all eyes fixed on her. She explained the situation. *To avoid panic,* she went on, *I've put the girls in a deep sleep...*

So what are we going to do? Sandra asked.

Nothing, Kate replied, *provided they don't try to break in.*

And if they do? Tania asked, emerging from her sulk.

The wards should take care of them.

And if they find some other way in? Tania persisted. It was as if she were spoiling for a fight.

We could try talking into their minds, Suzanne suggested. *That might spook them enough to have them run.*

You remember that African chant? Clara asked.

The one that's like the invocation of a spell? Christine asked.

Exactly, Clara replied. *I reckon that would scare the hide off them.*

Good idea, Kate said, chuckling at the thought.

And if that doesn't work? Tania persisted.

Then you'll defend us, Claudia shot back, clearly annoyed at Tania's insistance.

Tania's question was reasonable. But Kate didn't know how to respond. Clearly they wouldn't stand a chance if it came to a fight.

Can't we send for help? Sandra asked. *Couldn't you talk mind-to-mind to those people in the big house up the road?*

She'd never spoken to Lydia or Klaus that way and, despite the desperate circumstances, she preferred not to reveal the fact to them. Only one adult in Lucern knew of that ability, Viktor. Maybe he could alert the others. *I can't contact them,* Kate said, *but there is one other person I can try. Give me a moment.*

Viktor, Kate called out.

Peter? A drowsy voice replied.

No. It's Kate. Sorry to wake you but we have an emergency. She explained and asked him to contact Lydia. He promised to do so. Her conversation was interrupted by a pane of glass shattering. *Got to go,* Kate told Viktor. *They're breaking in.*

Eileen thrusted a broom into Kate's hands, one of those

old-fashioned ones witches used to ride. All the girls had one. Flanked by Eileen and Tania, they crept closer to the broken window. Impatience must have driven whoever was outside to break the glass, but frustration hadn't completely overruled caution. No one climbed in.

The girls waited unmoving, pressed against the wall next to the broken window, trembling from cold and fright. *Wait till they try to climb through,* Kate ordered. It was a long wait. Ten minutes must have gone by before a cautious foot ventured through the opening followed by a leg. Kate resisted the temptation to strike. She wanted the person caught inside. The moment the hips appeared and the feet touched the ground, Kate brought the handle of her broom up with all her force on the man's groin.

An ear-splitting scream shattered the silence, causing several of the sleepers to stir, but no one awoke. Outside, all efforts to scare them halted. The youth, he was hardly an adult, crumpled to the floor, writhing in pain. Kate dealt him a second blow, to the head this time, and he went still.

Hauling him to one side, hidden from anyone outside, Kate checked she hadn't killed him. He had several injuries, but his life was in no danger. *Can you tie him up?* Kate asked. Eileen produced a ball of twine from her pocket and she and Tania knotted the youth's wrists and ankles together.

"Jörg?" a male voice hissed at the broken window. "You all right?"

The girls waited out of sight with bated breath, their brooms at the ready.

More agile than his colleague the second youth sprang through the window and confronted Tania who clumsily tried to hit him with the broom. He ripped the handle from her hands and sent her flying. Armed with Tania's broom he turned to face the other girls, a grimace on his face. Presumably the ward was having its effect but he was trying to ignore it.

Kate stepped forward, driving up with her broom to parry a blow aimed at her head. She swung out with one foot and knocked the legs from beneath the youth who fell hard amongst the shards. He rolled over and sprang up, ignoring the blood dripping from his lacerated hands. He thrust forward with the broom narrowly missing Kate who side-stepped. Turning, she brought her broom down on his outstretched arms producing an ominous cracking sound. It was not his arms as she'd hoped, but the broom handle that shattered leaving Kate unarmed.

A grin of triumph spread across the youth's face as he raised the broom to strike again. It was at that moment the chanting began, not out loud but in their heads. The youth's free hand flew to his ears as if trying to drive away a hoard of flies. To no effect. The girls chanted on. In his moment of distraction, Kate darted in and kicked him in the groin before stepping out of reach.

Eileen tossed her a broom as the youth bent over in pain. Kate spun round him and swiped as hard as she could behind his knees causing him to collapse with a grunt to the floor. Sandra finished him off, smashing him over the head with her broom. Kate gave her the thumbs up as the youth sank to the ground, unmoving, blood pooling around his hands. Two down. How many more to go?

36.

A resounding crash echoed across the hall as a side door flew off its hinges letting in a flurry of snow and a rush of bitterly cold air closely followed by four youths. From scaring, they'd escalated to full-out attack. Luckily no sleepers had chosen to lie nearby as no amount of plugging could curb the draught.

Stay out of sight and keep chanting, Kate ordered. Taking Eileen and Tania with her, she dashed round the hall, keeping to the deepest shadows. The youths halted, apparently unnerved by the lack of resistance. Their heads swung this way and that in search of who ever had attacked their buddies. A couple held hands over their ears in a vain attempt to shut out the chant.

The move Kate had in mind was a desperate gambit, but they could never fight four burly youths and win. *Stand by me, your broom held handle up.* Kate showed them what she meant. *I plan to scare them. For that, we need to look absolutely sure.* Kate stepped forward, head held high, her expression determined. Eileen and Tania mirrored her.

Speaking mind-to-mind, she asked, *Do you know what happens to boys who mess with witches?*

I've heard their willies shrink, Tania replied, as if the question were addressed to her. *Some even say they shrivel up and fall off.*

Kate was disgusted at Tania's words and furious at her for butting in and possibly wrecking everything.

Three youths took a step back in horror but one held firm, the biggest. He was clearly the one to beat. "Don't talk nonsense little girl," he said, his tone scornful.

Kate kept a watchful eye on him while she spoke directly to the three edging away, *Don't let wild fantasies scare you. We're looking forward to getting to know you.* The moment she spoke, she realised that, in the light of Tania's taunt, her words could be misinterpreted. And they were. One of the youths turned and ran, a stifled scream on his lips, his hand clutching his groin. The other two looked at each other in horror then turned and ran.

Abandoned by his gang, the leader stood his ground. He was a tough number, a victim of violence himself. A scar snaked across his cheek and his nose was broken. His clothes, however, were expensive and fit well. The only odd note was a roughly hewed pendant dangling round his neck.

Come join us, Kate called to the girls who'd stayed back, *but keep chanting. Bring your brooms.*

The youth planted his feet in a fighting stance and crossed his arms over his chest, his eyes shifting from one to another, sizing them up. The chanting must be getting to him. He wouldn't hold out long before he attacked.

Interesting pendant, Kate said conversationally, seeking to gain time. *Looks like something a witch would make. So you know about witches.*

The youth scowled. He was about to reply when Sandra and the others arrived, forming a line facing him, each with their brooms at the ready.

Odds not in your favour? Kate taunted.

Defiance was still winning out over fear as the youth thrust forward his chin and glared at the girls. That he didn't fix her had her realising he didn't know who was talking. *Spread out and form a wide circle,* Kate told the girls. *Take it easy. No rushed movements. No heroics. Keep up the chant. Hammer it into his skull.*

Kate was about to speak when Tania beat her to it. *We weren't joking about your willies,* the girl said, unable to suppress a mad giggle. *We roast them, you know. They are a real delicacy. Unfortunately donors are never quite the same afterwards. But you look like the generous sort. I'm sure you'll...*

Tania! Shut up! Kate interrupted, speaking solely to the girl. *What're you playing at? This is not a game. We have to live with boys and men.* She thought of Peter. *You can't just threaten to take away their most treasured possession.* When she felt Tania readying to contradict her she said, *Not another word!*

The youth's face had blanched and he made a move as if he were about to force his way through the cordon formed around him.

I wouldn't do that, Kate said, hurrying to stop Tania causing any more damage. *Don't count on that pendant to protect you.*

The youth abruptly turned and slammed into Claudia sending her flying before dashing for the door. Sandra, who'd been standing next to Claudia raised her broom like a javelin and hurled it after him, letting out a triumphant battle cry. The broom shot between his legs and with an ominous crack he fell to the ground writhing in pain. Both Tania and Eileen dashed to finish him off. Kate left them to it while she knelt by Claudia, laying a hand on the girl's shoulder. The damage was not serious. A sprained ankle, bruised knees and cuts on her hands. Setting things right took no time.

Looking up, she saw Tania in a fury braining the youth with her broom. *For God sake, Tania, what's got into you. Stop that immediately. This is not about revenge.* Reluctantly the girl ceased, but not before giving him a parting kick in the groin. Not for the first time, Kate wondered if there was something seriously wrong with Tania. Eileen pulled the ball of twine from her pocket and lashed the youth's hands behind his back, fixing him to one of the pillars supporting the ceiling.

Is that all of them? Sandra asked, picking up her broom which had broken in half.

Dunno, Kate replied. *Six so far. With their racket I thought there were more.*

A faint crackling like paper being crinkled came from the back of the barn. It was not over. Kate sprinted across the hall dodging treacherous objects scattered haphazardly under foot.

She was closely followed by the others, some of whom were not so lucky and stumbled in the dark. It was a wonder none broke a leg. That the sleepers didn't awake was another miracle. The nearer Kate got, the greater her dread. A faint smell of burning confirmed her fears. The idiots were trying to set fire to the barn. *Buckets*, she barked. *And snow shovels*.

On it, Eileen shot back, roping in several girls to help.

Reaching the wall, Kate could feel the intense heat although the flames had not yet broken through. The fire must have started just the other side. Shoving open a nearby door she quickly removed the ward and stepped cautiously out. There were tracks everywhere visible in the moonlight, but no sign of the youths. They'd scarpered. From the smell, they'd used petrol.

Grabbing a large flat shovel Eileen handed her, Kate tossed shovelfuls of snow onto the flames. The others helped. Within minutes, her hands and feet were bitterly cold, but her face was scorched by the flames. At first their efforts proved futile. Flames licked up the wall, driven by a sharp wind. It was more the petrol than the wood that was burning. Then the wind abruptly dropped and it began to snow heavily. Within minutes the flames abated and finally only a smouldering, charred wall remained.

Retreating inside, they locked the door and huddled together in an attempt to get warm. During the short stay outside the cold had cut so deep, Kate had the impression she'd never get warm again. Her fingers and toes were the worst. They stung with cold, almost as if they were burning. Reaching inside, she eased the blood circulation and calmed the nerve endings till the stinging ceased. Then she showed the others how to alleviate the pain.

Claudia suggested hot chocolate as a nightcap, but a glance out the window revealed a sky tinged with reds and oranges. The snow had ceased, giving way to the first hints of dawn. *Breakfast, then,* Claudia said heading for the improvised kitchen area. Several girls followed.

Kate, Eileen, Tania and Sandra went to check on their three

captives. *You going to heal them?* Eileen asked as they crossed the barn.

Whatever for? Tania asked, indignant.

I'll ensure their injuries are not life-threatening, Kate replied. *But otherwise letting them suffer a while might serve as a lesson. We can always heal them before they leave so they can't blame us.*

The first two youths were awake. The moment they saw the girls they launched into a chorus of complaints. "I should be taken to hospital," one insisted.

"Can I kick him?" Tania asked, a malicious grin on her lips. At least she did ask.

"Tempting," Kate replied. "Acting like a snivelling vermin does invite violence. But we don't want to sink to their level." Turning to the two youths, she added, "You tried to scare defenceless girls. You planned to wreak havoc and maybe worse. And if that wasn't enough, your buddies tried to set fire to the place."

The two looked horrified.

"Count yourselves lucky we managed to put out the blaze. Seems like your friends were ready to abandon you to the flames. I wonder what the punishment for mass murder is."

"They'd probably be awarded a medal," Tania said. "After all, it was only girls. And orphans at that."

She might be right, but Kate wondered yet again where the bitterness came from. Surely the girl had not always been like that. "Let's move them to the stalls," Kate suggested. "We don't want their hate-filled faces frightening the girls when they awake."

The girls dragged the youths to the stalls where they lashed the two in separate pens. Before leaving to fetch the third youth, Kate removed the pendants from round their necks, making sure not to touch the metal.

"Do you know what these are for?" she asked. Both youths stared back, tight-lipped. Placing a casual hand on one youth's shoulder, she eased the sphincter on his bladder causing him to squirm as he wet himself. "You were going to tell me what these were for," she said brandishing the pendants. When no answer came she stretched a hand towards the second youth who blurted out, "They was to protect us if ever you lot used witchcraft."

"And who made them?"

"Dunno. We got given them just before we came."

"And who gave you them?"

"The geezer wot organised everything."

The other youth, the one who'd wet himself, strained desperately at the twine trying to get free. "Shut your mouth," he hissed, terrified.

"You realise I can easily get the information without you talking. It's just you might not be quite the same afterwards." She let the threat hang in the air. It wasn't true, of course. No damage would come of it. Not unless she was very heavy-handed.

"We was recruited by some bloke from the church. Said we were to do a good deed. To scare the..." he hesitated over the word, "...out of you."

"And did this man say you were to set fire to us?"

The youth shook his head in denial although guilt was etched on his features.

Let's go fetch the other one, Kate said to the girls and turned to go.

"What's gonna happen to us?" the youth asked, sounding scared.

"We haven't decided yet," Kate replied over her shoulder. "That depends partly on you."

The leader was slumped in a heap where they'd left him. Kate approached gingerly, fearful of some subterfuge, but he was unconscious. Both his legs were broken. His mind must have fled the pain, taking refuge in a coma. If they were to drag him they'd make his condition worse. For all their ill intent, Kate refused to deliberately handicap someone for life.

"We can't move him like this. I'm going to heal him," Kate said. "Suzanne will you help me?"

"Why waste your time?" Tania interjected. "Were they not ready to rape us if not kill us?"

"I'm a healer, not an executioner," Kate said with force. "If we start harming our enemies we'll end up a band of thugs like them."

Tania burst into tears and stomped away. "Could you talk to her, Christine?"

As Christine hurried after Tania, Kate knelt by the youth and Suzanne joined her. "We can't straighten his bones with him tied to that pillar. I'll put him in a deep sleep then you can untie him." The moment the youth was laid out, Kate set about healing him. With Suzanne's help they did a thorough job, even remedying other problems the youth had.

Suzanne was about to withdraw when Kate stopped her. *I want to understand why they did this and who sent them.*

But he's unconscious, Suzanne objected.

That makes it easier, Kate replied. *What I am about to show you goes with a heavy responsibility. Only use it sparingly and never for your own personal curiosity.* She felt a mix of anticipation and trepidation from the girl. *We're going to read his memories.*

37.

It's like skimming through a book, Kate said. *I'll show you.* She flipped back till the youth was outside the barn. Several groups peeled off and, wading through deep snow, headed silently for different places around the barn. *Of course, you only see what the person saw,* she told Suzanne. *If the person was distracted, the memories might be incomplete.* The youth's attention turned to the three who remained with him. It was those that had fled earlier. 'Where's your pendant,' he asked a youth who reluctantly pulled it from his pocket holding it at arm's length as if might bite. 'Idiot! Put it on. You heard what the Priest said.'

Kate halted the memories leaving him suspended mid-sentence. How odd. A priest gave them those pendants. *I thought the church was against witchcraft.*

Publicly at least, Suzanne replied.

Kate returned to the memories and scrolled back to the moment the youths tumbled out of a van. She recognised the spot. It was on the main road above the village more than a kilometre away, a long trek in deep snow. She shifted backwards and forwards hoping to get a sight of the driver, but the youth was worried he'd get stuck in the snow and never looked at the man.

Winding back even further she was rewarded by a scene where a priest in a dingy cloister was handing out pendants and issuing last minute instructions. 'Scare them as much as you want,' the man of cloth said, his grin making him look like a crazed troll. 'And when you've finished having fun, torch the place. We don't want any witnesses.' She felt the youth's pulse beat faster at being let loose on a pack of helpless girls in an isolated place, although he wasn't so eager about burning them.

May I? Suzanne asked. When Kate nodded mentally, she shifted back to the memory of the priest briefing the youths. *I recognise him,* Suzanne said. *He's one of the bishop's staff. He came to the orphanage often. A shifty bloke. When he looks at you it's as if he's undressing you. Girls tell bad stories about him.*

Do you remember his name?

Suzanne struggled, but the name wouldn't come. *Maybe Sandra remembers. She must have seen him often.*

Meanwhile Kate moved even further through the memories trying to find out about the youth. His name was Fritz. His parents were well-off, which explained his well-tailored garb. His father was a big-wig in a large pharmaceutical company and his mother was active in foundations linked to the church. Fritz had a religious up-bringing and his schoolwork was initially promising, but he rebelled in his early teens and had trouble with the police, brawling in public places, running a protection racket, threatening younger children. Only his father's status and money kept him out of borstal.

Father Jakob, Suzanne burst out, startling Kate who was engrossed in rifling through Fritz's memories. *That's who it was. Smarmy bugger. Ought to be in jail.*

Good, Kate replied, letting go of Fritz's memories. Emerging from her trance-like state, she saw Tania fixing her with an accusatory stare.

"That took an awful long time," she complained.

As Tania's constant suspicion was getting on her nerves, Kate didn't bother to answer. In her place, Suzanne replied. "We went through his memories. That takes time."

"And what was so interesting?" Tania asked.

"We'll tell everyone over breakfast," Kate said, turning back to Fritz. "Now let's get this lump tied up in the stalls."

Finding breakfast nearly ready, Kate said the magic word. The girls stretched and yawned, unaware that anything had happened, although one or two looked questioningly at the blankets nailed over a broken window or the smashed door held in place by planks.

"What's that smell of burning?" one girl asked.

"I hope it's not breakfast," another retorted.

"Sit down cheeky monkey," Sandra chided, "and you'll see how good a real breakfast is." She and the members of the council carried in the food and silence fell as the girls set about eating.

It was at that moment the main door burst open and Viktor hurried in flanked by Lydia, Klaus, Regina and Heinz. "Are you all right?" he exclaimed.

"Yes," Kate replied, getting up wearily. "You're just in time for breakfast. Do take a seat. I was about to explain what happened last night."

Once the newcomers were settled and served, Kate put down her tea, stood and turned to face the assembled group. "This night, unbeknown to most of you, we had an adventure." She didn't want to frighten the girls. Some were very young. "Long after you'd gone to sleep we had visitors who tried to force their way in but we sent them packing."

"How come we heard nothing?" a girl asked.

"I imagine you were so tired after the excitement of coming here and the party yesterday evening."

"Do we know who they were?" the same little girl asked.

"Yes," Kate replied. "But more about that later. Take your time, enjoy your meal. The snow has stopped. Maybe we'll be able to visit the village later. In the meantime, we need to talk to our guests."

Turning to the adults, she thanked them for coming. "I imagine it wasn't easy," she said, taking a welcome sip of warm tea. She felt so tired she could hardly keep her eyes open.

"You're not kidding," Viktor said. "The telephone lines were down and by the time we managed to reach Klaus and

Lydia's place it was almost dawn."

"Then there was waist-deep snow all the way here," Klaus added. "The snow plough wasn't working and we didn't have enough snow shoes for everyone."

"But I see you managed to deal with your attackers on your own," Regina said, then, lowering her voice, added, "I imagine there's a lot more to your story than you told the girls."

Kate nodded.

"You look exhausted," Lydia said. "Did you get any sleep?"

Kate shook her head. "If you've finished breakfast, let's go through into the stalls before I fall asleep. We have something to show you."

Kate opened the door to the stalls and, having peered in to check the three youths were still tied up, ushered the adults inside. Eileen, Suzanne and Sandra had come with her. Tania had been eager to come too, but Kate put her in charge of making sure the breakfast was cleared away properly, hoping she wouldn't make a mess of it.

Neither Lydia nor Klaus knew the youths but the others clearly did. Pointing to Fritz, who was now awake and would no doubt have been shouting abuse but for the gag, Regina asked, "What's he doing here?" Her tone made it clear he filled her with revulsion.

"Fritz and his merry colleagues broke into the barn during the night and would have attacked us, but we scared most of them away. These three we captured. The others tried to set fire to the building before they fled. Luckily the wood seems to have been treated against fire and heavy snow helped dowse the flames before too much damage was done."

"That's terrible," Lydia exclaimed. "Were any of you hurt?"

"Only minor cuts and bruises," Suzanne said. "All tended to."

"Do you know who's behind this?" Regina asked.

"Let's talk about this elsewhere," Kate said, glancing at Fritz who'd given up on his tantrum and was listening intently. She led them to a small office on the far side of the stalls. "We know who sent them," Kate continued, "a certain Father Jakob."

Heinz whistled between his teeth. Regina looked grim.

"I gather that's not good news," Kate said looking from one to the other.

Regina nodded. "He's been implicated in several scandals including suspected abuse of young girls, but he always managed to wriggle out with the help of the Bishop. Many people consider him to be the church's secret strong-arm man."

"He's a really nasty specimen," Sandra said, her lips pinched in disgust. "I saw him at work in the orphanage. I'm sure there are plenty of girls here who could testify against him."

"Good," Regina said. "We might be able to use that. It would also explain why he wanted to get rid of you girls."

Sandra looked doubtful. "I'm not sure the word of us girls would carry much weight against a man of the church," she said, her tone bitter. "We often complained to the nuns, but they did nothing."

"Apparently Fritz was no angel either," Kate said.

"True," Regina said. "His father has a lot of influence thanks to his company and him being a good friend of the Bishop. His son has been charged with many a crime, but he always gets off."

"So what are you going to do with them?" Lydia asked.

It was the one question Kate had been avoiding. "I'm not sure," she answered.

"It seems to me we're gathering a convincing collection of evidence," Regina said.

"For an act of accusation," Viktor said.

"An illustrated guide to the darker side of the church," Heinz said. "With photographic evidence and first hand witness statements, like we did for the orphanage."

"But will anyone believe us?" Eileen asked. "Surely they'll brush it aside, claiming we made it up out of some twisted desire for revenge."

"Not if we trap them," Sandra suggested. "That Father Jacob can barely control himself when he's around a young girl.

He doesn't exactly dribble, but I swear he trembles. Maybe we could lure him into revealing who he really is."

"That sounds complicated and dangerous," Lydia said.

"It might be worth exploring," Viktor said.

"Maybe we could do something with Jo's car," Eileen mused.

"Like some accusatory work of art," Viktor said. "Especially if we could get hold of the Bishop's damaged car and re-enact the aftermath of the accident."

Kate could feel the excitement bubbling over but no one answered the question: what to do with the youths? She wondered what damage it would do if they released them. Surely there was no way the church could twist this late night visit of a group of youths to an isolated encampment of girls in their favour. Then she remembered the veiled accusations about the girls running a brothel in the wilds.

"Your ideas are stimulating," Kate said. "But they don't settle our immediate concern. What do we do with those three?" She jerked a thumb in the direction of the stalls. "We can't keep them prisoner for ever. Either we let them go or we hand them over to the police."

"I wouldn't count on the police," Viktor said. "Look what happened when Peter was abducted."

"We'll end up being blamed," Sandra said. She was right of course. There was a clear hierarchy of credibility that had nothing to do with blame. Experts before lay people, rich before poor, men before women, adults before children, legitimate children before orphans, boys before girls. The whole situation seemed hopeless.

"I say we question them and let them go," Regina said.

"I partly agree," Kate said. "No decision is the right one. Whatever we do will come back and bite us. So let's question them then turn them over to the police. It's more or less what people will expect."

What she didn't say was she intended to make sure they had no tell-tale marks to justify claims of mistreatment. Of course that wouldn't stop them hurting themselves and blaming the girls. She also planned to wipe certain memories to curtail accusations of witchcraft. They'd gone overboard in their efforts to scare the youths. Not to mention Tania's excesses.

38.

Peter brought his explanation to a close and bit into the last sandwich. He'd only had that one because he'd threatened not to explain any more if they didn't set one aside for him.

"That's extraordinary!" Alexandria exclaimed. "I have so many questions. Is it easy? Can anyone do it? Can you teach me?"

"What I find extraordinary," Sarah said, leaving Peter no time to answer, "is that it requires none of that book-learning that doctors have to do. I always thought learning was about books. Even when it's a teacher teaching, she's doing so from a book."

"Books really are important," Eloise interrupted. "I love reading. There's so much to learn from them. Just think of all those worlds, real or imaginary, they give access to."

"True, but what I was going to say was that Peter's healing requires no books. Books even get in the way. Just look at doctors. All that book-learning leaves them out of touch with the body, making healing all the more difficult."

"So will you teach me?" Alexandria asked.

How was he supposed to keep healing a secret when so many clamoured to be taught? "Do you know why this form of healing has to be a secret?" he asked.

Alexandria looked surprised if not worried. "No," she muttered. You'd have thought Peter was a teacher who'd caught with her homework undone.

"It's because..." He didn't get any further because the door burst open and the headmistress barged in.

Bearing down on Eloise, she demanded, "What's going on?" Apparently Eloise still had some grain of authority, despite having been dismissed as a prefect. Intimidated, the girl was at a loss for words. "Dimwit!" Heartless exclaimed. "Why ever did we chose you as a prefect?"

"Because she has the interests of the girls at heart," Peter replied.

"Trust you to get it all wrong! On the contrary. That's why she's so bad. Prefects are not supposed to be interested in girls' well-being." She shook her head, disgusted, while one hand insistently massaged her belly. "God knows why I bother."

"Maybe because you are not your usual self," Peter ventured.

She spun round to face him, shooting him an appraising look. He kept his expression blank causing her face to turn sour.

"Get back to your rooms," she ordered. A look of consternation flickered across her face when no one moved.

"Is it wise to be up and about?" Peter asked. "You might have a relapse."

Heartless took a step back, although she quickly reined in her fear. Ceasing the incessant rubbing of her stomach, she straightened her back and forced herself to look determined. "I said..."

Peter didn't let her say a word more. "You don't look very well, Headmistress." Taking a step in her direction, his hand outstretched, he added, "Would you like me to help you back to the infirmary." She turned and fled.

The girls' expressions were troubled. Apparently, getting one up on the headmistress was both frightening and promising. "She'll be back," he said closing the door. He preferred to be realistic. It wouldn't do to let them believe they could get away with anything, especially not with someone as dangerous as Heartless.

"Let's do some healing," he said, joining the girls on his bed, "before that sour-face comes back and stops us." Alexandria rubbed her hands in glee and began bouncing up and down.

Peter put out a hand to restrain her. "Healing requires calm. Why don't you close your eyes and take a deep breath." Alexandria didn't do as he suggested, but she did settle down.

"My method involves learning by doing, so we need someone who's ill. Several people would be better. But whoever it is, we can't have them blabbing." There seemed little hope of that with so much tittle-tattle. The thought of people gossiping gave him an idea. "Maybe we can find someone with a problem she's ashamed of and would never dare talk about. Any ideas?"

Apparently any number of girls had reasons to be ashamed or embarrassed, although not all their problems could be fixed by healing. Peter had another reason for wanting a growing number of girls to be grateful. If he were to push Heartless out, he'd need as many allies as possible.

"But how do we approach them?" Eloise asked. "We can't just barge in." She was right. Discretion was needed.

"You'd be the best one to talk to them," Sarah said, "but, seeing as you are..."

She hesitated over the word, at which Peter muttered, "A pervert."

She shook her head and continued, "... an outcast, anything you do will appear suspicious." In the end Eloise agreed to contact the first girls, and, as the evening was getting on, she would do so while it was still possible without being collared by a prefect.

Ten minutes later, the door opened and Eileen entered closely followed by a short, overweight girl with tiny, beady eyes in a podgy face. She kept as far away from Peter as the small room would allow. "This is Gladys," Eileen said, taking her by the elbow and leading her closer to Peter.

"What's bothering you?" Peter asked. "Apart from me, that is."

The girl shot him a quizzical look before replying, "It's personal."

"That's a shame. We'll just have to find someone else to help," Peter said, turning away. He regretted using strong-arm tactics, but they didn't have much time. "If you can't tell us what's wrong, there's little we can do."

Both Eloise and Sarah were shocked, but he kept his expression neutral. As for Gladys, she looked crushed and turned to leave. "You shouldn't give up so easily," Peter said, causing her to halt. "If you want to resolve your problem, you have to dare take the first step. In this case, that means telling us what's bothering you."

"I can't stop eating," she said, her voice barely audible. "Everyone hates me. I hate myself. I'm so fat. It makes me so miserable, I eat even more."

"Would you like us to help?" he asked.

"I doubt you can. My mother took me to all sorts of specialists. They just made it worse."

"Let me explain," Peter began. " Every cell in your body knows what's best for you. But something seems to be stopping the healthy message getting through. What I'll do, if you agree, is help your body hear that message so it can get back on track. No potions, no creams, no special diets, no strenuous programme of activities, no painful operations. All we have to do is encourage every cell in your body to return to that healthy blueprint."

"How on Earth do you do that?" Gladys asked.

"It's a bit like payer," he replied figuring that, as a pupil in a religious school, she'd respond better to a familiar image. "With prayer you close your eyes, go inside and think of what you want. You can't insist God give you things, that wouldn't be right and it wouldn't work, but you can at least make your intentions known. So in a similar way, I place a hand on you, I go inside and encourage your body to return to the original blueprint that is synonymous with good health."

"Is that all?" Gladys sounded astonished if not incredulous.

"That's the most important part," Peter replied.

"Okay," Gladys said and timidly held out her hand.

"Good. You might like to sit down. The feeling can be a little strange."

Once she was seated, he sat next to her and took her hand

which trembled in his. The moment there was contact her fear was apparent so he set about alleviating it. "I'm teaching Eloise and Sarah to help me, so I'll ask them to touch your hand too." She nodded. "Now close your eyes. We need to concentrate, so we'll remain silent while we work." He didn't need silence, but he wanted to be free to talk mind-to-mind to Eloise and Sarah.

She's very afraid, he sent, *so I've diminished her fear.* He showed them how and let each try. *Now let's tackle the weight problem. Dealing with this is going to be more complex than I told her. Her body will need time to set things right, maybe weeks. But we have to show her tangible results. Giving priority to the blueprint will not be enough. We'll need to actively help the body rectify the problem.*

Some fifteen minutes later, they opened their eyes to see a transformed Gladys staring at them in wonder. Much of the swelling of her face was gone and the pasty colour of her skin had been replaced by a healthy pink. "That was extraordinary," Gladys exclaimed. "It felt so odd, as if you were moving things around inside me." She stared at her hands in wonder. Like her face, much of the swelling had gone and renewed tension meant that skin no longer hung loose over layers of fat.

"The whole process will take some time to complete," Peter said, "but you should immediately see a difference." He looked around for a mirror, but, of course, there wasn't one.

"Is this what you're looking for?" Sarah asked, pulling a tiny mirror from her pocket. She handed it to Gladys who, grasping the mirror in trembling fingers, eyed her reflection in amazement.

"I'm not the slightest bit hungry," Gladys burst out. "I haven't felt so good in years."

"Remember," Peter said, "it's important you tell no one."

"But everyone will notice!"

"You'd be surprised how few people do. Don't be upset. As for those that do see, you'll need to invent an explanation. A new medicine. A diet. More exercise. Prayers answered. A miracle. Chose one and stick to it."

"What if I notice that one of the girls around me could do with your help?"

"Don't approach her directly. Let us know."

All of a sudden the girl became shy and stared at her feet. Peter could guess what was coming. "Could you teach me to do what you do?"

"While the headmistress is still in place and she has the administrator, those prefects and some of teachers on her side, teaching too many girls to heal might alert her. This has to remain a secret. We don't want her to stop us helping each other."

"What do you mean by, 'still in place'?" Gladys asked.

Sharp girl! He had to be more careful. "Well, I imagine she won't be here for ever."

"I wish she were gone," Gladys said. "She brings only pain and suffering."

39.

Eloise had a slightly larger room on the ground floor, one of the perks of being a prefect, with its own tiny wash basin and a window looking out onto the park. It was there on assembled mattresses that Peter was to sleep with her and Sarah.

After Gladys, they'd healed three others. One suffered from acute period pains, another was plagued by acne and the third had a mysterious itch that refused to go away. Despite being sworn to secrecy, the message must have leaked as ever more girls slunk up to Peter's door in search of cures. It was late and prefects were on the prowl so they turned the girls away with promises of help in the morning. It was this influx of would-be patients that led Peter and the others to take refuge in Eileen's room.

Peter felt strangely elated lying sandwiched between two girls in their nightdresses, as if he were drowning in a sea of girlishness. Sleep might prove difficult. The girls, in comparison, seemed unbothered and in no way inclined to take advantage. Eloise was curled up with her back to him engrossed in a book. Sarah was lying on her back with her hands folded behind her head staring at the ceiling. "Were you serious about getting rid of Heartless?" she asked. He nodded. "Count me in," she exclaimed with enthusiasm. When he grinned, she asked, "So how do we do it?"

"Maybe we could scare her..."

"Like with ghosts...?"

"Something like that. But that would only be temporary. I'd

rather tarnish her name for good." He didn't want to admit it, but, by discrediting her, he hoped to get Christina reinstated and have the injunction against his adoptive parents lifted.

"That shouldn't be so difficult," Eloise said, sliding a finger between the pages of her book. "There are loads of girls who could testify to mistreatment."

"They'll only do that if they feel safe," Sarah said, turning on her side to face Peter. "And this place is hardly safe."

"We're changing that," Peter said. "Healing girls is a first step."

"I can't see how," Sarah replied, stretching out a hand to brush aside a lock of hair that had fallen over his eyes. When he stiffened at her touch she blushed and turned back to scrutinising the ceiling.

Pretending not to notice, he replied, "We need as many girls on our side as possible. Only then will those who've borne the brunt of her ill treatment dare speak up."

The sound of scuffling outside put an end to their conversation. Had someone been listening at the door? The prospect filled him with dread. The last thing they needed was for it to be known they were plotting against the headmistress.

A thud had Peter springing to his feet. Wrenching the door open he found two prefects dragging a little girl down the corridor. The girl must have found where they were hiding and been intercepted by prefects.

"Stop that!" he called out, hurrying after them. The prefects, who paid no heed, tightened their grip on the struggling girl.

"Help!" she cried out, battling to get free. "Help, please."

Several girls peered out from their rooms, intrigued by the noise. Peter caught up with the prefects, the growing number of girls in the corridor hampering their progress. Amongst them, he recognised several he'd helped heal.

"Stop bullying that girl!" Peter said, grabbing a prefect's sleeve to halt her.

She shoved him back, retorting haughtily, "What're you going to do about it?"

"We've had enough of your bullying," the girl who'd had problems with her weight said. A group of girls around her nodded in agreement.

"You must be joking," the other prefect said, her voice dripping with scorn. She turned to push the girl way forward, but the others tightened ranks. There was no getting through. "Get out of my way!" the prefect ordered, but no one moved.

She raised her hand to strike one of the youngest girls who stood in her way, but Peter deflected the blow causing her to stumble and fall. Those wearing shoes didn't hesitate. They kicked the fallen prefect with vicious determination.

"Stop!" Peter shouted, restraining one girl who was repeatedly kicking the prefect in the ribs. "It's not because she's been vile that you have to break her bones. On the contrary. You don't want to be like her and her fellow prefects. Being strong and in control doesn't mean you have to hurt or belittle those around you. That's what bullies do. You can do better."

The girls stepped back leaving a space around the fallen prefect. Peter knelt at her side and laid a tentative hand on her shoulder. She flinched, no doubt expecting him to inflict pain. "I'm not going to hurt you," he said. "I just want to make sure you're not seriously injured."

"Get away from her!" The other prefect said, pushing her way through the crowd.

"She has two broken ribs and internal bleeding," Peter replied. "If I do nothing, she'll have to be rushed to hospital and operated on. Recovery will take weeks. If I heal her she'll be as right as rain straight away."

"You?" the prefect sneered. "Who made you a miracle worker?"

"What do you know about miracles?" Sarah said, her voice firm as she faced off with the prefect. She looked so small and frail compared to the bulk of the prefect, but she stood her ground. "All you can do is hurt people."

"Get out of my way," the prefect said, shoving Sarah to one side. The moment she touched Sarah, she yelped and jumped back. The girl must have used the little she knew of healing to deal a shock to the prefect.

"Let her be," Peter said to Sarah as he helped the prefect to her feet. "She doesn't get it. Hurting her won't make her understand. We all need time to learn. You know that, you who put so much store in learning. It's just that some people are slower than others."

"Sure," a voice in the crowd said. "But Sarah doesn't go around deliberately hurting people. Not like that mean sod," the speaker, a tall, slender girl with a shock of black hair, emerged from the crowd and pointed at the prefect. "She goes out of her way to cause pain and suffering. I still have the burn marks on my arm. I say some people can only learn if they're punished."

Peter shuddered. His only experience of courts and judgement was Kate's trial. Her conviction had been a foregone conclusion, her execution inevitable. "I'm sorry. I didn't know," Peter said, struggling to keep his emotions in check. "We'll need to hear the evidence before we decide what to do. But please let me heal this girl first. If I don't, her condition will deteriorate rapidly."

"You can do that?" The lanky girl sounded both sceptical and hopeful.

"She sure can," the girl who'd had the eating problem exclaimed.

Her support was more than welcome and being called 'she' was an added perk. Not waiting for the response, Peter knelt at the prefect's side and Sarah came to join him. *Can you keep an eye on that other prefect*, Peter asked Eloise. *I'll relay the healing, so you don't miss anything.* There was a short pause, then the answer came back, *No thanks. Too distracting.*

Peter and Sarah placed their hands on the fallen prefect and, closing their eyes, set about righting bones and staunching the flow of blood in her abdomen. Peter kept up a running commentary to guide Sarah. She learnt quickly.

A hushed silence settled over the scene. You'd have said a holy relic had materialised in their midst. Everyone was awestruck. There'd be a long queue of girls begging to learn to heal the moment they finished. However had he managed to let himself be cornered into making such a public display? So much for keeping healing a secret. This wasn't how he'd envisaged winning the girls over.

Once the healing was complete the two got to their feet and helped a dazed prefect struggle up. "What happened?" the girl asked, a puzzled expression on her face.

"You were seriously hurt," Peter told her. "But now you're okay."

For a brief moment the girl's tone had been conciliatory but it rapidly turned sour and became suspicious if not belligerent. "However did I get hurt?"

"Let's worry about that later," Peter replied, forcing his voice to sound firm but soothing. "You must be exhausted. You need a goodnight's sleep after all you've been through."

"Who are you to order me about?" she retorted, indignant.

"I'm the person who just reset two of your ribs which were broken," Peter said mildly, "and who staunched the flow of blood escaping from several ruptured veins in your stomach. Without Sarah and myself healing you, you might have died."

Unimpressed, the girl turned on Peter, her fists readied to strike.

"I hate to admit it but..." he turned to the lanky girl who'd pleaded for judgement and asked, "What's your name?"

"Linda."

"I hate to admit it, but Linda was right, some people can only learn certain lessons the hard way."

The prefect chose that moment to strike, but Peter anticipated the move and stepped aside letting the girl fall forward at the feet of a none too friendly crowd.

"Don't break her ribs again," Peter pleaded, a smile playing on his lips. "We already pieced them together once. It's hard work." He offered his hand as if to help the girl up, but the moment their fingers touched, he sent a powerful wave of drowsiness over the girl who sank back and curled up, asleep. "I warned her she'd be tired," Peter said, hoping the girls wouldn't guess he'd sent her to sleep. It wouldn't do to have them terrified of his abilities.

Flanked by Eloise and Linda, the other prefect swivelled her head desperately in search of a way out. *Put your hand on her*, Peter told Eloise. The prefect dodged, trying to avoid Eloise's outstretched hand, but she was hemmed in on all sides by the crowd and the narrow corridor. The moment Eloise made contact, he used her as a conduit to send wave after wave of weariness washing over the prefect. *Catch her*, he said, *she's about to collapse.*

"She's faking it," one girl called out. "That lot would do anything to stop the truth coming out. Except you, Eloise, that is."

"Thanks," Eloise said. "I'm glad you don't consider me one of them."

Peter moved to take a closer look at the sleeping girl. "No. Her sleep is real enough," he said. "She must be exhausted."

"Where are we going to put them?" Sarah asked. "None of our doors have locks. Even if they stay asleep, we don't want the other two coming to their rescue."

"As night prefect, my room has a lock and I have the key" Eloise told them. "If we can block the window, we could keep them in there."

"No. We'll need your room. I don't think we should bother," Peter said. "The tide has turned. Their reign is over. I suggest we dump them in the entrance and let them sleep it off."

Once the two prefects were disposed of Peter led Linda down the corridor and asked, "Let me have a look."

Rather than offer her arm, which was what Peter expected, she just stared at him confused.

"Your arm, I mean. You said you'd been burnt."

"Oh!" she exclaimed looking embarrassed, but still didn't hold out her arm. "That was a longtime ago. I doubt there's anything anyone can do."

Wondering if she was shy about her damaged arm, he

suggested they go to Eloise's room but she refused. "I don't want to be any bother. There are surely many other girls who require urgent attention."

"I can't force you," Peter said, "but at least let me look then you can decide if I should heal you or not."

Reluctantly, Linda rolled up her sleeve gingerly. Peter couldn't help gasping. The girl's skin was peppered with burns as if someone had repeatedly stubbed out cigarettes on her. The marks were a vivid red and swollen. Several festered. The girl must have been in considerable pain although her mild face gave nothing away.

"You can't stay like that!" Peter said, his expression grim. "You'll lose your arm."

"It's not important," the girl insisted. "I can bear it."

"Listen," Peter said. "I have no idea why you refuse, but I can't leave you with your arm in that state. I could ask the girls to restrain you. But I'd much rather you let me heal you."

Seeing Gladys walk by, he stopped her. "Tell Linda what it's like to be healed," he said. "She won't let me heal her arm."

"It's wonderful," she exclaimed. "Just look at me! He did that."

"That's not strictly true," Peter corrected. "I helped your body do what it always wanted."

Gladys nodded in agreement "It feels odd at first, as if parts of me were shifting around. But it was well worth it. For the first time in years, I'm proud of my body."

Linda stared at Gladys's radiant face then, turning to Peter, she nodded.

"Let's go to Eloise's room. I need quiet to concentrate," he suggested. When she agreed, he added, "I'm teaching a couple of girls to heal. Do you mind if two sit in and help?"

"I'd prefer not," she said after a long hesitation, her voice barely audible. Tears sprang to her eyes as she added, "I'm so ashamed."

Peter was perplexed. How could she possibly be ashamed? Surely she should be angry. He chose not to respond. Once in

Eloise's room with the door shut, he said, "Maybe you should remove your blouse. Every time you roll up a sleeve you hurt yourself."

He attributed her reticence to shyness, but once the blouse off, he understood her shame. Her shoulders, her back, her breasts, even her stomach were covered with ugly red burns. She hung her head and began to sob.

"I'm so, so sorry," Peter said softly, placing a hand on her neck, one of the few remaining unmarred spots. Closing his eyes, he immediately dampened her pain and set about driving out the spreading infection. There were so many wounds, it was hard to know where to begin. Working systematically, he healed the tissue around the burns, helping the skin grow over the ugly mark.

When he became aware that her thighs and her sex had also been burnt, his nausea was so strong, he had to divert a little of his healing energy to prevent himself from throwing up. No wonder she felt ashamed. Her life, her feelings, her body had been negated. She'd been reduced to a meer object of someone's sadistic pleasure. All she had left was the pain and the shame.

His vision had long been blurred by tears, but when the final burn had been healed an involuntary sob burst from his lips. Never had he seen such a vicious attack on a fellow human being. The horror had him feeling lost and rudderless. When Linda took him in her arms to console him, he felt both her immense strength at surviving such an ordeal but also his own ineffectiveness and guilt at having done nothing to stop it. Him or the others around them. And even now she consoled him when he should be consoling her.

40.

Peter couldn't sleep, memories of Linda's pock-marked body haunting him. Despite extra blankets, he was unable to keep warm. In the end, both Eloise and Sarah cuddled up close, the warmth of their bodies slowly thawing the ice that froze his bones.

Eloise must have turned away during the night because, when he awoke, she was sleeping with her back to him, blankets pulled tight around her neck. Sarah, however, slept with one arm slung round his waist, her body cuddled next to him. Her warm breath on his neck ruffled his hair like a soft caress.

Peter, a familiar voice called in his head, startling him. His sudden movement startled Sarah too. She groaned, still half asleep, and clung to him, burying her nose in his neck.

I see I called at a bad time, Kate said. *You seem caught up in other things.*

The more Peter struggled, the more Sarah hung on, mumbling in her sleep. Finally Peter gave up and lay back unmoving. *I can explain,* he said.

I'm sure you can, but not now, I have to go. From her tone and the emotions underlining her words, it was clear she was upset.

Kate! he called out but she'd severed the contact. He sought to re-establish the link, only to receive the mental equivalent of a cold shoulder. Drat! She'd surely contacted him for a reason. She wouldn't have done so if it hadn't been important. Yet, in a huff, she'd left without sharing her news. And now she had a completely wrong impression and wouldn't let him explain.

His gloom must have shown because Sarah asked, "What's up? Don't tell me my snoring kept you awake." It was meant as a joke but he couldn't muster a smile.

When she stretched out to caress his cheek, no doubt intending to console him, he flinched. Her hurt was plain to see. "Oh dear," she said, "it really is serious."

Not only was he in a mess with Kate, but he was upsetting Sarah too. He sighed and shook his head. "I'm sorry." He should have explained, but he was afraid he'd make her more upset. He'd hardly given their friendship a second thought. Now he imagined all sorts of scenarios, every single one ending in disaster.

"Spit it out," Eloise said, surprising him. He'd thought she was asleep. "All those girls yesterday had the courage to expose their problems. Now it's your turn."

"I'm not ill," he muttered, sounding grumpy.

"Maybe not," Eloise said, clearly not deterred. "But like an illness, what's troubling you will only get worse if you don't confront it."

A part of him was inclined to ironise, 'When did you get so wise?' But that would be unfair. Knowing that didn't make it any easier to keep his ill-humour at bay. The angry part of him was indignant at being unjustly treated. The victim in him was miserable at being rejected by Kate. While the sensible part struggled to get the upper hand, knowing Eloise was right.

"Okay," he said heaving himself up till he had his back against the wall and the covers pulled up around him. "I upset my best friend," he began. The moment the words were out of his mouth, he was aware of their ambiguity. The girls might believe he was talking about Sarah. Damn it! The girl had been in his arms when Kate called and his guilt at being caught deformed everything. There was nothing between him and Sarah. Friendship, maybe. But no more. Nothing compared to what bound him to Kate.

"The girl in Switzerland?" Sarah asked. "Kate, isn't it?"

Was that sourness he heard in her voice? She was probably upset about him having another girlfriend. What nonsense. His imagination was running amok. "Yes. She called mind-to-mind. Just now. I ..." He couldn't go on.

Eloise patted him on the knee. The gesture was innocent enough, but it took all his willpower not to flinch. "It's silly," he admitted, "but I've tied myself in knots."

"Why don't you just tell us what happened," Eloise suggested, coming to sit next to him. Sarah remained curled up at his feet under a pile of blankets.

"When I awoke," Peter began, "Sarah was next to me with an arm slung around my waist. That was when Kate spoke. As you know, speaking mind-to-mind means you pick up a lot more than the person's words. She saw me in bed with Sarah cuddling up to me..."

"Ah," Eloise said. "I see. She thought there was something going on between you."

"Well there is, isn't there?" Sarah said.

"Not helpful," Eloise said, much to Sarah's dismay. "I don't mean to be cruel, but the beginnings of a friendship with you can't compare with the relationship he has with Kate after all they've gone through."

Peter nodded. "She was so upset, she broke the connection and refuses to talk to me." He couldn't help it. Tears welled in his eyes. "I feel so guilty." Looking at Sarah, who'd clearly been put out by Eloise's comment, he added, "This drama has poisoned our relationship. I don't think I'll ever feel completely at ease with you again."

"That's absurd!" Sarah exclaimed. "I've done nothing wrong. Why should I get punished?"

"Let him speak," Eloise said. "He's telling us how he feels. You might see things differently, but you can't deny his feelings. Only he can know what they are. That's where my parents got it all wrong. They thought they knew my feelings better than me. They had me doubting myself. There's nothing worse than being unsure about your own feelings. It's as if you're cut off from yourself. Their interference left me painfully shy and insecure. Only when I got away from them, did I gradually realise how misguided they were and how damaging their attitude had been."

"Eloise's right," Peter said. "I'm telling you how I see things, what I am afraid of." He paused to set his thoughts in order. "In fact, it's not even how I see things, but how I imagine Kate sees them. She thinks there's something untoward between you and me. Even though that's not true, the fact that she thinks it makes it a possibility where no possibility was before. And it is that possibility, real or imagined, that robs our potential friendship of its innocence. It may well even ruin the love between Kate and I."

A knock at the door put an end to their conversation. It was Linda. "You lot should get dressed," she said, peering round the door. The brilliant smile she gave him lifted some of his gloom. It was amazing what a good night's sleep could do. She was positively radiant, a far fetch from her haggard state the evening before. At least he got some things right.

"The girls are impatient," she continued. "They're thirsting for blood. I'm afraid they'll do something rash if we don't give them a trial soon." Being Saturday, there were no lessons to distract them and, as it was term time, none were allowed home for the weekend. What's more, persistent trouble with local girls meant most couldn't go into town. Those who didn't have homework often used the time to catch up on lost sleep.

"Have you found a suitable room?" Eloise asked. "Somewhere we won't be disturbed."

"The only place big enough is the chapel."

Peter shuddered. Holding a court in a consecrated space seemed like an open invitation to trouble. "Who's going to oversee the trial?" he asked.

"You," all three girls said in chorus.

Their unanimity surprised him. It wasn't a task he'd envisaged. "Why me?"

"You're the only one not directly involved," Linda replied.

If anything, he was intimately concerned. And anyway, how

was he supposed to run a trial? He'd only ever once attended one and he'd been so preoccupied with saving Kate, he'd paid no attention to the proceedings. Ah Kate! She'd know what to do. If only he could ask her. He shook his head. The thought of her flooded him with fresh waves of despondency.

"Don't worry," Eloise said, misinterpreting his gloominess. "All you have to do is coax out the facts."

"And make sure nobody gets lynched," Sarah added.

Both Eloise and Linda shot her an exasperated look. "You should add diplomacy to the list of things you have to learn," Eloise quipped.

Sarah response was to throw a pillow at her. It missed, hitting Peter instead. "Sorry," she muttered, not looking in the slightest contrite.

"Give us five minutes to get dressed," Eloise said. "We can talk over breakfast."

It being Saturday and long past breakfast time, the staff had left for their weekend pursuits, abandoning the canteen to a small group of girls clustered around Eloise, Linda and Peter.

As he chewed on a slice of bread and butter, Peter wondered about the forthcoming trial. The word was being tossed around as if it were self-evident, but he didn't like it. It implied judgement and punishment. He felt wary of venturing down that road. Who were they to punish? He much preferred the word 'inquest', a meeting to tease out the truth, to let everyone share what they knew, to become aware of what had happened.

So far, a deep-seated fear of revealing the truth had worked against them. Linda was a striking example. She'd suffered pain and humiliation, unbeknown to fellow pupils, making her torture a guilty secret she had to bear alone.

"What about the prefects?" Sarah asked. "Shouldn't they be cross-examined?"

"I don't think we need that," Peter said. "I can't imagine interrogating them. This is no court of law. Rather I'd prefer girls to bear witness. In all simplicity. To recount what happened. To get the whole mess out in the open. To put an end to the secrecy that has poisoned so many of your lives." He glanced at Linda who nodded in agreement, her eyes bright with tears.

"We'll need someone to take notes," Peter said, "as a memory of what was said." He wished Regina and Heinz had been there. They'd have known how to capitalise on what happened.

All heads turned to Sarah, who promptly looked over her shoulder as if to deflect their pointed attention. "Sarah it is then," Peter said, shooting a questioning look at the girl who nodded reluctantly. "You needn't note everything. Just jot down the important points."

"You realise that dragging up the past and taking notes will make no difference," Sarah said, her expression thoughtful.

Eloise was about to pounce, no doubt annoyed at Sarah's pessimism, but Peter held up a hand to silence her. "What do you mean?" he asked. His question earned him a dismissive shrug from both Eloise and Linda.

"In what way will pawing over stories of violence stop it?" she replied. "True, it'll be less of a secret. It might make us warier. We might even come to each other's defence more readily. But the exactions won't cease. For that to happen we need pressure from the outside, from the adult world."

"You're such a pessimist," Eloise chided.

"She may sometimes be," Peter said, "but in this I think she's spot on. We really do need adult witnesses." The idea was brilliant. Not only did it offer a possible avenue to depose Heartless, but it also provided a rampart should the headmistress try to interfere. "And I have an idea how to get them."

41.

When Eileen came to fetch her, Kate wasn't sure she'd slept. Not that the improvised bed on the platform perched above the barn was uncomfortable. On the contrary. She just hadn't slept well. She squinted against the bright sunlight reflecting off the snow out the window, her eyes struggling to focus. Her every limb felt leaden. When she tried to stand she would have keeled over had not Eileen caught her by the arm.

"Easy does it, Captain," Eileen said with a grin. "A little less rhum next time."

She was about to grin back when she remembered her stormy exchange with Peter. What a disaster! She'd just wanted to share her news, pleased they'd foiled the attack. How was she to know he'd be snogging with a girl? She tried to shrug off the memory of the young girl's arms sensuously slung around his waist. Or the way the little slut had clung on, her whole body pressed against his. The intimacy of it sickened her.

If Kate hadn't been so weary and strung up, she might have reacted differently. But she hadn't. And now he was angry. No wonder she'd slept badly. She freed herself from Eileen's grip and let herself sink onto the bed, her head in her hands.

"What's up?" Eileen asked, sitting next to her, slinging an arm around her shoulders.

Kate buried her head in Eileen shoulder and burst into tears. "What a disaster," she muttered. "How was I to know? And now of all times!"

"Tell Auntie Eileen," Eileen said, gently brushing a tear

from Kate's cheeks.

"It's Peter," she managed to say.

"What has the naughty girl done now?"

Kate was undecided whether to laugh or to punch her. In the end she did neither. "He cheated on me." The words burst from her lips before she could stop them.

"What makes you think that?"

Kate described what had happened.

"How long did you talk?"

"Less than a minute."

"And what happened to him before?"

"It's not hard to imagine."

"Therein lies the problem," Eileen said, getting to her feet to pace the room. "You caught a glimpse, a frozen moment, but what happened before and after? You could be right. But there are plenty of other scenarios. Was she ill or sad and he was consoling her? Or had they had a fright and were huddled together to stave off fear? Maybe he was telling her how much he missed you and she was commiserating. Who knows? Yet despite these many possibilities, you've singled out one version and won't let it go. Why didn't you ask him?"

"He wanted to tell me," Kate began, "but I wouldn't let him."

"Why ever not?"

Kate tried to recall. She hadn't given it much thought. "I don't know. I guess I thought he'd dream up some lame excuse."

"Is he the sort who lies to get out of a tight spot?"

"No." Kate could feel shame taking hold of her. She shook herself, trying unsuccessfully to get free. "No. That's not like him."

"So maybe there's another explanation," Eileen concluded as she ceased pacing and faced Kate. "Of course, if you enjoy feeling jealous - I gather it can be exhilarating - you can always stick to your explanation." She shot Kate a wicked grin. "If you do relish being jilted, I advise against checking your story against his. You might end up being disavowed."

"Enough!" cried Kate, a hint of a smile on her lips. "Stop poking fun at me and let me be miserable."

"Never!" Eileen exclaimed, offering Kate a hand to help her up. "Come on. We've got mischief to do, people to confound and music to make."

Kate took her hand, let herself be hauled to her feet and flung her arms around her friend. "Thanks," she said, then, relinquishing her hold on Eileen, she added, "Give me a moment."

Nodding, Eileen said, "Give him my love," and with a chuckle left.

Peter? Kate called out the moment she was alone.

Still angry? he asked. Beyond his brusque tone she could sense his relief at hearing from her.

I'm sorry. I kind of flew off the handle. She was tempted to justify her reaction, but silenced the words. *What's going on?*

When she heard of the torture Linda had endured, she was aghast. *Was that the girl in your arms?*

No. That was Sarah. He explained that he was teaching her and Eileen to heal and they had taken refuge in Eileen's room to escape the press of girls who demanded to be healed. *I couldn't sleep. That girl's pock-marked body haunted me. The thought of it froze me to the marrow. Eileen and Sarah leant me their warmth so I could sleep.*

I wish I'd been there to keep you warm, to cuddle up close and fall asleep in your arms. I miss you so much.

I miss you too. If all goes well, I should be on my way home soon. He told her about the inquest and how he hoped it would set things right.

What a coincidence! she said. She told him about the attack on the village and the Lost Girls plans. *Not an inquest,* she explained. *More of a performance or a revelation through a work of art, a cross between fact and dramatisation. To get the truth out.*

Both were reluctant to break the link, but they had responsibilities and urgent things to do. So they embraced mentally and Peter promised to return home soon.

Kate climbed down from her perch to find the new girls milling, impatience if not discontent erupting in raised words or scuffles. She went in search of Sandra. The girl was a likely candidate to lead the group. The new girls needed to organise themselves. If the Lost Girls tried to do it, they'd be seen as replacing the nuns and be greeted with sullen opposition. Kate found her in the kitchen trying to rope girls into cleaning up. So much for leading. Kate snatched a broom from a girl's hands before she hit another girl over the head with it. "That's for brushing the floor, not braining your friends," she said. Turning to Sandra, she said, "Can I have a word?" and led her away from the rowdy group.

"They're hopeless," Sandra muttered. "You'd think they were still in the orphanage. Maybe we should have left them there."

"You're right. In part. A few should have stayed under the yoke of the nuns rather than dragging their bad mood here," Kate said with a chuckle. "But don't despair. We'll find a way."

"I thought they'd be overjoyed to get away," Sandra said, looking defeated. "Instead they're bickering and fighting when they're not complaining about you lot for telling them what to do."

"Yes. I noticed." They'd retreated to the far side of the barn from where they could watch the mass of girls listlessly shifting around. "They need a goal, something to give a new sense to their lives."

"We could have them clean away the snow so we can visit those houses," Sandra suggested, although she wasn't over enthusiastic.

"Would they realise they were doing it for themselves?" Kate asked.

Sandra shook her head. "No. They'd probably see it as a chore imposed by you lot."

"I have another idea," Kate said. "Can you fight?"

Sandra took a step back, looking at her in alarm.

Kate burst out laughing. "Don't be alarmed. Here's my idea." The girl seemed to like what she heard, judging from her grin. "So we'll need a small group," Kate concluded. "People you trust."

Ten minutes later, Kate, Sandra and a few new girls pushed back the tables to free a large space in the middle of the hall. Kate had had time to warn Eileen what she was doing and all the Lost Girls had been informed. Some of the remaining new girls were intrigued but most kept a wary distance. Kate paid no attention. Instead she turned to Sandra's small group and said, "The attack last night could have been far worse. If you're to live outside the orphanage, you'll need to protect yourselves." She spoke quietly, forcing those spectators who wanted to hear to come closer.

"I'm going to show you a few basic moves that are useful in self-defence." She beckoned to Sandra who'd agreed to be her victim, saying, "Attack me as if you had a knife."

Sandra's attack was half-hearted. It was not her fault. She clearly had no experience with fighting. Several spectators jeered. Kate beckoned one of them over, a thick-set girl with a black eye, one of eldest of the group. The girl shoved her way through the crowd, scattering girls as she did, and swaggered up to Kate. Not waiting for an invitation, she threw a punch. Side-stepping gracefully, Kate lightly touched the girl who was off balance and sent her sprawling.

The crowd let out an appreciative roar as the girl sprang to her feet and threw herself at Kate. But no matter how hard she tried she couldn't get the better of Kate. Panting she came back for a tenth time, fists raised, but Kate held up a hand to stop her. "I admire your determination," she said. "but this is meant to be a demonstration, not a fight to the death. I have no grudge against you and nothing to prove. I'm not the one who kept you locked up in an orphanage for years. I'm not the one who beat you or starved you. I'm not the one who took pleasure in hurting you. I'm the person who set you free, who is offering you a place to stay where you'll have not only food and shelter, but the possibility to learn new things and determine your own way in life. Instead of venting your anger and frustration on me, why don't you help me teach these girls to defend themselves?"

"Why should I trust you?" the girl snarled.

"She was an orphan like you," one of the Lost Girls called out.

The girl responded with a rude gesture. "You don't look like no orphan to me," she exclaimed. "You don't talk like one either."

"Being wary of people, especially those offering gifts, is a wise strategy. I'm not asking you to trust me long-term, but rather to give us a chance. As I said at the orphanage, if you want to leave you're free to do so, whenever you like."

The girl hesitated a long moment, her hands on her hips. The gathered girls held their breaths. Then she stepped forward and held out her hand as if offering to shake Kate's. The moment the girl grasped Kate's hand, she yanked it forward and would have thrust her other hand in Kate's face had Kate not used the girl's effort to propel herself forward and, ducking, drove her shoulder into the girl's stomach.

The girl let out a grunt and toppled forward, rolling over Kate's back as she crouched in front of the falling girl. Kate extended a hand to help the girl up, a hand the girl took cautiously and clambered to her feet.

"Neat," she said with a crooked smile. "You got any more like that up your sleeve? Wanna share?"

"Sure. But not just you. With all the girls." She looked at the crowd. Eager faces, for the most part. "Don't worry. We'll start easy." She walked up to a terrified young girl and, placing an arm around her shoulder, led her to the middle, whispering encouragement as she did.

"The first step in unarmed combat is being aware of your body and its movements," she told everyone. Using the young girl as a sparring partner, Kate took her and then everyone through a series of movements that were closer to dance than combat. A fact more than one pointed out, half complaining, half appreciative. Despite the snide remarks, everyone finished by joining in and were soon whole-heartedly swaying and dancing.

Once the girls were warmed up, Kate had them in pairs, practicing simple moves designed to ward off frontal attacks. "Don't forget," she said, raising her voice over the animated chatter and laughter. "Use your opponent's energy to get the better of her." By the time they'd finished, it was late afternoon, the sun had set and everyone was tired and hungry.

"What's for evening meal?" one of the new girls called out. "I'm starving."

"That depends on you," Kate replied. "Your turn to cook."

"Me?" the new girl asked in alarm. "I've no idea how to cook."

"Do none of you know how to cook?" Kate asked, feigning worry. "How are you going to survive on your own in this village?"

"I can cook," a chubby girl said, her tone almost apologetic. "But only simple food."

"There are so many of us, you'll need help," Kate said. "Pick a crew and we'll loan you one of our's, but only to show you were the food is and to give you advice if ever you get stuck. You're the boss." Several people laughed. The girl gulped and would have slunk into the crowd had the others let her. "You look like you've just seen a pack of hungry wolves heading your way." Someone nearby growled for effect. "But don't worry, help will always be at hand."

42.

Their improvised cook found sausages and dished them up fried with mashed potatoes and an onion sauce. It might've been rudimentary, but it tasted delicious and, judging from the way girls shovelled it down, the meal was appreciated.

Kate asked the Lost Girls to mix with the newcomers. She'd chosen to sit next to the fighter, whose name turned out to be Granta. So she was alone at a table of girls she didn't know except for Sandra, who'd joined her. All were so engrossed in eating, no one uttered a word. Kate wondered if they were intimidated.

"I like that twist and kick move," Granta told Kate, downing her knife and fork, having cleaned her plate of any trace of food. Before Kate could respond, a dessert of stewed apples and cream was dished up, earning the cook generous applause.

"I don't get it," Granta said, once the noise died down. "Most posh girls like you never go near a fight. Where ever did you learn to fight?"

"Where I come from all girls and boys are taught to defend themselves. I was lucky. I had a very good teacher." Kate couldn't help feeling wistful at the thought of Zhuru, her arms master. "He was one of the best."

"Where was that?" Granta asked.

Kate wasn't about to tell her she came from another world. As it turned out, she didn't need to. The door to the barn flew open and a gust of icy wind and a flurry of snow burst in closely followed by Viktor. Shod in snowshoes and wearing a thick anorak dusted with snow, his eyes roved the room till they found Kate and he came lumbering in her direction. "It's Beth," he blurted out, gasping to catch his breath. "She's had an accident...."

Kate sprang to her feet and ran to the man, taking him in her arms. "What happened?" she asked.

"I'll tell you on the way," Viktor said, freeing himself. "She's at the hospital and asking for you." He pulled a set of snowshoes from his back where they'd been strapped and fitted them round Kate's boots. "Have you got an anorak?"

Kate shook her head. "Only a coat."

"You can borrow mine," Eileen said, dashing off, only to return carrying it.

"Thanks," Kate said, donning the anorak which was a little big for her.

"There are gloves in the pockets and a hat in the hood," Eileen said. "Here's a scarf."

"Keep an eye on things," Kate said, threading the scarf around her neck. "Co-opt Sandra and Granta to the council and keep the girls busy. Call me mind-to-mind if anything urgent comes up. I'll be back as soon as possible."

A gust of wind almost swept her off her feet as she stepped out into the snow. The sun had long set and the moon was obscured by leaden clouds. Were it not for Viktor's torch, they'd have been plunged in pitch dark. The narrow beam of light cast eerie shadows off branches bent double under the mass of snow. Several times they had to clamber over branches that had not withstood the weight.

They followed Viktor's earlier trail. The going was tough and she was soon out of breath. Viktor had to rescue her several times when she keeled over in deep snow.

Her legs ached, her gloves and trousers were sopping and her fingers frozen by the time they saw the lights of Lydia and Klaus's house. Who would've thought walking in snow demanded so much effort? Viktor was out of breath too which explained why he'd spoken so little. All Kate knew was that the brakes on Beth's wheelchair had failed and she'd plunged down the stairs with the chair tumbling on top of her. She'd been unconscious when they'd rushed her to hospital. They done several X-rays and an operation was scheduled for the next morning.

The idea of an operation worried Kate. For all their good intentions, doctors were liable to cause lasting damage. If only she could get to her adopted mother before they opened her up. It was that thought that drove her on.

"Oh! Poor dear!" Lydia exclaimed as she opened the door and hugged Kate even before she could shake the snow from her clothes. "I'll make you some hot chocolate."

"No time," Viktor said stepping inside. "We have to leave immediately."

Lydia took hold of Kate's hands, removed the soaked gloves and began massaging her painful fingers. "She's frozen! Surely you can spare five minutes to get warm."

"Okay. But no more. I'll go warm the car."

Lydia must have been planning hot chocolate because the milk was already heated. Klaus peered in to see how Kate was. "Rhum business that falling down the stairs," he said. "Odd those brakes failing. Beth's not the sort to neglect having her wheelchair checked. If I were you, I'd take a close look at that chair. Provided some helpful person hasn't got rid of it already."

It was plain what he was hinting at, but she couldn't believe anyone would sabotage a handicapped person's wheelchair. Surely not. Then again they'd caused Jo to have an accident and she was pregnant. She went to sip her chocolate, but it was too hot. "Can I take it with me?"

Lydia nodded. "I'd give you one for Viktor, but he's got to drive..."

Clasping her mug to warm her hands, Kate thanked her and headed out to the car. The snow had ceased but a bitterly cold wind coated every surface with ice.

Viktor had the motor running and the heating on full blast. He was so impatient, he set off before she was settled, causing the chocolate to slosh in her mug and almost spill over Eileen's jacket.

"Easy does it," she exclaimed as he swung the car off the gravel drive and onto the main road, the vehicle skidding as he did. She'd heard how Beth had come to be condemned to a wheelchair. A car accident on a snowy, icy night just like this. Viktor had been at the wheel with Beth next to him, just like Kate. He'd escaped with minor injuries, but she'd been handicapped for life.

Viktor accelerated, taking advantage of being alone on the road. Several times the vehicle lurched sideways on a patch of ice, but Viktor managed to wrest back control. Meanwhile Kate gripped the side of her seat. Evoking the dangers of driving in such conditions would've been cruel, especially with Beth back in hospital, but Kate didn't want to be the victim of a similar fate.

"Please drive slower," she pleaded, unable to silence her growing panic. "Let's get to the hospital in the car, not an ambulance."

Viktor grunted by way of response and eased up on the accelerator. Despite slowing, the car still slid sideways before coming to a halt with a jolt on the verge. He closed his eyes and rested his head on the steering wheel. "Oh my god!" he muttered, clearly shaken. "It was just like that. Only I didn't stop. I couldn't. And we hit that tree." He pointed up the snow-covered bank at a gnarled tree that leant away from the road.

Kate stared at the tree then at Viktor. "Have you never been back?" she asked. He shook his head, his hands trembling as he gripped the steering wheel. "Here," she said offering him her chocolate. "Drink. It'll help." When he relinquished his grasp on the wheel and took the mug, she placed a hand on his shoulder and did her best to channel calm and confident vibrations. It wasn't easy. She was spooked herself.

"To think it almost happened again." His whole body shuddered violently.

His reaction had her scared. She was afraid he'd fall apart

and she wasn't sure she could piece him back together. He'd always been such a dependable person. "You stopped," she said, her voice trembling as she took back the mug. "History didn't repeat itself."

He ran a shuddering hand over his face. "I was unconscious for a long time," he said staring off into the distance. "When I finally came round they told me Beth was dead. It was a lie concocted by her parents. All I could think was I'd lost my love." He glanced up at the tree. "Only now, parked in the very spot where the crash happened, in the same bitter cold and snow and ice, with you, her daughter in many ways, at my side, do I realise how much the accident cost me."

She wished she could hug him, but space in the car was limited and they were trussed up against the cold. Instead she said, "Let's go see Beth." And she thought to herself, and see how much we can heal. The idea of doing anything about Beth's handicap had never crossed her mind. The accident had been a long time ago, but something ought to be possible no matter how set her body was in its disability. She'd never attempted such a feat. She wished Peter were there. Such complicated interventions were best done together.

The remainder of the journey was uneventful with Viktor driving so carefully the car crept through the night. The bustle that greeted them in the hospital contrasted with the snow-laden stillness outside. Road accidents abounded and casualties were being wheeled in. Viktor ignored the milling nurses and worried relatives, fraying a path through the chaos towards the quieter private ward were wife and mother awaited them.

With the combined effect of painkillers and sedatives, Beth drowsed fitfully, making little grunts and groans. Kate sat at her side and cautiously laid a hand on the woman's arm. It was warm, too warm. She was running a fever, although not much. "Can you make sure nobody disturbs me," Kate asked. "I'm going to see what I can do." Viktor nodded and shifted his chair next to the door.

Closing her eyes, Kate plunged inside Beth. There were

multiple cuts and bruises but most important was an impressive number of broken bones. To her relief no vital organs had been punctured. There was so much to put right, she decided to deal with the new damage first, working her way systematically outwards from the bones and muscles to the skin.

By the time she'd finished she was exhausted. The breaks and sprains and cuts and bruises had been so numerous, helping the body heal itself had drained her. Several hours must have passed and she needed a rest if she weren't to damage herself. In some distant part of her mind she could hear Viktor in earnest if not heated discussion. He must be in trouble, but there was one last thing she had to do. A deeper cure of Beth would have to wait.

She shifted her attention to Beth's mind and sifted methodically through the woman's memories, only speeding up when she reached the accident. She didn't want to relive the full force of the trauma. Despite her precautions the pain was excruciating and she couldn't help moaning. She heard Viktor's distant voice ask, "Are you alright?" Another male voice added, "She's having some sort of fit. We must get her out of here."

Kate ignored them as she landed on the nether side of the accident in Beth's memories and began hastily rummaging through the woman's perceptions for any clue as to what had happened. She drew a blank. She turned back and moved ever closer to the moment Beth lost control and began her fall. Alarm surged in the woman's mind at the realisation the brakes didn't work and she couldn't stop rolling over the first downward step, an image flashed through her mind. A man tampering with her chair.

Kate felt a hand briefly on her shoulder and was aware of a struggle nearby, but she plunged even deeper into Beth's memories. Earlier the woman had had a visit from a cleric. Beth recognised the man and even feared him, but at no time did she think his name. Maybe she didn't know it. He'd come, he said, about some plan to renovate an ancient fresco. It was news to her. He'd offered to wheel her into the study and she'd accepted.

It'd seemed an unusually friendly gesture, a mark of concern she wouldn't have expected from him. Maybe she'd misjudged the cleric. Unfortunately the wheelchair had blocked for some reason and the man had to get down on his frocked knees and fiddle with the chair to release it.

A hand was back on Kate's shoulder shaking her in a none too friendly fashion. "Wake up, Miss," a man's voice said. In the last second before she was forced to return to herself, she caught a glimpse of the cleric's face and committed its every detail to memory. Ripped from her deep concentration by the person who was pulling her off Beth, Kate opened her eyes feeling nauseous and disorientated.

Her assailant was not a doctor, as she'd imagined, but a male nurse with an ugly scar on his face. "The woman is very ill," he said, his tone annoyed as he gripped her arm and yanked her off Beth. "You can't just sprawl on her like that."

Kate felt she was about to faint and in a last ditch effort that she'd no doubt regret, she mentally struck out causing the man to run screaming down the corridor. Sinking softly to the ground as darkness closed, she felt herself scooped up and heard Viktor's distant voice ask, "Are you alright?"

43.

Sheets rustled nearby but Kate kept her eyes closed. She was lying on a bed and, judging from the telltale smell, she was still in hospital.

"...you sure she's alright?" she heard Beth whisper.

"Whatever she did exhausted her," Viktor replied, he too talking softly.

"Well, she worked a miracle," Beth replied. Kate felt a soft hand stroke her face, the fingers lingering in her hair. The motherly touch filled her with nostalgia for something she'd never had. "I haven't felt so good in ages," Beth continued. "I could get up and leave if it weren't for that pesky doctor."

"He's had a hard night. What with you miraculously healed and a man disguised as a nurse running amok..."

"Sorry about that," Kate said, opening her eyes. "I was so tired, I couldn't think of anything else. He was hurting me."

"You're awake!" Beth exclaimed and flung her arms around Kate who found herself lying on a second bed flush with Beth's. "We were worried."

"I'm fine. How are you?"

"Couldn't be better," Beth exclaimed planting a kiss on Kate's cheek. "Thanks to you."

"I hadn't quite finished," Kate said, "but I was too weary to go on."

"Well I don't know what more you could've done," Beth exclaimed. "I could get up and walk out."

"Let's not exaggerate," Viktor said with a chuckle. "One

miracle at a time. Are you two hungry?" When both agreed, he called a nurse, a real one this time, and ordered breakfast.

"Where did you sleep?" Kate asked him.

"In this very comfortable armchair," he replied, his tired but happy look belying his assurances.

"You wanna lie down here?" Kate asked. "I'm done with sleep."

"Thanks," he said shaking his head. "I'll get plenty of sleep once we get home."

Kate wasn't sure it would be safe to return to their house, but she didn't want to spoil the moment. While they waited for breakfast, Kate laid back, closed her eyes and contacted Eileen. *How's it going?*

The girl sounded breathless. *Demanding. I don't have your stamina.* The tongue-in-cheek humour came over loud and clear. *Keeping the new girls busy is hard work.*

What you doing?

Clearing the snow. But what about you? How's Beth?

She's fine. Kate groaned mentally at the memory of the accident. *She was really messed up. It took a lot of work.* The cleric's ugly face flashed through her mind. *You need to be vigilant,* she said. *What happened to Beth wasn't an accident. These people will stop at nothing.*

Eileen gasped. *Tell me.*

I will when I see you.

When will you be back?

Sometime this afternoon. I'll let you know.

Breakfast was being wheeled in when Kate opened her eyes. "Yum!" she said, her mouth watering at the bowls of muesli, garnished with fresh fruit. The doctor turned up at that moment and insisted on examining Kate before she ate.

"Headache?" he asked, pressing his stethoscope against her back.

She shook her head.

"How many fingers?" he asked holding up four.

"Seven," Kate replied, causing both Beth and Viktor to

chuckle. The doctor wasn't amused.

"This is serious, young lady," he said.

"It will be, if you prevent me from eating."

"Yes. Of course," he said folding his stethoscope and sliding it into the pocket of his white coat.

"What happened to that nurse?" she asked, reaching for the muesli.

"That was no nurse," he protested. "We haven't been able to get any sense out of him. My guess is he escaped from an asylum."

"Has anyone been reported missing?" Viktor asked.

The doctor shook his head. "The police have no idea who he is. And they've no inkling why he picked on you."

Kate munched a large mouthful of muesli, nodding to acknowledge the man's words.

"So, can I leave once we've eaten?" Beth asked.

"I'd like to do some tests," the doctor replied, scratching his head. "I still don't understand how you were so miraculously healed. The doctor last night reported multiple fractures. Now you don't even have a scratch, let-alone a bruise."

"Maybe I have the favour of the Almighty," Beth suggested, a smile on her lips.

"Well if you can remember the prayers you said, I'd be interested." He reluctantly accepted she could leave providing she came back for a check-up in a week. "I gather they've started clearing the roads so getting home shouldn't be a problem."

"What about my wheelchair?" Beth asked.

"We can loan you one, if you like."

"What happened to mine?"

"Apparently a man from the police took it away. I imagine they'll examine it."

Them and me too, Kate thought.

Back at Beth's house, Kate glanced through the Sunday newspaper while Viktor installed Beth in bed. December 11th, 1960. Rioting in Algeria took up much of the front page as locals continued to battle colonialists. She wondered if her old world would ever regain its independence from the warrior priests. More likely it no longer existed, given that the author who'd dreamed it up had died, thanks to her. She had no way of returning there and even if she had, she doubted she'd go. What remained of her family and friends were dead. And technically she was no longer the same person. She was a sort of clone of a younger Beth.

Turning back to the paper, she learnt that an American guy called Libby had won the Nobel prize for some newfangled way of dating old bones. The association was not very flattering, but she thought of Beth and whether her mobility could be improved or if her handicap could be removed completely. Once again she wished Peter were with her.

Her mind on him, she thumbed through the pages in search of news about England. The only thing she found was the mention of a new television programme called Coronation Street. The journalist speculated how long it would last. The Lost Girls had no television and neither had Lydia and Klaus, so she found it difficult to grasp what the article was about.

"She wants to talk to you," Viktor said coming back from the bedroom. The room where the couple slept was on the ground floor so as to be readily accessible with a wheelchair. A double bed was the centre piece, to each side bedside tables were piled high with books. There were no bookshelves, however. Those were relegated to the study which was just down the corridor.

Kate had never been in their bedroom. She was impressed by a large modern painting that hung at the foot of the bed. Kate was admiring it when Beth said, "It's by Aloïse Corbaz. Have you heard of Art Brut? The expression was coined by a guy called Jean Dubuffet." She briefly explained what the term meant. The idea that people could do art without having to learn the techniques and the history of art appealed to her. It made her think of the way they healed. Beth tapped on the bed, inviting Kate to sit next to her.

"I wanted to thank you," Beth began, a trace of embarrassment in her smile. "I knew you could heal, but I had no idea the extent of your abilities. Who taught you?"

"Nobody. I was interested in healing but none of my teachers were much use. They were stuck in the same paradigm, like doctors here. In fact it was Peter and I that stumbled on a new approach that was far more effective and didn't require cutting people up or feeding them drugs." She told Beth how they realised they could adapt mind-to-mind travel to enter people's bodies and heal them from within. She described their discovery of the blueprint that underscored life and how they used it to heal. "It was that simple."

"That's extraordinary," Beth said. "And you're teaching the girls?"

"Some."

"Just think of all you could do if you had a team of dedicated healers trained in your way of working."

Kate shook her head. She was used to the enthusiasm their approach sparked, but she knew only too well the medical profession would never let a different way of healing emerge. "There's a major problem to that rosey future," she said. "The medical profession would never accept an approach that showed up their incompetence. With their testing, their scientific method, their book-learning and the relentless training they undergo, the vast majority would be incapable of healing like we do. It would be too simple and simple is unscientific, untrustworthy. They'd be incapable of accepting that it worked even if they saw it done."

Beth nodded. "I see what you mean. It's as if you've stepped outside the bubble they've so carefully crafted. As they can only think inside it, what you do is beyond their comprehension. You might as well be a magician or a witch or an angel. It's a shame."

"That won't stop us training the girls. We just have to be very, very cautious. All this trouble with the church is nothing compared to what would beset us if the medical profession and the pharmaceutical industry caught on to what we do."

"Healing me like you did in public was maybe not so wise," Beth mused. "That doctor was perplexed. It'll probably never cross his mind that you, a young untrained girl, can do what he is unable to achieve with all his equipment and learning. But such an inexplicable event will bother him till he finally comes up with an explanation, true or false."

"I know. I shouldn't have done it, but I couldn't leave you broken when I could so easily heal you."

"I appreciate your help all the more for knowing the risk you took."

"That leads me to an important question," Kate said. She paused. It was difficult and delicate and she was unsure how to advance. "I have a suggestion to make." The look Beth gave her was intense. Questioning, expectant, suffused with suppressed excitement, dread, hope. Kate wonder if the woman had guessed. "I'd like to try and heal some of your handicap."

Beth let the breath she'd been holding whistle between her teeth. "You don't do things by half," she said, her chest heaving with emotion. "You realise it's been years. All that time, being handicapped has been a key part of my life, of my identity. I can barely remember myself otherwise. Yet not a day goes by that I don't wish the accident hadn't happened. That I could walk and dance and swim. That I didn't need help to dress or to take a bath. I'd have given anything for such a miracle."

Beth brushed tears from her eyes, then lent forward and took both Kate's hands in hers. "If healing me in the hospital was rash, removing my handicap would be suicidal. I'm a public figure. Everyone knows me. How would I explain such a miracle? They'd find out. They'd hound you till they managed to get rid of you, the anomaly that challenged all they stood for, someone they couldn't bear to live with. Why do you think they nailed Jesus to a cross? Because he healed people, he worked miracles, he had a radically different way of seeing the world. I'd never accept that you sacrifice yourself just so that my life could be a little easier. You're one of the people I treasure most in the world. You're my daughter, my love."

44.

Christina? Peter said.

Peter! she exclaimed, her voice full of worry. *Are you alright?*

I'm fine. Is John with you?

Yes.

Ask him if I can include him in our conversation.

He heard her ask John and a mental nod came back.

Hi, John! Peter said, extending their conversation to include his adoptive father.

What's up? John asked, sounding uneasy.

We have discovered that the prefects, the nurse and probably the headmistress have been physically abusing the girls.

Christina gasped, but John growled. *I'm not surprised.*

I've seen things that would sicken you. Peter paused, making sure he didn't inadvertently relay images of Linda's pock-marked body. *We've decided to hold what I'm calling an inquest. To give the girls a chance to bear witness. It's a quest for facts, for openness, for understanding, not for retribution. We need to do this amongst ourselves, to confront these problems without wreaking bloody revenge. I am convinced we can and must, but it won't be enough.*

What do you mean? Christina asked.

We're aware this abuse has wider repercussions. That's why we need adults to bear witness, before acting on what they've heard and seen, carrying it forward into society at large with all the implications involved. For this to work, those witnesses need to watch, to listen, and possibly act later, but not to intervene during the inquest.

That's a tall order, John said, although Peter knew from the man's thoughts that he was already mentally drawing up a list of people.

I know, Peter replied. *I've thought about it a lot, but it won't work any other way. This isn't about justice, although that's important, but healing. These girls have to continue living and studying together.*

That's so thoughtful, Christina responded, her words suffused with love and admiration.

I think it's a excellent idea, John added, *although it's not going to be easy. When do you need these people?*

Ten tomorrow morning in the chapel.

The chapel? Christina exclaimed. *Are you sure? On a Sunday?*

I know, Peter said, letting his uneasiness colour his words. *But there's no other place big enough and it's normal for it to be used for assemblies.*

That makes sense, Christina mused. *And there's a balcony where the witnesses could sit unseen.*

Good, Peter replied. *So I can count on you?*

Yes, John replied. *I thought I'd invite...*

I prefer not to know, Peter interrupted. *Tell me afterwards.*

John chuckled. *Okay. We'll be there at ten.*

Pleased it had gone well, Peter lay on Eloise's bed looking up at the ceiling. One thing they hadn't discussed was the reaction of the girls. He had no idea if they'd go along. And how would they react to such an intimate discussion in front of a silent audience of adults? He'd already broached the subject with the others. They'd agreed. But had they been fully aware what it entailed?

Peter? a familiar voice called out. Kate. She didn't sound angry, but he had to check. To his surprise and delight she apologised. It was the chance he'd been hoping for. He explained what had happened and instead of flying off the handle she questioned him about Linda's injuries. He also mentioned the inquest, at which she said things were coming to a head in Luzern too. Out of necessity, their conversation was short, but he was relieved to have talked to her. It was with a smile on his lips that he got up and went in search of the others.

He found Sarah and Eloise seated with Linda and a few girls in the canteen. He collected his lunch from a lady at the hatch and carried his tray to join them. "How did it go?" Sarah asked.

"Much better than I expected. They agreed to get together a group of adult witnesses for ten tomorrow."

"Tomorrow!" Eloise exclaimed. "That's impossible. We'll never keep the girls in check till then."

"What we need is a distraction," Linda said. "Something to keep them busy."

"How about healing?" Eloise asked, grinning at her own suggestion. "There's no shortage of ailments. Just think of all those who came for help yesterday and had to be turned away. And you could continue teaching us at the same time."

"Oh yes!" Linda said, clapping her hands in enthusiasm. "Please."

It was a good idea and had the added advantage of winning over more girls to their cause. "Fine," he said. "Let's use my room as a surgery. That way we can take refuge in yours, Eloise, if ever."

At first only a trickle of girls dared come, but the more they healed the wider the word spread and the longer the queue grew. Everyone had something. Sores that wouldn't heal. Itches that drove one mad. Incapacitating pains that stabbed in the stomach or the back or down one leg. Not to mention headaches or full-blown migraines. The list was unending. With so much suffering, Peter wondered how life had gone on normally. Why on earth didn't the nurse cater for such ailments? When asked, girls were evasive.

During a pause he raised the question. "Whatever does the nurse do all day?"

"Not much," Eloise replied, sounding sour.

"I heard she had favourites and spent a lot of time with them," Sarah said.

"I'm not sure 'favourite' is the right word," Linda said, wrinkling her nose as if she'd smelt something rotten. "Unless of course you mean they did favours for her."

"Like running errands?" Peter asked, hoping against hope that she wasn't talking about sexual favours.

Linda's laughter was bitter. "More like..." She hesitated, looking completely disgusted. "...personal gratification."

Peter groaned. What a place! "Is this common knowledge?"

"I don't think so," Sarah said, "I knew nothing about it."

"I had my suspicions," Eloise said. "But I kept out of her way."

Peter wondered if Christina had known. She'd been at the heart of the workings of the school. Surely she'd have done something if she had. "Have we healed any of those girls?" he asked.

"Nope. They've been hanging around, spying no doubt, but none have come to see us," Linda said.

"I'd like to talk to one," Peter said. "Maybe we can convince her to speak at tomorrow's inquest."

"I doubt it," Linda said. "The nurse has a pretty tight hold on them."

"Blackmail, you mean?" Sarah blurted out.

"Something like that," Linda answered. "Or just guilt."

"Maybe they enjoyed it," Sarah suggested, earning her filthy looks from both Eloise and Linda. Sarah shrugged. "Why not? This is a pretty grim place. A little warmth and comfort from time to time must surely be welcome."

The girl had a point. "The question is," he said, "whether the nurse took advantage of their need for human warmth and company."

"I know one. She's got a bit of a squint," Linda said. "She might be tempted to come if she thought she could be healed. I reckon she's more likely to spill the beans than the others. I'll go fetch her."

The girl with the squint was called Pam but most people called her Pin. She was tall and resembled a skeleton with skin pulled over it. Peter wondered if she was anorexic. Why had no one tried to help her? He felt a surge of anger at the nurse. She must have known.

"Why are you disguised as a girl?" Pin challenged, her voice surprisingly forceful for someone so frail.

At least she had the courage to confront him. "I'm not 'disguised'," he replied. "I dress as a girl because, in many ways, I feel like a girl. If I wear girl's clothes, it's an affirmation of who I am. It feels right. I am complete."

"But you aren't a girl!" Pin objected.

"If you mean I was born in a boy's body, you're right. I don't deny that part of me is a boy, but a large part of me is a girl."

She shot him a disgusted look. "You're a freak!"

"I am as I am. Would you have me eliminated so you can feel comfortable with who or what you are?"

His words troubled her. She scratched her head and stared at the other girls before turning back to him.

"If you mean I am different from most people," he continued, "you're right. I'm in between. In a world where you have to chose between 'yes' and 'no', I refuse. I am both and neither."

The girl shook her head, but said no more.

"Tell me, how long have you had a problem with your eye?" Peter asked.

At the mention of her squint she lost much of her self-confidence. "Just after I came here," she muttered. "I looked in the mirror and there it was. I was so upset, I hid under the blankets."

"Did you see a doctor?"

"I went to the nurse. She said it was a lazy muscle. She prescribed massages. It seemed a good idea. When she offered to do them herself, I was delighted. It was always the high-point of my week. I was lonely and homesick and I had confidence. She was like a mother."

Peter could imagine the story unfolding, but he wanted to

deal with her eye first. "If you agree I'll set your eye straight. To do that, I need to place a hand on your hand or your arm."

The girl looked sceptical but nodded. He stretched out to touch her but she flinched. "I know. I'm a 'freak'," he said, saddened.

"No. It's not that." She seemed to struggle about whether to say more. "Last time someone promised to heal me, I ended up regretting it."

"I'm not going to take advantage of you." He glanced at Sarah, Eloise and Linda. "These three are my witnesses. I swear. Only one healing," Peter said, then he remembered the anorexia. "Well, maybe two. No more."

"Two?"

"The problem with the food."

"Oh!" Her face turned scarlet and she stared at her feet. After a long moment, she held out a trembling hand.

He took it, and quickly surveyed the state of her health. "I'm teaching these girls to heal. Do you agree to let them help?"

"It is bad enough having you mess with me. I don't want them meddling too."

All three looked disappointed, but no one complained.

At first her fear drove her to resist. He hadn't known the mind could deliberately oppose the body's blueprint. But now he'd experienced it, the phenomenon made sense. It explained why certain thoughts caused illness. He concentrated on easing the fear, then dealing with the squint was a piece of cake. Handling anorexia was more complex. He wasn't sure how to proceed. In the end, he worked on the natural need for food, strengthening it without causing her to overeat. He also worked on her vision of herself, alleviating some of the negative images.

He was about to leave her body, when he sensed a pain on the inside of her thighs and between her legs. Out of respect, he avoided those regions unless it was really necessary. He looked closer, but couldn't be sure what had caused the damage. Clearly the girl was badly bruised. He healed what he could, not wanting to linger too long.

"That was weird," Pin said as he relinquished her hand. "I expected to feel you grubbing about, but it was only at the end I felt anything. Did you think you could touch me up without me knowing?"

"I did not 'touch you up' as you call it. I healed the bruises on the inside of your thighs. Who did that to you?"

Pin looked at him aghast. "You saw that?"

"Not 'see'. Felt. Whoever did that used a lot of force. Those were pretty extensive bruises."

Tears welled in her eyes and she hid her face in her hands. "I said no," she muttered. "I said no, but she insisted."

"Who?" Peter asked.

She pursed her lips and refused to speak.

"So many bad things have happened here," Peter said. "But nobody dares mention them. Those secrets are poisoning us. It's time we shared. That's why we are holding an inquest. To give everyone a chance to speak up without fear of retribution. Why not take advantage and get this off your mind? I realise it won't be easy. It's not easy for anybody. But we'll all be stronger for it."

45.

"Do you think she'll dare?" Linda asked.

"I don't know," Peter said sipping a tea one of their growing number of supporters had brought. "When she hears others like you bear witness maybe that'll give her the courage."

"I don't regret you healing me," Linda said. "How could I? But in doing so you removed all the evidence."

"You're right. By healing everyone we are effectively effacing the proof of abuse," Peter said.

"Maybe we should have taken photos," Sarah suggested.

"There's a camera in the lab," Eloise said. "I'm sure we could borrow it."

A head peered around the door and whispered a warning, "The nurse!"

A hammering announced the woman's arrival. She shoved open the door, and stumbling inside, slammed it behind her. While the girls of Our Lady were looking increasingly healthy and a lot happier, the nurse appeared haggard, unkempt and thoroughly wretched. At a guess, she hadn't slept all night, might well have been drinking and looked to be on the verge of a nervous breakdown.

"Nurse?" Peter said. "To what do we owe this visit?"

"You know full well." Her words were slurred and she was none too steady.

Peter could sense the in-held breath as the others tensed for a storm. He was less anxious, having experienced threatening moments with outed adults before. Nothing unnerved adults more than no longer controlling the situation.

"Well?" the woman asked, putting out a hand to hold on to Eloise for support. The girl shifted out of reach causing the nurse to fall heavily to the floor in a disorganised heap of limbs. The girls stared in horror. Seeing this woman stripped of all dignity was like witnessing an institution crumbling. Here was one of the adults who ran their school, who was supposed to care for them and ensure their welfare and she lay snivelling on the floor. "Don't do this to me," she pleaded. "I'll never get a job again."

"Unfortunately, we can't help!" Peter replied, struggling not to sound triumphant. "We're too busy doing what you failed to do. If I were you, I'd try apologising. If you're lucky some might forgive you."

The woman scrambled to her feet, her abjection giving way to seething anger. "I'll destroy you," she spat, taking a threatening step towards Peter, "you filthy pervert. I'll tell everybody who and what you are."

"Go ahead," Peter said, trying not to cringe at the reek of alcohol. "I'm quite happy with who I am. As a rapist of young girls I'm not sure you could say the same."

She halted and stood, her mouth open, staring aghast at him. "You what?" Her voice had risen an octave making her sound like a pig realising its throat was about to be cut. "How dare you?"

"He's just stating the facts," Linda said.

"Your dirty secret is out," Eloise added.

"If I were you," Sarah put in, glancing at the door, "I'd run."

The nurse looked from one to another horrified. All of a sudden the tables were turned. Here were girls who would never have dared say a word, calmly exposing her, the nurse, for wrong-doing without the slightest hint of fear or anger. No wonder she stared at them uncomprehending. It was a nightmare. She turned on her heals and teetered in the direction of the door.

Once she'd left and Eloise had closed the door, everyone sucked in a deep breath.

"Well I'm blowed," Eloise managed, astonished. "Something momentous just happened. I doubt I'll ever be the same. It's as if the line between me as a child and her as an adult just went up in smoke? Does that mean I've become adult?" The idea seemed to horrify her.

"Yuppie! No more being bossed around," Sarah said with unrestrained glee.

"I wouldn't get too cocky," Peter said, looking around for his mug of tea. "Not all adults will fold like her. And anyway, the vast majority are not so bad. What they say often makes sense, even if we don't like it. Remember, we have to live with them like they have to live with us." He turned to Eloise. "I've no idea if that means you're becoming an adult. We all cross that line at some time." Yeah, he thought, you're a one to talk. Like his namesake Peter Pan, he wanted to dwell for ever on the child's side of the divide. How else could he remain both girl and boy?

"I see what you mean," he continued, setting aside his own preoccupations. "As children we have a distorted view of adults. For many it's a rosy picture, but for a minority it's more somber. Our naivety, our implicit trust and, for some, constant wariness, is partly why we unwittingly become complicit, if not victims." That said, if being disillusioned with adults was any indication, he'd very definitely crossed that line a while ago.

With a growing queue of girls waiting outside, they couldn't tarry long. All three were getting proficient in handling simple ailments and Peter was glad to step back and let them work. They'd learnt quickly thanks to the direct way working mind-to-mind enabled. Rather than trying to imitate a complex action seen from the outside, he had them feel what it was like as if they'd done it themselves.

They were nearing time for the evening meal when a tiny head peered round the door and hissed, "Headmistress" before disappearing. Indeed the headmistress strode in, not bothering to knock. She was flanked by the prefects.

Ignoring Peter and addressing only Eloise, she demanded,

"What on earth are you up to?"

Unlike earlier, Eloise did not cower. The experience with the nurse had changed her. "We're making the most of our time to help our fellow pupils," she replied.

"Well, I've come to order you to stop. You're disturbing the school. The weekend is supposed to be a time of rest. You're upsetting the girls. If you persist, I'll have to take drastic action. This cannot continue."

Peter wondered how Eloise would react. The girl hesitated, as if weighing her options. The prefects guarding the headmistress took a step closer, their arms crossed over their chests, their lips pinched in an angry snarl.

"What makes you think the girls are upset?" Eloise asked, her eyes fixed on the headmistress.

It was the headmistress's turn to be taken aback. Defiance, on the rare occasions there'd ever been any, never took this calm confident form.

"Who said we were upset?" Linda asked, moving to stand next to Eloise.

Peter did the same, although he kept quiet. Out of the corner of his eye, he saw Sarah slip out the half-open door. He couldn't help feeling disappointed. Surely the girl wasn't chickening out at such a key moment?

"I don't need to justify myself," the headmistress said, apparently over her momentary surprise. "Your insolence is insufferable. Come with me. I'll deal with you in my office." No one spoke. No one moved.

"No you won't," a voice said from the door. It was Sarah, her words ringing clear in the silence. The headmistress spun on her heels to face Sarah who stood in the doorway. Flooding into the room around her were many of the girls they'd healed or helped. They looked grim and determined. Angry even.

"The only thing we're upset with at the moment," Gladys said at Sarah's side, "is you and your prefects."

"Yes!" several voices hissed.

Peter's tiny room was already packed and more girls, who

were massing in the corridor, struggled to get in. Despite the crush, a tight ring isolated the headmistress and her prefects. Nobody wanted to touch them, for the moment at least.

"I'd leave if I were you," Eloise suggested, "It'll be safer for everyone."

"Go pack your cases," someone called out from the back, causing several girls to snigger.

Eloise ignored them. "The prefects can join us if they wish, providing they cause no further trouble. Or they can chose to side with you."

A number of girls bared their teeth and growled, no doubt unhappy at welcoming them. Peter couldn't blame them. After all, these were the very girls who'd mistreated so many of those present. The press of girls was now so great, the prefects were squashed up against the headmistress, their expressions of disgust revealing their intense discomfort.

"This is not the last you'll hear of this," the headmistress said, in an attempt at defiance,

"I'm sure it's not," Eloise said with a grin. The tense laughter that rippled through the room clearly spooked the headmistress who turned to retreat but the way was blocked.

"Let them out," Eloise ordered.

Immediately the mass of girls shifted and reformed, some withdrawing to the corridor, others tightening ranks till a narrow passage opened. The headmistress marched between the rows of girls, her head held high, to the sounds of hissing and booing. Nobody dared touch her, although Peter spotted a number of raised fists.

The prefects didn't fare so well. Elbows prodded them in the ribs, fists jabbed out, nails clawed at bare flesh, feet sought to trip up, some even spat, copiously. It was an ugly sight. He was afraid the pack would tear the prefects apart but they made it out, albeit cut, bruised and dripping with spittle. The crowd in the corridor was almost as dense and no less forgiving. The prefects ran the gauntlet all the way to the front door.

When the headmistress and her entourage had fled and

the cheer that followed had died down, Eloise raised her voice and said, "Now let's get something to eat." Her words sparked another cheer and the crowd began to disperse amid chatter and laughter.

Once the girls had vacated his room, Peter gave Eloise a hug, saying, "Well done. You too," he told Sarah, hugging her as well.

"What about me?" Linda piped up.

"You were all wonderful," he said and he meant it. Linda insisted on a hug. In the end, they formed a congratulatory huddle and for a long moment their worries receded in a joyous expression of triumph and a growing awareness that girls too had potential and could wield power. Peter was enveloped in a heady girlhood that accepted him for what he was. It felt good.

For the first time since he'd landed in Our Lady of Grace he had the impression he could slip away and everything would be alright. Well, it would be, provided they succeeded the inquest. Now they'd dealt with the nurse and the headmistress, albeit temporarily, Sunday's inquest could go ahead unhindered. That didn't make managing it any easier. He thought of the twisted faces spitting at the prefects and wondered if he and his new friends could contain the anger the inquest would set free.

46.

Drifts of snow sculpted unfamiliar landscapes as Viktor drove her up to Lydia and Klaus's house. Access by car to the village was out of the question. She'd have to hike through the snow. Elated as she was after her talk with Beth, she was looking forward to the walk.

During the ride, Kate told Viktor that Beth's wheelchair had been tampered with. When he insisted on knowing more, she related what she'd seen in Beth's memories.

"No wondered they took the wheelchair away," he said.

"Keep an eye on her," Kate warned

Finding neither Klaus nor Lydia at home, Viktor would willingly have accompanied her to the village but he was worried about Beth. So, borrowing a pair of snow shoes, she set off alone. It was sunny and the forecast predicted good weather.

Eileen, she called out. *I'm leaving Lydia's on foot. I should be there within an hour.*

Eileen offered to meet her, but Kate declined. *I need to think. We'll have plenty of time to talk once I arrive.*

The track wound through a small forest of pine trees. She was reminded of hunting with her arms master. They'd stalked deer. There'd been no snow, of course, but the watchful silence was similar. Instinctively she slowed her pace, making as little noise as possible. She paused regularly to listen. All was still except for the occasional thud of a clump of snow tumbling from a branch.

She was wondering if there was game around their village

when a twig snapped to her right. She froze, every sense alert. The sound of a second twig snapping followed the first. If it was game, it must be big. A bear maybe. She shuddered. She could fight, but not a bear. Several more snaps convinced her it couldn't be a bear. An animal would never make so much noise. It must be a person. Surely none of the girls would have ventured so far from the village.

"Bloody idiot," a whispered hiss said. "Mind where you're walking." The speaker was male and to her right just where the twigs had snapped. So there were two of them. Youths judging from the voices.

"How am I to see branches covered in snow?" the other youth replied. Snow might have muffled sound, but in such overriding silence their words were clearly audible.

"Put a sock in it!" a third voice exclaimed some thirty yards to her left. She strained to hear if there were any more. She heard the footfalls of at least one more person. She was surrounded. If she'd been strolling along the track, they'd have seen her. Luckily, in reminiscing about hunting, she'd taken to keeping concealed. She wished she had her bow. She was a good shot. In her world, she'd never have ventured out without it. But in Peter's world she had little use for one.

Eileen, she called out.

Trouble? Eileen replied, no doubt sensing the alarm in her voice.

A group of youths prowling through the forest. They're heading for the village, not on the track but through the woods.

Where are you?

About half way. In that little forest.

Should I send a band of girls?

Kate was tempted to refuse. If they barricaded the entrances, they might weather an attack. But she'd rather fight on her own terms. *Send half the choir along the track with drums and fifes. Have them make as much noise as possible, as if they were marching to war. Scare the living daylights out of the bastards. Keep the rest of the choir to organise the new girls if ever the youths skirt round and attack the village from behind.*

While she'd been talking, the youths had moved on and Kate shifted to follow them. Despite their slow progress, the youths would soon leave the forest and she'd be without cover. If she was going to act, it was now. She caught sight of a youth not far away. One of his snowshoes had come loose and he was sitting on a log struggling to re-fix it.

Can I help? she asked casually mind-to-mind.

The youth sprang to his feet in alarm, his head swivelling in search of whoever had spoken. Nobody was in sight. He took a step, forgetting he was wearing only one snowshoe and his foot sank deep into the snow causing him to tip over. There was an ominous crack as his leg broke. His scream shattered the silence causing his fellows to blunder through the snow in search of him. There were indeed four of them.

The tallest towered over his colleague writhing in the snow, berating him. "Bloody fool. Can't you be more careful?" None of the youths made the slightest move to help. "We can't waste time on this," the leader said. "We have a job to do. You'll have to stay here. We'll pick you up on the way back."

"At least help me onto that trunk," the youth pleaded between gritted teeth.

The leader nodded to the other two who hauled the injured youth out of the snow, causing him to wail, and dumped him on the trunk. He gripped his leg as if that would assuage the pain, but, judging from his face, it only made things worse. One of the two pulled a flask from his pocket when the leader was not looking and stuffed it in the injured youth's hand. She'd been going to attack him next, but his gesture made her change her mind.

It was at that moment the distant sound of drums and fifes reached them along with an eerie wailing. The choir! Even she was spooked. The youths spun round in the direction of the music, terrified. "What the hell's that?" the leader asked, unable to mask the tremble in his voice.

If I were you, I'd run, Kate whispered in his mind.

"What the bloody...?" he began and clamped his hands over ears.

Still here? Kate asked in her best imitation of a witch's voice.

"D'you hear that?" he asked, tapping the flat of his hand against his head as if that would drive the voice out.

"What?" one of the youths asked, sounding even more afraid. "All I hear is that blasted music."

"The woman's voice!" He sounded on the verge of panic.

"What woman? Ain't no woman here."

Kate was so close she could hear their laboured breathing and smell the reek of alcohol. Provided the youths didn't come any closer, they'd never see her, although behind the tree was not the best of hiding places. A dried branch stabbed her in the side. She thought of healing herself but instead shifted slightly. When branch snapped with a resounding click she swore silently. All the youths spun to look at her.

"That one!" the leader said, triumphant as he strode forward and grabbed Kate.

There was no point in trying to flee in deep snow wearing snowshoes. She let him drag her over to the others, making the most of the contact to flip through his memories while making him nauseous at the same time.

"Stop whatever you're doing witch or I'll break your arm," he growled. He must have realised touch had something to do with her power over him, if only intuitively, because he let go and took a step away.

Witch? She'd brought that on herself. *Eileen,* she called out. *Careful how you approach, they've caught me. There are four of them, but one is badly hurt.*

Okay, Eileen replied. *Be there soon. Hold on.*

"So Bruno," she said making use of the information she'd gleaned from his thoughts, "that cleric's not going to be very happy."

"How the hell does she know that?" one of the youths blurted out.

"Shut your mouth," Bruno snapped.

"If you don't get help soon for your colleague," she nodded towards the injured youth, "the badly fractured leg and frost bite will get the better of him. They'll probably have to amputate."

The youth moaned, causing Bruno to snap at him. "Don't pay her no heed. She's just trying to scare the shit out of you."

The marching band and choir was so close, Kate could make out individual voices. She didn't know who'd come up with the weird wailing chant, but it was brilliant. The youths, even their leader, were completely unnerved. They stuck their fingers in their ears, but to no avail. A part of the chant must have been communicated mind-to-mind. No wonder they were terrified. They couldn't escape.

Rather than march up to the youths, the girls stopped just out of sight and intensified their singing, punctuating the drawn out musical phrases with a roll on their drums. Several were playing fifes that wove a strident call in and out of the chant.

"Have them stop," one of the youths pleaded.

But the girls were relentless. They hammered away at the youth's minds. Kate expected them to run, abandoning their injured colleague, but they stood frozen to the spot, their faces twisted in pain and distress. One was even dribbling.

She pulled out a length of cord from her backpack and lashed the three together, attaching their hands behind their backs. The leader was the only one to resist, but his efforts were feeble.

Okay, she called out, *you can stop. They are under control.*

That's a shame, Tania replied. *I was enjoying that.*

Weird! How could anyone enjoy making such a painful sound? Eileen, Tania and Sandra tramped into sight. "The others are on the track," Eileen explained. "We didn't have enough snowshoes."

"We found a sledge in the village," Tania said, "so we pulled it with us. I gather one of these boys is injured."

It was a thoughtful idea, although Kate suspected Tania was angling to get her claws in the 'boy', always avid to procure anything new for herself. "We'll heal him before we move him," Kate said much to Tania's disappointment.

Sandra, Eileen and Tania led the three youths stumbling away while Kate tramped over to the remaining youth. He'd fainted. Mending his leg with him curled up in a heap was out of the question. Alone there was little she could do. Finally she hit on the idea of trampling the snow till the area was big enough to lay the youth on.

She'd just managed to shift the unconscious youth onto her prepared place when Eileen called. *You alright?*

Healing such a bulky youth in deep snow is a bit of a struggle. She didn't need to insist, Eileen could hear her laboured breathing.

Tania and I will come and help. We were waiting for you anyway.

Make sure those three are well tied up.

Eileen chuckled. *Don't worry about them. We've removed their snowshoes.*

Bring a blanket, if you've got one, Kate said before breaking the connection.

Examining the youth's leg, she realised that it was so badly fractured that no amount of effort from nearby muscles would shift the bone into place. She was forced to physically help. Watching the progress from inside, she pushed and twisted the bones from outside with her hands. She'd never attempted anything like it before and the feeling of being both inside and out was profoundly disorienting.

She'd just managed to manoeuvre the parts into alignment after a long struggle not only with the bones but with the muscles and tendons when her concentration was shattered by the arrival of Tania.

"I was sure you'd be touching him up while our backs were turned," the girl accused.

In a burst of fury, Kate snapped, "Blithering idiot! Can you think of nothing else than your own paltry pleasure? There's a lot more in the world than bloody boys."

Tania stumbled back as if Kate had slapped her. The surge of anger had caught Kate off guard. Several times recently such outbursts had surprised and shocked her. She hated to admit it, but she'd become touchy since Peter left.

Arriving late on the scene, Eileen too was astonished at Kate's anger. "What's up?"

"This idiot here," she pointed at Tania, "just wiped out ten minutes of difficult effort with her clumsy insensitivity. Now I'm going to have to realign the broken bones again."

As Kate turned her attention back to the bone she was vaguely aware of Tania stomping off and Eileen calling after her. She shut out the distractions and concentrated on the healing. A quarter of an hour later, the bone was pieced together and the tissues were knit to Kate's satisfaction. When she opened her eyes, the youth was staring at her in wonder.

"Whatever did you do?" he asked.

"I reset your bone. It should be okay but you'd better not put any weight on it for a couple of days. Bones take a while to heal, even with a little help from me."

"But... you're no doctor ... and you're so young ..." he stammered.

She was glad he hadn't added that she was a girl, even if he'd surely thought it. "If it makes you more comfortable," she said, "imagine it was a miracle." She helped him to his feet only to realise there was no way he could get through the snow without putting weight on his leg so she called Eileen and they brought the sledge.

Back on the snow-covered track Kate looked for Tania but she was nowhere to be seen. "Where's Tania?"

"No idea." Eileen shrugged. "I thought she would come here."

She clearly hadn't. Kate called out mind-to-mind, but, although she sensed the girl's presence, Tania refused to answer. *We're heading back to the village,* Kate sent. *Don't stay out too long. It's getting cold and night'll fall soon.*

The sledge went first, pulled by several girls. Someone had

suggested roping the youths in like oxen, but they were hopeless at pulling in the snow. Still strung together, the three came next and the rest of the choir followed. Eileen and Kate brought up the rear.

"That chant was impressive," Kate said.

"It was Clara's idea," Eileen replied.

"Did she think of mixing sound with mind-to-mind?"

"No. That was me." A broad grin brightened her face.

"You're right to be proud," Kate said, slinging an arm around the girl's shoulder. "It was a master stroke. You realise we could adapt the idea to happier chants and perform them in concerts. It'd be like playing on people's emotions as one might an organ."

47.

Night had fallen and it had begun to snow. Kate was worried. "Any news of Tania?" she asked for the third time.

Eileen shook her head.

"I'm going to contact Lydia. Maybe she went to their place."

Lydia?

Kate's call was greeted by a loud crash and Lydia swore. *You startled me. I dropped a baking tray.*

I hope it was empty?

Luckily. I'd just removed the biscuits. There was a brief pause as she picked up the tray. *I suppose you're looking for Tania.*

Kate nodded mentally.

She's not very happy and doesn't want to talk, especially not to you.

Kate felt indignant and was tempted to justify herself, but instead she said, *Tell her I called and that we were worried about her.*

I will.

Thanks for looking after her.

No problem. By the way, Regina called. The two are coming to visit you this evening. Apparently they've borrowed a small snowplough from a friend. They plan to open the track. Regina said they've got good news.

Well that's something to look forward to.

If you're short of anything, just say. With the trail open, Klaus could bring supplies over.

Thanks. I'll let you know.

"Well?" Eileen asked.

"She's with Lydia." Kate relayed the news about Regina and Heinz.

"I'll make sure we keep some soup for them. We could meet at the guardian's house."

Not understanding, Kate asked, "The what?"

"Sorry. I forgot to tell you. We cleared it out earlier with the new girls."

"How are they?"

"Fine," Sandra said, striding up. "They're hungry! As am I." She paused to give instructions to one of the new girls. "Are we supposed to feed those thugs?" She sounded disgruntled.

The three had been tied up in the stalls and gagged. The fourth lay on the sledge which had been dragged into a spare corner of the barn. Rather than complain, he'd repeatedly apologised. His behaviour had earned him a blanket and a bowl of soup.

"He's asking to see you," Sandra said, her smile barely concealed.

Kate groaned. She didn't need to ask who. Since she'd healed him, he'd clung to her. Well, he would have if he'd been allowed to get up. "I'll go talk to him. Eileen, why don't you come along?"

"Need a chaperon?" Eileen quipped.

Kate sighed. They were going to have to do something about the absence of boys. The hysteria at the slightest boy would drive her mad. With the Lost Girls, a girls-only regime had worked. Well there was Peter. But he was almost a girl. Now there were so many girls, having only girls was proving to be a problem. "No," she replied. "Just a witness."

"Should I bring a note pad and pen?" Eileen continued to tease.

"Bring whatever you like," Kate said, fed up at having fun poked at her.

The youth lounged under a heap of blankets, propped up by

a couple of cushions, a mug of tea grasped in one hand. His eyes lit up at the sight of her. "My saviour!"

Eileen nudged Kate in the ribs whispering, "He's talking to you."

Kate ignored her jibe and her jab. "I see you're well cared for." The girls were out-doing each other to coddle him. "I gather you wanted to talk."

"Yes. I've been thinking..." He hesitated as if not daring to go on, then blurted out, "Could you teach me this healing business?"

His hopeful expression had her smile. He reminded her of an old dog begging for favours, but she couldn't accept. They were already too exposed and saying yes would bring a total stranger into the fold, a boy at that.

"That might be difficult," Kate replied. "We are concentrating on girls healing girls." Peter was the exception, but he was an almost-girl. "Healing was once almost exclusively in the hands of women and they were particularly skilled in caring for other women. Now medicine is dominated by men, many of whom see women as men with a bit missing."

The youth smirked.

Typical! "You can laugh, but such an attitude has serious consequences for the health of girls and women."

"What about nurses? Surely they play a part."

"You're right. They do. But what they do and how they do it is largely dictated by men and by science seen through the eyes of men, for men."

"Wow! Where do all those ideas come from?"

"I take what I do seriously. Don't you?"

He laughed nervously. "I try not to think too much. I've always seen life as a chance to have fun."

Kate shook her head, muttering half to herself, "Boys really are a race apart." To be honest, many girls in this world were just as flippant. Maybe it was an effect of childhood. She suspected such a forced period of irresponsibility was debilitating. It hadn't existed in her world.

"Something intrigues me," she said. "Why were you creeping through the forest? Was it for 'fun'?"

The youth looked away, embarrassed. "I'm so sorry," he repeated.

"Yes. You've said. Several times. But you haven't said why. What were you planing to do ?"

"Er..." He looked away, embarrassed. "It wasn't my idea."

"Listen, we're not going to execute you if you spill the beans." She sighed. He was infuriating. "But I might strangle you if you say sorry one more time." He flinched. "It's important. We need to know."

"We were to scare you," he said, looking like he'd confessed to a deadly sin. What a hopeless ditherer!

"How were you supposed to do that?" Kate asked, making no effort to conceal her impatience.

"Drag some of the girls off into the wood..."

"And?"

He squirmed, reluctant to say. "You can imagine..."

"No," Kate said, intent on forcing him to say. "I can't. Tell me."

"Touch them up..."

"Assault them sexually you mean?"

He seemed shocked at hearing it put so bluntly. "Just playing around," he said staring anywhere but at her.

"Do you 'play around' with girls much younger than yourself often?"

He shook his head, ashamed.

"If I had a magic wand I'd turn you into a girl and force you to experience how terrifying boys' 'fun' can be." In reality, she didn't need a wand. Words were enough. She spoke of the prying hands roaming her body. Imitating what the choir had done earlier with their scary chant, she let her disgust and shame flow with her words causing the youth to whimper and cringe. Eileen and Sandra were also horrified and disgusted and angry as Kate's tale washed over them.

"Not only do you not think what you do, but you have no

empathy. Well now you know. Maybe you'll think twice next time."

He looked haunted. "I'm so..." he began, but halted before he could say the word. "I could never have imagined," he said, his voice trembling.

"Who put you up to it?"

The question scared him. "I can't say."

"Do you want to continue feeling like a boy's plaything?" she threatened.

He shuddered. "No. Don't. I'll tell you."

She was glad he gave in. She had no wish to pursue those feelings.

"It was a bloke from the church. I never met him. Bruno knew the guy. He'd done jobs for him. He told Bruno where to go and what to do. He promised a reward."

"That's interesting," a woman's voice said, startling Kate. She'd been so engrossed she hadn't realised they had company. Spinning round she saw Regina standing with Heinz.

"Well met!" Kate exclaimed and embraced the woman. Heinz gave her a hug too. "Thanks for coming despite the snow."

"No problem," Heinz said.

"We thought we'd bring you some good news!" Regina added. "But it seems you have news of your own. Who's your friend?"

Kate groaned. "This young man, who's no friend of mine, is one of four youths who thought it would be 'fun' to sexually molest young girls and hear them squeal."

The youth protested that he'd done nothing, that he'd changed his mind, that he would never do such a thing, but Regina ignored him. "Let me guess, they were sent by a man from the church?"

"Right again," Kate replied.

"Time to unmask that man before he gets someone killed," Heinz said.

The youth gasped. "I wouldn't do that if I were you."

"Why ever not?" Regina asked.

"He's dangerous."

"I thought you never met him," Regina shot back.

"I haven't. But he has a reputation. Bruno told us if we valued our lives, we shouldn't cross him."

"Well you're in a pickle," Heinz said. "I imagine he's not very happy about your failure to deliver."

The youth cringed, glancing hastily over his shoulder."

"You'd stand an better chance if he were in prison," Regina pointed out.

"But he's not. And he's got god on his side."

"I wouldn't be so sure of that," Regina replied. "Even the church has to submit to the law, in the end."

"Why don't you add your testimony to the growing body of evidence against him and his accomplices," Regina said. "It's probably the only way of protecting yourself."

"I don't even know the bloke," the youth objected. "You'd be better off getting Bruno to talk."

"We will," Regina said, gifting him a smile. "Don't worry about that. But your word counts too."

The youth shook his head.

"Surely you're not going to let Bruno have the final word," Kate said. "Isn't he the guy who was going to leave you stuck in the snow with a broken leg."

The youth's brow darkened but he wouldn't give in. Kate was fed up with his delaying. They had other things to do. "We'll talk to you later. In the mean time, I advise against walking on that leg. It could well break again." It wasn't true, but it was a handy way of making sure he didn't scarper.

Eileen led the way outside and along a narrow path cut through the snow that took them to the guardian's house.

"Neat!" Regina exclaimed, looking appreciatively around the cosy interior. The room was small with a tiny fireplace in which a fire burnt bright. A couple of worn armchairs flanked the blaze and there was a small table under the only window which looked out onto the snow covered street. The girls had not only cleaned up, but they'd decorated the room with sprigs of holly and mistletoe. There was even a bouquet of medicinal herbs in a jar on the mantelpiece. Kate recognised thyme and rosemary and sage. There must be a herb garden nearby. She helped Eileen carry through several mismatched chairs from the kitchen till all had somewhere to sit.

Sandra had brought a large thermos of hot vegetable soup, a basket of homemade bread along with bowls, spoons and a ladle. "It's a bit frugal," she apologised. "But I assure you, the soup is delicious."

Once everyone was settled and soup and bread had been served, Kate turned expectantly to Regina. "You said you brought news? Good news, I hope."

"Indeed," Regina replied. "But first, what happened to your friend Tania? She looked wretched when I saw her at Lydia's."

"I shouted at her," Kate said, feeling ashamed. "I know I shouldn't have. But she's so annoying. She's so caught up in herself, she's insensitive to others and what is happening around her. When she burst in with her silly jokes about boys, I'd spent a quarter of an hour aligning the fragments of bone in that youth's leg. Her distraction meant I had to begin all over again. It was the last straw. I told her what I thought of her."

"Well now you're going to have to piece together the bits of Tania," Regina said.

Kate sighed. Tania was an additional burden she didn't need.

"You realise she's madly in love with you," Regina said, matter-of-factly. "Not that I'm blaming you, but your sharp words cut her to the quick."

Kate shook her head, not out of denial but because it was exasperating. "I know. I know. She fell for me when we first met at the orphanage. Her love and the demands that puts on me are just another example of how she's wrapped up in her own world."

"She's not entirely blind to what's happening," Eileen said. "She knows full well you're in love with Peter. That's why she tries to get between you."

Kate couldn't help blushing, even if her love for Peter was common knowledge. She liked Tania, but she didn't love her. Not the way Tania wanted. How was she supposed to react?

"You're the leader," Regina said, her tone in no way accusatory. On the contrary, she gave Kate a warm smile. "Some of your followers are bound to be smitten by you." She grinned at Kate who groaned. "As a leader, it's your job to deal with it. I'd willingly help, but I have no such experience. One piece of advice I can give, though. Don't ask men. Most are pretty hopeless at dealing with adoration, lest it be to exploit or hurt those who admire or love them."

48.

It was getting late. They couldn't spend all night speculating how she should handle Tania. "I'll talk to her," Kate said, then turning to Regina added, "you mentioned you had good news."

"I have. We've traced Beth's broken wheelchair. It was clearly tampered with."

"Did you manage to get photos?" Kate asked.

"Better than that," Heinz said, grinning. "We've got the chair itself."

"Not only that," Regina said. "We have a friend who owns a garage and it just so happens the bishop sent his car to be repaired."

"And you've got that too?" Kate asked, delighted.

"We have," Regina replied, triumphant. "All we need now is to implicate Father Jacob."

"How about my idea of a trap?" Sandra asked.

Kate was extremely wary. Whoever acted as bait would be in serious danger. "It's too risky," she insisted. "We can't ask girls to volunteer to entice a vicious pervert."

"You won't have to," Sandra said, her chin thrust forward in defiance. "It's my idea and I volunteer."

"No!" Kate exclaimed, horrified. "You can't. It's too dangerous. This guy has already tried to kill Jo and Beth. He twice sent thugs to abuse us, if not to set fire to us. You can't."

"Kate is right," Regina said. "There are serious risks, but I think we can mitigate them."

It was very late when they finally agreed to Sandra's

suggestion. They'd discussed at length how the trap would close if and when the Father rose to the bait. Kate still wasn't happy, but Sandra insisted and the others felt they'd countered the greatest risks.

"If you don't want to return home this late, you folks can sleep upstairs," Eileen said as they got up to leave. "We've cleaned the bedroom and bathroom. It's small but cosy."

Regina glanced at Heinz who nodded. "Thanks," she said. "It's true, the roads are treacherous."

"And we can interview those boys tomorrow and get some photos," Heinz added. "If we're to bring off this performance we need to be quick. Who knows what else the church might throw at you?"

It was not a comforting thought. "I'll do the rounds with a couple of girls before we go to bed," Kate said. "We'll lay wards to deter visitors." The two adults weren't aware of the full extent of their capacities, so Kate trusted they'd understand 'wards' as some form of physical deterrent and not ask questions.

That was not counting with Regina's inquisitiveness. "I'll join you, if you don't mind," the woman said. And of course Heinz had to come too. There was no dissuading them.

"Let's get this done," Kate said. Turning to Eileen and Sandra she said, "Could you get Suzanne and Clara to join us?"

Trussed up in their warmest clothes, five girls and two adults trod one after another along the narrow path the new girls had cut through the hard-packed snow. It circled the entire village. A couple of shooting stars darted across the star-studded heavens. Their gasps were the only sound in the dense silence of the snow-shroud scene.

Kate halted where the path crossed the track from Lydia's house. "We'll place the first ward here," she said, gathering the girls around her. "I say 'ward', but it's more like creating a guardian who will watch over this road and the countryside around." She felt a shiver of excitement ripple through the girls, extending to include the adults. Speaking to the adults, she said. "We'll work in silence, but it shouldn't take too long."

She switched to mind-to-mind communication and spoke only to the girls. *We need to conjure up a presence.* Making wards had been a speciality of her father who'd favoured defence over attack. Their house had been heavily warded, but that hadn't stopped the warrior priests who wielded potent magic. She didn't expect to have to ward against magicians in this world. *I'll show you how.* She imagined a massive figure, imitating one her father had used, and shared the image with the others. *Now let your breath flow into it, giving it life.* Creating a form separate from yourself was always an odd feeling, so she was not surprised when several girls lost their concentration. She coaxed them back and encouraged them to feed the ward with energy. *Not too much,* she said to Sandra. *Keep some in reserve for the others.*

She looks a bit like a giantess, Suzanne said, looking up at the form towering over them.

Now we have to give our guardian some instructions, Kate explained. *This is a bit like making spells, the wording is key.* Her father told her the tale of an apprentice magician who created a ward that chased the youth because he'd muddled the instructions. Her father had had to rescue him. But she didn't want to scare the girls. *I'll use the words my father employed. I'll teach you them some other time. You'll have to learn them off by heart.*

"Done?" Regina asked, seeing the circle of girls break up.

"Yes," was Kate's reply.

"I don't suppose you could...?"

"Sorry. No," Kate replied with a chuckle. "Trade secrets."

"I thought as much," Regina said. "But I appreciate you trusted us this far."

"So you plan to unmask these villains in the form of a performance?" Clara asked. When Kate nodded, she went on, "I'd like to involve the choir. Not just the Lost Girls, but the new girls. Just think how impressive that would be. Seventy girls singing."

"It's tricky," Regina said. "You're bearing witness. What

you have to tell is not theatre but reality. It's dramatic in itself. You don't want people imagining it is fiction. It's a delicate balance."

"The two modes I have in mind should fit," Clara said. "First as a backdrop, quietly adding to the gravity. And secondly as interludes, short pauses in the story."

"Yes," Regina said, sounding enthusiastic. "That would work. The last thing we want is for people to believe it's a musical or a concert."

"Another thing I've been mulling over," Clara said, "is the stage. It's a barrier between the audience and the players. In telling this tale, everyone is a player. What if we set the action in the middle of the audience on the same level?"

"The advantage of a raised platform," Heinz said, "is that more people can see."

"Then have a raised platform stretch out amid the audience, like a walkway," Clara replied.

Kate halted at a slight widening of the path about a quarter of the way around the village. She'd planned four wards at the four cardinal points. "We'll set the next one here." The second time was easier. The girls were accustomed to the procedure and managed to maintain concentration throughout.

"What'll happen if anyone approaches these wards?" Regina asked.

"Two things," Kate replied, setting off along the path with the others following. "Intruders will be unable to get through."

"Unable?" Regina asked.

"They'll feel repelled. Not so much physically as mentally. They won't want to go any further. They might be disgusted. Or fearful. Or forget why they wanted to continue. Or just lose interest."

"You said there were two things," Eileen prompted.

"Yes. All those who made the ward will be alerted that someone is trying to get in."

"What if Lydia or Klaus turn up?" Regina asked.

"When we're alerted, we can chose to let people in."

"Even if we're asleep?" Eileen asked.

"Yes," Kate replied. "Sorry."

"That's really neat," Heinz said. "You should rig up something similar when we do this performance. To make sure the bad guys don't wreck everything."

Several people winced.

"I'm not sure how effective that would be," Kate said. "The first batch of yobs Father Jakob sent were wearing charms against wards. So I reckon the good Father knows something about magic."

"Are we in danger?" Sandra asked, her expression troubled.

"I don't think so. Those charms were pretty low-level."

Judging from her expression, Sandra was not reassured.

After they'd set the third ward, Sandra said, "I've been thinking of our evidence against this Father Jakob. My testimony won't be enough. The words of girls carry so little weight. Is there no way we can take photos and project them on the walls like in the cinema?"

"Sure," Heinz replied, clearly excited at the suggestion. "We can rig up a dia show."

"Can we do that without the machines getting in the way?" Sandra asked. "It shouldn't be a distraction, but an underlining of what is said."

"Easy. Suspend projectors from the ceiling and control them at a distance."

"Good," Sandra said. "We could also ask for volunteers amongst the new girls to add a few words about how this man mistreated them or their friends."

"Great," Regina said. "That would be very effective."

They halted to set the final ward. The starlit sky had clouded over leaving only distant lamps by the barn to light their path. More snow was on its way. "Let's get this over with," Kate said, "and retire to our beds before a snow storm catches us." The ward was in place and the girls were turning to head home when the sound of glass shattering caught their attention. Someone had broken the stalls window and was clambering out.

"Those three thugs are escaping," Eileen whispered.

"Maybe we can overpower them," Heinz suggested.

"No need," Kate said. "They won't get very far. I set a ward to watch over them. If they try to escape it'll whisper nonsense in their heads spreading confusion and fuelling fear till they have no idea where they are or how to get from there to anywhere else."

When Kate and the others approached, the youths skittered away like terrified children and cowered behind a rubbish bin. "Come on, boys," Kate said in her best nanny voice. "Mummy's waiting inside with a mug of hot chocolate." She took the leader by the arm and led him confused but unresisting inside. The others followed.

Once they'd tied up the youths and nailed planks over the broken window, the four girls joined Christine and Claudia and went on a tour of the barn, checking their new protégés were safe and sound. It was late and many had already gone to bed, tired as they were after a day shovelling snow.

Meeting Regina and Heinz near the entrance, they retreated to the caretaker's house with a thermos of herbal tea, a fistful of mugs and a bunch of unanswered questions. "You realise," Regina said, once they were settled around the glowing embers, "I'm not sure exactly what you did, but if this warding business were to get out you'd be in dire trouble."

"Warding?" Claudia asked, perplexed.

"We created 'wards' to protect the village against intruders," Eileen explained.

Claudia looked even more puzzled. "I still don't understand."

"Think of wards as imaginary beings conjured up to watch over us," Kate said.

"Ah!" Claudia said, intrigued. She clearly wanted to know more, but before she could speak, Sandra asked, "Why did you say we'd be in trouble?"

"Because using what is patently magic would be seen as a far worse crime than any committed by Father Jakob and his mignons," Regina replied.

"That doesn't make sense," Sandra complained. "How could repelling ill-intentioned people, not with guns or traps or explosives but simply by mentally shooing them away, possibly be a crime worse than rape or attempted murder?"

"Because people are deeply suspicious of things they can't explain or control," Heinz said. "Remember the church tortured and slaughtered girls and women suspected of wielding magic not so long ago."

Kate groaned and held her head in her hands. "It's all my fault. I learnt to use magic in a world where wielding it was not only natural but esteemed. I knew I was taking a risk introducing it here. But if I hadn't, a number of people dear to me would be dead or maimed for life. And anyway, I saw how it could be used for good, in healing for example."

Regina gave her a friendly pat on the shoulder. "I understand," she said. "It must be exasperating. You acted out of necessity, in good faith, but with time your enthusiasm got the better of you. You've ceased to be cautious enough. In reality, you can only use your skills with the utmost of care and in absolute secret. I see no other way."

"Don't put yourself down," Heinz said, smiling at Kate, "I too was encouraging you. Did I not suggest placing wards to protect our event? The truth is you have wonderful abilities. They could save lives. But like all abilities they could also be misused."

"It's not just you ... or us abetting you," Regina said. "It's society. We live at a time when science, rationality and economics reign. Even the church has come down against anyone who challenges what it sees as its unique right to be the conduit to all the lies beyond the rational."

"You lost me there," Claudia said.

"Me too," chimed in Sandra.

"Let's say that in this world, on the surface at least, seeing is believing, science has a monopoly when it comes to explanations and value is measured in money," Regina said. "With me so far?"

The girls nodded.

"Anything that can't be seen, that can't be explained, that can't be measured by its weight in gold is suspect if not highly dangerous. Like healing by thought or warding with imaginary beings. They would be seen as unhealthy or criminal if not evil. Those who did them would be reviled and hounded out."

"But surely much of what people do is irrational if not incomprehensible," Eileen protested. "What about those boys who tried to set fire to us? Nobody can claim their behaviour was rational. How can you possibly say that attempting to murder seventy people is less of a crime than healing one person by an unfamiliar method?"

"Isn't something terribly amiss with a society that acts on such warped values?" Sandra asked.

"You're right," Kate said. "Not only is this world adrift, but it's unjust. By holding our event we stand up against those who would bully us. At the same time, we cannot live apart from society. We have good things to bring to the table. Think of our choir. Think of our skill with herbs. Think of the healing we could do. We need to find ways to play our part but also co-exist with those around us."

49.

Peter had not seen the adults, although he knew they were there. That was how he'd planned it. Seeing but not seen. Hearing but not heard. The people John had invited, whoever they were, were on the balcony out of sight as the girls jostled for places in the chapel below.

He was nervous. A lot hinged on what they were about to do. If it worked he could return home and be with Kate. Despite having talked to many girls, he was unsure how they'd react. The slightest misstep might spook them, they'd clam up and no one would bear witness.

"It'll be alright," Sarah whispered, squeezing his hand. Eloise was across the corridor with Linda, making sure the girls entered in an orderly fashion. They were also to prevent the prefects or the twins entering should they turn up. He glanced at Pin who was waiting with them. She looked pale. Nervous no doubt. She was to be the first to bear witness.

Ready? a voice whispered in his head. It was Christina. She was with the adults.

Almost, he replied.

Girls were still queuing, waiting to enter the chapel. Finally, only Peter, Sarah, Eloise and Linda remained outside. "Time," Peter said. The girls nodded and followed him inside. As he stood on the steps before the altar, his eyes roving the girls, silence slowly settled.

"Greetings," he began. A murmur of greetings echoed back. "We're gathered to bear witness about recent events, to share what has largely been kept secret. It's our chance to heal deep wounds. Doing so will not be easy, especially for those who come forward. They're the courageous ones and we're grateful to them." He paused to let his words sink in.

"In what we're about to do, there'll surely be anger. There'll also be sadness and regrets. We'll best succeed if we can describe what happened without blame or accusation. If it helps, imagine we're trying to heal wounds so we can move forward together. Our job is not to pass judgement. If judgement and punishment are needed, that'll be the task of others. That is why a number of adults have been invited to listen to our discussion."

A murmur went up as girls twisted in their seats trying to catch sight of the adults. Peter raised a hand for silence. It was a while coming. The news that adults were listening troubled many. "Those adults have been asked to remain silent and not to manifest their presence. We're not talking for them, but for ourselves." Once again Peter paused. The tension in the room was palpable. The girls were fearful but there was also hope.

"Volunteering to talk takes courage, especially when you're the first. That's why I asked someone to start and Pin has graciously accepted. Her story is both terrifying and heart-wrenching, so I ask you to treat her with respect."

Pin has been sitting on a hassock at Peter's feet. At his invitation, she pushed herself up and stood facing the school. She was deathly pale, her hands clasped in front of her, as she desperately tried to stop them trembling. After a long pause, she took a deep breath and said, "I was abused by the nurse." Her words sent a wave of shock through the gathered girls. Several gasped. Others looked pained. Many looked terrified.

"I had a squint," she continued. "The nurse said she could treat it with a face massage..."

Several girls sniggered. "Please," Peter said. "There's nothing funny about what happened to Pin. If what she says disturbs you, there'll be a time to react. For now, just let her tell her story."

"I was young and naive and desperately lonely. That

woman's attention was like water to a thirsty plant, but very quickly she insisted on touching me elsewhere..." Peter was afraid there'd be more sniggers, but no one made a sound. "I tried to resist, but she insisted, she forced my legs apart and ..." Pin burst into tears. "She made me do things, disgusting things that made me feel ashamed and dirty. I told no one. I kept to myself and cried myself to sleep at night. What made things worse was the taunting. Girls insisted I was the nurse's favourite. They had no idea."

Pin sat down, her head in her hands, sobbing. Sarah slung an arm round her shoulder and hugged her.

A voice from the back of the chapel said, "The nurse toyed with me too." A chubby girl with a round face got to her feet and came to join Pin, giving her a hug. "Like you, I was taunted for being her favourite. Like you she forced me to do terrible things. I tried to scrub myself clean, but no amount of soap and water could rid me of her touch."

"This is awful. Why didn't you tell me?" a friend from the back asked, sounding distressed. "We tell each other everything."

"I was frightened. She threatened me... And I was sure it was my fault."

Several girls had similar tales to tell but then there was a lull. In the silence, Linda got wearily to her feet and turned to face the girls. "It was not the nurse with me, but one of the prefects." She described how a prefect delighted in burning her skin with a cigarette, much to the horror of the girls listening. "She said she loved to hear me squeal. So I held in the pain and said nothing. My silence made her furious. She began burning the inside of my thighs and finally between my legs." She choked over the words and had to take deep breath before she could continue. "It went on for months."

"Why did you say nothing?" one of older girls seated up front asked.

"Like Pin, I was frightened. I was sure it'd just get worse if I said anything. I had no one to turn to. I felt terribly alone. Do not most of you feel alone and isolated?"

Heads nodded. Several girls muttered "True" or "Me too."

"Did you know about this, Eloise?" a girl called Judy towards the back asked. It wasn't so much an accusation as a request for information.

"No. I had my suspicions. But they never did anything in front of me. I had little to do with them. They always picked on me. When they put slugs in my bed, I was so disgusted I chose to sleep elsewhere. They even called me a slug, saying I was slimy because I preferred the company of you girls to them. They gave me what they thought were the worst jobs. Like night duty. I preferred that, knowing I could protect you, at least a little."

It was then that an astonishing thing happened. A couple of girls clapped and ever more joined in till all the girls were applauding an embarrassed Eloise. Some even stomped with their feet, an odd local custom when you appreciated a particular person or performance. "Thank you," she muttered when the clapping finally ceased.

Many girls spoke of exactions committed by the prefects, although none of them were as spectacular as Linda's. The emerging picture was of extreme bullying and what could only be called insane behaviour that ran unchecked. Apart from the nurse, nobody had as yet mentioned the complicity of the teachers or the headmistress.

As if in answer to Peter's thoughts, Judy, who'd questioned Eloise earlier, got to her feet and came to stand next to Eloise and Peter facing the school. "If you ask me," she said, "it all began when that abomination of a headmistress turned up."

"Why do you say that?" Peter asked. This was exactly what he wanted, but empty accusations were of little use. "Did something happen?"

Judy shot Peter an angry look that scared him. But, to his relief and amazement, she turned away and spat on the chapel floor, causing several girls to gasp. Peter was about to warn her to respect the holy place when Judy spoke. "That woman destroyed my life!"

There was a pause as she collected her thoughts. No one spoke. Only the spluttering of a candle on the altar could be heard. "My parents sent me here because I was in love with a boy. They wanted to stop me seeing him. Being locked in Our Lady of Grace was like being in a prison. I was desperately unhappy. I tried to run away several times, but the headmistress, who sided with my parents - what do you expect? They gave her a lot of money - sent a detective after me. I blamed myself for the mess. I felt so rotten, I imagined ways of ending it all. I would have done it, had not Christina, who was still working here, sensed my misery and spoke to me. Her kind words changed everything. I believe she had good advice for many of us."

A murmur of agreement rippled round the chapel. "Then that hag kicked Christina out." The girls hissed in disapproval. "The headmistress even boasted one day when she was drunk that she got rid of Christina because she was too soft. 'What I need,' she told me, 'is a firm hand.' She kept a wide leather belt in her desk." Several girls gasped. "She made me lift my skirt and pull my knickers down..." She couldn't go any further. Eloise took her in her arms and cradled her while she sobbed.

Refusing to let the emotions get the better of her, Judy pulled free and angrily brushed the tears from her eyes. "That was the first of what she called 'corrective treatment'. It went on for months. The weals on my backside began to infect and sitting down was torture. I could tell no one and I dared not go to the nurse. I'd heard the rumours. I resorted to stealing salves from the infirmary and did my best to heal myself." She turned to Peter. "When I heard you and a couple of others were healing girls, I was tempted, but I was too ashamed and afraid of showing anyone the mess my backside had become."

She had suffered so much, Peter was tempted to heal her then and there, but it would be folly in front of so many witnesses. "Come and see us afterwards," he said.

"I said it was all the headmistress's fault," Judy went on. "I didn't just mean the way she treated me. She encouraged her prefects to be hard on the girls." She nodded to Eloise. "The four. Not you. I never saw you there. She invited them to her study and got them to tell tales of girls they'd hurt. I know. I was there. She'd tie me up in a corner with my bum bared for the girls to admire the damage. She also exchanged stories of abuse with the nurse."

"She's stark raving mad," someone called out from the back. Mutters of agreement rippled round the room.

"How many others have been strapped by the headmistress?" Peter asked. Hands shot up around the chapel. Aware that the unseen audience could not know how many responded, he said, "Could you stand one after another and call out your first name. Then remain standing."

Judy began, then one by one they stood with dignity and defiance, calling out their name as if it were an act of accusation, but also of self-affirmation. Anna. Olga. Kathy. Frida. Brigit. Susan. Carmen. Petra. Martina. Sally. Dee. Hanna. Jeanne. Heidi. Nina. Ali. Tania. Ely. Indigo. Mary. Grace. Magdalena. The names went on and on, a roll-call of more than half the school, the girls standing in silence, acutely aware of the others standing around them. Sarah, Linda and Eloise were the last to stand and pronounce their names.

Peter was about to say, 'Look around,' but the girls were already doing so. The lucky ones who were still seated got cautiously to their feet till everyone was standing. Girls turned to girls, tears in their eyes and hugged. Sarah and Eloise and Linda formed a huddle around him but he gently broke loose and stepped away. Not that he didn't feel a part of the drama. He did. But he was convinced it had to end as it had begun, with singing. He took a deep breath and launched into a lullaby he'd sung with the Lost Girls. Apparently the song was well known in England. More and more girls joined in till the chapel was overflowing with girls' voices.

When the last note faded like a sigh, the girls burst into applause and stamped their feet. As that in turn dwindled, a ripple of laughter shivered through the gathering and the girls began to chatter in small groups.

Well done, Christina said in his head. *You were wonderful. I am immensely proud of you.*

50.

There was a festive air as the girls chatted and laughed, although the Christmas decorations were not yet up and Eloise had been unable to convince the kitchen staff to serve a special meal. Peter was seated with Eloise, Sarah and Linda along with several girls they'd healed. There was a constant flow of girls coming to thank him. He tried, and failed, to deflect praise onto Eloise, Sarah and the others.

Peter had his back turned, so he had no idea who had arrived when the girls began clapping. Turning to look, he spotted Christina carrying a large tray. She placed it on a table. "I thought you'd appreciate something special on such an auspicious day." Her words set off a cheer as the girls rose to fetch a piece of chocolate cake.

Getting to his feet, he went to give Christina a hug. "You were wonderful," she said. "Everyone was shocked, but impressed at your inquest."

Peter took her by the hand and led her to his table. "You all know Christina, my Mum," he said, his voice trembling at the word.

"Mum?" Sarah exclaimed. All the girls stared at the pair, incredulous. "How can that be?" Sarah continued. "I thought you..." Eloise elbowed her in the ribs, stopping her saying the unsayable. Everyone knew Christina's son had died shortly after birth and that her daughter had been shot much more recently.

Christina put an arm around Peter's shoulder saying, "I am so glad we adopted you." Peter pulled up a chair and she joined them.

"What's going to happen now?" Eloise asked.

"I'm not sure. The judge, the head of police and the schools inspector went off to discuss what to do."

"They were here?" Pin exclaimed. "Oh dear! I won't get punished will I?"

"No, dear Pin," Christina said. "Can I call you that?" The girl gave her a shy nod. "There's no question of punishing you girls. You've been punished far too much already."

"What'll happen to the nurse?" Pin asked. There was solicitude in her voice.

"I imagine there'll be a trial. What she did was wrong. Those who commit crimes are punished."

Pin looked downcast.

"Why are you so concerned?" Peter asked. "She tortured you for months."

"I know it sounds odd, but I wouldn't want her hurt. True, she did evil, but she also..." she hesitated over the words... "kept me company when I was dreadfully lonely."

"Well at least you won't be alone any more," Peter said, glancing round at the groups in lively conversation.

"No. You're right. And you were right about the healing," Pin said, "This school sorely needed healing and you were the one to do it." She lent forward and gave Peter a peck on the cheek, much to his surprise and not a little embarrassment. "I'm sorry we treated you so badly. It was mean. The headmistress told us such terrible tales. We knew how nasty she could be, yet we still believed her."

As if on cue, the headmistress strode in and halted, clearly astonished at the atmosphere. A tense silence fell and many a girl looked fearful. However, having got over her initial surprise, the woman paid no attention to the girls. Her eyes latched onto Christina and a feral roar burst from her lips. "I told you never to return," she shouted. "How dare you enter my school?"

Christina got to her feet and smiled. To anyone else her smile would have been disarming, but Heartless was not like other people. She bared her teeth and growled.

"I think you'll find this is no longer your school," Christina said calmly. "You've been dismissed."

"What nonsense. Who dismissed me?"

"For a start," Christina replied, "all the girls in this room."

Heartless surveyed the girls, an expression of contempt and disgust on her lips. "This useless lot!"

Eloise got to her feet and pointed silently to the door, her arm outstretched. Sarah, Linda and Pin followed suit. Then, little by little, the groups stood and pointed to the door. Although the girls were determined, it was clear they were terrified.

The headmistress stared at Eloise and then at the others. She seemed to hesitate between fear and fury. It was the latter that won out. "You'll pay for this insolence." She shot a look of hatred at Eloise and then at Peter. "You two in particular."

"Don't make empty threats. It'll only make things worse," an authoritative female voice said from the door. Peter didn't recognise the woman standing there flanked by two policewomen, but Christina whispered she was head inspector of schools. "We've heard a lot of disturbing evidence about how you run this school..."

"What evidence," the headmistress spluttered.

"The astonishing and damning testimony of the girls of this school," a man said, stepping up to join the woman between the two policewomen.

"The head of police," Christina whispered.

"You can't possibly believe this rabble," the headmistress countered.

"Oh, but we do. For over four hours many of these girls spoke of your atrocious behaviour and that of your nurse and prefects. I commend them for their courage in talking of painful experiences with such level-headedness and clarity."

"What nonsense," the headmistress blustered. "It's a plot against me orchestrated by that woman." She shot a blistering glare at Christina.

"I doubt the jury will agree with you," the head of police

said.

"Jury? What jury?"

"The one that will likely send you to prison," the chief of police said. "Take her away," he told the two policewomen.

Heartless lashed out at the policewomen as they moved closer, but they seemed accustomed to such behaviour. In no time the headmistress was led away, handcuffed, swearing in language not at all appropriate for the former head of a school which, according to the glossy brochure, was for girls 'of the very best families'.

The girls had finally settled after their excitement and triumph at seeing the back of Heartless, when the door opened and an a spritely lady entered dressed in a well-tailored pinstriped jacket and matching skirt. She headed straight for Peter's table and Christina.

"Meet Mrs Hale," Christina said, getting to her feet to greet the woman. "She's chairwoman of the Board of Trustees of Our Lady of Grace."

Shaking hands with Peter, Mrs Hale said, "Young lady, your leadership today was exemplary." Peter promptly blushed, mainly with pleasure at being taken for a young lady. "I want to thank you for bringing this sorry state of affairs to our notice in such a thoughtful way. I can assure you, we had no idea a disaster was playing out behind our backs. The headmistress always gave glowing reports..." She spoke at length about their shock and surprise at learning the truth.

She might have gone on for ever, Peter feared, but Sarah interrupted. "What are we going to do without a headmistress?" Trust Sarah to get straight to the point.

Where other adults might have taken umbrage at being so rudely interrupted, Mrs Hale took it in her stride, smiled at Sarah and replied, "That will be no problem. As chairwoman of the Board, I have decided to appoint Mrs Grant here," she turned to Christina, "as interim headmistress, if you accept. At the next Board meeting we'll decide on a longer term solution."

A broad smile lit up Christina's face. "I'd be delighted. I've enjoyed working here. Having the girls' interests and education at heart has always been my main concern."

Mrs Hale launched into a monologue about girls' education and the need to prepare them for the modern world and all the false ideas about the liberation of women and the shocking turn taken by women's fashion and unrest in universities even amongst girls which was no doubt due to failings in their earlier education... As a teacher she would have been the type through whose lessons you could easily snooze with impunity were it not for her habit of abruptly addressing a question to an unsuspecting listener.

"I trust you won't be like that when you are older," she said to Peter. The irony of her words was not lost on him. Unless there was a miracle, he certainly would not be like 'that'.

Once Mrs Hale had left, the chill in the atmosphere thawed and the buzz of conversation rekindled. The news spread about Christina becoming acting headmistress and a stream of girls jostled to congratulate her. The relief was evident on their faces. Heartless's presence had been a constant threat. In comparison, Christina was approachable and they knew and liked her.

"John's not going to be happy," she confided to Peter in a quiet moment. "Now we're both heads of a school."

"Of course he'll be happy," Peter exclaimed. "How could he not be? This is wonderful news."

She shook her head and for the first time there was a look on her face that said 'you're a kid, you'll learn'. "You'd be surprised how many men in positions of power are all for the empowerment of women till their wife or colleague suddenly reaches the same level or higher than them."

It wasn't the first time he'd heard Christina sound sad and resigned. It had been far worse when Fi had been killed, but that she was disappointed about her husband who had always been a source of joy and encouragement made Peter sad too. He flung his arms around his mother's neck and hugged her tight. When a new wave of girls approached to congratulate Christina, she freed herself and kissed him on his forehead.

"So?" Sarah asked, now Christina had left to amble from table to table chatting with the girls.

"So what?" Peter asked, distracted.

"What are you going to do now?"

"I haven't thought about it," he said, watching Christina, still preoccupied by her sadness.

"You know that's not true. You'll be running off to that girlfriend of yours." Her bitter tone shocked him and he looked at her closely, struggling to understand. Not for the first time, he wondered if her odd behaviour was due to a growing attachment.

"Leave him alone, you bully," Eloise said, playfully pushing Sarah away. "Why shouldn't he want to return to the one he loves? I would if anyone loved me."

"Poor you," Sarah responded, her tone dripping with irony. The more she spoke, the bitterer she seemed to be getting.

"Poor you!" Eloise retorted.

"Stop that," Peter said wearily. "What's wrong with you. I know we've had a hard day but it's also been a very successful one. We should be rejoicing not fighting. Just look around. Behold the first seeds of friendship. The fear and hate that prevailed before were toxic. Everyone deserves to be loved."

Sarah pouted. "Well no one loves me."

Peter was tempted to counter, 'Of course people love you!' He was convinced of it, but instead he asked, "What do you mean by 'love'?"

"Now there's a tricky question," Christina said, arriving at that moment. "I once heard a vicar spend a whole sermon enumerating the types of love and I doubt he managed to embrace them all."

Peter grinned at the unintended pun.

"You know what I meant," Christina said, giving him a playful shove.

He nodded, still grinning. "I asked Sarah about love because she said nobody loved her," he said, "and I wondered what kind of love she was lacking because she's clearly got the love of her friends."

Sarah looked thoughtful, if not a little annoyed, but said nothing.

"I'm guessing your question put her on the spot," she said to Peter. "Let me turn the tables. Do you love me?"

It was Peter's turn to look thoughtful. "I do indeed. You have become my mother." The word still felt awkward. "You are my mother. I trust you. You are a friend. You were the mother of my best friend. We are family."

"Do you love Kate?"

Peter couldn't help a broad smile blossoming on his lips. A deep feeling of longing filled his chest. "Of course I do. She's my soulmate. We fit together. When she is not here I feel something is missing. I long to be with her. To feel her hand in mine ..."

Christina interrupted. "I think we get the picture. And do you love Sarah?"

Peter looked at the girl, embarrassed. "I like Sarah a lot. She's fun. I enjoy being with her. I appreciate how her questions get straight to the point, like with Mrs Hale. She's a good learner. She's intelligent."

Sarah was pouting again. "You see. He only likes me. He doesn't love me."

Sarah tried to snatch her hands away as Peter leant forward to take them, but he caught them and held on. However, once her hands were in his, she made no effort to get free. She just sat and looked him in the eye. "It is true that I don't love you like I love Kate. I'm pretty sure there can only be one such person in your life. I'm lucky I found Kate so early. Maybe you'll have to wait a while. But I do see you as a good friend, someone I can count on, someone I enjoy being with and talking to, someone who will prod me in the ribs if I do or say something silly."

Sarah grinned. She looked like she wanted to kiss him but didn't dare, so she hugged him instead.

"Am I interrupting something," Peter heard John say.

"No. We're all good," he replied. "Am I right?" he asked Sarah.

She nodded and stepped back. "We're good."

"Congratulations," John said to Peter.

"For having Sarah as a friend?" Peter asked, a twisted smile on his lips.

"Indeed. You are lucky to have such a good friend." It was Sarah's turn to grin. "But I meant for your 'inquest'. It made a huge impact on the adults." He glanced around the room. "It's clearly had a big impact on the girls too."

"You should congratulate, Mrs Grant," Sarah said on cue. How did she always manage to raise the one subject others didn't dare mention? "Christina is our new headmistress."

John didn't look at all surprised. "I though they'd name her." He turned to Christina and added. "It makes sense. You were the logical choice. You have all the qualities the job requires. They couldn't have chosen a better person."

Christina shot Peter a tear-filled glance and flung her arms around John's neck. A cheer went up from the girls and there was much appreciative stamping of feet. Christina ignored the racket and kissed John.

When the two finally disengaged Sarah muttered, "Showoffs!"

John ignored her jealous remark. He pulled an envelope from his inside pocket and handed it to Peter, saying, "We'd much prefer if you'd stay a while longer but we understand you have reasons to hurry home. This should help."

The hormones! In the run up to the inquest Peter had completely forgotten the threat hanging over him. Could it be a prescription? If it were, he wouldn't need to dash home. He ripped open the envelope but it wasn't a prescription. It was a train ticket. No. Not one. Three. He looked questioningly at John, "So you and Christina are coming too?"

"We are," John said. "But those extra tickets are not for us." He glanced at Sarah and Eloise. "They're for your two friends. I understood they wanted to travel with you."

Sarah, who'd been listening in on their conversation, let out a squeal of delight and flung her arms around John, hugging him.

51.

Kate sighed. Everything was as ready as it could be. They'd spent three days preparing. Heinz had been a great help, suggesting links between the scenes, assembling slides, overseeing lighting. Seating arrangements had been a problem, but a social centre had loaned foldable chairs. Decor was Viktor's pitch along with music. He worked with Clara to prepare the choir and persuaded theatre friends to help with the decor. In turn, they gave Heinz a hand with the lighting.

Invitations had been written and hand-delivered, Beth and Isla putting their address books to good use. Everyone who was anyone would be present. Local councillors. Representatives of the authorities. Judges. Heads of schools. University professors. Business men. Journalists. Theatre critics. Authors. A brace of famous people who'd taken root in town. Not to mention Isla's influential women, although Gertie Styles remained recalcitrant. Only the Bishop would not be present. The news that he was still detained in Rome was a relief.

Then there were the rehearsals. Not that everything could be rehearsed. Some parts had to be spontaneous. Only the very last scene remained untold. The trapping of Father Jakob. Who knew if that would work?

And of course, there was the television. They fussed and got in the way, demanding this or that, requesting changes to suit their needs, seemingly unaware of what they were dealing with lest it be as material for television. So much so, Kate was on the verge of sending them packing. But Isla smoothed things over. The TV people finally accepted it wasn't their show. Kate walked the director though the event. He was flabbergasted. Rumour had it he was in admiration of Kate's leadership. At least, that's what Tania said. She'd been persuaded to return from exile at Lydia's house having been put to work baking cakes and tarts for the guests.

Kate's rumination was interrupted by a noisy huddle bursting into their improvised theatre. Clearly someone was getting a royal reception but she couldn't see who. Then the girls parted revealing a thin schoolgirl she didn't recognise. Only when the girl, who looked quite nervous, smiled coyly at her did she realise who it was. "Peter!" she exclaimed and took a hesitant step forward. With him were two girls dressed in the same uniform, one taller and older, the other shorter and probably younger. The three were flanked by Christina and John, grins all over their faces.

"Kate," Peter said, sounding unsure.

He was hanging back. "Have I changed that much?" she asked and on the heals of her question came another, unspoken one, 'Have you changed so much?'

"Go on ninny," one of the two girls, the shorter of the two, said and pushed him forward. "You've been waiting for this for ages."

Peter stumbled, recovering just in time to halt in front of Kate. Standing at arms length, they looked long at each other. There were dark shadows under his eyes and he had lost weight. Kate glanced over his shoulder at the crowd egging them on, grins plastered on their faces. "Aren't you going to kiss me, you silly girl?" Kate asked. A broad smile lit up his face and, taking the remaining step, he placed his hands on either side of her head and pulled her face to his till their lips touched.

A chorus of whistles and catcalls came from the gathered crowd. Kate waved them away with an outstretched hand but did not break the kiss. *I missed you so much,* she said mind-to-mind.

I missed you too, Peter said, *but I was afraid you'd have moved on. That I'd no longer have a place in your life, in your heart.*

You've been constantly in my thoughts, she replied. *You can't imagine how often I wished you were by my side to help me, to give advice, to amuse me when I felt glum....*

Hand in hand they returned to the group and Kate embraced both Christina and John. "Lovely to see you again," she said in hesitant English.

"We thought we'd bring you an early Christmas present," Christina joked.

Peter tugged at Kate's hand. "Come and meet my friends," he said in Swiss German. Switching to English, he indicated the taller girl, "Meet Eloise."

The girl appeared shy and intimidated. "I've heard so much about you," she said offering to shake Kate's hand. Kate took her hand but pulled her into an embrace. "Well met," she said.

Peter then presented the other girl, the shorter one with mousy brown hair and swarthy skin. "And this is Sarah."

The girl dispensed with the handshake, moving straight to the hug. "Grüetzi" Sarah said. "Did I get that right?" she asked Peter.

"You did indeed," Kate replied, in English.

"Peter has been teaching us Swiss German," she explained.

"You must be tired and hungry," Kate said. Calling over Eileen, she told the visitors, "This is Eileen. She'll find you a place to rest and something to eat and drink. She speaks a little English."

Sarah looked around the room and at all the girls busy preparing the evening's event. She stared amazed at the television crew setting up their cameras and the two wrecked cars. "Amazing!" she exclaimed. "This is so much more exciting than Our Lady of Grace."

Kate looked questioningly at Peter.

"The girls' school we were attending," he explained. Addressing Sarah, he pointed out, "Our Lady was exciting too but in a more scary way."

Kate doubted anyone had attempted to murder the girls in their precious school but she refrained from setting Peter right. "You've come at a very important time," Kate told them. "A lot depends on the success of our event. So please excuse us if we're so busy and ..."

Seeing her search for a word, Peter guessed, "Preoccupied?"

"Exactly," Kate said, giving him a broad smile. "We are preoccupied, but we'll have plenty of time to talk tomorrow."

Kate was a little irritated to see how the two girls clung to him. They finally released their hold when John and Christina offered to accompany them. "You might not think so, but they can be very resourceful," Peter said when he and Kate were alone, apparently reading her thoughts. "It's just that being in a strange place where you don't speak the language can be intimidating."

Kate took him on a tour of the preparations, explaining briefly each part of their tale. "Who could have imagined?" he exclaimed as they finished. "And I thought I'd had it difficult at Our Lady."

"I have one more urgent thing to deal with," she informed him.

"I'll tag along," he said.

"Sorry," she said. Halting, she placed a hand against his chest to stop him. She could feel his heart beating fast beneath his bra and flimsy school blouse. "That won't be possible." When his expression changed from surprise to disappointment, she withdrew her hand and added, "It's complicated and dangerous. I'll explain later."

"It's as I feared," he said, sounding dejected, "there are things I'm excluded from."

Kate sighed. "Okay. I'll explain, although I really don't have the time. The main villain in the plot is a man with a penchant for young girls. We've set him a trap. It's a dangerous gamble. If our event this evening is to work, the trap must snap shut around him without hurting the girl who's volunteered to be bait. Very few people are involved. It has to remain a secret." She sensed he wanted to insist. It wasn't like him. His stay in the English school seemed to have had a bad influence. "If you want to help, find Viktor and see if we can't work your kidnapping into the story. And Clara might have something for you to sing." The idea of singing seemed to appeal to him and he set off, leaving her to hurry to meet Sandra.

The bedroom they'd rigged to trap Father Jakob was bleak. The only furniture was a single bed, a small dresser over which hung a mirror and an old armchair in which Sandra sat huddled under a blanket. "How do you feel?" Kate asked.

"Terrified," Sandra admitted.

"Listen," Kate said. "I'm not going to let you do this alone."

"But we agreed there was no other way. I have to be on my own."

"I know. And you will be. But I'll join you in your mind. It's something we used to do with Peter. Not only will I be able to give you moral support, but if ever he attacks, I can take over and defend you."

"Take over? That sounds alarming," Sandra said, turning even paler.

"I'll show you, but for this to be like the real thing I need to be in another room," Kate said. "I'll just go next door. Hold on a sec."

Heinz and Regina let her in when she knocked. Several cameras had been set up facing what looked like a window onto the room where Sandra sat. "A one-way mirror," Heinz explained. There was also a tape recorder. Several microphones had been planted in the adjacent room. Heinz had persuaded a technician from the radio to help.

"I need to try something," Kate said. She lay on the bed which had been shoved into a corner. "Don't let anyone disturb me," she said and closed her eyes.

Sandra? she said.

Yes Sandra replied. Kate could feel her pace racing.

I'm talking to you mind-to-mind. Now I'll jump to your mind. She did so, eliciting a gasp from Sandra.

This is really weird, Sandra said. *My head has always been my own. Nobody gets in. It's my sanctuary. I'm not sure I like having someone share it. Can you see what I see?*

Yes. I can also hear what you hear and feel your body and your emotions.

Can you ... read my thoughts?

Kate could feel the girl's trepidation but opted for the truth. *Yes. It can be very useful in a difficult situation. We don't need to talk. Thoughts are enough. It's lightening fast. But let me teach you how to hide those thoughts and memories you don't want to share.*

Five minutes later, Sandra was proficient enough to mask her thoughts. Kate congratulated her, the girl was a quick learner. *I'll leave you for a brief moment. I want to talk to Heinz and Regina. I'll be back before he arrives.*

When Kate opened her eyes she noticed the sound engineer had stepped into the next room for a moment. She sat up and hurriedly explained to Heinz and Regina what she planned. They were flabbergasted but had no time to discuss because the sound man returned and the walkie-talkie that hung at Heinz's side buzzed. He put the device to his ear only to announce, "He's on his way up."

"I'm going back," Kate said as she lay down and closed her eyes.

He's on his way, she told Sandra. The girl's pulse spiked, her hands trembled and she broke into a sweat. Kate did what she could to allay her fear, but being in the girl's body she shared her feelings.

The door creaked open and a man in a cassock peered in. His eyes lit up at the sight Sandra and he licked his lips. Sandra cringed, scuttling as far away on the bed as she could. Father Jacob stepped inside and lent on the door, pushing it shut behind him. The click had Sandra whimpering uncontrollably.

Kate had a hard time keeping her lucid. The girl was terrified. *We need to get him to talk,* Kate said, battling to restrict the hormones from running wild.

"What do you want?" Sandra asked, the trembling of her voice making her words barely comprehensible.

Father Jacob stopped, taken aback that his victim should question him. "Fear not child," he replied, his voice like syrup. "I wish you no harm..."

"I've heard about you," Sandra interrupted. Talking gave her a hint of confidence. "The girls whisper you do nasty things to them."

"Whoever said that?" he asked, sitting down next to her. He placed a hand on her bare knee and squeezed.

She tried to push him away, but he tightened his grip. In pain, she dug her nails into the back of his hand and clawed sideways, drawing blood. He cursed and slapped her hard, sending her sprawling across the bed. Her hands flew to her cheek, the sting excruciating. Finding her defenceless, he forced her legs apart and climbed on top of her, his weight crushing the air from her lungs. Placing one hand around her neck he began to squeeze while he fumbled between her legs with his other hand.

Enough, Kate said to Sandra. Seizing control, she drove her knee into the priest's groin. He let out a pained grunt and relaxed his strangle hold. Kate twisted her hip forcing the man tumble to the floor. She sprang off the bed as he scrambled to his feet and turned to face her, his expression furious.

"So you like defenceless little girls?" she taunted. "How many have you had?"

He lunged at her, but she side-stepped and sent him sprawling into the wall. Righting himself, he nursed his hand.

"I bet you've had loads," Kate continued. "Do you count them?"

"Many more than you could imagine," he snarled, flinging himself at her. She dodged again, this time tripping him before planting a foot in the small of his back as he tried to get up. When he did manage to right himself, blood was dribbling from his nose.

"Is it hurting the girls that appeals to you?" she asked.

Something in his mind must have snapped because he

growled deep in his throat and tensed ready to spring. "The more it hurts the better," he snarled and threw himself at her, his madness giving him added speed. She was not quick enough to dodge his grasping hands. He snatched at her blouse and ripped it from her body sending her spinning into the wall.

Kate braced herself as best she could, but the impact was so violent it winded her. Her senses darkened and she was afraid she was about to faint. Frantically healing Sandra's body, she was just able to avoid his grasping hands as he tried to tear her skirt from her. Lunging forward, he grabbed her by the wrist and was about to pull her into his embrace when she slammed into his mind. His fingers went limp and he crumpled in a heap to the floor.

The door flew open and Heinz and Regina rushed in. Heinz swore and shoved Father Jakob away, but the priest, his eyes rolled up in his head, his expression blank, was no longer a danger.

"Poor thing," Regina said as she helped Sandra to her feet and took the trembling girl in her arms. "We should never have let you to do this." Kate relinquished her hold, sensing Sandra breakdown and sob as she shifted away.

Even in the safety of her own body, Kate was unable to stem the trembling as the spectre of the priest's grasping hands and his greedy eyes continued to haunt her. She took a moment to heal her own body that was complaining bitterly as if it had fought the fight. Then she opened her eyes to see the sound engineer standing over her, a worried look in his eyes. For a brief moment she imagined he was about to attack her and cringed, but reason prevailed and she let him help her up.

"Are you alright?" he asked, his words full of compassion.

"Just a little shaken," Kate replied, praying he wouldn't ask what she'd been doing.

Instead of interrogating her, he grimaced and said, "Your friend is very brave. I could never have done what she did."

52.

People were already queuing when Kate arrived. She skirted the building and entered at the back. Eileen and Clara were waiting, worried looks on their faces. "Sandra's badly shaken," she announced, "but she'll be okay. And before you ask, yes, we got what we wanted." The two sighed in relief.

"The television people are having cold feet," Eileen told her. "They've suddenly realised what a risk they're taking. Beth and Isla are talking to them."

Kate had just peered out from behind a curtain to find almost all the seats taken when Isla hurried up. "It wasn't easy but we managed to convince them," the woman told her. Good. The broadcast was important.

When the opening chorus came to an end, Kate strode between the rows of spectators and stepped onto the stage. "Apart from the music, nothing of what you're about to hear was invented." She paused to let her words sink in, scanning the audience as she did. "Don't be misled by the stage. This is not theatre. This is real. Laid end-to-end these botched plots and near-fatal misses might seem far-fetched. But they're based on real events. We have the evidence to prove it."

KIDNAPPING, the caption was projected on the wall above the Lost Girls who stood centre stage and sang. Peter, concealed behind them, sang a solo only to break off mid-phrase. The girls' singing faltered then parted leaving him alone as they filed off stage. "We were in St Leodegar," Peter said, lit by a single spotlight. "I was singing a solo, unseen by the audience. Men surged from the dark and held a cloth over my face. The world went dark."

The spotlight shifted to Viktor. "A lackey from the church wanted to oblige our young friend to return to England. We feared he'd take her by force. I was in the vestry keeping a watchful eye when men overpowered me and knocked me out."

Shifting once again, the spotlight highlighted Heinz. "Camera at the ready, I stood outside, unseen by the men who, with the complicity of the local police and the church, bundled our young friend away." Pictures of the kidnapping flashed on the screens. Here and there, members of the audience gasped and muttering could be heard.

Peter, dressed in his Our Lady uniform, joined Viktor and Heinz. "I was held hostage in a church school in England and tortured. Only now have I managed to escape." They left the stage but the photos continued as the choir in the wings took up their song, uninterrupted this time.

A single word, POISON, was projected on the screens to the sound of the choir singing like angels. Kate spoke. "The church announced they would no longer let the Lost Girls sing in churches." The angel song shifted to a minor key and became unsettling. "I petitioned the Bishop, but he insinuated the girls had a dubious reputation. He offered no proof, instead he fed me tea and a bitter-tasting cake."

Suzanne joined Kate on stage, saying, "Shortly after her return, Kate fell ill. Her fever spiked, her body sweated profusely and her limbs were trembling. We feared for her life." A single photo of Kate ill in bed appeared on the screen to shocked muttering from the audience. "Thanks to her perspicacity, Kate had kept a small piece of the Bishop's cake in her pocket and we were able to identify the poison. Strychnine."

"Surely not!" someone exclaimed.

A photo of the piece of cake in a napkin bearing the Bishop's insignia flashed on the screen. "Luckily we had the antidote and Kate recovered. A subsequent analysis of the cake and Kate's urine confirmed our diagnosis." An extract from the laboratory analysis appeared on the screen as Kate walked off stage to the soft crooning of a lullaby by the choir, leaving Suzanne in a single ray of light.

THREATS the projected word declared. Surrounding the audience, the choir of all the girls took up an indistinct muttering like a host of gossips. "The Lost Girls sing," Suzanne said as the gossiping ceased. "But they also work on healing, in particular herbal remedies. We grow plants and prepare them in our laboratory." A slide of the laboratory appeared on the screen. "In their effort to discourage the Lost Girls, the church sent a delegation of priests, supposedly to look for the devil. I tried to stop them, but they were too strong and too many." A series of slides depicting enraged priests smashing the workshop could be seen on the screen accompanied by the choir intoning pianissimo a question-response that resembled a wordless Gregorian chant.

"That's outrageous," a woman called out.

"How dare they?" another exclaimed. "What a waste."

"In a fit of rage, they destroyed everything," Suzanne continued. "They said they were in search of the devil, but I had the impression they brought him with them." A number of spectators sniggered, their laughter taken up by the choir and amplified into a sinister cackling before dying away to silence.

ASSASSINATION was the next word to appear on the screens as Jo walked on stage, her belly swollen with child. "I was close to term when my editor sent me to investigate reports of children running away from an orphanage. Rumour had it they were trying to reach the Lost Girls. I talked to the Lost Girls and wrote an article about how the church was hounding them and smashed their workshop. My editor refused the article insisting it was all lies despite the photographic proof. Then he fired me. How was I to know he was such a good friend of the Bishop? Alone and distressed, I welcomed an invitation to dine with the Lost Girls. On my way home, my car was rammed by another car. The driver drove off leaving me and my unborn baby injured and unconscious."

Suzanne joined Jo on stage. "We were able rescue Jo and

her unborn baby and care for them till they were no longer in danger. The police came to question her the next day. They were insistent, rude even, claiming she had driven off the road and was probably drunk. Neither were true. When asked, they said they saw no skid marks on the road." A photo projected on the screen clearly showed the marks leading to the wrecked car.

Heinz climbed on to the stage. "On a hunch," he said, "I checked the Bishop's fleet of cars and found one that had the front bumper driven in."

"That's preposterous," a man in the audience objected, getting to his feet. Kate recognised him as a leading journalist from Jo's former paper.

"Judge for yourself," Heinz challenged. The curtains at the back of the stage drew up revealing two cars interlocked in collision, one bearing the crest of the Bishop.

The man who'd challenge Heinz sat down embarrassed, muttering "Well I'll be blowed!"

As the lights faded and the curtain fell back into place, the choir took up Silent Night, singing softly, their voices like the rustle of snow falling. A new word lit up the screens, ARSON.

It was Eileen's turn. "Snow was falling heavily on an isolated village where the Lost Girls were entertaining the girls rescued from the orphanage. Some seventy girls were camped in a barn awaiting the renovation of the cottages. In the middle of the night, a dozen drunken youths forced their way in. A guard of girls repelled the attack, taking three youths prisoner. Frustrated, the remaining youths tried to torch the barn before fleeing. Luckily heavy snow extinguished the fire."

Photos of the three youths were projected on the screen causing a stir. They were clearly known to many. Viktor climbed onto the stage accompanied by an unwilling Fritz. "This young man was the ring-leader who tried to set fire to seventy young girls," Viktor said, his voice trembling with anger as he kept a firm grip on the youth's arm. "Weren't you?" Fritz replied with a sullen silence. "I say ring-leader," Viktor continued, "but he was not the boss. The attack was masterminded by a priest called

Father Jakob." A ripple of fear tore through the audience.

A stocky man, one of the top business invitees, elbowed his way to the front. "Is this true son?" he demanded, his voice trembling with rage. The youth stared at his feet in silence. "Speak up!" his father ordered.

"Yes father."

"Did Father Jakob make you do this?"

The youth nodded, still refusing to look his father in the eye.

"Why, for god sake, did you accept?"

"Father Jakob has been ... helpful," Fritz muttered. "He said we'd have fun and he offered to pay..."

"How much did he pay to set fire to those girls? Seventy of them, for Christ's sake!" When the youth shrugged, the father turned to Viktor. "Take him away. Hand him over to the police. I want no more to do with him." At which he stormed out and Viktor marched the youth away.

As Beth wheeled her chair up the ramp onto the stage, some members of the choir tolled a baleful knoll with handbells while the rest of the choir intoned a hesitant funeral march. The word MURDER filled the screens. "I had just had a visit from a priest, a certain Father Jacob, and was at the head of the stairwell when the brakes on my wheelchair failed," Beth began, "precipitating both myself and the chair down the stairs. In the flash of a second before I blacked out, I remembered wondering why the priest had fiddled with my wheelchair. I came to in the hospital surrounded by Viktor and Kate."

As she mentioned them, the two joined her with Viktor pushing a wheelchair in front of him. "I was tending Beth," Kate said, "when a male nurse, brandishing a syringe, tried to haul me away. I resisted and he rushed off screaming down the corridor. A doctor told us later the police had apprehended the man who was no nurse."

"When my dear Beth told me of her suspicions," Viktor said, "I went in search of the wheelchair. It had been impounded by the police. I was told they had disposed of it because it was so badly damaged. By a subterfuge, I found the wheelchair hidden in a storeroom at the back of the station. This is it." He indicated the wheelchair he had brought on stage. "As you can see it is not irremediably broken. Such chairs are very strong. They have to be. But the brake wires have been cut."

Beth waited for the gasps and the indignant muttering to die down before she said, "I was lucky my dear husband and my lovely new daughter were at my side..." The three stood unmoving, as if posing for a family photo. The tampered wheelchair lay abandoned to one side. The choir hummed the carol, I saw three ships coming sailing in...

Beth wheeled herself off the stage with Viktor following, pushing the damaged wheelchair. Only Kate remained. The choir had ceased and all was silent. The words FUN WITH THE BOYS appeared on the screens. "It was snowing," Kate began. "I was making my way back from tending to Beth, plodding through deep snow, when I heard voices, boys' voices, laughing, chatting as they stalked through the forest. Like me, they were heading for our improvised home, but theirs was no social visit."

The tension in the audience was palpable. After all that had befallen the girls, they must have feared the worst. "When one of the youths slipped and broke his leg, the others abandoned him, talking of a mission, an attack. With part of the choir, we were able to apprehend them..."

"However did you manage that?" a man in the audience called out in disbelief.

Kate made no attempt to reply. Instead, the sound of fifes and drums could be heard coming ever closer accompanied by an uncanny wailing. The sound was terrifying. Kate was filled with pride as the Lost Girls marched onto the stage, two by two, heads held high, majestic.

A solitary youth sidled after the choir, head down, shoulders hunched, hands in his pockets, and came to halt some distance from Kate. "I was the youth that broke his leg," he said eliciting a hiss from several people.

"Let him speak," Kate said. "It's not easy."

"It was supposed to be fun," he mumbled.

"Speak up if you want them to hear," Kate said.

"We were told there were loads of girls for the picking. It would be fun."

"Fun?" Kate asked.

The youth cringed. "You know ...kissing ... touching ..."

"Molesting young girls is fun?" Kate asked.

"I thought it was... before I met you."

"And who sent you?"

"I never met him."

"But you know who it was."

The youth hesitated, glancing around afraid, then nodded. "Father Jacob."

As indignant cries broke out amongst the audience, the hall was plunged in darkness and those on stage moved silently away to free the space.

RAPE. The single word was a silent accusation multiplied from screen to screen. When dim lights came on, Sandra was shuffling onto the stage, a blanket huddled round her shoulders. "I..." she began, but faltered. "It was so horrible..." She broke down and sobbed. All the orphans joined her on stage as newly developed pictures of her being molested lit up the screens. The violence was evident even if the photos were cautious in what they revealed. Outraged cries went up from the audience. Several stood and shook their fists, only to be restrained by those around them.

The presence of the girls seemed to give Sandra strength. She took a hesitant step forward and let the blanket fall. "More than half the girls on stage have been been molested if not raped. Most of them by this man." Her voice rose in anger as she pointed an accusing finger at the photo in which Father Jakob was clearly visible. "With the complicity of the nuns, this man was the worst offender. His hands on us have marked us for life."

A number of the audience once again sprang to their feet gesticulating, crying out, scandalised, objecting, but most watched in shocked silence. "Please be seated and hear me out,"

Kate said as she wheeled Father Jakob gagged and attached to a wheelchair onto the stage. "As I said in my introduction, nothing of what you've heard this evening was invented. Sandra and a large number of girls from the orphanage were beaten, abused and even raped. Jo, Beth and myself were almost murdered and many others narrowly avoided being burnt alive. Why? Because a few men in power, in the church, in the police and in the press felt threatened by a group of young girls or wanted to have 'fun' at their expense."

She paused to indicate Father Jakob who was now conscious and struggling to get free. "This man not only faithfully executed the orders of the Bishop. He was also an inveterate abuser who preyed on young girls with impunity because those in authority and those with a duty to care turned a blind eye."

As she spoke, the seventy girls behind her linked arms and closed ranks. "In the eyes of society, we are only children, girls at that. Unwanted orphans. Expendable some might think. We have no say. And as future women we will have no vote in this country. Yet we girls stand up and refuse to be beaten into submission. We say yes to life, to the future and a resounding 'No' to all those who would abuse us."

"Our question to you here tonight, to those watching at home and to those reading this in a national newspaper supplement is, are you going to be complicit and turn a blind eye, abetting these men in their criminal acts. Or are you going to stand up and say 'No. We refuse.' You run society. Not us. You are the adults in the room. It's your choice. But our path is clear. The future lies with us."

Epilogue

"It's odd," Peter said, cradled in Kate's arms. They'd raided Beth's stash of dresses in Lydia's house and were both done up as if they were off to a ball. But there was to be no music to sway their hips, no pretty girl to dance them off their feet. Just two girls curled up on a bed in a flurry of satin and silk, recovering from trying on so many dresses.

"When that parcel arrived," he continued, "I thought my luck had turned. I imagined discovering how to stay forever girl and boy. So much for wishful thinking. Things turned out differently. I am still no closer, although finding a solution gets more urgent everyday."

She ran her fingers through his hair admiring the earrings that hung from his newly-pierced ears. "You may not have done what you planned, but what you did was awesome," she said. "From frankly hostile, you got those girls to accept and appreciate you. With their courage and determination, you managed to outwit evil adults and their minions and heal an ailing school."

"You did pretty well yourself," he said. "All those high-society grown-ups fell over themselves to praise you and right the wrongs those men had done." He paused to give her a kiss. Engrossed in the taste of cinnamon and salt and the feel of her fingers roving over his dress, he completely forgot what words were to come next. When their lips finally parted and she ceased her explorations, in a breathy whisper he urged her, "Go on." But her attention was already elsewhere. They weren't talking mind-to-mind, but he could sense the drift of her thoughts.

"You refuse to chose between girl and boy, and I willingly embrace that, you naughty girl." Peter grinned as she straightened their dresses. "Lingering in the no-man's land before puberty, you refuse to become adult, not wishing to submit to the dictates of biology. Events of the past weeks have shown we both refuse adulthood in another way. We have taken on heavy responsibilities and confronted difficulties, we have transcended ourselves, we have learnt to lead others without lording over them like our subjects. Some might say we've become adult. But, in truth, we refuse the passage from child to adult. Adulthood sucks the vitality out of people, leaving many yearning for a lost paradise. Whereas we, in comparison, can be both serious and playful, courageous and fearful, responsible and carefree, if not reckless. Who else would heal a dysfunctional school by holding an 'inquisition' amongst girls with adults condemned to watch on in silence? Who else would stage a 'play' for a captive audience of influential adults to end violence and oppression against girls?"

He nestled his head between her breasts, breathing in the scents so characteristic of her. He could feel her heart beating and the passionate rise and fall of her chest. "I love you my wild and wonderful beauty," he purred.

"I love you too." Her words echoed his in a rush of warm breath that tickled his ear. "You know what?" He didn't answer. Her question didn't require one. She was going to tell him and anyway he already knew the answer and was happy to be a part of it. "With all we've achieved," she said, "we girls really do show the way..."

Annexes

380   Alan McCluskey

The Author

Alan McCluskey lives amid the vineyards in a small Swiss village between three lakes and a range of mountains. Nearby, several thousands of years earlier, lakeside villages housed a thriving Celtic community. The ever-present heart-beat of that world continues to fuel his long-standing fascination for magic and fantasy.

Whether it be about Sally, Brent and Keira in The Storyteller's Quest or Peter, Kaitling and Fi in Boy & Girl. In Search of Lost Girls or We Girls, all Alan McCluskey's novels tell the story of young people who, despite the immense difficulties that abound, discover and develop their own astounding talents and manage to do the exceptional.

We Girls is the third in the Boy & Girl Saga. The other two books are Boy & Girl and In Search of Lost Girls. Alan McCluskey has published three YA novels in The Storyteller's Quest series: The Reaches, The Keeper's Daughter and The Starless Square. The fourth book in the series, World o'Tales is awaiting publication. In addition, he has published two other novels, Chimera and Stories People Tell. The sequel to the latter, Local Voices, is awaiting publication.

Boy & Girl Saga Book 1
Boy & Girl
2020 edition
Alan McCluskey

Boy & Girl
The Boy & Girl Saga - Book 1

When Peter awakes in the head of a girl, he is both delighted and alarmed that his secret yearnings have become reality. Very quickly, however, his error is apparent; this girl is not him. Kaitling –that's her name– is twelve years old, like Peter. She's the daughter of a magician, a prominent figure in another world. Boy and girl travel back and forth from each other's minds, but have little time to get acquainted before Kaitling's island is overrun by warrior priests and she has to flee. At home, a conflict erupts in Peter's family forcing him to take refuge at a friend's place. Meanwhile at school, a haughty new girl goads him about his girlishness and, spitting in his face, vows to rid the earth of people like him. The stage seems set for a desperate struggle to survive, but will ingenuity and youthful fervour be enough against folly and fanaticism?.

Boy & Girl Saga Book 2
In Search
of Lost Girls
2020 edition
Alan McCluskey

In Search of Lost Girls
The Boy & Girl Saga - Book 2

Listen carefully. You can just hear the mournful tolling of a bell over the shuffle of girls' feet as they traipse to Mass, nursing bruises and numb despair. No one cares. No one is there to stem the torrent of injustice and abuse. They are lost and forgotten. In another world, the cathedral still reverberates to the melody of angelic voices as the mourners file out, heads bowed, words hushed. If only they knew that the two girls whose music delights them so were really boys in disguise, sanctity would flee in the face of raging indignation. Then a gunshot threatens to put an end to the girls' lost cause. The scene is set. The author picks up his pen with trembling fingers and begins to write. Time to tear Kate and Peter apart. The thought of making her life hell has him dribbling in anticipation. Age is no excuse. He ought to know better. Things rarely turn out as an author expects.

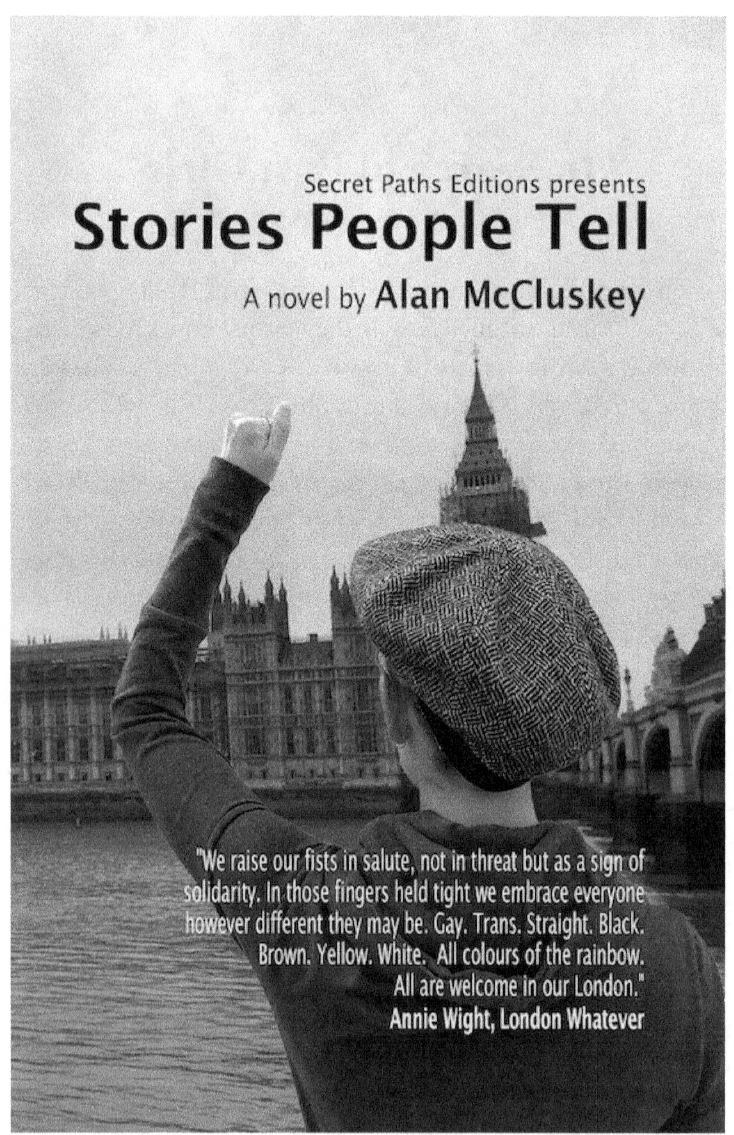

Secret Paths Editions presents
Stories People Tell
A novel by Alan McCluskey
"We raise our fists in salute, not in threat but as a sign of
solidarity. In those fingers held tight we embrace everyone
however different they may be. Gay. Trans. Straight. Black.
Brown. Yellow. White. All colours of the rainbow.
All are welcome in our London."
Annie Wight, London Whatever

Stories People Tell

Stories People Tell is a tale about Annie Wight, a shy schoolgirl who, despite sustained, cruel treatment and personal doubts, blossoms into a major voice in the grassroots movement 'London Whatever' celebrating gender diversity while struggling to end violence against women and care for the weak and marginalised.

Annie wasn't expecting to fall in love with a girl or to shoot to notoriety when she got swept up in 'London Whatever'. Nor could she have known that, right from the outset, she would become the number one target of Nolan Kard, the homophobic Lord Mayor of London. who was campaigning to 'Keep London Straight'. She bore the brunt of attacks from his rogue police, not to mention from a sinister gang of ghostwriters, the nightmare of all Kard's enemies.

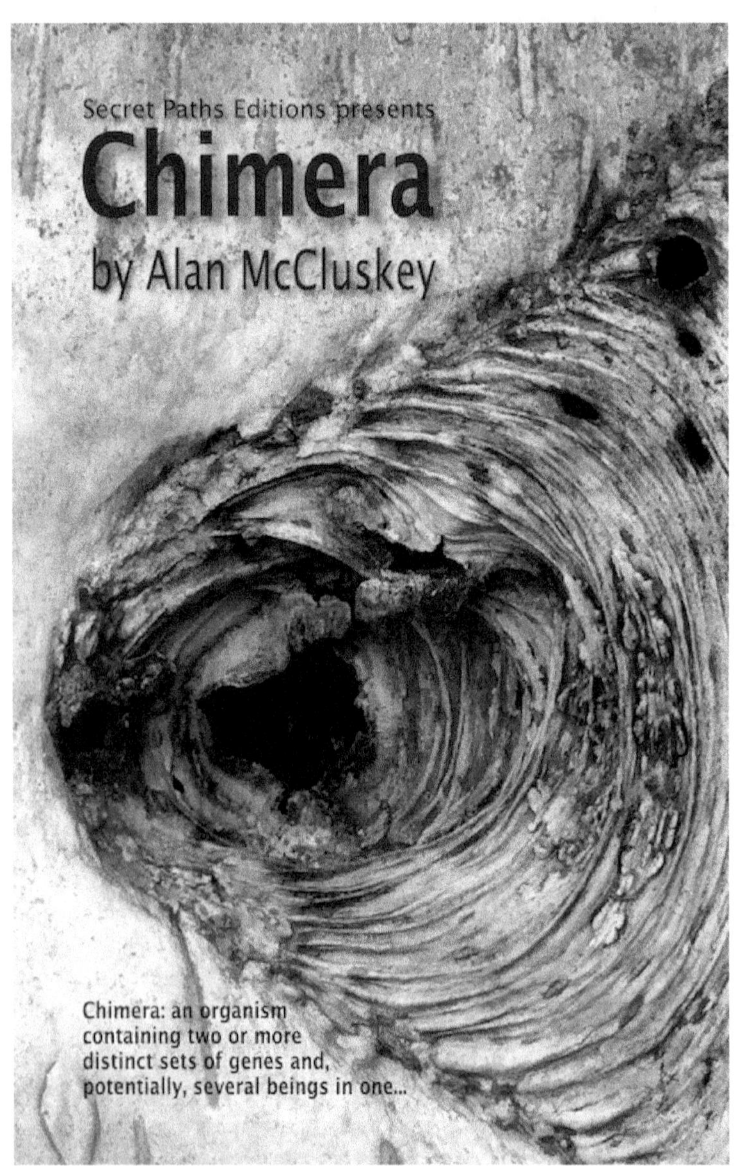

Secret Paths Editions presents
Chimera
by Alan McCluskey
Chimera: an organism
containing two or more
distinct sets of genes and,
potentially, several beings in one...

Chimera

A chimera is an organism containing two or more distinct sets of genes and, potentially, several beings in one. Sami and Sam are a chimera, two people in one, a girl and a boy, a leader and healer of people sharing a body with a brilliant but autistic child.

Sam talking to himself on discovering he is one half of a chimera...:
:: not being able to speak, to move - such was the price I had to pay - to cut out the chaos and confusion from a world run wild - a raw satisfaction - being barricaded in my head these past twelve years - all for nothing - that blasted girl has ruined everything - surging out of nowhere - pirating my body - bridging the gap between me and the others - letting chaos rush in - beguiling everyone with her codswallop - not me - I'm not impressed - some say she's destined to be our saviour - as if the block-head could save a fly - I just want her gone

Sami's first ever words to her teacher and her father...:
"I … need … to explain. Words come with … difficulty. I must … be brief. Sam and I are a … chimera ... there are two of us... Sam is the boy you know. New things terrify him. He cannot speak … out loud. He stumbles. He falls. I am new. I just awoke. I am a girl. I play piano I talk. I walk. As for that violence you just saw, that was Sam trying to kick me out"

The Storyteller's Quest ~ Book One
The Reaches
Alan McCluskey

The Reaches
The Storyteller's Quest Bk 1

The quiet town of Avan with its port, its provincial university and its conservative seafaring folk would hardly be the place you'd expect to run into an adventure and frankly neither Brent nor Sally nor Keira were going out of their way to have one. At least nothing more than the occasional torrid love affair and the awkward self-questioning typical of many young adults like themselves. Sally was finishing her studies in the Theosophy Department of the University hoping to become Professor Rafter's assistant, Keira, Sally's best friend and lover, was a young librarian who occasionally sang in a popular folk group and Brent was a would-be writer who couldn't quite get his act together and who spent hours wandering the streets and lanes of the town in search of inspiration. Yet unbeknown to them forces had long been at work that would throw them together in a series of adventures that were going to tax them to the extreme forcing them to develop abilities that went way beyond what would seem possible during a voyage from the real world to the realm of dreams and on into another world called the Reaches that at first sight looked deceptively like their own.

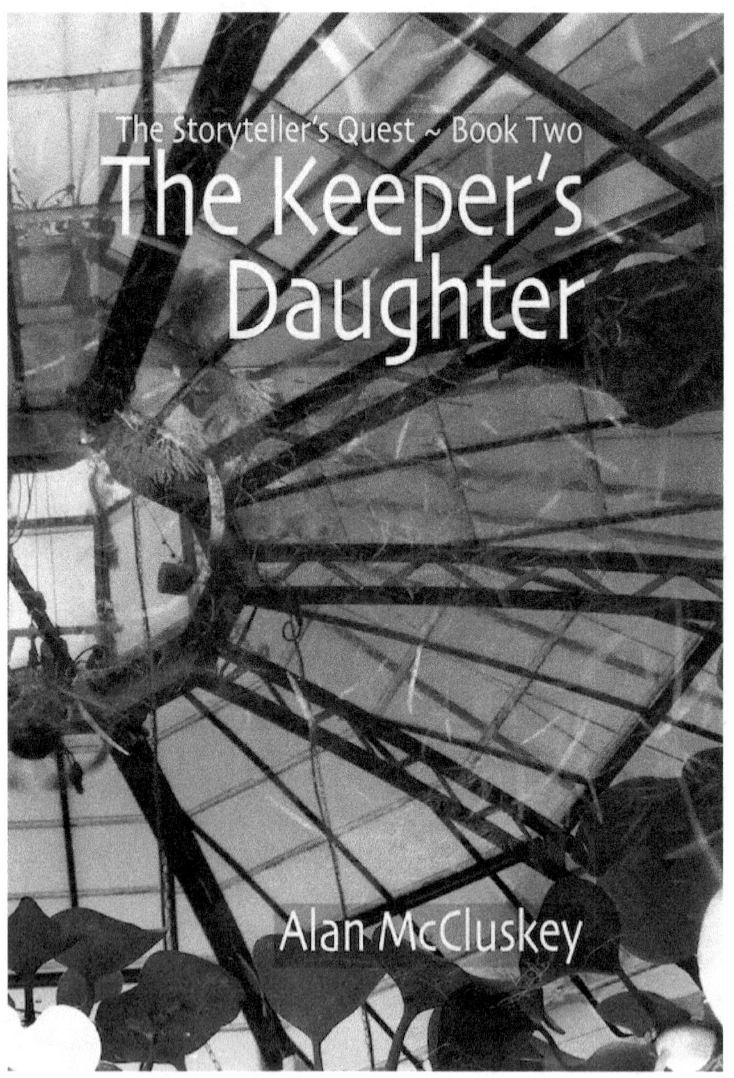
The Storyteller's Quest ~ Book Two
The Keeper's
Daughter
Alan McCluskey

The Keeper's Daughter
The Storyteller's Quest - Book 2

It wasn't Brent's fault if he was stuck in the form of Jake the Owl, at least he didn't think it was as he sat on a branch preening despondently. The threads of all his stories had become inextricably muddled in his owlish head. To think that he'd once prided himself on being a storyteller. His stories had become adventures and some of those adventures had become nightmares, and now he was stuck with them. He'd flown in search of his friend and lover, Mia. She'd been dragged off by a band of thugs just when it was time for them all to return to their world. Only Sally, their mutual friend and lover, had made it back from the world of the Reaches to their hometown of Avan. Hearing her story, despite the dangers she'd had to face, her friends suggested Sally teach them to travel to the Dream Realm and beyond to the Reaches. The idea appealed to everybody. Not that Sally knew how to get back to the Reaches, but the idea of a 'dream class' as they called it pleased her and, above all, she wanted to return to the world where her newly-found half-sister lived and where her two friends had so abruptly disappeared.

The Storyteller's Quest ~ Book Three
The Starless Square
Alan McCluskey

The Starless Square
The Storyteller's Quest - Book 3

A weekend of joyous festivities! Such was the Theosophy department's response to a group of fanatics bent on destroying their reputation and having them shut down. Theosophy? Professor Rafter, head of the department, calls it "the study of our direct relationship with that which is beyond and above the normal range of human experience". He could just as well have been describing the adventures of a group of young friends who have been called back from their travels in another world to defend their department with their new-found abilities. But how could entrancing singing or breath-taking storytelling or exquisite cooking possibly stand a chance when pitted against the evil black cloud that threatens to obscure the Starless Square?

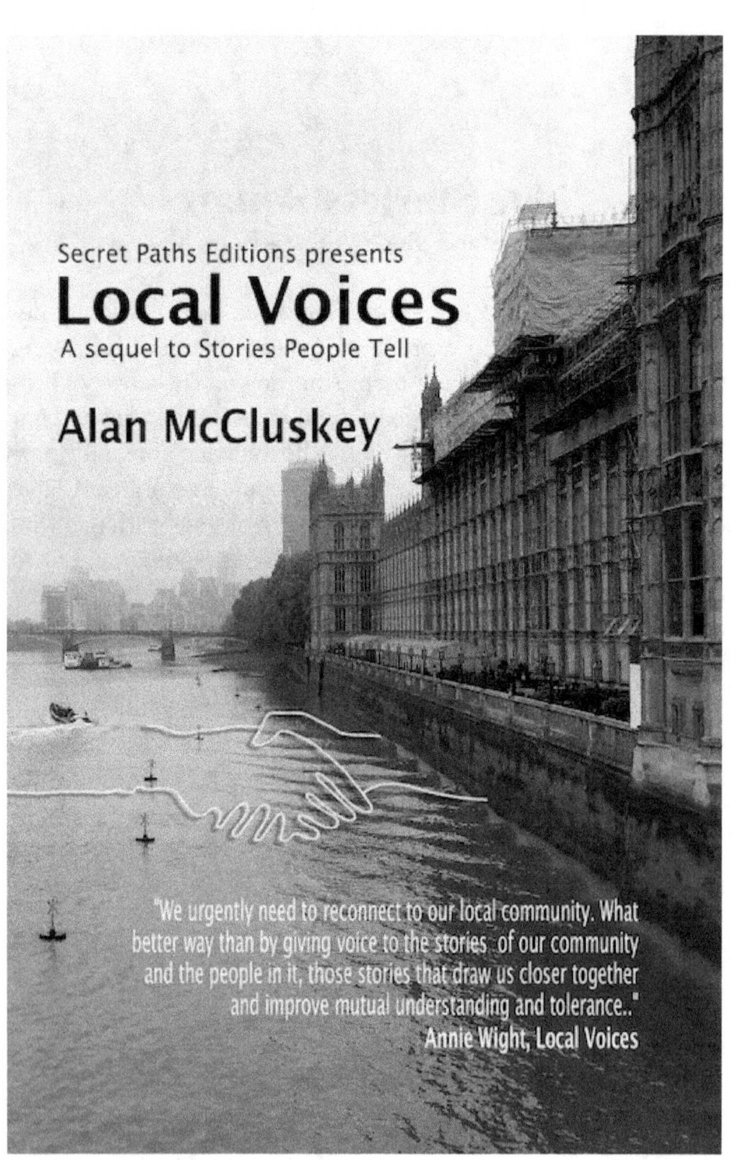

Secret Paths Editions presents
Local Voices
A sequel to Stories People Tell
Alan McCluskey
"We urgently need to reconnect to our local community. What better way than by giving voice to the stories of our community and the people in it, those stories that draw us closer together and improve mutual understanding and tolerance.."
Annie Wight, Local Voices

Local Voices

Coming soon: a sequel to Stories People Tell

In her campaign to re-assert and strengthen the role of women at the heart of hearthside healthcare, seventeen-year-old Annie Wight finds herself pitted against Health England, a conservative think-tank backed by pharmaceutical giants and private healthcare providers. Pretexting the defence of the National Health Service, they stop at nothing to stamp out Annie's efforts. They target not just her but those close to her, wreaking havoc in friendships and affairs of the heart. As part of her response, Annie launches a project to share the stories of those that never figure in the spotlight. By celebrating local voices, the project fights against isolation and disempowerment.

Online

Secret Paths: https://author.secret-paths.com
Facebook: https://www.facebook.com/Secret.Paths
Instagram: https://www.instagram.com/secretpathseditions/
Twitter: https://www.twitter.com/Almacme